In Which Our Dashing Duo of Derring-Do Arrive at a Foreboding Conclusion

"I want your men to check any and all of the enemy dead here, solid or otherwise, and I want them photographed."

"Yes, Agent Books," O'Neil said, giving him a salute before ordering his men to pass along his words through the ranks.

"Sorry, darling," Wellington said, giving Eliza a weak smile. "I should have let you take command as you are the senior agent."

"Old habits." Eliza patted him on his shoulder before turning to Vania. "Inauthentic æthergate technology, a man presumed dead taking up arms against the empire, and all the elements in play to throw India into chaos. What do you think, Agent Pujari?"

"Usher," she replied.

"We're going to need to see those photographs as soon as they are ready. Alert Director Smith, and send word to the home office. Inform them of the situation."

"Yes, ma'am," Vania said before heading back to the barracks.

"Well then," Wellington began, "the House of Usher is apparently supplying rebels with inferior, supernatural technology, India is on the brink of war with Mother England, all while a madman possessing the ability to turn ordinary people into ten feet monsters is on the loose."

Eliza bobbed her head, her lips bent in a smirk. "Just another day at the Ministry."

"Shall I go put the kettle on?"

"Please."

THE
GHOST
REBELLION

BOOK FIVE
OF
THE MINISTRY OF PECULIAR OCCURRENCES

PIP BALLANTINE & TEE MORRIS

Imagine That!
STUDIOS

www.ministryofpeculiaroccurrences.com

For the Kickstarts
of 2015

Your enthusiasm for the series

inspires us daily.

Because of you,

the adventure continues.

ACKNOWLEDGEMENTS

When we approached the end of *The Diamond Conspiracy*, we asked ourselves, *"Are we done, or do we have more in the tank?"*

It didn't take us long to answer. We absolutely love this world, these adventures, and these characters.

We also knew there was a good chance we would be on our own. More than any other installment in the series, though, *The Ghost Rebellion* has taught us that books are a collaborative effort.

In making the best adventure possible, we turned to a collection of incredibly talented people. There's Sarah E. Daniels, MA Soviet History, keeping us on the right path of snow, language, and geography. We also owe big thank you to Suna Dasi, founder of Steampunk India (www.steampunkindia.com) for making sure we knew all about proper chai, the best fashions of Bombay, and the effects of the British Raj. And a very special thanks to Michael Spence, author of "Why the Sea Is Boiling Hot" from *Tales from the Archives: Volume III,* for providing a wonderfully infernal device that found its way into our fifth adventure.

For the mechanics of the story, we owe so much to K T Bryski and Jennifer Melzer, and their talents of developmental and proof editing of this, the most far flung of all the Ministry books to date. Thanks for getting down in the dirt and wrangling words with us.

As the snow piled up in Virginia this winter, we are most thankful for our "captive" peer readers, Christina Payton and Verena Vorsatz. Granted, for captives, they were most meticulous when it came to continuity, character complications, and—of course—giving the fans what they *really* want.

Once the story is ready, the cover arrives; and the team behind our cover exceeded all expectations. Tamara Barnett of Tennille Makeup Artistry worked her magic, Michael Ward of Go ForWard Photography shot the cover, and Starla Huchton of Designed by Starla brought all the elements together, including the all-important light rays through the fingers. And a hearty huzzah to our European cosplayer turned cover model, Verena Vorsatz, quite an adventurer herself in trusting us to come all the way from Germany, and bringing eerie life to Eliza D Braun.

As steampunk is all about the accessories and the arsenal, special thanks to Jared Axelrod, Piper J Drake, and Kevin Houghton for providing all this; and bounteous gratitude to our behind-the scenes wranglers and photojournalists, Wendy Ward, Matthew J Drake and Christina Payton. You do have to keep the hired help in order.

Finally, there is you, the supportive patrons of the books, the podcasts, and the role-playing game. When we set out to crowdfund our fifth book, we had very modest goals, but our backers blew all that out of the water, funding not only this book, but a novella (of a rather dubious nature, coming in December 2016) and *Operation: Endgame* (coming in 2017) as well. If you ever wonder at the end of our stories *"Do the authors have as much fun as I do when reading these adventures?"* the answer is yes.

Most assuredly, yes.

CHAPTER ONE

✦⟫═◉═⟪✦

Wherein a Delightful Luncheon Is Cut Short

Wellington Thornhill Books took in a deep breath, sparing just a moment to collect his wits. Otherwise he risked not living to see dessert.

The archivist-turned-agent dabbed at the corner of his mouth with his snow-white napkin, and draped it carefully over his lap. Outside the window the gleaming Atlantic rolled under their ocean liner, the *African Sunset*, but that was not the view that held his attention. His focus remained with the dandy in front of him. Since their first meeting, the bombastic lord seemed rather taken with the sound of his own voice, which was why the change in his dining companion's demeanour came as such a shock.

If an attack should come, Wellington still had his dinner knife and fork. Both hardly suited for close-quarter combat, but still useful. He was also in possession of a glass of wine, half finished—a pity to use, since it was a delightful vintage and paired perfectly with the duck—that could blind his opponent for a few valuable moments.

His lunch date kept a hard glare fixed on him, the monocle digging into the folds of his cheek. Rather unexpected to Wellington, Lord Hieronymus Featherstone had run out of things to say, and was now giving him his undivided attention.

Wellington thought he had shown unending fortitude while being subjected to Featherstone's eternal droning on about his recent excursions across Africa, India, and Siam. He now knew to what far reaches Lord Featherstone had traversed in the name of Her Majesty—which might be useful.

Yet now Featherstone sat before him, no longer the awful, droning chatterbox. The gentleman's jaw twitched as he kept his ice-chip blue eyes trained on Wellington, demanding satisfaction.

"Well," the lord spoke, his voice booming from his barrel chest, "answer me, man."

Sod it, Wellington thought as he picked up his glass. *At the very least, I will finish this excellent wine.*

"You obviously mentioned her name during one of your riveting stories when crossing the Serengeti," Wellington replied before taking in a good, long sip of his wine.

"My dear Bernice does not care for heat."

"Then perhaps you mentioned her joining you as you crossed the Canadian Rockies?"

"Nor does she care for the cold."

Mrs. Bernice Featherstone did not sound either lovely or agreeable, a perfect match for her husband, it seemed.

Nodding in resignation, Wellington cast another quick glance across the table, taking note of the knife and fork. "M'lord, we could speculate for the entirety of the afternoon on how I came to know your lovely wife's name, but why don't we just cut this clever banter short and try a more direct form of engagement?"

"Which would be?"

"The truth." With a final dab at the corners of his mouth, Wellington dropped the napkin on the table, swiping up the fork and placing it in his lap. He positioned the silverware for a quick thrust as he began. "Lord Featherstone, it is no lie when I say your company has been enlightening. I have genuinely enjoyed our spirited and scintillating discussions whilst we journeyed around the Ivory Coast. However, to say we 'met you' by chance would be disingenuous." His grip tightened on the fork as he said, "My associate and I have been tracking you since your boarding in Conakry."

"Really?" Featherstone said, with a slight huff. "Does this have something to do with my position in Her Majesty's government?"

"In a manner of speaking." Wellington's thoughts scattered when he caught a glimpse of the dessert tray; there were two slices of cake that looked utterly delightful passing by. Swallowing disappointment, he continued. "It is not your position with the War Department that interests us, so much as your choice of physicians. A rather dastardly gent by the name of Henry Jekyll." Featherstone's expression tightened, but he remained silent. Wellington took that as a sign to continue. "I am sure you will defend the character and the skill of dear Doctor Jekyll, but I can assure you that my dealings with him go further back than yours. You believe him to be a miracle worker, a saviour, and a friend. However, the man is both figuratively and literally, a monster."

Catching sight of the waiter, Wellington motioned him over. Out of the corner of his eye, he could see Lord Featherstone silently stewing, probably outraged that a man of his station was being spied on like he was common criminal. "Do bring the dessert tray around again, please." And with a quick glance to Featherstone, Wellington added, "Do not dally. I'm in a bit of a hurry."

"You have some cheek, Mr. Canterbury," Featherstone growled, while his face turned an interesting shade of puce.

"Actually, it's Books." He polished off his glass of wine. Yes, a most delightful vintage. "Wellington Thornhill Books, Esquire."

"And to whom do you answer?" he snapped.

"That you will soon discover, but needless to say we know you have been recently contacted by Doctor Jekyll. It's doubtful he did so out concern for your health, but more likely because you are Royal Engineer for Her Majesty's military. I understand your specialty is experimental weaponry. The amount of secrets you carry, m'lord…well, I'm sure Doctor Jekyll would relish obtaining many of them."

Featherstone's breathing grew laboured. Wellington had often observed people forced to face uncomfortable truths had trouble controlling themselves in that respect. His free hand still gripped the fork in his lap, since it never hurt to be prepared just in case things went "tits up" as Eliza put it. Wellington grinned in what he believed was a disarming way. "The only way to finish a meal as splendid as this is with a cordial and some dessert. After which, we will retire to my cabin, and there, my associate and I will outline the best way for you to untangle yourself from Doctor Jekyll relatively unscathed."

He could see the dessert tray approaching. Wellington was fairly sure he saw a dish in the corner that might possibly be a crème brûlée. A silver lining, to be sure.

The snap of glass cracking ripped his attention away from the approaching steward.

Lord Featherstone's face was beetroot red, but that did not alarm Wellington so much as the crack that had appeared across his monocle. The sheer pressure between his brow and the top of his cheek continued to press against the eyepiece's rim, bending it until the brass casing and shattered glass fell off his face. Featherstone was a burly gent to begin with, but the changes he was going through were entirely unnatural. His already-broad shoulders were spreading fast, filling out his smart uniform.

It was no illusion. Featherstone was growing.

"You seem to have forgotten your place," Featherstone growled, even as people in surrounding tables scrambled to vacate their seats.

Very well, Wellington decided, *the fork it will be.*

The archivist swept his makeshift weapon out from under the table, and Wellington's aim was—as usual—spot on. The prongs of the fork struck the flesh between the index finger and thumb. With the amount of force and the fork's momentum, Wellington's blow should have pinned the man's hand to the table. However, the skin was intact. The fork, however, was nothing but bent prongs. Staring at this slight deviation in his plan, Wellington observed the hand grow even larger while the seams of Featherstone's military coat split.

"Stings a bit," Featherstone chuckled, thick foam seeping from between his lips and teeth. "Nothing like I am going to do to you, though..."

Oh bugger, Wellington thought quickly. *Here we go.*

Pushing hard against the floor, he tipped his chair backward, putting him out of reach of Featherstone's massive arm, now thrice the size of what a normal man's would be.

The right cross had narrowly missed Wellington, but it did connect with a passing waiter. Wellington was in the process of hitting the floor when Featherstone picked up the poor man and threw him across the length of the dining room. Unfortunately, he crashed into an exquisite mirror, shattering the glass and probably gaining seven years' bad luck.

Wellington tucked his knees into his stomach, which gave him momentum needed to tumble back and away from the table. It was a prettily timed move as Featherstone promptly flipped the table onto the chair Wellington had been sitting on. With their disruption, a shattered mirror, and the fate of the poor waiter, this was quite a bad day for dining on the *African Sunset* all around.

Patrons were now more hurriedly making for any exit, regardless if it led to the outside decks or the kitchen. Featherstone's howl could be heard over the screams of the female passengers. He grew larger and larger with each passing second, his teeth now too big for his mouth.

"So, Mr Books, what am I to do with you?" Featherstone asked with a snarl as he looked down on him. "Should I break your legs so you can't run, or just rip you in two?"

"I think you should hold your breath," he suggested.

Featherstone blinked and cocked his head. "What?"

"Hold your breath," Wellington repeated with some care.

From behind him, the signature whine of a Lee-Metford-Tesla Mark IV started up. Wellington rolled away from the sound, reaching inside his jacket to draw his own sidearm, an experimental of Axelrod and Blackwell's design. Its crystal-clear chamber flared to life as Wellington brought the pistol up, but he was beaten to the punch. A cerulean ball of plasma energy exploded against Featherstone's chest, sending this member of the House of Lords backwards into the far wall of the dining room. His hulking form left an impression where it hit, and the impact shook the whole dining room.

Eliza stepped out from the doorway, lifting her tinted goggles to let them rest against her forehead. They were the only practical part of her attire, though her plum-coloured day dress was quite lovely. She flipped a series of switches to put the generator into a cycling mode as residual electricity crackled between the coils of its conical barrel. Since that blast had been considerable, it would be a few moments before the rifle could do it again.

A racking cough from Featherstone widened the smile across her face. "He told you to hold your breath," she called out to him.

Wellington rolled on his shoulders, wincing. "I was truly hoping this lunch would unfold differently. I never even got to dessert. Did you see what happened to the crème brûlée by any chance?"

"I think it is gone, darling," she said with a grin as she flipped the safety off the rifle and glanced around the dining room. Until the generator showed green, it would be high calibre shells now. "But console yourself with this, it could have been worse. It might have been a repeat of Lyon."

Her lovely skirts swished as she approached him, a combination of elegant and deadly.

"To be fair," Wellington began, "that was our first patient on the list."

"True," she said with a nod, adjusting her tiny hat around the goggles. "We didn't know what to expect."

"And we have learned so much since then."

The growl interrupted their conversation, and both Wellington and Eliza jumped to one side as a table flew at them. The shattering of wood and fine china, accented with the ringing of silverware, was yet another affront to the exquisite dining experience that the *African Sunset* offered. When they drew aim on where Featherstone had been, Wellington saw only a blur of muscle shouldering its way through the exit leading to the Promenade Deck.

Wellington shot a glance at Eliza. "Didn't expect that."

"That is a lovely thing about serving in the Ministry of Peculiar Occurrences, Welly," Eliza said, shifting the modified rifle in her grip, a sure sign she was about to begin pursuit. "We are always seeing something new."

He followed Eliza through the luxurious corridors of the *African Sunset*. Tracking Lord Featherstone was hardly a challenge. All they needed to do was follow the screams and signs of destruction.

As they went Eliza eyed the smashed oak panelling. "Jekyll's cocktails tend to show all sorts of negative side effects he fails to mention in his ledgers."

"I suppose," he replied, somewhat resigned to the uncertainty, "the term 'negative' is a rather subjective one."

They stepped out into the midday sunlight and caught a glimpse of the lumbering lord sprinting—as much as his mutated mass allowed him to—for the bow of the ship. It was difficult to deduce exactly what Featherstone's endgame was, but regardless Wellington and Eliza needed him alive.

As their own footsteps pounded against the deck, a soft counterpoint to Lord Featherstone's, Wellington checked the experimental in his grip. The charge was full, and the strange flare of energy spun madly within the tempered glass. He had no earthly idea what this gun would do, nor even if it would work.

However, since they were running out of ocean liner he knew he was about to conduct his first field test in a moment or two.

The mad lord was now grabbing random tables and unsuspecting passengers and tossing them behind him. Hurling gentlemen, Wellington could not deny, was a very effective distraction. Eliza managed to sprint a few paces ahead, and with one hand she pulled at the waistband of her lovely skirt, one jerk, buttons flew and it billowed and flew away. Eliza was very hard on her fashion, but he had gotten rather good at sewing buttons back on.

Then sliding across the polished wooden deck, she came to an abrupt stop at an overturned table, drew aim with the Mark IV, and fired.

Lord Featherstone lurched forward, and for a moment it looked as though he might tumble to the deck. Instead, he stopped and snorted like a bull considering the amount of force needed to charge.

"Bugger me!" Eliza ejected the shell and worked the bolt back to a firing position.

"Have you got a full charge built yet?"

Eliza glanced down and shook her head. "Still working up to that, love. Considering the first shot only winded him, a half-charge might just twirl his moustache a bit."

Wellington brought up the experimental, its energy pulse out-flashing the sunlight around them. "Then I guess we don't have many options, now do we?"

"You can't be serious?" She sounded both shocked, and a little aroused.

"If you come up with an alternative strategy in the next five minutes," he said, continuing forward, "you will know where to find me."

The closer he got to Lord Featherstone, the more he tightened his grip on the experimental, hoping it would still the tremor in his hands.

It didn't.

"Cute little toy you got there," growled Featherstone. "You and your lot must have some right smart clankertons on the job."

Actually, they dance the line between genius and lunatic quite deftly. "We must be prepared for anything we encounter in the field, present company included."

Featherstone's chuckle sounded like stone rubbing against stone. He was hoping to maybe calm Featherstone and relax him to a point to where Jekyll's serum would lose some of its impact. However, one look in the monster's eyes told him that the Doctor's hold was complete. Wellington chanced a look around; terrified passengers were huddled against the bow of the ship.

So it was to be a last stand.

Behind him, he could hear the *Sunset's* defensive crew taking up positions. He was able to identify the bolt actions being worked behind him as Lee-Metford standards. Then by the sound of metal-scraping-metal he knew they had magazines too —probably the newer Emily models, firing .303 calibres with an improved design to accommodate for greater heat and pressure generated by its cartridges.

Busy man, that James Paris Lee. Better he was not here to see his powerful 303s perform no better than slingshots against this behemoth.

"Pull your crew back, boatswain!" Eliza's voice was calm, but also deadly serious. *Better listen to her, lads, as she's got the Mark IV and knows how to use it.* "I've got a man in there!"

"Sir," called a White Star officer, "step aside. We have the monster cornered."

"Along with passengers, you git!" Eliza's voice went up a notch in volume. "Hold your fire, and get those people clear! My man will handle this!"

"Oh now, she *is* a little darling, isn't she? A delicate flower of the South Pacific, from that accent." The monster's words dripped with lechery. "I will tear through this lot like they were nothing more than a cheap penny dreadful, but her?" A line of drool dripped from the corner of his mutated lips. "I'll take my time with that little treasure."

Wellington felt a prickle under his skin. Splaying his fingers around the butt of the experimental, he kept his aim at Featherstone's chest. *We need him alive,* he had to remind himself. "Stand down," he stated evenly.

The passengers huddled behind the monster flinched when Featherstone's wild, bloodshot eyes fell on them. "I count eleven. Twenty, if you include the crew. You can watch them die first. Then I'll take me that fine lady friend of yours."

"My apologies then, M'lord," And Wellington pulled the trigger.
Click.

The energy within the glass chamber still danced merrily, but that was all it did. Wellington would have pulled the trigger a second time, but it was now locked back.

Featherstone took another step closer. The man was bloody huge. "Guess your toymaker isn't as skilled as you thou—"

Wellington felt the tingle in the handle first, and that instinctively brought his arms back to their full length. The experimental's concussive blow was not loud, but low. A deep, resonant bass that echoed through his body.

Then he was knocked backward and into the reinforcements from White Star Line.

Though there had been no flash, there was a definite disruptive field; a concentrated electricity that distorted into something resembling fairy lights. He saw all this in a matter of seconds before knocking down the *Sunset* sailors like nine pins. His slide across the deck was only halted by a bulkhead.

Slowly, Wellington rocked up to a sitting position, and that was when he observed Lord Featherstone still in the air. He seemed to hang in the æther for a moment before plummeting like a stone. He hit the water hard, but then there was as second, more muffled impact. The passengers for all their terror were peering over the side, and then came the screams. One or two took time out from doing that to throw up on the deck.

"Welly!" Eliza called, worming her way through the crush of sailors that were still getting to their feet. "Welly!"

"I'm alive," Wellington groaned. He looked at the pistol in his hand. There were muscles he didn't know existed that ached, and he had been on the *shooting* end. "What on earth do Axelrod and Blackwell call this?"

"I believe Blackwell called it the Mule's Kick."

"Aptly named," he said, craning his neck. "Featherstone alive?"

"Not bloody likely," Eliza said, with a tilt of her head. "I saw the ship's bow mow him down, then he disappeared under the keel. I doubt Jekyll's serum gave him gills, even if by some miracle the ship didn't cut him in two."

"Dashitall," Wellington said. "We needed him alive."

Eliza let the Mark IV rest on her shoulder. "Guess we'll have to go through Lord Featherstone's suite. I believe his was Number Twelve."

"Will you need a key?"

She jerked her head towards her rifle and grinned. "I always travel with some way of getting in."

"Well then, let us not stand on ceremony." Wellington motioned back towards the rest of the ship. The gesture hurt. He suspected everything would hurt for quite some time.

"Oh, and I'm sorry you did not make it to dessert, darling," Eliza said, putting a hand around his elbow. "I know how much you love crème brûlée. Maybe we can get the chef to make you some more."

"I fear, my sweet Eliza, that the time for brûlée has well and truly passed."

In Which a House Falls Under New Management

Mr Jeremy Elliott tapped his fingernails on the long, mahogany table in front of him. Time was money, and it had been far too a long an airship journey from Manchester to Toronto to be kept waiting like this. A swift glance to each side of him confirmed to the Englishman he was not the only one with this thought: all of the men seated in the boardroom looked uncomfortable or completely outraged at being kept waiting. They shot each other covert looks over their starched collars and perfectly knotted ties.

The hotel being so unfamiliar had put them all on edge to begin with, but discovering the hotel staffed as it was only elevated the tension. Usually they met on airships, or on a House of Usher submersible. Their current surroundings were almost banal in comparison. A lone grandfather clock in the hotel's boardroom ticked on interminably. Jeremy did not know how much longer the eight of them could possibly stay seated, and in silence. The Lord of the Manor had never before taken such liberties with the board's time. No one mentioned it, but the chair India's Mr Cobra would have occupied was eerily empty. Jeremy was curious about how he'd managed to deny the Lord's summons. Unless he was dead.

Mr Badger shifted in his seat, stroking his moustache, and spoke with his broad French accent. "How much longer must we wait? We all have business to attend to, I'm sure." He pursed his lips and then sneered to underscore his displeasure.

Always one to break the ice, Mr Badger.

Jeremy—Mr Fox to those around him—was not surprised in Badger's sign of weakness. Silence made Badger nervous. It was a vulnerability many of the board members took advantage of in open debates. They might all be part of the House, but that didn't mean any of them liked each other. It was hardly out of the ordinary to have board members attempt to eliminate others. Strictly business, of course.

Mr Bear was, however, not as circumspect as Jeremy. The big Russian leaned back in his chair, making it creak alarmingly. "This is Holmes. Ever since Lord of Manor saved his hide from noose in America, things have been like this. Difficult. Inconvenient. What can be so urgent to call a board meeting like this?"

The predatory aliases were an affectation. Most of the men in this room had ferreted out the names and histories of the others—Jeremy certainly had. Yet like many things in the House, it was all done in the shadows.

"Perhaps this is pertaining to House finances," grumbled Mr Lion, a tall, bald man seated at his right. His tanned skin would be outrageous in London society. "My coffers have been nearly drained dry, and seeing as how our diamond market has been supporting operations of late," he said, casting his eyes around him while slowly tapping on the fine mahogany table where they all sat, "I would like to open discussions on where exactly our finances are going."

Brazen. Blunt. These traits, along with being the board's oldest surviving member, made Mr Lion the most formidable man in the room.

That did not mean he was immune to opposition. "You are not the only one with fiscal concerns," spoke Mr Dingo, the representative of their Australian operations. "Our own silver and opal markets are finding it hard to keep up the growing demand from the Lord's office. Do not dare regard your problem as a unique one."

Jeremy leaned forward and took a cigarette out of the silver box in front of him. Through his initial puff of smoke, he observed Mr Lion lean over and whisper to Mr Dingo. If those two were setting aside old rivalries, the end result could not be good.

Bear gave a slight sniff. "Perhaps we should open discussions concerning this 'grand asset' from your part of the world," he suggested to Jeremy. "Seems to eclipse all else."

All the board members shared a look, to which Jeremy released a derisive snort in reply. They all believed the archivist to be nothing more than a key to the secrets of the Ministry, and that was what he wanted them to think. Only the Lord of the Manor and Jeremy knew of Project Achilles; an astounding creation of breeding, training, and scientific manipulation. The template for Tomorrow's Soldier. *Their* soldier.

Unexpectedly, Wellington Thornhill Books had not turned out to be nearly as compliant as advertised; and that non-compliance was demanding from the House a high price. Project Achilles cost them one of their finer agents, Evelyn Primrose, after Arthur Books, in an apparent fit of rage, or spite, or perhaps a touch of both, eliminated her following the project's departure. Then, after finally obtaining their prize, came the loss of their Antarctic outpost. Finally, there was the recent catastrophe that was Operation Poseidon, proving that Books would continue to be a menace to the very organisation that had commissioned his creation.

Mr Tiger glanced his way, and he knew what the Chinaman was thinking. Jeremy's obsession with Wellington Books and its toll on the House was his fault. The Ministry, this "Maestro" nonsense, and the assassin's defection—all being laid at his feet. As if Mr Wolf, in control of the Americas, was completely immune, even though Operation Poseidon had been his responsibility.

Mr Badger couldn't quite keep the smile off his lips, shooting Jeremy an arched eyebrow through the smoke. The Frenchman had nothing to be smug about—Books had been in France when the Ministry of Peculiar Occurrences enacted Phantom Protocol. Another opportunity to capture their elusive prize. Lost.

"I hardly think we are here to discuss the Ministry," Mr Scorpion said softly, his fingers steepled in front of him. "Being summoned all the way to..." He looked around, his scowl deepening, "Toronto."

"Perhaps not as rich in history as your beloved Egypt, but believe me," a smooth voice appeared among them as quickly as a hawk stooping might, "this city is quite a treasure trove of delights, I assure you."

It was not the Lord's voice, though he stood next to the speaker. A chill crept up Jeremy's spine, not on seeing the elder statesman of the House of Usher, but on locking eyes with Dr Henry Howard Holmes.

Jeremy tried to keep his face in an unreadable mask as he looked at the interloper, but he caught from his fellow board members the faintest of straightening in their seats. He preferred not to meet the gaze of Holmes. It had been a trip to Chicago in 1892 when Holmes captured the Lord's attention. What developed quickly between them was a relationship of opportunity, primarily for Holmes. The American might stand at the side of the Lord of the Manor, but he had not earned the right to be there.

They all watched as their leader strode to his place at the head of the table. It was the forced march of a man trying to conceal any weakness. Jeremy doubted any other man in the room was fooled by it. Holmes took his place quietly behind his right shoulder and gave them a pleasant smile.

"Gentlemen," the elder began, but then suddenly his brow knotted. His lips moved, but no words came from them.

Watching Holmes gently take hold of the old man's shoulder made Jeremy's skin tingle. With a nod from his charge, Holmes turned and addressed the assembled directors. "An unexpected gathering, yes? Mr Cobra sends his regards as well as his regrets for not attending. An unfortunate complication has arisen in his current operation. The Lord of the Manor granted him leave to deal with it. As for the remaining corners of the world, all are represented at this table."

"Da," grunted Bear, "most impressive. Now we ask, again, why?"

"Since the failure of Operation Poseidon, we have been—"

"*We?*" Jeremy asked, his apprehension yielding to his contempt for Holmes.

Holmes' reply was a polite, civil smile. So civil, in fact, that Jeremy suddenly grew aware of the pistol he had concealed in his right sleeve.

"The Lord of the Manor confided in me his concerns about the House of Usher and its current direction."

"We seem to be struggling forward." Wolf shook his head as he took a final drag from his cigarette. "If we have a direction at all."

Holmes gave a sigh of delight as he pointed at Wolf. "How very apt, Mr Wolf. Keen insight, indeed. I would expect no less from the esteemed Adams bloodline."

Jeremy watched as Mr Wolf, his real identity Milford Scott Adams III, reddened with anger. Rather daring for Holmes to allude to Mr Wolf's true identity so openly amongst the other boardmembers.

Holmes continued, ignoring Wolf's outrage. "*If we have a direction at all.* My own observation, as well. Seems that we have been tripping over ourselves, particularly when the Ministry of Peculiar Occurrences is involved." Holmes paused, looking at each of the board for a moment before continuing. "It was the topic of conversation just before we entered, was it not?"

Tiger sat upright, his frown deepening. "I do not care for being spied upon."

"Oh, please." Holmes waved his hand dismissively. "You all have spies within your branches, perhaps even double agents and—knowing you lot—triple agents. You see, this is what happens when an institution lacks direction. A shame it should happen to the House of Usher."

"Who are you to scrutinise us?" Lion said, straightening in his chair. "You are an assistant to the Lord. His valet. You have not served the House over the years as we have."

"No, but therein lies your problem." Holmes stated. He did not address them as superiors or even equals. He was amused by them all. "You are too close to the issue at hand."

"What issue," Badger said, interlacing his fingers together as he leaned forward, "is at hand, *monsieur*?"

"You are all so close to the House of Usher, to its history and reputation, that you refuse to acknowledge its decay from the inside, this mistrust of each other." Holmes let that assessment hang in the still air of the room for a moment. "The House of Usher has become something of a jaunty music hall number, now hasn't it? Reduced to a laughing stock in the intelligence community."

"I beg your—"

Holmes ignored Scorpion's protest. "You have lost direction as you have lost your foundation. The House of Usher was never intended to be some fat git's getaway from the missus, now was it?" Bear, a man of considerable carriage, bristled a bit at Holmes' words but the Lord's right-hand continued. "To be the society the House of Usher desires to be—undeterred, undaunted, uncompromising—you must have a foundation."

"I assume," Wolf began, "that you are intending to rebuild this foundation you pine for, yes?"

"Indeed," Holmes replied, his smile almost illuminating the room. "A foundation such as the one for this hotel is but a simple thing—stone, mortar, dense cornerstones. I believe the House can be great once more if you all focus on three things."

His fingers pressed against the surface of their shared table, and a panel Jeremy had not noticed on earlier inspection slid back. Behind it were three rows of buttons and switches, each row a singular colour. One row of buttons was white while another was a deep green. The final row nested between them was red.

In that moment, Jeremy finally took a prolonged notice of their leader. He was smiling, bobbing his head as if to some invisible tune, his eyes catching and following specks of dust that floated in the air before him. The Lord of the Manor was not just getting feeble in his advanced years; his wits had quite left him.

"The first rock we must lay in this new foundation is Authority. You all must believe in your leadership." He then looked over his shoulder to the Lord. "Sir, it's time."

His eyes jumped to Holmes, and a clarity Jeremy had not seen since his entering filled the old man's eyes. "Very good, Holmes. If you are ready, carry out my order."

Holmes nodded. "Serving you has been beyond pleasure. Thank you."

The Lord of the Manor released a small titter of excitement as he breathed, "Oh, you are most wel—"

Holmes flipped the red switch within the crook of his index finger and light flared and danced from underneath the head of the House of Usher. Their leader was trying to scream, but his muscles all locked and stiffened against the violent convulsions overtaking his body. While quick flashes continued to pop and flicker from underneath the old man's seat, sapphire tendrils of electricity leapt across his face, fingers, and neck.

The clamour and chaos of the assault ended, and the Lord of the Manor slumped back in the chair. Holmes pressed the green button just underneath the switch that had killed the elder, and the corpse descended into the floor. He took a deep breath and announced, "I hereby formally accept this unexpected appointment as Lord of the Manor."

Surprisingly, Tiger lurched to his feet, but hesitated as Holmes' finger now rested on another red switch. Keeping his dark gaze on Holmes, Tiger returned to his seat once more. Next to Jeremy, both Lion and Dingo took stock of their own seats.

"Edison had been such a delight to work with during Operation Poseidon," Holmes said, his chuckle mingling with his words. "While his first electric chair may have been something of a disaster, I dare say he has perfected it."

The slightly charred chair—the Lord's body notably absent from it— now rose from the floor to lock back into place.

Badger recovered first, pointing a finger at Holmes. "Exactly what makes you think we will follow you? You are not one of us."

"Have I gone through your ridiculous initiation phase, memorised your impressive but somewhat stagnant history, and endured your melodramatic rituals?" Holmes gently caressed with a single finger the tops of the scarlet switches. "You are correct; I have not been anointed by you—but that is the Usher of old. We must rebuild on this new foundation comprised of Authority." His finger stopped. "And Accountability."

Holmes' fingertip pressed the white button underneath it and the floor collapsed from underneath Mr Bear, both chair and occupant disappearing from view. There was a rush of metal against wood, and then all went quiet again, though not for long as Bear's shouts rose from under their feet. The whole board was out of their chairs now, but remained rooted where they stood.

Dr Holmes smiled. A handsome, terrifying smile. "Accountability is key, gentlemen, if success is to be obtained. We have a new initiative currently underway in Russia, and it has fallen woefully behind schedule. The Lord of the Manor—my apologies, the *former* Lord of the Manor—was rather indulgent when it came to patience. I, however, am not."

Holmes gently stroked his moustache, as underneath the table Mr Bear's curses filtered upward, muffled by the wood and—based of the echo of his vulgarities—size of the room.

Mr Lion cleared his throat. "Mr Holmes, if you have learned anything about the House of Usher in your time caring for our recently-departed elder, you know we are about more than mere survival."

"What I do know is that the House up to this point has been barely existing." He calmly took the Lord's place at the head of the table, the control panel well within reach. "Your collected incompetence has pushed the House to the brink of collapse. You all have been plotting and scheming against each other for how long now? Years? Decades? Forming alliances within when you should have been *united* under the raven's crest. My country knows all too well the cost of division."

Mr Bear's curses paused at that moment, and then came a strange, high-pitched whine followed by the sound of something slicing the air. His screams erupted anew, but this time they were not of outrage and indignation, but of agony and terror.

Their new leader motioned for the remaining predators to resume their places at the table, even as the screams turned bloodcurdling, the quick cuts through the air growing louder and faster. One by one, they took their seats again. After all, they were of the House—screams were their stock in trade, but even Jeremy had never heard such fresh anguish as this.

Nausea welled within him. Casting his eyes around the room—Bear's screams now laborious pleadings—did nothing to calm this strange sensation of vertigo. The hotel's valets. The Lord of the Manor's seat. The room below them. It made sense. This was not an Usher safe house where they met. This was a structure commissioned after Holmes' rescue years ago. Money from all their lucrative ventures had been funnelled into this project: a recreation of his killing house in the White City during the Great Exhibition.

And the heads of the House of Usher were all presently inside it.

What Wolf blurted out made Jeremy nearly scream. "A fine way to show your gratitude, Mudgett, since I believe you were saved by the House. Hardly the sign of an aimless organisation possessing the resources to find someone to take your place at the hangman's noose?"

Using Holmes' actual name may have been Wolf's attempt at retaliation for using his real name openly, but the intended insult only had the effect of making the man pause and close his eyes for a moment. The breath he took seemed to last forever, prolonging Bear's final wail. He gave a slight shrug. "I would have enlightened you, Milford, on my intentions for the House. I would have gladly enlightened all of you, but I don't feel a pressing need to disclose anything to a syndicate of cutpurses, charlatans, and ne'er-do-wells peddling snake oil at carnivals."

At that moment Jeremy was certain the remaining board members were about to be swept into the same dark chamber as Mr Bear.

"My first official act as the new Lord of the Manor—eliminate this *ridiculous* title. 'Lord of the Manor' makes me sound as if I should be adorned with ornate robes, blood-soaked proclamations in one hand, and a glass of wine in the other." Holmes rolled his eyes, groaning softly. "How utterly Baroque."

"What should we call you then?" Mr Tiger asked.

"I can think of a few things," Mr Lion offered.

Holmes replied to Lion's slight with a wry grin. "Something more practical. Chairman."

Now it was Mr Lion who groaned. "How very American."

"I like it," Wolf replied.

Jeremy tightened his jaw. Adams had always been a right bootlicker.

"So, let me see,"—and the entire table flinched as Holmes reached into his coat pocket. He produced a small notepad, which he flipped to what Jeremy could see was a list of items. Holmes made small checks as he read off— "the induction of new leadership, disciplinary action carried out on Mr Bear, title change. Any other pressing business, gentlemen?"

The boardroom remained silent, as did the room underneath.

"A rather productive first day, if I do say so myself. Well then, as Chairman, I hereby bring this meeting to a close. We will convene here again in—shall we say—a month's time? In order to give our Russian associates ample time to find a replacement?"

"I will see to that straight away," Tiger stated. Then he added, "Chairman."

"Most kind of you." Every board member cringed as Holmes' finger slipped deftly to an amber button at the top of the console. "The staff will see you to the door."

With a final nod, the directors all stood in unison.

"Mr Fox," Holmes said, "Stay for a moment, if you please."

Each representative regarded Jeremy for a moment. The primitive part of his brain screamed at him to get up and run for the door. It wasn't that far. Easy distance to cross. The more logical part assured him he would be dead within three steps.

"But of course," Jeremy replied, easing back into his own chair.

The door opened, and three men filed in. Though they were dressed in the typical dark suits of the House, they were much taller—all over six and a half feet. They also had curiously white hair for young men. A shudder ran down Jeremy's spine as he observed how their eyes remained fixed on unseen points in space above them. As their faces were elevated slightly, it was impossible for the dim light of the room to not catch the milky substance that undulated within their pupils.

"You rang, sir?" the lead valet asked.

"Yes, Barnsley," Holmes said, opening his journal to a blank page, "please escort the board members out."

"Safely, sir?" he asked, his query capturing everyone's attention.

Holmes jotted down a few notes in his pad, and then replied, "This time, yes."

Barnsley nodded curtly and stepped back, motioning to the door where the remaining valets, blind as their leader, stood on either side.

Sharing uneasy looks with one another, the leaders of the House of Usher disappeared from view, leaving Jeremy alone with Holmes.

"Mr Jeremy Elliot," Holmes said as he leaned back in his chair, "as it is only you and I present, I am making the rather bold assumption I can drop with the alias pretence. Fox, Dingo, Wolf, Bear...a bit trite, don't you think?"

"The less we know about one another—" Jeremy began.

"Yes, yes, I know—plausible deniability, secrecy maintained, but really, it's traditions like that which keep the House anchored in its own past. Besides, you lot spy so incessantly on one another, you all not only know one another's true names, you know their families, their intimate acquaintances, and probably what they had for breakfast this morning." Holmes shook his head. "And yet we call ourselves 'brothers' and 'sisters' when we know so very little about each other, about our passions..." He leaned forward. "Our obsessions. This archivist I have heard tell of—" Holmes returned his attention to the ink still drying against the open page. "Wellington Thornhill Books. I want to know everything about him."

Jeremy stumbled on this new title. It would take some getting used to. "Chairman..."

"Henry, please," he said.

Jeremy cleared his throat. He was desperate for a drink. "Henry, as head of the House, you now have access to mission dossiers. I beli—"

"Jeremy," Holmes sighed, and on that exhale Jeremy's flight response bucked and kicked like a wild horse trapped in a pen, "I am sure there are some fascinating reports at my disposal, but that is not what I want. I want the third element of our new foundation. We have Authority. We will have Accountability. What I want is what you want: Achilles. I want to hear your personal thoughts concerning this great hope of the House of Usher. I want to hear of what had been promised to us decades ago, about the progress made by both Arthur Books and Dr Henry Jekyll, and about the boy that grew to become Wellington Thornhill Books, archivist for the Ministry of Peculiar Occurrences. I want to understand your obsession." Holmes urged, his pen at the ready, "I want to hear all about it, from the beginning."

CHAPTER TWO

When Our Colonial Pepperpot and Dashing Archivist Set Foot in India, a Land of Many Surprises

Bombay in January was a lovely change from wintry London—though granted it was still crisp, reminiscent of the beginning of spring or autumn back home. While the climate was certainly a dramatic change to what she was accustomed to at this time of year, it was their current mission that gave Eliza D. Braun pause.

Wellington was still on board, retrieving from the First Officer's log the final co-ordinates on where Featherstone had gone down. It was a very small chance he'd survived, but a Ministry submersible would be sent to the area, just in case. With Featherstone lost to the watery depths, the only tenuous hope remaining was to track down where he was staying and whom he was meeting in India.

Eliza was already eager to get back to their pursuit of Dr Henry Jekyll, but her stomach fluttered with uncertainty. This was not London, there were no sharp-eyed Ministry Seven to help out, and it had been many years since she'd been here. Gaining local insight was going to be the first call of business.

From what she understood, the Indian Branch—the largest divisional office outside of Great Britain—had taken quite the pounding from the Department of Imperial Inconveniences. Those tossers in tweed had been responsible for the deaths of many good agents, including its director, Kamod Tandon. However, with the reinstatement of the Ministry of

Peculiar Occurrences, the India office was getting back on its proverbial feet, and operations were slowly returning to normal.

Sadly, the same could not be said for their ruling monarch. Freed of the effects of Jekyll's serum, Victoria had reverted to a quiet, if slightly difficult, old lady. Doctor Sound had confided to her and Wellington, just before leaving on their hunt for Jekyll, that the side-effects of the serum had probably shortened Her Majesty's life by a few years. *"She would be fortunate to live into the next century,"* he had told them.

The domino effects when Victoria inevitably passed on Eliza could not predict, but as she looked around the dock, she suspected they would be wide reaching. Victoria was Empress of India, and even though she had never set foot on the continent, her death would surely bring changes.

All those concerns aside though, Eliza would never forget the immense satisfaction of punching the ruling monarch of the British Empire square in the face. Quite fulfilling. A story for grandchildren.

Turning around, Eliza looked towards the city of Bombay itself. She did not know India well, her work only bringing her here on two occasions, and she did not much like the idea of chasing Jekyll over unfamiliar ground. With climate and culture in mind, she had dressed in linen pants which were cut for the female form, along with a simple cotton top. Perhaps the blouse might show off a fraction too much of her breasts for London or even Indian society, but it kept her cool.

With a glance to her pocket watch, she turned back to scan the wharf for Wellington. He had probably got into some technical discussion with the First Officer and Navigator and forgotten all about the time. Still, Eliza didn't like him being out of sight. Despite his skills, he was still an archivist at heart, not a field agent. Besides, as soon as their contact arrived, she wanted to be away.

The wharf in Bombay harbour bustled and pulsed with activity. The flotilla around them was disgorging all sorts of cargo: spices from other regions, beer for the military, building materials from Europe, and ice from Scandinavia. Meanwhile, Indian products were being loaded onto other ships, especially cotton, silk and tea. The *African Sunset* was moored alongside other pleasure craft, but theirs appeared to be the only one presently disembarking passengers. So much chaos provided all kinds of ways for the two agents to be blindsided.

Eliza sighed softly and strode over to what could serve as the most advantageous tactical position: by the luggage, close to their boat, slightly set aside from the hubbub. This position offered the best of the terrible sight lines. As she smoothed down her trousers, Eliza checked by habit the location of her pistols under her jacket. Wellington had been gone some time, and that meant her mind conjured all sorts of things happening to him.

Then a voice broke though, tearing her away from the horrific phantasmagoria. "Eliza?"

At the sound of her name, she spun around, hand already reaching for her pistol, but then she stopped. Those who approached were practically on top of her, but thankfully they were friends. One of them at least, while the other looked strangely familiar.

"Now the Eliza D Braun I am familiar with," began Agent Maulik Smith, his artificial vocal apparatus unable to remove the mirth in his tone, "would have never let me sneak up on her like this."

"Long voyage," she returned with a twist of her lips.

"A pleasant one, I hope."

She managed to keep her face still. "More like eventful."

"Oh dear," he said, "I am surprised the ship is intact."

Maulik looked the same as ever, his entire head encased within the large mask he was forced to wear. He never talked about the mission that sentenced him to a life within a walking respirator. Besides, it was not as if his abilities in the field were ever dampened by this disability. He was as formidable now as he had been the day she first met him—just in different ways.

Things, however, had changed following the Diamond Jubilee. His battle with the Maestro had bought Wellington and Eliza precious time to escape with Queen Victoria, but had cost him his ability to walk. Before their departure, Eliza had seen her friend in a wheelchair, provided by the hospital. This one looked as if it had been provided by R&D.

"You mentioned returning home to India," Eliza began, extending her hand to him.

"I did, but not quite as I would have imagined," he chortled, bringing her hand up to where his lips would have been.

"Come again?"

"What Director Smith means," said the young female protégée at his side, "is that retirement did not suit him in the least."

Eliza stared at Maulik. "*Director* Smith?"

"Shortly after you and Wellington went off gallivanting across England and such," he began, "Director Sound approached me with a proposition. He was rather dismayed about losing me, it seemed, so he asked me to take the reins here."

Eliza released a delighted laugh. "Then congratulations, Director Smith."

The masked agent shook his head. "No. Still not used to hearing that."

"Do not let this modesty fool you," said the Indian woman tending to him. "He rules with an iron fist."

Maulik turned his head to the agent and held up one of his hands. "I prefer leather-encased fist, thank you very much."

"The work he has accomplished in these past few months has been a true credit to the Ministry," she said, patting him on the shoulder. "Director Smith has been an inspiration to all of us here at the India office."

The dark-skinned girl, her features seemingly plucked out of a memory, continued to distract Eliza. What was it about this young lady?

"I take it you are an agent of the Ministry then?" Eliza brazenly asked.

"Oh, where are my manners?" Maulik said. He then motioned to the diminutive girl at his side. "May I introduce Field Agent Pujari? Your liaison for the length of your stay."

The name from the past almost knocked Eliza back a step.

"Pujari?" she asked, offering her hand to this new, yet familiar face. "I take it you are—"

"I am Vania. Ihita was my sister," she replied, her grin somewhat tight.

All of a sudden, Eliza did not know where to look. Ihita, one of her closest friends in the Ministry, had not been the first agent killed in the field, but her loss had hit Eliza particularly hard. Her death had been painful and completely unnecessary.

"She was a fine agent," Eliza stated, her voice suddenly sounding frail even to herself, "and we in the London office still miss her very much."

"Of course she was, but she is missed by more than just the Ministry." Vania's words sounded rehearsed, and as if they had been repeated over and over again.

A healthy dollop of guilt with a dash of regret was not quite the arrival to India Eliza had been anticipating, but there it was.

"I say, Eliza," Maulik said, his voice sounding louder than what would be considered proper, "is that Books?"

She was not one to be so easily distracted, but here she was being caught hot-footed again; first, being snuck up on, and now face-to-face with Ihita's sister. Eliza might as well have been naked and dancing a can-can down the streets of Bombay. Instead, she turned and looked up the gangway. Wellington Books adjusted his fine brown bowler, which now carried the added accessory of tinted goggles wrapped about its hatband, and tapped the shoulder of a passing porter. Even though distance denied them any chance of overhearing what was said, she already knew the subject matter. He was once again reminding some poor employee about how important—and extremely delicate, from the look of his gestures to the porter—his luggage was. The man did love his devices, and even if he had been unable to bring the *Ares* with him, he had not left London empty-handed.

"Why yes," she replied lightly, quite relieved to see her partner, "that would be him."

From Maulik's vocaliser came a soft chuckle that burbled and rumbled through the pipes of his life support. Eliza guessed he was smiling. Maulik and the archivist had formed quite a bond during the battle for London, and so when Wellington's feet touched the soil of India, he was pulled downward to be enveloped in a hug.

Eliza got a great deal of satisfaction in watching her partner's face twist in surprise and embarrassment. It was strange how much she had come to love Wellington Books, and yet still enjoyed working his levers. Despite everything that they had been through, he still managed to hold onto the very correctness of his English upbringing. At least in public.

She let out a little sigh, thinking of their more private time on this journey. As always, it was not nearly enough. *Priority,* she thought whimsically. *Find more time alone with Agent Books. Not Mission Critical, but definitely Me Critical.*

When Maulik released Wellington, she found herself guiding him over to their liaison. "Agent Wellington Thornhill Books, may I introduce Agent Vania Pujari, our liaison."

Wellington's eyebrows shot up, almost disappearing under his bowler hat. "Pujari?" She wondered what was going through his mind, and if he would possibly bring back the awkwardness that his arrival had so conveniently pushed aside. "The pleasure is all mine."

The young woman's face softened a bit. It seemed that Wellington's wide-eyed charm was irresistible. "Likewise, Agent Books. Welcome to Bombay."

Well done, my love, Eliza thought, with a smile.

"Let's move along then," Maulik said. "Not the most secure location to talk business."

The three of them nodded, and Maulik took charge of things after that, ushering them through the chaotic streets of Bombay. Eliza saw British military made up a large portion of the crowd, their uniforms in stark contrast to the explosion of colour around them. Loose cows wandered through the press, finding their own paths. Bicycle bells rang noisily, barely heard over the angry snarl of motorbikes and the calls of vendors at the edge of the crowd. Bombay was a far cry from the staid composure of London. Noisy and impossible to ignore, Eliza recalled why she liked India so much.

Apparently, Wellington was just about to find a reason to like India too. When Maulik raised his arm, a large gleaming brass trunk rose in the air and let out a trumpet that sent the crowd scampering. The automaton elephant lumbered up to where they stood, quite snatching Eliza's breath from her. One glance at Wellington, and she knew she had competition for his affections.

"They do have that effect on people," Vania said to Wellington, grinning like hers was fit to crack her face. "Director Smith thought he'd show you the best Indian ingenuity could do."

Wellington's gaze apparently didn't know where to linger, but he finally recovered the ability to speak. "It's...it's magnificent." Then he blinked. "Wait a moment—*Director* Smith?"

The driver slid down a ladder artfully concealed behind one ear, and hooked open the belly of the beast. Inside was a red velvet interior, a pot of tea steaming cleverly secured on a narrow table, and a small slatted window keeping out most of the sun. Vania, Eliza and Wellington climbed in, while Maulik's chair was attached to a lift and placed inside. The belly closed moments later, and they set off. Even with its odd swaying stride, their magnificent transport was still very smooth.

Maulik let out what sounded like a satisfied wheeze as he pressed a button on the table, and freed the pot of tea from its base. "These auto-mahots and their creations are the latest thing in Bombay. They may not be fast, but they are comfortable." He shot a glance at Eliza. "I know you usually prefer fast."

Eliza let out a contented sigh. "For the moment I forgive you, Maulik. This is delightful."

Wellington was too busy poking the innards of the elephant, muttering equations to himself. He then looked at the teacup on the table, which was remarkably still. "Magnets?"

"Press the button by the saucer to release it," Vania said, motioning to the table. "Do not fill your cup too high, though."

"Yes," Maulik said as he filled his own cup halfway, "because you never know when..."

The elephant lurched suddenly to the right, sliding Eliza into Wellington's lap. Not that she minded. As if by reflex, her hand darted under her jacket and drew one of the pounamu pistols.

"...that will happen," Maulik said, returning the pot to the table with a hard *thunk* as the magnet took hold. "You can holster the weapon, Eliza," he said, with a low, soft chuckle. "It's not an attack, just the dreadful state of the roads."

She took her seat again and smiled. "I guess that whole affair with the Maestro and the Department has made me rather jumpy."

Wellington squeezed her hand, just for a moment, throwing aside protocol. He then tried his very best to draw attention away from her mistake, but in an entirely inappropriate direction.

"So, Director Smith, how have you been managing—" Wellington began.

"Really, Wellington?" Eliza said with a roll of her eyes. "I don't think that is a question you should be—"

He arched an eyebrow as his eyes locked with hers and continued—"with your new duties here at India Branch?"

Maulik chuckled. "Books, I think you need to spend more time with Eliza here. She can be quite protective of her mates. It's most endearing."

Eliza was now the one blushing. "My apologies, Welly."

"No, quite alright," he replied. "I'm sure you still see me as the newly-appointed field agent bumbling his way across the Americas."

"You were a bit clueless when it came to that tart Lovelace," she muttered.

"To answer your question," Maulik interjected, his tinted lenses looking to Wellington, to Eliza, and then back to the archivist, "I am adjusting. Paperwork and administration are hardly my strong suits though."

"I can only imagine," Wellington said, dropping a single cube of sugar into his cup.

"Stuff and nonsense," Vania piped up, releasing the teapot and pouring Wellington a safe amount of tea. "Director Smith had R&D design him a weaponised wheelchair."

Eliza inclined her head to one side. "What? You mean with his Queensbury Rules housed in one of the armrests?" Vania looked over to Eliza, her smile very sly. "You can't be serious."

"Darjeeling?" Vania offered, pouring Eliza a half-cup's worth.

"Maulik!" Eliza snapped. "You were told to slow down! For your health!"

The director raised a hand in surrender. "Old habits, my friend." He detached a small tube Eliza never noticed before in his left sleeve and stuck it into the cup. She watched wide-eyed as the tea slowly slipped through the tube and directly into his arm. "I have enjoyed my time working for the Queen. The mission against Methuselah's Order, seen Hill to the end of Operation Corazón, and of course, the battle with the Maestro himself—if my life as a field agent has taught me anything, it is to be prepared for the unexpected."

"But, Maulik, if I may be so bold," Wellington continued, "why did you not allow Axelrod to fashion mechanical legs for you. They work very well for Eliza's maid."

Eliza screwed her eyes shut. *It is his choice, my darling,* she thought with a wince.

"Well, after that brouhaha with the Maestro, I had suffered so much muscle damage that not even Axelrod's automatronic legs could work. So I decided on an enhanced wheelchair instead."

Wellington nodded. "And the intravenous tea delivery system?"

"That's Blackwell." Maulik shrugged. "Little vices."

"Ta," he returned, toasting him with his own teacup.

Maulik tapped his fingers on his knee. "I take it Doctor Sound is still operating headquarters out of Whiterock?"

Wellington nodded. "At the moment. With Miggins reduced to rubble, it seemed best. There is a threadbare detachment running a small office in London, but all operational matters are coming from my old home." He adjusted his glasses. "Once we have settled on a new location I will remain quite busy with reconstituting the archives."

That simply wouldn't do, Eliza thought as she cleared her throat. "Agent Books, you have field status now, and tidying up this Jekyll mess is your first priority."

He shot her an almost embarrassed look. "Yes, quite."

As Eliza finished her tea—and a delightful brew—their extraordinary vehicle lurched to a stop. Through the window, Eliza observed a rather modest corner building, such as she might have seen lining the River Thames. It bore a rather faded canopy with the words "Miggins Antiquities" just visible. Perhaps it was nostalgia, but she couldn't help smiling.

Their mahout opened the belly of their beast, and they descended to the ground. After slipping their driver some coin, Maulik rolled towards the building. "Vania, if you would please escort our guests upstairs. I'll be taking the lift."

"Certainly, sir," and she gave him a slight tip of her hat.

They watched as Maulik trundled up the ramp leading to the back of the shop's gallery, and then Vania motioned for the two of them to the exterior stairs of the building. "The lift was specifically built for Director Smith. There's only room for one."

They followed Vania the rest of the way, and entered the upstairs "Receiving" area of Miggins Antiquities. Looking around, Eliza almost forgot she was in India; the desk and office décor were identical to the former London office. However, at least half the occupants of said desks were Indian, with the rest being made up of either the tanned complexions of British folk who had been on the continent for some time, or the bright pink ones who had obviously only just arrived.

Eliza silently reminded herself to lotion once she reached her lodgings. Her family were more of the frying variety rather than the tanning.

"Welcome to India Branch," Vania said, motioning to the other agents.

"I knew this area of the Empire was busy, but—" Wellington's words stopped abruptly, and he even paused mid-step. Eliza always did like watching her walking analytical engine seize up. It reminded her that despite his cleverness he was not without fault. "This office is as large as London's."

Vania gave a slight chuckle. "Well, it is on account of the population, Agent Books. We are kept busy here, as India is a rather big place."

"You were expecting the Egypt Branch, Books?" Eliza inquired, with a slight twitch of her lips.

"Well...yes," he admitted.

She patted her lover gently on the back. "Don't worry, Agent Pujari, despite the antics in America and Europe, I am endeavouring to get him out more."

Wellington shot her an unamused look. "You really count our jaunt across Europe as time in the field?"

"Considering we were running for our lives whilst protecting seven children and a maid? Yes, I do," Eliza replied tartly.

Wellington nodded. "Point taken."

"So, Agents Books and Braun," came a mechanical voice from their left. Maulik was now rolling free of the private lift and into an office immediately to one side of him. "If you would follow me?"

Unlike the luxuries of Dr Sound's office in Whiterock, Maulik's office was dramatically different. Mounted on the walls were a variety of weapons and devices Eliza recognised as equipment he once used when out in the field. Instead of a world map, one wall featured a detailed map of India. Magnets depicting different agents on assignment, a device Eliza knew from other offices, decorated the map. Along with reminders of his years in the field and the active cases on the map, his office offered a breathtaking view of the Bombay harbour.

Perhaps Maulik Smith was uncomfortable with the responsibility of a directorship, but he seemed by all outward appearances to be settling into the position quite well.

"Have a seat, everyone," he said to the three of them. As they got comfortable in their chairs, Maulik came to a stop behind his desk. "It's just so bloody big!"

"You know how to handle large objects I am sure," Eliza said, unable to ignore an opportunity to flirt.

"Enough of that, you wicked lass," he replied, with a gurgle in his breather. "Oh yes, before I forget…" and he slid a folded paper to her. "From Section P. For Your Eyes Only, Eliza."

"What is that?" Wellington asked.

She shrugged. "Good news, Welly."

Wellington crooked an eyebrow.

"Keeping a promise, as it were," she assured him. "Good news, have no fear."

"So," Maulik said, capturing their attention once more, "exactly how did your isotope trail lead you to our modest doorstep?"

Eliza exchanged a glance with Wellington. "We were rather led here."

"Last time I saw you both, you were set on the trail of Jekyll," Maulik said, fixing them with a hard look. "You think the dark doctor has set foot here?"

"We boarded the *African Sunset,* following the trail of the isotope," Eliza said.

"The isotope is still working, then?" Maulik's hand twitched on the controls of his chair. "I'll be buggered. Axelrod and Blackwell actually made something that exceeds expectations."

"In a matter of speaking," Wellington said. "We knew the isotope wouldn't last for more than a month or two, and as expected, we lost his trail in Madrid. What we had not accounted for was how the isotope somehow infused itself with Jekyll's sweat glands. At least that is Doctor Blackwell's theory. Anyone the mad doctor comes into physical contact with is also marked with the isotope," he said, motioning to the goggles resting on his bowler.

"A pair of fingerprints on one wrist's pulse points, and a full hand imprint on Featherstone's coat sleeve, was all we needed," Eliza added.

"Featherstone?" Maulik asked. He glanced over to Vania, and then back to Eliza and Wellington. "Lord Hieronymus Featherstone? He was the one you were tracking?"

"Yes," Eliza replied, feeling like there was something about to be dropped on them. She slipped her hand into Wellington's.

Maulik ran his hand along the black canvas hood covering his head and then slapped an open palm on his desk. "Damn."

A strange silence fell over what had started as a delightful visit to the India Branch. It was, of course, protocol when Ministry agents arrived in other territories to notify head offices just to make them aware—on a "need to know" basis—that operations were underway.

Maulik's odd outburst, however, was far from expected.

Wellington's hand tightened on hers as he began to speak. "So by that rather colourful proclamation, are we to assume you are familiar with Lord Hieronymus Featherstone?"

You are, Eliza thought, *a delightfully ridiculous man sometimes, my darling.*

Vania cleared her throat. "Lord Featherstone has been supplying us weapons for months. The Ministry, as a courtesy, has also been working with him to see what we can do to aid the Queen's army in their peacekeeping operations."

That was, indeed, a surprise. "Welly, when you introduced yourself formally to Lord Featherstone, he didn't—"

"Lord Featherstone acted as if he had never heard of the Ministry," Wellington stated.

"Well now," Maulik said, lightly thrumming his fingertips against the polished surface of his desk, "shall I book for your stay two separate rooms, or a single suite?"

Eliza didn't bother to glance at Wellington as she spoke for them both. "Single suite."

⤖

Wherein the Ministry's Finest Face Their Greatest Challenge for Crown and Empire

Life at Whiterock was growing bloody tedious. Watching new recruits run by the back verandah in the freezing rain entertained Agent Bruce Campbell enough on the second, and even third, pass, but dining on their pain and suffering could only sate his appetites for so long. Besides, watching the anguish in their faces was laughable. They had no idea what was ahead, and God help them all when Cassandra Shillingworth got her hooks into them.

It had only been three weeks since his last mission, and it hadn't been an easy one by any stretch. Wales might have a reputation for being a little dull, but retrieving the wedding ring of Owain, the Lady of the Fountain, sounded easier than it had actually been. He and Brandon Hill had spent a lot of time running through the wilds of Wales chased by someone he was fairly sure had been some kind of grey lady. Usually Bruce liked ladies, but not when they wanted to rip his flesh from his bones.

Three weeks at headquarters, though, was threatening to make Bruce go mad with boredom. At first he'd hit the training fields with other agents recuperating from assignments. Weeks of shooting, boxing, and becoming familiar with new technology had finally become dull. Even that bloody karate nonsense that Agent Killian had brought back with her from Japan had ceased to be interesting. When yesterday he walked by the library and seriously considered picking up something to read, Bruce knew this was a sign that the walls of Whiterock were closing in. He had to get out or risk starting a brawl in the dining room just for fun.

"Well," Bruce muttered to himself just before taking a sip of his coffee and leaning back in his chair, "I suppose I did make a bit of a cock-up of the Queen's Jubilee."

He grinned. That operation was, indeed, the best of times. In fact, it was operations like the Diamond Jubilee that reminded him exactly why he joined the Ministry. The clean-up, the investigations, and the reconstruction of the Ministry that followed had kept all of them busy. Most veteran agents were training new junior agents in the field who would take the places of the ones killed during Phantom Protocol. The missions were becoming less dangerous, or at least less dangerous than the Diamond Jubilee. Bruce stared out the window into the gloomy Yorkshire weather. He always hated the dull calm following a successful assignment in the field.

"Bruce!" a familiar voice called out his name from behind him.

He knew who it was without turning, but did so anyway. Standing in the door of the conservatory, giving him a cheery wave, was Agent Brandon D. Hill. He had with him a bowl of what looked like almonds. Brandon loved almonds, pecans, and all sorts of nuts. *You are what you eat,* Bruce thought with a smirk.

They really were a mismatched pair, but somehow the two of them in the field created pure magic. During the Ministry's reconstruction, Bruce and Brandon had to part ways for a few months in order to take greenhorns out into the field to get mud on their boots. Scenario training and drills were all very well, but there were things that happened on missions that could not be trained for. Field work sometimes demanded improvisation. That wasn't taught. It was simply experienced.

The mission in Wales had been just the two of them, and that was a welcome change.

Bruce took his boots off the table. "Morning, Brandon, how'd you sleep?"

Capital, he will probably say, Bruce thought. *He loves it here at Whiterock.*

"Oh, capital! I love it here at Whiterock!" Brandon said, taking a seat by Bruce. His breath reeked of almonds. "Such a delightful change from Miggins Antiquities. So serene, and what magnificent landscape views."

"Country life isn't for the likes of you and me, mate," Bruce stated. He polished off his coffee and set it on the small table between them. "Books' homestead is posh and all, but too much time here would drive me batty. Don't you think there's a reason he doesn't live here himself?"

"Well, Hebden Bridge is quaint enough. Far from the madding crowd, as it were." Brandon took in a deep breath and exhaled with delight. "And fresh country air. Good for the bowel movements."

Bruce frowned at his partner. "Come again, Hill?"

"Bowel movements. Why do you think spas and sanitariums are located far outside a city?" Brandon clicked his tongue as he set his snack next to Bruce's empty cup. "All that smog and soot in the air. Mark my words, those toxins will be the death of the Empire!"

He knew he would regret asking, but Bruce believed the best way to make a connection with a partner was to understand what was on his mind and how he deduced matters. With Brandon, though, that could be a true descent into madness. He braced himself. "And what exactly does this have to do with bowel movements?"

"Damn it, man, you should really indulge more in reading the science page of the *London News*." Brandon waved his hands madly between his stomach and crotch. "Your bowels are incredibly sensitive to not just what you eat, but your demeanour, your diet, and—yes—the excitements in the very air. As wonderful as London is, all its pollutants aggravate your bowels, causing the toxins *in your body* to back up." He was now making fists and slowly wringing them over his stomach. If it were anyone else, Bruce would have told him to stuff it and let him enjoy the silence. But this was Brandon. He wanted to know where he was headed with this fresh slice of insanity. "All that waste backs up and weighs—you—down. But here? In the country?" And he inhaled again, threatening to suck all of the crisp, clean air around them. Bruce hoped he would, as the lack of oxygen would make them both fall to the vapours. "The excitements are pure. You are refreshed. You are relaxed. Ergo..."

"Your bowels are relaxed. And you're lighter because of it." Bruce rubbed the centre of his forehead, trying to fight the desire to ask; but he was one for giving into those. "Where do you pick up these sort of ideas, Hill?"

"You're a fine man to have in a brawl, Campbell," Brandon said, clapping his hand on the man's massive shoulder, "but you really should broaden your horizons and read a bit. That recent mission of mine, just after that brouhaha with the Jubilee..."

"The one that took you to Vancouver with the greenhorn?"

"With *Junior Agent* Mallory, a fine lad, very eager..." Brandon shrugged. "Talked a bit much, for my liking." Bruce shook his head at that, but Brandon didn't notice. "While I was over there, some chap from the United States—Kellogg, that was his name—was giving a series of presentations on wellness and overall health. Revolutionary, this Doctor Kellogg. Fantastic breathing exercises, mealtime marches…." He tapped the small bowl of almonds as he said, "And encouraging more nuts in your diet. Lovely source of protein."

"So's a good cut of steak, mate," Bruce returned with a wink.

Brandon shook his head emphatically. "Doctor Kellogg believes cutting back on meats is best. More vegetables, and yoghurt. Best after an enema. Yoghurt, you see, replaces any intestinal flora lost during the procedure, creating what he describes as a *squeaky-clean* intestine."

"You lost me at 'enema,' mate."

Brandon took up a few almonds and popped them into his mouth. "Oh, I almost forgot to tell you, Doctor Sound wants to see us."

Bruce gave a start. "What?"

"That's why I came down here to begin with." He crunched a few more nuts before adding, "I think he has a mission for us."

"Just us?"

"Mmm," Brandon replied with a nod.

"Then why the bloody hell are you on about with enemas and squeaky-clean intestines when the Fat Man's waitin' on us?" he asked, scrambling to his feet.

Brandon held his hands out, exasperated. "You asked me."

Dammit, Brandon was right.

"Well, come on," Bruce said with a huff, motioning to the corridor at their back. "Let's not keep the man any longer."

Brandon's face fell a bit. Knowing him as he did, Bruce suspected that his partner in the field had more to say about the brilliant and enema-centric Doctor Kellogg. Finishing the mouthful of nuts before rising to his own feet and cupping the small snack bowl in his hand, Brandon joined Bruce in the walk to the Director's Office. Unlike their previous headquarters at Miggins Antiquities, there was no lift to speak of. Everything was accessed by either stairs or a dumbwaiter, which meant Bruce and Brandon had their fair share of stairs to climb. Brandon loved it, but Bruce appreciated modern conveniences and wished that someone would have fronted the funds to install auto-lifts. From the looks of Whiterock, that toff Books could afford it.

They entered a small office where the Ministry's formidable secretary, Cassandra Shillingworth, dutifully reproduced the day's roster, recent reports, or relevant titbits the good Doctor would need in order to get through the day. The Hansen Writing Ball had apparently survived the mad dash from London, or it had been replaced with a band new one. Bruce snorted, thinking, *They won't install a proper lift here, but they will give ol' Cassandra whatever she desires?*

When Cassandra's cold gaze locked with his own, Bruce remembered why the woman's requests were never taken lightly.

Those riveting blue eyes softened a bit when Brandon stepped from around him. "Oh, Brandon, shall I tell Doctor Sound you're ready to see him?"

"That would be lovely, Cassie, yes," Brandon said cheerily.

Shillingworth rose from her chair and disappeared through the solitary door.

"Cassie?" Bruce asked.

Brandon shrugged. "That's what some people call her, from what I understand."

"Cassie?" Bruce asked again, completely dumbstruck.

"Delightful girl," he remarked, popping a few more almonds into his mouth. "Quite keen with a blade as well."

This time, Bruce gave a light snort. "Right handy with a stiletto, is she?"

"Rather," he said, smiling warmly as he turned his eyes to the door, "but what that lady can do with a Bowie knife is nothing less than exquisite."

Bruce guffawed, but stopped as he noted the calm expression on his partner's face.

"You didn't see her at the Diamond Jubilee," Brandon continued, his gaze distant and dream-like. "A neat bit of knife work as I've ever seen, not bad with a rifle either."

He was about to question Brandon—since he had apparently missed quite a bit in London—when the door opened, causing him to jump slightly.

"Gentlemen, Doctor Sound will see you now," Shillingworth said.

"Excellent," Brandon said with a smile.

Bruce took in a deep breath, a feeble attempt at best to clear his mind, which immediately scattered on casting a glance at Shillingworth.

"Agent Campbell?" she asked him, her voice low and soft.

"Yes, thank you..." and clearing his throat, he added, "Have a lovely day, Miss Shillingworth."

Tick-tock-tick-tock-tick-tock...

Any other time, that bloody clock of Sound's would work under his skin. After the brush with his extraordinary and terrifying secretary though, Bruce found the rhythm calming. He looked over to where the Fat Man usually sat, but the chair behind the grand desk was empty.

"Gentlemen," the portly man proclaimed from the opposite side of the room.

Bruce and Brandon turned around to find their director, Doctor Basil Sound, standing in front of a grand map covering the entire wall of his office. It made sense that there would be such a map; Bruce had heard this had been the classroom once in Wellington Books' younger years. All the tools for a posh education expected from a privileged pommy like him were lying about.

That survival instinct of Bruce's suddenly whispered to him. At first Bruce couldn't understand why, until he noticed Doctor Sound placing a marker on Calais. It was one of those team markers cut into a silhouette of two agents standing next to one another. It snapped against the wall with a dull, metallic *snap*.

Whiterock, for all its fancy dressings and demeanour, really did not need much done to it to become ready for the Ministry's use. In fact, it served as a training facility and base of strategic operations far more aptly than Miggins Antiquities. They most certainly would not have been able to run drills with new recruits down by the Thames.

"Campbell." Bruce started at hearing his name. Sound, fortunately, was looking at Brandon when he acknowledged his partner, "Hill, so happy to have you back at Whiterock in one piece."

"None the worse for wear, sir," Brandon replied cheerily before snapping a salute, though that wasn't Ministry protocol at all. "And this Hebden Bridge air does help clear one's mind when returning from the field."

"Yes, quite," Doctor Sound said, placing the rake back into its holder before motioning to three chairs by a grand window overlooking the grounds. "Please, join me for a brandy."

"A brandy?" Bruce said, surprised and a little impressed. "At this hour of the morning?"

"Believe me, Agent Campbell, you will need a sturdy libation on hearing the mission I have for you lads." He turned back to the decanter and poured three glasses, two-fingers' worth. "I refuse to allow my agents to drink alone." He then offered up in a toast, "To your health, and continued success."

They touched glasses, and Bruce took a healthy sip as he watched Sound take his seat across from them.

"Gentlemen, we are, as I'm sure you know, in a very delicate state of reconstruction." Sound swirled his brandy around in the glass. "Following the Diamond Jubilee, we have been trying to restore order to the crown, but it would appear that Jekyll's foul serum took a severe toll on Her Majesty's health."

"You're saying the Queen Mum is ill?" Brandon asked, straightening up as if struck by lightning. How his partner still managed to hold onto an affection for the old bird even after the Jubilee remained a mystery to Bruce.

"Quite." Doctor Sound's gaze shifted to the view of the grounds. "In the months following the events in London, the queen has aged dramatically." He then took a deep breath and large gulp of the brandy. "The royal physicians have informed me, if we do not produce a serum that can counteract Jekyll's, the queen will be dead within a month."

"Crikey," Bruce whispered, "a month?"

"Yes, quite troubling." Doctor Sound pursed his lips as he stared off into the horizon. "This is why I am turning to you gentlemen."

"We are at Her Majesty's service," Brandon stated, setting his bowl of almonds alongside the brandy decanter.

Sound smiled at the agent's enthusiasm. "The physicians have identified key elements in the queen's bloodstream that Jekyll must have administered, and we know where we can collect what is needed for a counteragent. Something to keep the queen alive, possibly cure her."

Bruce tapped a finger against his snifter. "With all this good fortune, I'm waiting for the bad news that is sure to follow."

"What we need," Sound began, his eyes going first to Brandon and then to Bruce, "is located in the forests outside of Grójec."

Bruce sank back into his seat. "Tell me you're having a go at us, Director."

"Grójec?" whispered Brandon.

"I'm afraid not, Agent Campbell," the director said, taking another sip of his brandy.

Bruce reached across Brandon, flipped the stopper off the decanter, and lifted it by its neck. "Switch to gin. I'm taking the bloody bottle."

"Manners, Campbell!" snapped Brandon. "This is for the empire, after all!"

Bruce stopped pouring. "Grójec, Brandon. We're being sent to Grójec in January."

"To save Her Majesty and preserve the empire," Brandon replied with pride.

His eyes narrowed. "You haven't a sodding clue where Grójec is, do you?"

Brandon went to answer, paused, and went to answer again. He then looked over to Doctor Sound. "Director, I hate to seem ignorant, seeing as

I'm the one who usually reads the field reports and retains mission details, but I am afraid I don't—"

"The Russian Empire," Doctor Sound stated. "Near Warsaw and the Vistula."

Brandon's smile faded as did the colour from his face. "Russia?"

Even though his heart was sinking, Bruce leaned over to his partner. "Let me top you off there, mate."

"Gentlemen," Doctor Sound set his snifter on the small end table and rose from his chair. "I know this may seem a lot to ask of you..."

"You are sending us in middle of winter into the Russian Empire. With all due respect, director"— Bruce downed a huge gulp of brandy— "get stuffed."

"Now see here, Campbell—" snapped Sound.

"No, I think Bruce is absolutely right in this moment," barked Brandon, clinking his glass with Bruce's. "Get bent, ya' toff."

Bruce expected this sort of reaction. At least, from him. Brandon? Maybe, but perhaps not until he was into his second snifter.

The director considered the both of them carefully, but he pressed on. Bruce steadied himself as Doctor Sound approached the map and took the rake up in his hand.

"The plan is thus—you will rendezvous with agents of Section P in Danzig." Going to the map he slapped down a marker labelled "Campbell/ Hill" on the German city. "They will see you into the town of Toruń where a contact will get you safely across the Russian border. Don't ask how, they have their own methods, and I trust them."

"But of course," Bruce said, toasting Sound with his glass. "Who needs logistics, I say."

"Your objective is to obtain a Firebird feather. We have confirmation that there is a factory somewhere in the vicinity of Grójec. Once obtained, you will need to signal us for extraction." He moved their marker to a small city closer to where the German and Russian empires met. "Based on the terrain and location, Łódź would be the logical choice. You will have two days to reach the extraction team once a signal is sent."

Bruce's glass froze in mid-journey to his lips. "Two days," he asked, "across three days' worth of Russian territory?"

"Again, your ingenuity will out," Sound offered with a smile Bruce interpreted as a smirk.

"Oh, this mission is getting more and more promising as we go," Bruce seethed.

Leaning forward Brandon took the crystal bottle out of Bruce's grasp, refilling his glass. "Worst Case Scenario—not too much of a stretch as we are heading into the Russian Empire in winter—what if we can't find these Firebird feathers, or they are not readily available? What then?"

"Then the fate of the empire," Sound stated, his voice distant and dark, "remains uncertain."

"Right then, no pressure, just the fate of the monarchy and the British Empire hanging in the balance, another day on the farm, eh wot? Cheers." The Canadian gulped back a generous swallow of the brandy.

"Lads, I know what I am asking of you appears difficult, but I know you can handle it." Sound returned to his own chair before the two agents. Bruce knew the Fat Man was well within reach of a right hook, but he was concentrating on holding his glass. Apparently, the drink was beginning to take hold.

The beautiful thing about brandy when drunk like beer—it worked quickly. He glanced over at another decanter. "I take it that is scotch?"

Sound glanced at the crystal bottle, nodded, and removed its stopper. He took in a deep whiff of the dram. "Fifty years old. Usually reserved for my counterparts abroad and visiting dignitaries."

"I have no doubt," Bruce said, taking the bottle out of Sound's hands, "but today it is the select drink of Agents Bruce Campbell and Brandon D. Hill, Saviours of the Empire."

"Dear Lord," Brandon muttered as he tipped the brandy decanter upside-down, draining it of its final drops, "we're all done for."

Wherein a Charming City Hides a Spider

There was no place more beautiful or irritating in the whole world than Bruges, Agent Beth Case thought as she was paddled through the historic canals of the ancient city by a glum gondolier. Everywhere around her were tourists, carrying parasols, rifling through maps, and making cooing noises over their quaint surroundings. The sky, even overcast as it was, served as the perfect backdrop to the breath-taking gothic architecture all around them. If there was a lack of sunshine, it was more than made up by the people of Bruges, smiling and welcoming to a fault.

Meanwhile Beth sat in the back of the boat, keeping her arms wrapped around herself, as they passed under little arched stone bridges, the scowl on her face deepening.

The Ministry had sent her orders once Phantom Protocol was lifted, to ferret out any agents still in deep cover, and such had been her life for the last four months tromping around Europe. The fate of eight agents still remained uncertain. Her objective: Bring these brave agents in from the cold.

As she stared miserably around herself, she considered how she might have been back in London, enjoying a proper high tea, if only she could tell the director his brave agents—all eight of them—were dead. Unfortunately, Beth would then have to tell him how she knew that. This was where her plan became complicated. How did she know these agents were dead?

She had done it, and it had been easy. They had trusted her, and that had been their mistake.

It was hard to calculate how much longer she would have to linger in this godforsaken sewer before she could return to London and give a reasonable story as to why she'd been unsuccessful in finding the underground agents. Beth thought longingly of the airship port only a few miles outside Bruges, which had to be drier and better appointed than this particular conveyance.

The canal boat finally reached the dock, and Beth joined the tourists clambering off. She bought some fresh chips from little friterie by the canal, adorning the delicacy with a touch of aoli. Then, holding the paper cone close to warm her hands, she popped a few into her mouth and relished the treat's saltiness. The chips would have been a reminder of home had she been able to top them with malt vinegar. *When in Rome, or in Bruges,* she lamented as she joined the flow of tourists towards the Grote Markt.

The town square was a vast cobbled space, surrounded by pointed-roofed brick buildings gleaming with water. It bustled with far too much life even in the chill of winter. Many a meeting of vapid and dull tourists was conducted here, and the spot was positively rabid with little horse carts.

And these locals were so bloody *cheerful.*

Then there was the plethora of little tables and chairs set out for French, English, and even Americans to sit about drinking coffee and show how urbane they were. On the other side of the Markt, local vendors had set out fresh produce and handmade trinkets to bilk the tourists with. The Belfry of Bruges loomed over them all, with the grey-towered Provincial Court and Post Office finishing off the officious, dull nature of the place. In front of the court were two statutes of some Flemish heroes. One was a butcher, the other was a weaver.

"Typical," Beth muttered to herself. "Even their heroes are dull."

Deciding it was safe enough for her to circle about and return to her hotel—just in case any Ministry operatives were to happen upon her by chance—Beth set her weary feet on the path back to her room. That was when a gleam of brass in front of the court snagged her gaze. Quite the contraption had been set up in front of the grey building, and a small crowd was gathering. On one side of the stage was a gleaming brass and bronze contraption resembling a five-foot wide metallic spider. Unlike an arachnid, though, this device held spun wool in all of its multi-jointed arms. It was hard not to admire the mechanical cleverness of it.

On the opposite end of the stage was a loom. The contraption, looking ancient in comparison to the other, was made of polished wood. Beams were bolted together to frames and limbs, all of these connected to a variety of cross beams that eventually led to a series of foot pedals set before a long bench. Threaded through hooks and stretched between two of these beams were many colours of wool strands.

Beth curled her lip and wondered why two such incongruous designs were placed so close together. The loom belonged in the museum, the brass device in a humming factory. The answer was quickly revealed when a tall, handsome gentleman stepped up on the stage next to the brass machine.

"Ladies and gentlemen, gather round…gather round," he said cheerily, his voice holding a light French accent, "I see many visitors in amongst the ranks of the more curious citizens of this lovely canal city, yes? You all are strangers, but strangers united through one commonality." He held up his index finger and slowly drew it across the crowd, his eyes holding contact with random people, his smile never faltering. "Curiosity."

A showman obviously cut from P.T. Barnum's cloth, Beth thought with a wry grin.

"You see upon this stage the trusted tools of a trade," he said, giving his hands a slight flourish as he motioned to the loom, "and the wonders of modern technology," and his hands flickered towards the brass spider. "I am here today to give a demonstration of my latest invention, an innovation for artisans here in Bruges and for those of you travelling abroad. Ladies and gentlemen, without further ado, I present the Weaver's Web!"

As if on cue, the clouds parted, allowing for slivers of sunlight to illuminate its brass body.

Beth craned her neck, and noticed a line of round little businessmen standing at the front of the crowd, observing the showman with hawk-like intensity.

"To show how soundly my device trumps any human in skill and speed, I have one of your city's finest weavers to compete against." He turned towards the stairs, and a woman shambled up onto the stage. The tattered dark blue shawl and bent back of this decrepit creature didn't speak much to her skill. If she was making any money as a weaver, she was not spending it on herself.

Beth let out a little snort of derision, however the crowd was watching the weaver keenly. She sat before her loom, adjusting its bench so that her feet were at a comfortable distance from the pedal array. The salesman missed this reaction from the locals, but Beth could easily label it as respect. Whoever this weaver was, she had a reputation.

Their Master of Ceremonies, wrapped in the confidence of his ilk, yanked back a cloth, revealing an over-sized hour-glass. His grin looked fit to break his jaw.

"Both your local artisan and my Weaver's Web will have half an hour to show how much they can create in that time. Your very own mayor will be the judge to the quality of the work." His glance at the old woman dripped with dismissiveness. "Are you ready, madam?"

The old woman gave the slightest of nods, but did not even look in his direction.

He blew the silver whistle, flipped the glass over, and then stomped on a pedal by his foot. The metallic spider leapt to life as it began clicking and clacking, the legs spinning, retracting, and reaching while on the other end of the stage the old woman began smooth, practiced movements of her own. The audience cheered on the old maid and the machine, the locals cheering a fraction louder for the old woman that seemed undeterred by the strange machinery weaving without any signs of slowing. At first Beth was riveted by the hypnotic dance of the device's eight legs. The way the thread moved and spun through the abdomen was entrancing, each retraction and extension appearing as if this collection of metal, pistons, and bolts had served as an apprentice to the greatest of weavers. The rug that was being crafted was a beautiful scene of the market itself.

Then Beth glanced over at the old weaver, and swiftly realized she had been missing the true wonder on the stage.

She sat quietly at her loom, her eyes neither glancing at the audience nor at her competition, as the shuttle flew backwards and forwards between the threads. The old crone embodied determination and focus, her own patterns in the rug appearing conservative in comparison, her chosen colours whites, greys and blue.

As skilled as the old woman appeared, Beth could see the showman's creation was swifter, moving at a pace a flesh and bone creature could not possibly match.

Despite her love for mechanical wonders, she felt a sharp pang for the crone, and a part of her demanded that she turn away from this old woman's fall. It was evident how the people of Bruges revered this weaver, but the mayor and other rotund gentlemen in attendance remained preoccupied with the Weaver's Web. In a matter of moments, this salesman would collect a fine commission while the accomplished artist would fade into obscurity.

Beth had half-turned away to find her hotel, when cries and gasps of horror rippled through the crowd. She spun around to see the old weaver slump. Her hands and feet still worked the loom but fatigue was taking hold. Was this old woman to breathe her last on the stage before them? The weaver was waving the shuttle in one hand over her head, her hand shaking, and her body trembling.

Dramatic.

A bit too dramatic for Beth's liking.

Her gaze narrowed on the weaver's other hand, which hung lifeless, as well as upstage of the action, and obscured.

The weaver's limp right hand twitched once, then again.

Then she let out a tiny cry and pulled herself back up, the crone's eyes finding their focus again. Her teeth gnashed together and her jaw set as she continued her motions, commanding the loom to continue; and in her emerald gaze, she would be satisfied with nothing less than victory.

Those hard, emerald eyes…

Just when that realisation flashed into Beth's mind, the contraption's clicking grew louder. Then harder. The clockwork precision was degrading to a grating rattle that came from deep within the machine. The showman glanced nervously around, but Beth already knew that his demonstration was not long for this audience. Joints that had once bent slowly and with the skill of an artist were now snapping and whipping out and around, as if the machine thought it had fallen behind the crone. Attention began turning to the shiny creation and its demise. Its legs jerked and seized, curling into themselves like a dying man's hand, while the body from where its legs sprouted now shuddered and smoked. As the showman ducked and dodged the Weaver's spasms to find out why his machine was suddenly failing him, the old woman worked on calmly as if nothing was happening.

The sand finished in the hourglass, and a hush fell over the audience as the Weaver's Web gave one final *bang* before listing to one side, sparks and super-heated pieces of metal falling on its rug and catching it on fire. Its creator was now earning a fair share of chuckles as he stomped out the small flames dotting its half-completed rug.

Then the silence returned as the old weaver stood and walked to one side of the loom. Carefully, she removed the rug from her device and held it up for the audience to see. At first, there appeared to be nothing there, apart from white and grey smudges. The old woman then stepped into the light that had been turned on the Weaver's Web, and that was when the details of the rug came to life.

Vétheuil in the Fog, painted in 1879 by artist Claude Monet.

With the swelling adulation of the crowd, the show and the competition was over. Moments later, the crowd evaporated, chattering around the rest of the market. Some small clusters remained to watch the showman scramble about the remains of his failure, others had returned to their tourist maps for ideas on where to venture next.

The old weaver tidied up her belongings into her bag and shambled down the stairs, not even acknowledging the showman. She'd made her point. As she made her way across the market towards the tangle of streets, Beth noted how the crone kept her head down. She now appeared exhausted, and in desperate need of rest.

Beth helped herself up on to the stage and walked around the remains of the machine. She knelt, placing one hand on the Weaver's Web and the other on the showman's shoulder.

"An impressive display, to be sure," she said.

Her other hand searched for what she believed had been the old woman's secret weapon. Her fingers then brushed across the edge of a disc. She trapped the circle of metal between her fingers and wiggled it. The magnet popped off the housing and into her palm.

"Perhaps next time, *monsieur*," she said, clutching the device in her fist so as not to reveal it.

Spotting the bent, frail form now far from the attention of tourists or locals, Beth followed the weaver deeper into Bruges. Rain started to fall, the additional darkness reducing her target to a formless shape against shadow. Beth's heart began to race as she increased her pace, her eyes taking in any possible doorways or alleys that could mask her pursuit as a foolish English tourist lost in the city.

A pair of boys barrelled out from a corner, sending her to her knees. They raced past her, calling out rude words in French, having no earthly clue how lucky they had been that she had not slit their throats. With a few choice curses of her own, Beth pulled herself back on her feet and pushed onward, her eyes peering ahead for her quarry.

Turning a corner, Beth caught sight of a bent old woman with a dark blue shawl over her head bustling away. The canal was on her right, dark and slowly flowing past just beyond a low stone wall. This corner of the canal city presently belonged to herself, and her prey.

"Mistress!" she called out.

The old woman stopped.

Beth slipped the knife back into her sleeve as she approached the old weaver. The woman oddly seemed to be shrinking the closer Beth drew. "Can I help you, child?" a creaky voice asked.

"I just wanted to return what belongs to you," she said, holding up the magnet.

The old woman slowly turned, lifting her slender hand up to the cowl covering her head.

Beth stepped back as she locked her stare with the weaver's. These eyes were not the ones she caught a glance of at the Markt.

Stars flashed in her vision as something jammed into the back of her neck. Beth stumbled forward, and opened her eyes in time to see the old woman making the Sign of the Cross to her, the cloak she had been wearing left behind in a puddle at Beth's feet.

She needed to turn around. She needed to reach the knife she had out only moments ago, or the gun just under her wrap, but her fingers wouldn't move. Beth collapsed into the street, landing face down. The impact should have broken her nose, but she felt nothing. Hands grabbed her by the shoulders and turned her over, and now rain gently fell on her face.

Once, during her idle years of youth, Beth had kicked a tortoise over on its back just to watch it wriggle. Now it was Sophia del Morte that watched her, and suddenly Beth felt terribly guilty about tormenting that tortoise as she had.

"Your eyes," Beth said, and her voice grew more and more raspy with each word. "I recognised you by…your eyes."

"Shhh…" Sophia perched herself on the other woman, knees on each side of her, dark hair blowing slightly. "You've been injected with the Family Kiss," she purred, holding a small syringe before Beth's eyes. "Paralysis is immediate. Death, somewhat slower—and a great deal more painful. If you answer a few questions for me, I can make your passing much quicker and more pleasant than you deserve." The assassin leaned closer until the subtle smell of her rain-kissed skin wafted over Beth. "Does the House know I survived the Jubilee?"

Beth nodded.

"Is there a bounty on my head?" the assassin asked, her head tilted to one side.

Beth gave her another nod, hoping that would give Sophia a fright.

Sophia's lip curled. "I hope it is a big one."

"Huge," Beth ground out through her tight throat.

"Well, I shall take comfort in that." Sophia tenderly brushed away a curl of hair from Beth's forehead. "Did you tell anyone you saw me?"

When it came to deception and misdirection, Beth's skills could not be matched. It had carried her through her life as a double agent, had allowed her to dispatch eight agents, and now at the edge of death she would deploy it with relish. "A dead drop," she managed. "The House of Usher will come for you. They will…not…stop."

Those words took effort to speak, and she slumped back into the stones under her, grasping for what tasted like final breaths. The world had now narrowed down to just Sophia's eyes. Such beautiful green eyes, but as cold as a raven's. No remorse or regret even as she rifled through Beth's pockets.

"I keep my promises," Sophia whispered to her, her breath caressing Beth's cheek. The slice of the blade was quick against her throat. The world was quickly slipping away, but not so fast that she was denied the welcoming chill of the canal, wrapping itself around her in a loving embrace.

CHAPTER THREE

In Which the Mettle of Her Majesty's Infantry Is Tested

"Lord Featherstone's designs and recent innovations have all been field tested and approved here in India," Vania shouted over the throaty report of the motorcar's engine. "The Ministry and the military have been in dire need of any and all advantages as insurgents have been taking arms against the Empire with renewed vigour of late."

"Insurgents?" Wellington asked, just before being jostled back against Eliza. Again. Not that he minded, but he was reminded with each rumble and shudder of India Branch's motorcar at how his own *Ares* handled. "A rather harsh word to describe resistance factions, don't you think, Agent Pujari?"

"Resistance factions, Agent Books, is too polite, especially in the case of recent events in Bombay. Civilian targets are becoming more common, and that captured the attention of Parliament. Featherstone undertook the challenge with great delight."

"How long—" and then Eliza was sent sliding into Wellington. He adjusted his bowler, hideously off-balance as he had forgotten about the isotope detectors still resting across the hatband. "How long has Featherstone been involved in the making and manufacturing of weapons for the Empire?" she asked, straightening her tiny hairpiece.

Vania opened a folio resting on top of a modest pile of case files and flipped through a few pages. "At least three years."

"That corroborates with our own notes concerning Featherstone. He had been referred to Jekyll by the Duke of Sussex." She then looked into the dossier Vania had open before her. "Have you all had any reports of malfunctioning munitions? Any sort of accidents or problems in the performance of these new weapons?"

"None," Vania said.

Wellington caught glances of various photos and schematics. Rifles, pistols, and even personnel armour, all of it carrying the signature of Lord Featherstone. Jekyll would have known about all of these technological marvels from inception to application. So much trust had been invested into Featherstone, and now every soul in the British Army and the Ministry were in potential danger.

Vania looked up. "What did you discover from Featherstone while on the *African Sunset?*"

"Not a great deal," Eliza said. "His room on the cruise ship yielded an appointment book—from the looks of the notes he kept, they were all of a deeply personal nature—and he was to meet with Jekyll two days from now."

"He has an apartment," Wellington said, "in a rather questionable section of Bombay, from what I read."

Vania closed the dossier. "Then I suppose you have a bit of time to take in a few sights while we wait for Jekyll to appear."

"I have no intention," Wellington stated, his tone low but still audible over the noise, "of waiting for the doctor."

An uncomfortable silence settled between the three of them, but Wellington did not mind it so much. Agent Pujari knew only of Jekyll through field reports. He did not have that luxury.

Through thick tuffs of steam rising from their transport's undercarriage, he noticed they were now crossing an open expanse just outside of the port city. Larger mountains could be seen in the distance, while the uneven land, greener than he would have expected but punctuated by hints of brown and beige earth, made their travel that much more difficult.

"We're just on the outskirts of the Hornby Vellard," Vania said, also taking a look outside her window. "We have an appointment with Lieutenant General Lawrence Southerby, the officer in charge of the troops in the Bombay area. The only person above him in India is General Sir William Lockhart, who is Commander-in-Chief at Fort William in Calcutta."

"Being in charge, wouldn't he prefer to command the troops from inside Bombay itself?" Wellington asked. Eliza furrowed her brow at the question. "It is not uncommon for a Lieutenant General to live outside the fort in a somewhat more salubrious accommodation."

"Lieutenant General Southerby is an uncommon commander," Vania said, "or he believes the Empire is at war. He insists on staying close to his men."

"Really?" He sat back in his seat, pulling at the hairs of his close-cropped beard. "Rather telling, I would say."

Eliza folded her arms. "So, how is Southerby a person of interest?"

"Southerby was a direct contact of Featherstone's." Vania said. "If Featherstone ever had new designs or was making a delivery here in Bombay, he would only speak to the Lieutenant General."

A muscle in Wellington's jaw twitched. Vania looked at them both as she returned the folio back to her satchel.

"Why am I detecting a hint of concern?" she asked.

Wellington gently tightened his hold on Eliza's hand as he replied, "None at all. Just recalling my luncheon with Featherstone. I'm hoping contact between this Southerby chap and Jekyll was never physical. Would prefer to avoid those particular unpleasantries."

Their transport rumbled forward once more, but much slower. They were now amidst the finest of the Empire. Soldiers on both sides of the car worked on what appeared to be machinations of war while other groups marched from point-to-point in drills, and smaller, more isolated units all practiced either marksmanship or hand-to-hand combat.

Not one Indian amongst them. All of the soldiers, male.

As it should be, a ghost whispered in his head.

Wellington shoved the wandering memory back as he took stock of the troops.

"Seems Southerby still holds onto some traditions," Eliza commented, the pointed civility in her words most evident. Naturally she would notice the lack of women in the ranks.

Vania shrugged as she took a different folio from the pile and tucked it under her arm. "The British Indian army is not exactly known for being progressive."

"Ladies," Wellington implored as their car came to a halt, jostling them all slightly, "open minds, if you please. Lest I remind you that while the Ministry embraces change and technology, some of Her Majesty's subjects are less than enthusiastic when it comes to progress."

The glare of India's noonday sun reminded him of Egypt, only without the heat considering the time of year. His eyes had finally adjusted to the light when he noticed the ladies were nowhere around him or the car. Wellington looked to his right, and then to his left.

"Ah, there you went. I was thinking," Wellington said, coming up between them as he consulted his pocket watch, "as we are quickly coming up on eleven, the best way to approach Southerby would be to suggest a light repast. As he is a traditional sort of fellow, Vania, would you agree?"

He looked up from his watch. Neither woman regarded him. Both just stared upward at the motor pool just right of the garrison's main headquarters.

"What?" he asked, before following their wide-eyed gazes.

What he saw caused him to start slightly. Lumbering across the open space usually reserved for transports or other varieties of vehicles was a marvel of modern technology, its large cannons coming round to bear on the entrance. "Good Lord," he heard himself whisper over the rhythmic *thump-thump-thump* of its massive, metal feet.

The soldier suspended in the air over the three of them chuckled as if he were enjoying a day out in the park playing cricket with the lads rather than piloting a technological wonder. The engineering feat that surrounded the soldier reminded Wellington of those damnable Mechamen of Havelock's, only this military monster was a hybrid between the smaller Mark I automatons and the larger Mark IIs. This war machine was a walking, lumbering contradiction in itself as the cannon and gigantic Gatling gun all seemed powered by the diminutive human at the core. From the central cage, the driver operated the entire creation via two gear shifts, his left hand operating basic forward-backwards motion while his right turned his enclosure left and right. When the soldier lifted his left arm upward, the titan's left arm did just the same. The legs were of a similar design, but basic motion required more rotors, gears, and pistons as their clacking and whining struggled to keep time in mimicking its operator.

"It looks as if the military engineers have been burning the midnight oil in India," Wellington managed.

"The Enforcer," came a voice from behind them. "Quite a view from the pilot's seat. Best one to have in a battle."

They turned towards the voice, and Wellington saw Eliza straighten just a fraction. The young man before them carried a pith helmet in the crook of his right arm and the rank of lieutenant across his shoulders. What Wellington found so startling from this young, handsome man was how he carried such a high rank against the darker colour of his skin. Such things did not matter to him, as Wellington's main concern from soldiers were their skills in the battlefield and their character in the barracks. He knew several men in Africa he would have gladly promoted to ranks equal to his own; but those above him put more value on breeding.

Much like his own father, come to think of it.

The soldier's smile he found quite disarming. A good thing, too, as the closer he approached, the larger he appeared. He was of a solid frame, to be sure.

"As we are charged with the well-being of India, we are always first to get the latest inventions from the War Department," he spoke with a rich baritone. Wellington wondered if this man indulged in music—preferably singing—as a hobby. If not, what a shame. "The Enforcer is just that. Innovation extraordinaire. Featherstone's finest, I have no doubt."

Wellington extended his hand. "Wellington Books, Minis—"

"Ministry of Peculiar Occurrences, yes, I know. Your office sent notice you were en route. Agents Eliza D. Braun and Vania Pujari, yes?"

"You have us at a disadvantage, Lieutenant," Vania said, her smile reflecting his.

"I'm a soldier," he said, placing a hand on his chest and giving a slight bow. "I prefer keeping the advantage."

Eliza gave him a wry smile. "I would think just walking in a room would do that."

The soldier cleared his throat in some kind of embarrassment. "So I've been told." He extended his hand to Eliza. "Welcome to Fort St Paul. I'm Lieutenant Jahmal O'Neil, secretary to General Southerby."

The same question flashed through Wellington's mind, but it was Vania who blurted it aloud. "Jahmal O'Neil?"

"Yes, Irish father and officer in Her Majesty's corps, swept off his feet by a jewel of India. I inherited my mother's looks, I assure you," he said with a wink.

"What did you inherit from your father?" Eliza asked.

He looked at Eliza with those dark eyes and grinned. Now it was the New Zealander's turn to blush. "I can drink any man here under the table." They all shared a chuckle at that. O'Neil replaced his helmet and motioned for them to follow him back to the barracks. "The general is currently reviewing the troops, so I've been asked to serve as your liaison here."

"Excellent," Wellington said, following them all into the modest office.

Fort St Paul did not appear out-of-the-ordinary for an Indian outpost, this building in particular doubling as offices for administrative duties and living quarters for the troops, as well. It was as Wellington would expect, until he noted the amount of experimentals this outpost of the empire had in stock. Wellington observed a corporal cleaning a rack of weapons on one side of the room. A few Crackshots, the Mark IVs of the Lee-Metford-Teslas, a few experimentals he did *not* recognize, and Webley-Maxim Mark IIIs, all in immaculate condition. Such an arsenal would have been a delight in Africa.

"Are you preparing for war against your countrymen?" Vania asked, her eyes also fixed on the weapons cabinet.

"Preparing," O'Neil assured her, setting his pith helmet on a vacant desk. "Not fighting. We need to be ready as Bombay is a high-value target. We keep order within the city quite well, but if a threat were to come from the outside, we are the first line of defence," he said. He went to add something when his attention fell squarely on the soldier tending to the weapons. The corporal was staring at Vania in a most unfriendly way. "Harris, is there a problem?"

"Didn't care for her tone, is all, sir," the corporal said, his eyes narrowing.

"I don't particularly care for yours at present," O'Neil warned. "We're all a hodgepodge here of Indian and English, but we are all Her Majesty's subjects. Now, back to your work." The corporal remained still, his eyes fixed on Vania. "Would you prefer my discipline, Harris, or the general's?"

That seemed to snap Harris back. "Yessir. Sorry, sir." The corporal then went back to tending the weapons cabinet, only this time taking up a magnifying glass and looking at the arsenal with focused attention.

"What was that all about?" Eliza asked, while trying to be inconspicuous about peering at the weapons.

O'Neil shook his head. "We have all been on high alert for the last few months. I am assuming that is why you are here."

Wellington blinked. "I beg your pardon?"

"The Ghost Rebellion, or at least that is what the men have been calling it. Gossiping like fishmongers, they all are, over spirits returning for revenge, refusing to rest until India is free." O'Neil chortled dryly as he shook his head. "Doesn't matter if you are white or not, Christian or Hindu, everyone here is waiting for something to happen." He paused as his eyes went to each of them. "You all have no idea what I am on about, do you?"

Wellington began to feel rather awkward. It seemed they were talking at cross purposes. "I'm afraid…"

"Isn't this what you do: chase ghoulies and ghosties and long-legged beasties and things that go bump in the night?" O'Neil asked, wriggling his fingers in front of his face.

"What we do," Eliza seethed, "is a bit more complicated than that."

"We are conducting an investigation of Lord Hieronymus Featherstone," Vania said, tapping on a dossier in her hands. "Just a few questions for the general."

"You're investigating the Royal Engineer for Her Majesty's military?" O'Neil asked. He then looked to Eliza. "When you say 'complicated' you weren't exaggerating, were you?"

The door to the office burst open, making all four of them jump. Even backlit by the brilliance of the noonday sun, Wellington could follow the dark, deep lines etched in the man's pale skin, incredible mutton chops joining at an impressive moustache that almost glowed on account of the sunshine. It was an amazing feat in how he could keep his facial hair and his uniform so flawless. Commendations polished to a dazzling brightness decorated the man's chest, reminding those around him how sterling his service had been to Her Majesty. His numerous decorations coupled with the rank he wore also reminded anyone within hearing his voice that his opinions were to be regarded as law.

And considering the man's present volume, "anyone within hearing his voice" meant anyone within the walls of Fort St Paul and possibly all of Bombay.

"—and as I am told it is the future of warfare, it would be a grand assurance if we could find someone besides my secretary who could drive the bloody thing," the general roared, waving a swagger stick as if it were going to find someone's head.

"Attention!" O'Neil called out, snapping to attention.

Even Wellington leapt to attention. He glanced down at Eliza, who looked at him with elevated eyebrows. *Old habits,* he mouthed to her.

"As you were, lads," the general said with an almighty roar, before removing his own pith helmet and shoving it into the small servant-boy at his side, "The future apparently needs a man to operate it!"

"I am sure a woman could lend a hand, if called upon," Eliza stated, striking a posture just as assured as the Lieutenant General's.

Wellington closed his eyes and took a deep breath. *I could think of better ways of introducing ourselves...*

"Not if I have a mind about it," Southerby barked at her, his tirade losing no cadence whatsoever. "Regardless of what nonsense those suffragette harridans blather on about, the battlefield is no place for a proper lady of the empire."

Wellington dared to reach out and pat Eliza's hand. The look she shot him could have melted metal.

Then the tirade ended, and the general's grey eyes examined the only three in his office that were not in proper uniform. Wellington could feel his heartbeat pick up a pace. If there was something the military hated, it was government agencies offering their assistance—or what those in the military referred to as interference.

"Our guests from Bombay?" Southerby asked.

"Yessir," O'Neil announced. "Agents Books, Braun, and Pujari."

Southerby studied the three of them for a moment, then his head snapped in the direction of the open office. "Unless I have sprouted a second head, I believe you have seen me here and there in this fort before! Return to your duties and stop goggling!"

There was a rustle of movement, a quick shuffling of paper, and not a word uttered as the soldiers all returned to their duties.

"Lieutenant General Archibald Southerby," he said after a moment's silence, crossing over to O'Neil's desk. His cold gaze locked on Eliza. "Is it a safe assumption whatever agency you represent, the women there are as outspoken as you?"

"No, General," Eliza returned, doing absolutely nothing to mask her defiance, "I am more than outspoken for ladies everywhere. It's a gift."

Wellington snapped a salute out of respect, and also to grab the general's attention away from her. "Agent Wellington Thornhill Books, Lieutenant General." He then motioned to Eliza and Vania. "We represent the Ministry of Peculiar Occurrences."

"Wellington Books?" Southerby's eyes raked over him from head-to-toe. "Captain Wellington Books, is it not?"

Warmth rose in his cheeks. He cleared his throat before answering, "Retired, sir."

"I see." The general huffed through his moustache as he took a seat. "Couldn't quite cut the mustard, eh Books?"

"Begging your pardon, Lieutenant General," Eliza spoke, the edge in her words as sharp as a bayonet prepared for a push, "but Agent Books here is more than capable of holding his own anywhere in the Empire, I assure you."

Southerby now looked over Eliza with full consideration. "No, not Australia, couldn't be. Not nasally enough to be Australian. New Zealand then. I should have gathered as much from your impertinence." The commanding officer shook his head before returning his ire to Wellington. "I had my fair share of assignments in the Dark Continent, Books. Was very aware of your exploits over there. Perhaps you were not the man you led people to believe."

The gentlest of touches against Eliza's wrist just managed to keep her rooted where she stood. "Perhaps I just had my fill of following orders that appeared nothing less than brilliant in a war room, but lost a step or two on the field." The old man's cheeks grew ruddy in stark contrast to his white mutton chops. "A career in Her Majesty's Army takes a certain passion."

"That it does, Books," Southerby said, his words even and controlled.

"Agent Books," he corrected. "Still in the service of Her Majesty, but now my uniform comes from Saville Row." He glanced back at Eliza, and her smile only reinforced his confidence. "We need a moment of your time, concerning Lord Hieronymus Featherstone."

The general motioned with his swagger stick in the direction of Vania, but kept his eyes on Wellington. "Was bringing the brownie really necessary?"

Eliza's victorious grin melted away.

Vania cleared her throat gently as her grip on the folio tightened. "The particulars of our investi—"

"Agent Books," Southerby interrupted, "whatever transgressions this wog has convinced you Lord Featherstone is to be held accountable for, I assure you her understanding of any particulars is far from what currently plagues us here in India."

"Then if you please..." Wellington's gaze met Eliza's. It seemed that they were sharing a tether now as a couple. Wellington admitted to himself he was about done with this arrogant toff. "Enlighten us."

Wringing his hands against the stick in his grasp, Southerby's face twisted in disgust. "Ministry of Peculiar Occurrences, indeed. A pain in the backsides is what you are." He got back to his feet, O'Neil shadowing him. Wellington, Eliza, and Vania remained where they stood. "As my guests," Southerby began with false civility, "I would like to show you something."

The invitation, hollow as it was, served as motivation enough for the agents to join the general. Once more they found themselves looking across the training yard. "India is more than just a part of Her Majesty's Empire," Southerby spoke over his shoulder. "It is the centre jewel in the Queen's crown. Bombay is my responsibility, and I will not falter in my duty."

"Yet you have a problem. Lord Featherstone," Wellington stated. "If you would spare but a momen—"

"Do not presume to know that gentleman as I do," Southerby said with a low growl, waving them off with a free hand as if they were simple flies bothering him at a picnic. "I will entertain your visit, but whatever accusations you hurl against our Royal Engineer I will take with a grain of salt considering all that he has done for us here."

Vania fished out from the dossier in her hands a photograph of Henry Jekyll and held it out towards him. "General, we need to know if you have seen this man in the company of Lord Featherstone?"

Southerby's eyes continued to inspect the Enforcer now standing motionless in the motor pool, its maintenance crew conducting a visual inspection.

"General," Wellington began, amazed he could still speak what with the tension tugging inside his neck and jaw. He knew he was merely a breath away from losing his composure. "Agent Pujari asked you a question."

The old man's eyes dressed down Wellington as if he were in his regiment. "Whose side are you on, Books?"

"The Queen's," he replied evenly. "And the Empire's."

Southerby glanced at Vania as if for the first time, and then fixed Books with a stare. "Then act as such."

He was the same height as the decorated officer, but his posture had stiffened on the challenge. This old relic of the Empire's heyday was hardly worth the attention, but dashitall if Southerby were not working under his skin presently.

Then Wellington suddenly remembered the goggles still around his hatband. Perhaps Southerby could still answer the question presented.

"Your Ministry believes Lord Featherstone to be a threat, even after providing Her Majesty's finest with weapons of the latest engineering advancements?" Southerby asked, his chin elevating slightly.

The mannerism gave Wellington the impression he thought himself on a stage towering over them all, which was fine. The more self-involved the accomplished soldier remained, the more time Wellington would have to slip the isotope detectors down and see if any signs of Jekyll were present.

"If I may, sir," O'Neil began, and the officer's sudden courage to speak on the Ministry's behalf caught even Southerby by surprise. "I believe Her Majesty's agents are not looking to tarnish Featherstone's good name. They just have a few questions."

"Do not test my limits, O'Neil," Southerby warned. "I may be indebted to both you and your father, but that does not give you carte blanche."

O'Neil lifted his hands in surrender. "I would never dare to presume as such, General. These agents are merely following—"

"Stuff and nonsense," the old man seethed. He then rounded on Wellington. Perhaps out of the three of them, Southerby felt more a "connection"—contemptuous as it may be to him—but any such connection was lost when he looked at Wellington now wearing wide, dark lenses over his eyes.

"And…" Wellington said, running his eyes up and down Southerby's tall, wide form. "No, General, you have not met Doctor Jekyll," he said, replacing the goggles back above the brim of his bowler.

"What—in—the—name—" the general stammered.

"Please, General." Wellington held up a single finger, somehow silencing the bombastic man. "Lord Featherstone was a patient of Jekyll's, and this doctor is dangerous. On several fronts. We have no idea how deep Jekyll's influence ran with him."

Southerby glared at him for a moment before replying. "Did I meet this Jekyll you are looking for? No. I did, however, work closely with Featherstone, a man who has done more for the Empire than all the branches of the Ministry combined. Now, you come here to tell me that Featherstone was perhaps compromised in some way? Sabotaging his own work? Selling secrets to the enemy? I do not believe that Featherstone has ever been disloyal to the crown—"

Wellington was certain the lieutenant general's next words were to be "…*and I do not intend to start believing that now!*" or something to the effect, but his attention turned to the gooseflesh rippling along his arms as a sudden chill swept across his skin. The smell, a scent reminiscent of summer thunderstorms at Whiterock, filled his nostrils and excited his tongue.

Then came the flash of light, and before their eyes the fabric of reality began to fold upon itself.

◈═◯ ═◈

In Which Miss del Morte Makes a Move

$\mathcal{S}$ophia took each stair, slowly and carefully. A pair of tourists, a man and a woman chattering to each other, passed her without a glance.

Still she waited until she reached the top of the stairwell before glancing over her shoulder. No one was following her. No one was casting a glance up to see where she had been. She was just an old woman with laboured breathing who had to take her time to reach the top of the stairs.

Just as Sophia wanted.

Continuing the illusion up another stairwell, Sophia finally arrived to the third floor. She looked up to the room numbers as she trundled by each door. On reaching Room 312, Sophia slipped the key into the lock, waddled inside, shut the door, and then whipped off the shawl around her head. She glanced out one window, ran over to an opposite window, peered through the curtain, and then took a deep breath that felt like her first.

"Damn!" she whispered, looking around the stranger's room.

Months of hiding in Bruges, months of building the perfect cover, months of building an identity, and her own vanity had caught up with her. The urge to break something—furniture, a mirror, a complete stranger's arm—welled up in her. Her instincts warned her all along taking up that shlockwork's ridiculous challenge had been a bad idea. Yet she had done it anyway. Some part of her wanted to show the world the skills her aunt had taught her. Weaving had always been her family's sanctuary of calm and centring, the exact opposite of what her life had been before going dark.

Another part of her was so desperate for some excitement that she'd found a stupid weaving challenge irresistible.

Complacency had led her to the Grote Markt, and dumb luck had placed an agent of the House of Usher there at the same time. She had craved for excitement, and Fate certainly had an interesting sense of humour.

"Who are you?" Sophia muttered as she turned to examine the luscious suite.

The woman had certainly spared no expense for herself—but then again this was the House of Usher. They believed in only the finer things. If they ever achieved their goal they would undoubtedly do it from opulent surroundings.

Sophia's attacker had surrounded herself with velvet drapes, gilt mirrors, and a huge four-poster bed.

The end tables on either side of the bed yielded nothing, aside from some books to which Sophia could only shake her head in disgust. However, she also had a huge wardrobe full of the latest Parisian fashions, so she was not without some sense of taste.

There was no evening finery to speak of, but plenty of choices for her to appear as an innocuous tourist. On the shelf above were three hat boxes. Sophia stood on a nearby stool and climbed up to have a closer look. Reaching between them she rapped her knuckle on the wall behind the boxes. All was solid, until she struck the panel to the left of the last box.

Pressing gently against it, she heard a latch unlock while springs popped it open. Then pushing aside the hat boxes, she reached into the compartment, and found several bound leather folders, a seal bearing the raven burned into each of them. She felt deeper into the cubbyhole and discovered a small box.

Hopping down from the stool, she scattered her finds across the bed. Before diving into this hidden treasure trove, Sophia retrieved from her satchel the other items she had lifted from the dead Usher agent: a passport, a map usually issued to tourists, and a small wallet carrying a modest amount of currency.

The map was worn, frayed. It had been opened and folded closed repeatedly. Sophia opened up the passport, and now this Usher agent had a name: Diane Elizabeth Case. From the looks of the currency she carried, Agent Case had plenty of lavish tastes that went beyond this hotel room.

"Tell me more, Agent Case."

Pulling the tie free, she opened the folder to stare at a woman she did not recognise. The photo was an image of her standing against a brick wall. The accompanying notes identified her as Fiona Brannagh, an agent of the Ministry of Peculiar Occurrences. Flipping through the other pages, there were additional images of Agent Brannagh wandering streets Sophia knew from her time in Bruges. These photos had been taken without her knowledge.

The final photograph in the dossier was of this woman with her throat cut. Clipped to the photo was a note bearing the crest of the raven. The message read:

```
Please send a postcard. Father would
love to see what you are up to in
Europe. Take all the time you like.
Your work abroad is exceptional.
```

Sophia knew that code all too well. Agent Case and she shared much in common, it appeared.

She opened another file. This time the subject was Ignatius Daniel Wadsworth, another Ministry agent. Again, a photo taken in front of a brick wall. Again, images of him captured wandering throughout Bruges, taken without his knowledge. The final photo, Agent Wadsworth dead. Same message attached.

She glanced up. There were six other folders, all secured like this.

Time to examine the box. Giving it a quick look for anything out of the ordinary—this woman was skilled enough to have dispatched eight Ministry agents and kept it secret—Sophia flipped open its latch. One item inside immediately caught her eye and caused her stomach to turn over. It was a small fold of leather with the stamp of an eagle and a dragon on it—the crest of the Ministry of Peculiar Occurrences. Inside the small wallet was the face of Diane Elizabeth Case, and her credentials as a Field Agent for Her Majesty, Queen Victoria.

Sophia pressed her hands to her forehead for a moment. When she had killed Agent Case, she knew her as an agent of the House of Usher. Now, Agent Case's secret was out, but only to Sophia. She was a marked woman by two agencies. The Ministry would believe she had killed one of their own, and not a double agent.

What was she to do? The possibility of returning to her family's village flitted through her mind, but Sophia dismissed it quickly. It was one of the del Morte's rules. If there was trouble, never take it back to the family. Never.

That left the only people she trusted to watch her back. They possessed true honour, honour that her own family would no doubt respect, and perhaps be glad of their assistance as well. The challenge would be locating them before either the Ministry or the House of Usher found her.

She checked inside the box for anything that could aid her in that search. Sophia found there were messages from "Uncle Basil" that looked to be sent via æthermail. No doubt from the communications office in the town plaza. She remembered her neighbour Febe telling her of an analytical terminal being installed there. With the amount of tourism in Bruges, that came as no surprise.

Before taking flight, she would have to become herself again. Her illusion was on borrowed time, she knew that, but she would take up as much of that time as she could.

The dossiers stretched the seams of her modest satchel even after she emptied it to make room for them. The box she would have to carry by hand. With the extra weight, it would be a long, agonising walk through town. Perhaps she would see a neighbour or a farmer willing to take her home, granting her a few precious minutes.

Leaving the hotel room, she shut the door carefully, and returned the way she had come. When she reached the ground floor, her mind was already working on her route out of Bruges.

"Mona!" a voice called from across the marble lobby.

Sophia froze halfway towards the door, her honed instincts preventing her from releasing one of her lethal cogs from its launcher and sinking it squarely in the head of the person who had called to her from the concierge desk.

The young woman standing in the lobby, causing many unwanted eyes to turn to Sophia, was Febe, a neighbour who had always been eager for advice from Mona, the "kindly old weaver" that Sophia had been playing for months. As usual, she was bundled up like a sore thumb, with her bright red hair sticking out at all angles. The young woman's grey eyes were wide and innocent, her cheeks naturally ruddy, and that sweet face staring at her contained only endless innocence. She knew nothing of the world outside of Bruges, but Bruges she knew intimately.

Sophia did not care for redheads, but as she was a foreigner in Bruges, she did need at least one person to feed her gossip, which Febe never lacked. It was the most adventure the simple woman knew.

"*Bonjour*, Febe," Sophia replied, pulling the small box in the crook of her arm closer to her. Hopefully, the shawl concealed it from view. "What brings you here?"

"I should ask the same," the woman said, her hand motioning to the hotel all around them, attracting even more attention. "Such a fine establishment for simple folk like us."

Sophia shook her head. "Oh, Febe, you have so much to learn of the world. I was just meeting with someone who had taken a shine to my work."

Febe's eyes suddenly lit up with delight. "I saw you coming in here, and I did wonder. I just had to find out what you were doing."

The girl was far too curious for her own good and had absolutely no shame about it either.

Sophia frowned, and took a couple of steps away in an attempt to get Febe outside, and shut the woman up. "We were discussing a commission and payment."

Febe clapped her hands, and Sophia knew her limits were being tested. "Oh how exciting!"

"Yes, yes, yes…" Sophia said, allowing her words to trail off as she waved a free hand towards the door. "But I think the day is catching up with me."

"Would you care for a ride back home?" she asked.

Finally, the peasant comes in use. "Splendid."

Outside, the horse and cart awaited them. Febe helped Sophia up to her seat, then she joined her, clicked her tongue, and off they went.

For the entire ride Febe talked. And talked. And talked. It was the usual gossip of town, which was no longer of interest to the assassin. Sophia nodded, but used the opportunity to glance around, and reassure herself that they were not being followed. On this trek to her modest hovel, though, the only thing eventful was Febe's news; and according to the peasant, it was the only thing worth knowing about.

"And then there is you," Febe said suddenly.

Sophia blinked. "Whatever do you mean, child?"

The girl burst out laughing. "You don't know it, do you?" Febe, shaking her head, sighed. "Oh, Mona, what you did in the Markt today is the talk of the town. You beat a machine, Mona. *A machine!* So many weavers are praising your name, and I think the *Gazette* wants to feature you!"

Sophia shook her head. *Damn.*

"We will have to sit down and talk about how you will charge people for your wares. After all," she said, "you are now a local treasure. A celebrity!"

It had to be now. She needed to leave Bruges now.

Their cart trundled up to Sophia's house, the modest dwelling she had called home all this time. She patiently waited for Febe to help her down from the cart. With a gentle nod to her friend, Sophia began her slow walk up to the front door. It had never appeared so far away.

"Poor thing, you must be exhausted," she heard Febe say from behind her. "Let me help you."

"I may be old," Sophia barked over her shoulder. She had to get rid of Febe. "I am not helpless."

"Don't be so silly," the girl said, cutting in front of her, "I insist."

Perhaps it was the uneven ground underfoot, or Febe's excitement making her move faster than Sophia had ever seen before, but the light jostle between Febe and Sophia for the key in Sophia's hand knocked the small box out of her hidden hold. It landed at their feet with a dull thud, and did not go unnoticed.

"Mona," Febe asked, turning the rectangular object over in her hands, "whatever is this?"

The hand slapped firmly across Febe's mouth as they both slammed into Sophia's front door. Sophia unlocked the door, pushed her neighbour into the dark dwelling, and shut it behind them in one fluid motion.

"Not. One. Sound." Sophia's warning was returned with a muffled whimper and a rapid nod.

She had to kill her. It was the sensible thing to do, especially now that she had tipped her hand with the "Mona" disguise. The girl was a knot left untied, a dangling thread, where Sophia did not want to leave a trace.

With a shove against Febe, Sophia stepped back, and then reached for a lantern sitting on a table by the door. She lit it, hung it up, and then took the matches to another lantern suspended across from them.

"Mona?" Febe finally gasped out.

"I said, not one sound!" Sophia snapped, causing her to flinch.

Sophia checked the curtains to assure herself they were drawn. With a deep breath, she stripped off the grey-haired wig, then worked her fingers underneath the hidden seams of her elaborate mask, which extended to her neck, and she began to pull. The second skin stubbornly held on, but she continued to tug at it until a good portion of it was free. She tossed the section of her disguise at Febe's feet.

The young woman let out a tiny cry at the portion of neck, cheek, and nose lying there. Sophia could only imagine the fresh horror she emulated with tatters of another face remaining on her actual one. She continued to pull at the false skin on her nose until finally the remains were gone.

Febe remained rooted where she stood, her eyes tracing over Sophia's true face. Yet—even in this moment—she couldn't quite stop herself from talking. "Mona...how...why? All this time..." Then she swallowed, and said in a raspy voice, "Who are you?"

Sophia could end all this, either with the stiletto hidden up the right sleeve or a single razor-cog from her left. As the assassin's eyes narrowed, she couldn't help but think of the two of them. They'd sat out in the courtyard, carding wool, chattering and gossiping. Febe had a widowed mother and three younger brothers; and though they drove her mad, she loved them. Sophia knew everything that went on in that house. The arguments, the joys, the minutiae of a normal life. It was all so lovely, in an honest, sincere fashion.

"I am sorry I have put you in this situation," Sophia said to the wide-eyed girl, "but you and your family must leave Bruges immediately."

"Leave Bruges?" Febe asked. If the woman was not careful, she would faint, considering how hard she was breathing. "We cannot just leave."

"Your spectacle at the hotel has tied you back to me," she said in a hard tone so that Febe would understand that this was serious. "When I disappear, when Mona disappears, people will talk about who was last seen with her. This means you and your family must disappear." Sophia went to the centre of the kitchen and stomped hard against the end of a floorboard. The plank lifted, and she reached into the hole and produced a pair of saddle bags. Flipping one open she rummaged through it and fished out two wrapped bundles of what she knew was currency. "There is enough there to start a new life," she said, tossing Febe the money. "Do so. Tell no one what you have seen tonight, or where you are going. If you do, the people I was hiding from will kill you all."

Febe just stared at the money in her hands, definitely the most she had ever seen in her life; and then back to Sophia, her mouth agape.

Her left arm shot outward, and the razor-sharp teeth of the cog sunk into the wood of the door just behind Febe.

"Go," Sophia uttered.

The girl spun on her heel and scrambled out of the hovel. Sophia honestly hoped she would take her advice, and that her own pity would not end up coming back on her.

She went to the solitary mirror suspended over the basin, and removed the last scraps of Mona from her skin. She then scooped up the remnants, dropped them into the basin, and with the strike of a match, lit the disguise on fire. Perhaps that was a silver lining in all this: she would not miss the ritual of creating this old crone.

Returning her attention to the saddle bags, she winced at the amount of generosity to Febe, but this was not the girl's fault. Sophia still had enough money to keep her on the run, hopefully enough time to find her allies. When she found in the second saddle bag her assassin's gear, her lips lifted in a surprised smile. Life certainly took some strange turns, but perhaps this one could still be interesting.

Be careful what you wish for, Sophia thought with a wry grin.

As she swung the bags over her shoulder, removed the cog from the door, and finally glanced around the small house that had been her home, Sophia let out a soft sigh. *Ah well*, she thought to herself, *Bruges lost its charm awhile ago. Time to go find some friends, or at least allies.*

But first, a quick stop at the communications office. Considering the security in Bruges, it would be a brief detour.

CHAPTER FOUR

✦⊷══◓ ◖══⊶✦

In Which Our Colonial Pepperpot
Finds Herself in Most Comfortable Trappings

"Get down!" Eliza screamed just at the moment the training yard around them went white. When her vision began to clear it was to see figures emerging out of the glare—worse still, armed figures.

Wellington was going to be very cross, Eliza thought as she yanked at the edge of her wrap skirt, and buttons went flying. Yet she was now lighter, agile, and far more nimble in her tight leggings beneath. It also meant she could better access her pounamu pistols and a small baton holstered against her left thigh. Eliza slipped both pistols free and brought them to bear on the rebels now charging.

Three men dropped in quick succession, but there were too many to dispatch quickly or efficiently. As she continued to fire, Wellington dragged her by the elbow towards a storage facility, while Vania followed.

"Whomever they are," Vania said, looking in the opposite direction of the attack, "they will easily flank us from the other side."

"Then we need to get back inside the office," Eliza said, peering around the corner. She could see a small group of these invaders break away from the line, only to disappear from view. "Here they come."

Wellington drew from inside his coat the modest experimental, barely larger than a Remington-Elliot. Where there should have been a hammer, there was instead a clear cylindrical chamber lit with a faint glow.

Eliza's jaw twitched. "You really should stop with those clankertons' toys, you know that?"

"I'll provide cover. You and Vania make for the door."

"With that?"

"Just trust me, my darling. Oh, and don't look in my direction once you start moving." Wellington's fingers splayed around the handle of the gun. "Ready?"

Eliza glanced over her shoulder, and Vania gave a shrug. "As we will ever be."

Wellington gave his sun spectacles a quick adjustment, took a deep breath, and whispered, "Go."

Then, calm as you please, he stepped out into the firefight.

Eliza and Vania sprinted back for the office, but the door felt like it was farther and farther off with each step. Then, everything around her disappeared in a brilliant white flash. Even the sandy ground underfoot vanished, leaving her and Vania running through a white void. Eliza tripped, her toe catching something in the ground. She toppled over, pulling her colleague on top of her. She placed a hand on Vania's back and could make out the agent nodding. *Get up,* Eliza thought to herself. Slowly, texture and shape were returning.

Steps. This was the stoop just in front of the barracks door.

"Go on," she shouted. "I'm right behind you."

Pulling herself back to her feet, Eliza could now make out a door handle and the dark cool interior of the command offices. Against the glare, she could see soldiers loading pistols and rifles. Those inside were calm, but visibly rattled by this surprise attack. She only took two steps before a pair of hands grabbed her from behind and shoved her through the threshold.

"Close the door!" Wellington ordered as he released Eliza and dropped her on a bench against the wall. He plopped onto his backside on the floor at her feet.

The dead giveaway was the slight sunburn on his face.

"Welly, what was that?" Eliza demanded.

He winced slightly. "Just an idea I had been bandying about for a spell. Something akin to the Mule's Kick, only using light. Haven't christened it yet." He glanced at the small pistol in his hand. "Went rather well for a first field test."

Eliza scowled. "Remind me to have a serious talk with you about how 'the field' is not the optimal place to test your weapons. Especially during a firefight."

"Bloody wogs are everywhere," grumbled a voice alongside them.

She whipped her head around to see Lieutenant General Southerby working his arms into a mechanised device Eliza suspected was a small backpack of ammunition. The strand of bullets fed to a small Gatling gun mounted on a chest plate covering his midsection. It was easily recognisable as a variation of what the Maestro's Grey Ghosts wore in their assault on the Diamond Jubilee. *Lord Featherstone,* Eliza seethed. *Must have worked with Jekyll in the scavenging and adapting of the departed Peter Lawson's technology.*

Behind the backpack, O'Neil was engaging several locks that connected hoses and hydraulics. With a final look, he came round to face Southerby.

"The Gatling Garrison is at the ready, sir," O'Neil stated. "My men will provide cover fire from the left flank, as ordered."

"Good man, O'Neil. Fight the good fight," Southerby replied with suitable relish.

"Whomever these rebels answer to, they are using technology we are familiar with," Eliza said to Southerby. "I speak with unwavering confidence that your boys have never seen the like of it."

"Young miss, as you can see,"—Southerby yanked back the bolt of the Gatlin's custom safety, beginning the feed of bullets into the weapon's chamber—"we are not ones to dismiss innovation. These savages can try to lay claim to Her Majesty's base, but their efforts will all be for naught."

O'Neil pulled back a heavy lever, and just audible over the gunfire and explosions outside came a rush of steam, the click and clacks of gears, and the hum of hydraulics. The wall in front of them bumped outward slightly, split in two, and slid to either side, giving the Gatling Garrison a wide berth.

"Follow me, my lads" Hefting the weapon on its swivel-mount, Southerby clomped over to a group of ten soldiers also wearing the portable arsenal. "Let's give them what for!"

With a hearty huzzah, the Gatling Garrison charged. Pistons, axels, and chassis granted the lumbering soldiers amazing speed as they pressed deep into the battle. Those that remained behind hoisted sidearms, both standard and enhanced, to provide covering fire. Eliza, Wellington, and Vania sank lower to the floor as bullets struck maps and framed pictures hanging from the far wall. Papers and bric-a-brac flew into the air while bullets shattered teacups that had been left idle on the odd desktop. Two soldiers lurched back as rebel fire found its mark.

"Lieutenant O'Neil," Wellington called out, "you have to send out a distress signal now. You're going to need reinforcements."

"We are ordered to hold the line." O'Neil looked at Eliza, and she could see the frustration in his eyes. "Standing orders from the Lieutenant General." With a final check to his rifle, he looked to his regiment. "You know what to do, lads! For Queen, country, and the Empire!"

O'Neil took a position at the barn doors' threshold with a Lee-Metford-Tesla and fired off a quick blast, full charge, following the burst with several shots from the rifle while his soldiers sprinted across the motor pool. Once the last man was out, O'Neil slipped the rifle over his shoulder and began his own dash into the skirmish.

Bullets tore through windowpanes, sending Eliza, Wellington, and Vania back to the floor. Bits of glass and wood rained over Eliza, each shard and splinter that pelted her making her angrier and angrier at the complete pomposity of this Lieutenant General Southerby.

"Welly," Eliza shouted in the lull between gunfire, "I am rather sick of this all."

"Oh dear," he said, craning his neck up to the tatters of the windows and wall overhead. "Makes me almost feel sorry for whomever is raising arms against Her Majesty."

From outside came the *pop-pop-pop* of rifles along with the throaty snarl of Gatlings, but it was the retort that make Eliza's blood run cold. Every return volley grew louder, a dense thunderclap of defiance. With a quick jerk of her head to Vania, she crawled across the room to the still-open gun cabinet. Remaining were a pair of Webley-Maxims and a pair of Samson-Enfield Mark IIIs. She also found a crate of "Crimean Caterwaulers" much to her delight. Southerby might have been a prat, but at least he was a well-armed prat.

"Right then," Eliza began, grabbing an empty bandoleer from a peg in the cabinet, "we have a Webley-Maxim, a Samson-Enfield Mark III, and grenades. Pick your poison."

"Cover fire then?" Wellington asked.

Eliza rummaged through the cabinet, eventually finding bullets suited for her own pistols. "I'm going to get behind one of those Enforcers before these blighters do so," she said, slipping bullets into the bandolier across her chest.

"I call grenades," Vania spoke up, taking two of the Caterwaulers.

Wellington and Eliza glanced at one another. "Are you sure?" Eliza asked.

"Trust me," Vania stated. "You want me to handle these."

"I'll take the Brass Knuckles then," Wellington said, taking the Webley-Maxim. He ejected the clip and felt the weight of both clip and weapon. "Ten shots and three shells."

"You lay down that suppressing fire, Books," said Vania, crawling back to the barn door opening. Once there, she stood behind it. "I'll make sure Miss Braun gets to the Enforcer."

Eliza turned back to Wellington and touched his cheek for a moment. *Not today, darling,* she thought, just before following Vania's crawl to the barn doors. She waited for a lull in the gunfire before crossing to the other side of the opening.

"Ready, are we?" she asked, slipping the baton free from her left leg holster.

"On your word, Agent Braun," replied Vania.

"Very well." Eliza fixed her feet underneath her, ready for a sprint to the Enforcer. She waited as Wellington released the safety on the Brass Knuckles' compressor and gave her a nod. Her heartbeat sounded in her ears even over the sound of gunfire. "Darling, if you please?"

Wellington popped up on one knee and began firing. Eliza cleared the threshold by the third shot, heard Vania scrambling behind her by the fifth, but she stopped counting as she continued her dead run for the massive machine only a few hundred yards away. She heard more pops and reports from Gatlings, but Eliza pressed onward towards the towering war machine. Was it getting any damn closer?

The sudden explosion caused her to stumble a bit, but she kept her forward momentum. Her feet were back under her once more, and on the second grenade explosion, her pace never faltered.

Bloody hell, Eliza thought on seeing the plume of smoke ballooning upward. *Vania's got a fantastic arm!*

The rebels emerged from the garage closest to the Enforcer. One of the group motioned for the youngest to make for the massive war machine while they charged at Eliza. Taking a deep breath, she pressed the green button on the cylinder in her grasp. The device released a thin wisp of steam as each end extended to the length of a quarterstaff. The *taiaha*, a gift from her mentor Aroha Murphy after the excitement in London, spun in Eliza's hand before striking the ground. Eliza leapt upward and extended her right foot forward. Her boot connected with the rebel's jaw. The momentum of her landing gave her follow-through with the staff extra power, causing the second man to spin like a top. That left the leader, who was now lifting his pistol up to her, his finger squeezing the trigger.

She heard the gun fire, but she felt no shock against her corset or any sudden rush of pain in her exposed shoulders. Eliza brought her taiaha around for a strike and spun wildly off-balance. Meeting the ground unexpectedly winded her for an instant, and she heard the gun shot again.

Or did she? It didn't sound quite right.

Eliza looked up at the rebel who had her without question, since he was standing over her at point blank range. He pulled the trigger again, and the gun...fired. But it *didn't* fire. She saw the muzzle flash, but the concussive sound of gunfire did not sound like a standard Webley revolver. Nor did it sound like an experimental of Wellington's. It was—

Then she suddenly recalled she was in the middle of a firefight with a rebel keen on killing her.

Eliza launched a roundhouse kick that should have taken the man off his feet, but instead she rolled on to her stomach. Without pausing, she thrust her taiaha outward, grasping it at one end to allow for maximum reach, and brought it around in a swift backhand attack.

What Eliza saw should not have happened. It was impossible. She hadn't missed. Her weapon had passed *through* him.

The soldier had noticed it as well, stumbling back as he stared no longer at Eliza, but at her taiaha. He tightened his grip on the pistol and pulled the trigger once more. The gunshot sounded as if the weapon had fired underwater.

Her staff came around again, but this time, Eliza stopped her weapon inside the soldier. Her thumb slipped to the blue button on the baton. The rebel suddenly lurched as electricity shot out of her taiaha and into his body. What was unexpected, and assuredly more horrifying, was how the man flickered as if he were part of a strange phantasmagoria, blinking in and out of existence and lost in vapours. He finally screamed, a broken, shattered cry mimicking his corporeal appearance. Then in a burst of wind, ozone, and cascading light, the interrupted man vanished before her eyes.

A succession of gunshots brought Eliza back to the chaos that was continuing around her. No time to try and nut out what had just happened. She had to get to the Enforcer.

Rolling back to her feet, she continued her sprint. The fourth man was attempting to climb up the war machine, but his hands kept passing through the rungs built into the Enforcer's leg. Eliza thrust the taiaha forward, driving it into the man's back, but he didn't react until her thumb pressed the blue button. Her baton's final charge had the same effect: the rebel arched back, his entire body flickering in and out of existence, and then disappearing in a flash of silent fireworks.

The baton retracted in Eliza's hand as she took hold of the rungs along the Enforcer's left leg. She swung herself into the central cradle and grabbed hold of the bar above her head. The cage secured shut with a hard *ca-thunk*, and gauges jumped to life as systems suddenly powered up.

"I've got power. Splendid." Her eyes jumped all around her as she secured herself in the command chair's harness. By God there were a lot of buttons and levers. "Now how do you work exactly?"

The control cage, she quickly assessed, established some kind of coupling between pilot and machine. The arms of her chair, she noted, had sleeves connected to an array of mechanisms—hinges, pistons, and hydraulics—reaching throughout the Enforcer. Eliza shoved her arms through the sleeves, and breathed easier seeing as she could still reach the control sticks with each hand. The stick mounted before her right had a small array of switches, two red, two yellow, one black, running along its outside. Her left stick had a single trigger set inside the grip.

"If you are weapons," Eliza muttered to herself, "then you must be what makes me go?"

She took a quick look around her and noted above her head a small bar similar to the accelerator in Wellington's car. It meant having to pull an arm free of its sleeve; but when she eased the bar away from her and pushed the stick in her right hand forward, the Enforcer lurched in that direction.

"Very good," Eliza said with a nod, "we have momentum. Now I just need weapons."

From the left, an explosion—that of a Caterwauler—caught her attention. Pulling back on the accelerator and shoving her arm through the sleeve once more, she turned her Enforcer in an awkward arc to loom over the invading army. She gave her right arm a slight tug and all around her pistons, gears, and cogs whined and rumbled with life as the machine's massive right arm also lifted up, a huge Gatling gun coming to bear. Eliza glanced over to the left control stick and pulled the trigger.

The left arm shuddered as its Gatling gun fired round after round into the ground in front of her.

"Oh, bugger it!" She flipped the first red switch off, threw the second red switch, and then pulled the trigger once more.

The *right* Gatling rained down a tempest of bullets on the hostile rebels. Her metal monster lumbered forward, the abundance of gunfire sending invaders scattering in all directions. Some were cut down in moments, but others were flickering in that strange manner she had seen up close.

A red light suddenly buzzed next to a gauge tracking her ammunition. The right arm was about to be depleted.

"Very well then," she said, flipping the second switch off and turning the first yellow switch to the "On" position. "What exactly do you do?"

The Enforcer's left arm slowly rose, and from underneath its own Gatling, a plume of flame erupted. Eliza couldn't help letting out a little yelp of delight as she engulfed a good portion of the motor pool in flames. Some rebels scrambled for cover, while others screamed out in agony under the elemental assault. It would have overcome Eliza to witness such grotesque deaths if not for the poor souls running through the flames unharmed. One moment they were there, and the next they were not. These men trapped between this world and the æther looked around themselves in confusion as flames passed through their bodies without harm.

A sudden blast of hot air buffeted Eliza through the Enforcer's control cage. From her vantage point she saw reinforcements pouring out from the æthergate. Her attention turned back to Southerby's men now advancing on her position, attempting to finish the job she had started. They couldn't see what she could: these sheer numbers would easily overwhelm Fort St. Paul.

Another explosion—a grenade of some description—kicked up dirt and rocks that lightly pelted Eliza through the cage. She turned back to the gate, and her breath caught in her throat. These reinforcements were not charging at Southerby's remaining men. They were charging at her.

Eliza looked at the weapons array. "Red is machine guns. Yellow is flame throwers." That only left one option. "And black?"

On throwing the unknown switch, the Enforcer's massive arms went slack. The control panel above her head suddenly went dark, save for one row of lights. Ten red lights.

No, wait...*nine.*

Eliza heard sirens. Where were they coming from? They sounded close.

Her eyes jumped back to the row of lights. *Eight* were now lit.

Something was moving in the distance. It was Southerby's men. They were abandoning their portable Gatlings and falling back. A full retreat. They were screaming to one another, but it was impossible to hear over the siren what exactly they were saying—undoubtedly, it wasn't good.

The Enforcer was starting to tremble, reminding her of the familiar earthquakes that rippled through New Zealand. Then something underneath her disengaged. A series of clamps, she was fairly sure. Then another set behind her.

Her eyes returned to the panel. Six...that flickered to only five.

And in that flicker, Eliza's breath was stolen away as the world disappeared from around her and she ascended into the clear skies of India as if shot from a cannon.

In Which the Ministry's Finest Cross into Unfriendly Territory

The boiler hatch groaned as it opened. Brandon, holding a small lantern by his face, peered in and cocked his head to one side. "Bruce, do you want to come out now?"

"Gonna have to give me assistance, mate," Bruce managed, extending a hand to his partner.

Locking arms with him, Brandon braced his foot against the side of the boiler and heaved. Bruce slipped halfway out of the iron container, which was about two feet shorter than his height. If his counterpart had not been there, Bruce would have faced a real challenge in trying to escape.

It took all of Bruce's control not to slap the cheerful grin off his partner's face as Brandon helped pull him out of the damned boiler.

"One more," Brandon said, "and heave!"

Bruce tried to push with his legs, numb as they were, and the boiler vomited him out. Brandon landed with a dull thud against the freight car floor and Bruce landed on top of him.

"Sorry about that, mate," Bruce groaned. "My legs are damned near frozen solid."

"Oh, right." He gave Bruce a pat on his back. "Well, take your time, my friend. Feel free to roll off whenever you like."

"Damn Germans," he grumbled. "They definitely gave you a better boiler to travel in."

"Well, maybe you could have been a bit nicer to our colleagues," Brandon replied cheerfully.

"Colleagues? Those blighters from Section P had it in for me the moment they laid eyes on my face."

Bruce reached into his pocket and produced a key one of the Section P agents gave him just before setting off. Unlocking the only crate secured with a padlock, he pulled out the smaller of two long coats and passed it to Brandon. Bruce then slid into the remaining one, popped a fisherman's cap on his head, and slid the boxcar door open. He looked about the rail yard—not that different from the border station rendezvous—and handed a similar cap to Brandon.

This had not been Bruce's first trip to Russia, but he did not remember the Russian Empire being this dark.

"What time is it?" he asked, slipping on a pair of leather gloves.

Checking his Mapping & Webb, Brandon replied, "Just past midnight."

"Six hours on the rail. Did you manage to get any sleep?"

"Actually, yes," Brandon answered with far too much vigour. "Been following that Kellogg regimen, don't you know? I tell you, I feel fan-*tastic!*"

"I swear," Bruce warned, stretching his back a bit, "if the word 'enema' leaves your lips, I will punch you. Hard. In the colon."

The bitter cold of Grójec made this whole mission just that little bit less enjoyable. Three days ago, he was enjoying a coffee at Whiterock, and now he was sore, irritable, and on the verge of throttling his most-trusted field partner. Spies were supposed to enjoy the dark, but in his experience it only meant offering some bastard an opportunity to sneak up and stick a knife between your ribs.

"Luckily we have been equipped for local conditions." Brandon, since he had enjoyed a little more space on their journey, had carried a rucksack with field necessities in it. He handed Bruce a pair of Starlight Goggles. He slipped them on, and immediately after activating them, things improved. Bruce could now make out the long line of the train extending out before them, humps of snow piled high to the right, and behind them, the freight station itself.

And somewhere in the darkness of Grójec was their contact.

"Don't suppose Blackwell packed any of those little chemical packs to stick inside your gloves?"

Brandon shook his head, even as he pulled his jacket up tight around his face. "They turned out to be a little...unstable."

"Unstable?"

"Flammable," Brandon added. "The Director told her not to risk any more agents—or agents' fingers to be exact."

Shoving their gloved hands into their coat pockets, they resigned in toughing it out. The coats would be enough to maintain their body temperature, even in the Russian winter, but it wouldn't be pleasant. Bruce always preferred things to be pleasant.

"Where's our bloody contact?" Bruce asked, staring out into the long lines of snow and train cars before them.

"The Director was a little vague on how he was going to find us." Brandon sounded only slightly concerned, but that might just have been the muffling effect of all those layers he wore. Still, he was the kind of bloke who would sound cheerful even if his fingers fell off from frostbite.

Just as Bruce was contemplating the risk behind going to the freight station—after all, a fistfight could not only keep them warm but effectively stave off boredom—a faint light moved in the distance. It was really just a pinprick among the darkness and could have gone missed without the Starlights. Brandon pulled a small torch from his pocket and flicked it on, then covered the light with his hand, revealing its glow three times in succession.

Wrapped like a mummy in a museum—which would be a lot warmer than present—Bruce judged his fighting form would not be at his best, and Brandon's knife skills might be impaired in this wintery environment. He felt for the Bulldog holstered by his left breast. Most of their experimentals had been left behind, since in these temperatures they would be useless or dangerous. Blackwell had been most put off that they wouldn't fire her æther-oscillating "Scarlet Pimpernel" in the cold of Russia. Having been at the receiving end of one of the mad scientist's dry fires, Bruce had no desire to see what it would do in sub-zero conditions.

A small form emerged from the shadows and snow, and moved cautiously towards them. It was impossible to tell if the form was male or female, friend or foe, since all he could make out through the Starlights was a bundle just as they appeared. They would have to wait until this unknown element got close to find out. Hopefully what they would discover would not prove fatal.

At his side, Bruce could feel Brandon's tension. Many times they had been in this situation, and it never got any easier. In few too many instances, this kind of meeting had turned downright nasty.

Finally, the figure reached them, the new arrival removing her goggles and motioning for Brandon to use the torch. Bruce got a pleasant surprise when the modest light flickered on. A pair of stern blue eyes examined them both, and there was a hint of bright red hair tucked under her hood.

So their contact was an attractive woman. *Finally,* he thought, *a saving grace in this mission.*

Bruce then looked at Brandon. "Mate," he whispered, "what's the security code?"

Brandon went to reply, then paused. "Oh, um, Section P never gave us one."

"*What?*" he asked in a harsh whisper.

"They said it wouldn't be necessary."

"Wouldn't be necess—*we're in bloody Russia, you git!*"

"They gave us a…gesture."

He pulled Brandon back a few steps to make sure they could not be heard by the stranger. "Come again?"

"She is supposed to identify herself with this," and Brandon—concealing his hands with his body so she could not see it—covered his right hand with his left, and dealt himself a handshake.

Bruce knew this gesture.

His thoughts scattered on hearing a fist slam twice against a train car. They both looked at the young woman before them, who delivered the gesture Section P had said was their designated greeting. Brandon repeated it to her. She then jerked her head over her shoulder in a silent invitation to follow. She obviously expected them to follow as she immediately replaced her goggles back across her eyes and turned her back on them.

It wouldn't be the first time he and Brandon had simply put their lives in a stranger's hands. So, the two Ministry agents trailed after the silent woman. She had carefully stomped a path for them, and they dutifully stayed in it, though keeping their eyes on the surrounding hummocks of snow. They rounded a particularly tall one, and now out of sight of the station, the woman's means of travel was revealed.

"Well," Bruce thought with a nod, "beats riding in the belly of a boiler."

A snow vehicle unlike anything Bruce had ever seen towered before them. It appeared to be part of at least four other machines. At the heart of this thing Bruce could discern was a tractor, but he also saw what appeared to be the bow from an ironclad welded on the front. The back end looked cobbled together from a potbelly furnace, an array of meat grinders, and…

Was that a giant ceiling fan fitted into the face of a massive clock?

The odd configuration of the snow tractor meant that Bruce and Brandon were crammed into the rear, while their driver took the front. From where they sat, Bruce tried to make sense of the formidable collection of levers and gear shifts that surrounded the steering wheel. He would not have known where to begin in finding which was the throttle, which served as a brake, and which could be an accelerator. In their snug backseat, windows provided them some protection from howling winds and shifting snow. They were warming up quickly. The driver had less protection, but with her seat right next to the boilers she would be fine. Their contact reached underneath the tractor's dash and flipped an unseen switch. The vehicle shuddered and rumbled around them, and then after a baffling sequence of levers pulled and pushed forward, they lumbered forward into the snow.

Stuffing his hands under his armpits as best he could, considering he was jammed up against Brandon, Bruce leaned forward and over the growing storm and the hammering of the machine yelled, "Are we far away from shelter?"

Either she didn't hear him or chose to ignore him. Controlling this beast in this weather must have been quite enough for her to deal with, let alone putting up with a yammering Australian sitting in the back. At least that was the impression Bruce got as the tractor lurched to the left.

"Let her concentrate, for God's sake," Brandon suggested ever so helpfully. "One wrong move and we'll tumble into an unsafe snowbank or ditch, and then no one will find us until spring."

"Thanks, Brandon." Bruce uncurled his shoulders a little, crunching his partner just a fraction. The rucksack was lying across their knees, adding to the discomfort. Wind railed against the tractor, snow blasting the window and scattering against the glass in a fashion that rendered Starlights useless. Their silent driver, however, piloted their vehicle so assuredly, showing plenty of local knowledge where solid ground instead of loose snow would be. The woman's confidence reminded Bruce of a mad uncle who lived on a farm outside Melbourne. He drove his tractor with the same kind of reckless assurance. Of course he also had his tractor equipped with something he called the "Oh Shit!" handle for his occasional passengers. This contraption had no such convenience.

Finally, after inclines, declines, and controlled skids, Bruce could see a faint light in the distance. It was not much, just what a house might let out.

"Signs of civilisation," he said, pointing it out to Brandon. "Or a bit of warmth at least."

His partner tilted his head. "You didn't come to Russia expecting to be warm all the time, did you?"

"Just thinking of my poor todger and tackle mate," Bruce said, squirming where he sat. "I might want to have some more kids one day, and all this cold might freeze the whole package off."

Brandon snorted. "How about we focus on the mission and not on your balls for a bit?"

"You have your priorities, I'll have mine, mate."

The vehicle came to an abrupt stop right before the only light in the snow-tossed blackness, a low wooden building with only two shuttered windows on either side of the door. Hardly a fortress, but Bruce had long ago given up judging buildings by their initial impressions. He'd seen too many ruined castles serve as House of Usher lairs and the slums of London offer fronts for mad scientists.

Following their driver out of the snow tractor, they stomped their boots in front of the door before following her in. This time, Bruce found, initial impressions were very accurate. It was, to put it bluntly, a hovel. Those two shuttered windows were the only ones in the entire building. The rest was mud, wood, and not much warmer than outside. The light that had given him such hope came from a fireplace in the far corner of the building. Lines of clothes hung around it and provided so much cover that it took him a moment to realise that there was in fact a little wizened man in a chair in front of the hearth, snoring pleasantly.

"Good evening," Brandon said in accented Russian. Still, it was better than Bruce's.

Their contact, still remaining quiet, had started stripping off her snow-kissed gloves and top coat. She was much more of Bruce's type of woman, though he decided not to mention that immediately. Petite, tiny really, but he wasn't letting her outward appearance fool him. He had known his share of Russian women, and from those painful encounters he considered them far more terrifying than the men. He still recalled one particular incident with a platoon of Russian female aerial marines, and it was that recollection which stayed his impulse to deliver her the usual smile and line. Personal growth was possible, apparently.

As she shook out her ginger hair and brushed the snow from her shoulders, Brandon spoke. "Thank you for your assistance back there."

Her hands, now free of the bulky gloves, flew and arched, forming shapes that Bruce recognised. No wonder the security gesture from Section P seemed so familiar.

My name is Ryfka Górski, the woman signed to them. *Welcome to the Kingdom of Poland.*

The sudden paleness that Brandon took on caught Bruce by surprise. Usually the Canadian had Bruce beat with languages, so he was pleased to feel the boot on the other foot.

"She's deaf then?" Brandon asked. He then looked at her and spoke louder and slower, "Par-don-me, but-if-you-are-deaf-how-do-we-com-mu-ni-cate?"

I can read lips exceedingly well, Ryfka replied.

"Oh dear Lord," he said, flustered. "Right then, I know some sign language. Basic, mind you, but I can do this."

He cleared his throat and began signing.

We are full of cat, Brandon signed awkwardly. *I am a delightful pillow of bananas from a kangaroo.*

She signed and mouthed simultaneously, *What?*

Bruce chuckled. That was enough watching his friend struggle. *I'm Bruce Campbell and he is Brandon Hill,* he signed. *Forgive my partner. The cold has taken a toll on his wits.*

The way she glanced between them was challenging, but with the kind of spirit he could only admire. She gestured them over to the fire, and the three of them managed to get some warmth from it. All this time the old man sitting the chair didn't stir.

That is my grand-uncle Leib, Ryfka said. *He isn't deaf, but he sleeps most of the time.*

Had you been waiting for us long?

Ryfka shook her head and smiled. *No, for once the German trains were on time.*

They grinned at each other, while Brandon looked between them. "Ummm....hello...what are you saying? Bruce, you really are a terrible translator."

"Oh, sorry, mate. This is Ryfka Górski, and this is Grand-uncle Leib," he said, motioning to the old man snoring away in his chair.

"Right then, now out with it. How are you fluent in sign language, and sign language that she can understand?"

Bruce smiled. "Ya know, I kinda like this. I know a practical skill that you don't." Brandon shot him a glare cold as the winter they had left outside, to which Bruce rapped his hand lightly against Brandon's chest. "Aww, c'mon, mate, let me enjoy this. And to answer your question, she's using British Sign Language. Guess she's multi-lingual."

"And you know sign language because..."

"Because I had a cousin who was deaf. He..." A muscle twitched in his jaw. It had been a long time since he had seen Trevor. "Good bloke. Both sides of my family could have been better to him. I bothered to learn sign language so I could talk to him. Also helped to handle any blighters wantin' to make Trevor uncomfortable."

Brandon gave him a warm smile. He wasn't tearing up, was he? "That's beautiful, Bruce. Especially from you. I never knew."

He shrugged. "It's not like I should wear a sign around my neck reading 'Oye! I know sign language!' wherever I go. A bit much, don't you think?"

A soft knocking came from the hearth. Ryfka looked to Brandon, then to Bruce, and signed, *Where are the rest?*

Bruce furrowed his brow. "The rest?" he spoke while signing, in order to keep Brandon informed. "The rest of what?"

The rest of your team. For the assault.

"Assault?"

"Assault?" Brandon asked. "What assault?"

Ryfka started signing. "Oh, bugger," he groaned. "Apparently, Ryfka was expecting us to lead an assault on some factory around here. She's been watching this facility for a spell, that it's the Russian Empire enslaving locals and working on building up the military. Looks like the Czar is wanting to give mapmakers some work updating where borders fall."

Brandon shook his head. "That's not what we do!" He then turned back to Ryfka and bellowed, *"That's-not-what-we-do!"*

"She can read lips, mate," Bruce winced. "All you accomplish by doing that is making it hard for me to hear out of that ear."

Ryfka stomped on the floor, earning a sharp *snort-snort* from Grand-uncle Leib. *Why are you here?*

"Her Majesty the Queen is ill," Bruce began. He could feel himself sweating, and knew the sweating had nothing to with how long he had been standing by the hearth. "We're supposed to be getting Firebird feathers, kept somewhere in that factory, according to Section P. You're supposed to get us in, and then get us out."

The once sweet-looking, pretty face twisted into the kind of anger that made both Bruce and Brandon step back. She paced by Grand-uncle Leib, her hands and arms flying in front her in sharp, precise movements.

"So what she's saying, Brandon..." Bruce began.

"No need to translate, my friend," Brandon said. "I've got the gist of it."

Bruce watched Ryfka explain the problem, and his heart sunk. Firebird feathers had not sounded too difficult back in Whiterock, but as usual nothing was ever as it seemed. Perhaps he should have just stayed in the boiler.

✦⟫◉⟪✦

Wherein Our Agents of Deering-Do Test the Fantastic

Wellington's heart leaped into his throat as the central cage protecting Eliza—more or less—from possible gunfire shot upward into the skies, the rockets underneath her carrying her higher and higher away from the battle. She was still gaining altitude even as the flames erupting from underneath her fizzled out.

"Move! Now!" a voice screamed.

It was Lieutenant O'Neil, waving madly, and motioning towards the barracks as if life itself depended on it.

Hands grabbed at him, yanking him backward. His eyes locked with Vania's.

It was most definitely time to go.

Wellington stumbled backwards, and while his mind was preoccupied with Eliza, his feet seemed determined to follow Vania. Other soldiers were sprinting for the open barn doors of the base offices, while some disappeared into the nearby alleyways created by other buildings. Everyone was scattering, trying to find a new place to defend.

No, that wasn't quite right; they were not looking for new defensive positions. Everyone was ducking for cover and looking for places to hide.

Once back inside the office, Wellington claimed a bare patch of the floor alongside Vania and Southerby's men. Mere seconds after he stopped moving, the explosion ripped through the air. Windows shattered, walls buckled, and parts of the roof rained down as the floor rippled underneath them. Shards of glass and pieces of metal were hitting his back, and outside men began to scream. It reminded him of too many terrible things in his past.

Daring to look up at the ruined windows above his head, Wellington saw sunlight coming in through holes big and small. Dust from this mighty show of ordnance surrounded them, making it hard to see anything else in the room. His ears rang, but just through the high-pitched whine in his head he could still hear the steady drone of fire. "What was that?"

"The Enforcer is armed with Gatlings and flame throwers, as you saw," O'Neil said, picking himself up and brushing the debris from his uniform. "There is also, in the event of a total conversion of enemy forces or no-win scenarios, a self-destruct mode."

Vania's brow furrowed. "Has Agent Braun received formal training in the Enforcer's schematics?"

"No," Wellington said, pulling himself back to his feet, "she just has quite the innate talent for mayhem and destruction." He then motioned to the opening of the building's barn door. "Once more unto the breach, Miss Pujari? I believe after that impressive display we should have the enemy turning on their heels."

English soldiers were already back in the fray, as Eliza's final act of defiance had taken out most of the invading rebels, their bodies slashed and torn apart by the explosion or shrapnel from the Enforcer. The survivors were gathering themselves up and attempting to retreat to the portal.

Now able to get a good look at it, Wellington immediately recognized it as an æthergate. The English had collected their ranks and were firing in fluid, precise lines, their bullets claiming a fair number of these soldiers attempting their escape. Others were running through the arch of white-blue energy revealing on the other side another world, or at least another part of India. Where the gate led, Wellington could not ascertain on account of lingering smoke and soot.

The gasp from Vania caught him in mid-stride. Perhaps she had never seen æthergates before. Perhaps it was the sight of people running through them and not appearing from the other side. To the uninitiated, æthergates were a wonder defying all sciences, but her dark eyes told Wellington what she was witnessing was less of a marvel and more of a horror.

Then he saw it for himself. A pair of insurgents were sprinting for the portal, reaching their escape only to vanish in a wild flash of light and cerulean fire. They did not continue on through the other side, nor did they explode as if struck by ordnance. They simply...*disappeared.* Another group of rebels were making for the gate when British riflemen expressed their displeasure. Many of them dropped, but three others flickered. They blinked in and out of existence as soldiers continued to open fire on them. These three reached the gate only to meet the same bizarre fate at the others.

"We must find Eliza," Wellington said, his eyes scanning upwards.

Vania turned about, peering at the sky through smoke and flame. "There!"

A few hundred feet above them, a small cage attached to four large parachutes descended back towards the fort. Wellington reached into his coat pocket and produced a small case no larger than his palm. His thumb brushed over a small switch that popped it open, revealing a small pair of opera glasses. He slipped his sun spectacles off and brought the telescopic lenses up to his eyes. He had to be sure.

"I can just make out movement in the cage." Wellington's shoulders dropped slightly. "She appears to be laughing."

"Laughing?"

"Hysterically, as a matter of fact," he stated, snapping the small binoculars shut and returning his eyes to the protection of the sun spectacles. Relief made him feel quite light-headed. "I will wager you a shilling that she will ask me to build her one."

A flash, followed by a sudden chill, stole Wellington's attention from the sky. He turned just in time to see the æthergate begin to close. With a great rush of thunder, light, and electricity, the portal bent and twisted until reality returned to normal. Those rebels attempting to escape now faltered in their run, crying out to no one sympathetic to their cause. They had been abandoned and turned to face British infantry. Their hands raised into the air as they fell to their knees.

"What was that?" Vania asked, her voice shaky.

"Come along, Miss Pujari." Wellington gave her a nod. "We can explain it all, but presently, we should welcome Miss Braun back to this earthly plane."

The Enforcer's escape pod was still descending easily and steadily, an occasional strong breeze toying with it as it fell. It pitched slightly to the left and then struck the open motor pool with a dull thud. Wellington and Vania ran for Eliza as the parachutes collapsed and fluttered to the ground. Over their own footfalls and the whispers of silk, Wellington could hear Eliza's blissful laughter. She was enjoying herself. Beyond reason.

"The woman is mad," Vania said with a grin, pushing aside one of the parachutes.

Wellington chuckled as he pressed billowing fabric aside. "I believe it is a necessity in this job."

The chutes parted just as Eliza threw back hydraulic releases that popped the front of her cage open.

"That," she began, unbuckling herself from the command chair, "was amazing! Welly, you must build me one of these with all speed!"

Vania looked from Eliza to Wellington, then back to Eliza. Sighing, she reached into one of her belt pouches, pulled out a shilling, and slapped it into Wellington's hand. "Agent Braun, are you well?"

"Exhilarated, Vania!" Eliza made a swooshing noise, and raised her hand. "The rockets...the acceleration...."

"Did you happen to see the other side of that æthergate?" Wellington asked.

"Afraid not," Eliza replied, stepping free of the metallic cage. "Too much distortion on the event horizon."

"Æthergates in India. This complicates things tremendously."

"Let's not be too hasty," Eliza said. Then she shook her head. "Ye gods, I do hate when I sound like you, Welly."

He shrugged. "I find it quite endearing, actually."

Eliza crooked an eyebrow, then brushed a single finger against his nose. "Back to the scene of the crime, my Archivist-Agent-Engineer. I'd like to see if either my mind is going, or if you truly are rubbing off on me."

Wellington glanced over to Vania, and with a tiny nod to her, they followed Eliza back to where the æthergate had appeared. They came upon a rebel lying on his side. He did not appear to be wounded, but the wretch fought to breathe, and there was something definitely strange about the man. They were standing in front of him, close enough to see the ornate details of his white and scarlet robes.

"Poor sod," Eliza said, crouching down lower. "It's getting worse, isn't it?"

"Not so close," Wellington hissed.

"It's all right," Eliza said, referring to the dying man in front of her. The rebel's eyes were now darting in all directions. At moments, Wellington believed he saw him, but the man's face was a concoction of panic and puzzlement. His eyes couldn't focus on one point. "I've seen the rare daguerreotypes of this order," Eliza said, now motioning to the fallen soldier's clothes. "If memory serves, this is one of the factions looking to unite the continent with plans to install an emperor back on the throne."

Vania leaned forward and pointed to the markings in his robes. "Markings of the Mughal Empire?"

"Is that what we were facing?" came a voice from behind them all.

Lieutenant O'Neil removed his pith helmet and lightly dragged his palm across his smooth, bald head. Behind him was a group of ten men.

All of them looked relieved that the battle was done, but also confused, trying to fathom exactly what had just been unleashed on their base.

"I was rather impressed with Agent Braun's efficiency behind the Enforcer." He gave her a polite salute. "You are a natural."

"It really was a bit like driving my uncle's tractor." Her lips pursed for a moment, then she added, "Well, provided that tractor was armed with a flame thrower and Gatling gun."

"And a self-destruct mechanism," O'Neil added, wagging a finger at her, "lest we forget." His smile faded on seeing the dying rebel before them. "My God. That's Phani Talwar."

"You know this man?" Eliza asked.

"I...killed him..." O'Neil spluttered. "Six months ago. A firefight on the docks."

"But that was an engagement with Free India," Vania said.

"I know it was, but that was where I last saw Talwar. My men and I had him pinned down. No one from FI walked away from that firefight."

Wellington glanced at both Vania and Eliza before asking, "Did you see the body?"

"It was pandemonium, Agent Books. Quite a few bodies—both FI and British Empire—fell into the bay. Not all the bodies were recovered, but I did see him take a bullet."

"Did you see a body, Lieutenant?" Wellington pressed. He knew there were many things beyond what a simple solider might have experience with. Things that the Ministry dealt with almost daily.

"Missing," O'Neil stated, "presumed dead."

"False presumption, I'm afraid," he said, turning back to the man on the ground.

"So it would seem," Eliza said, removing her taiaha from its holster.

"Any ideas how someone like Talwar and his lot managed to get their hands on æthergate technology?" O'Neil asked, his hand tightening on his pith helmet.

Wellington peered over his spectacles. "Pardon me, but how do you know about æthergates?"

"The War Department spares no expense for us. We tend to serve as a proving ground for various inventions, and the idea of an æthergate was presented to us. Featherstone showed us schematics, looked promising, but Featherstone's offer was suddenly rescinded. Never really given a reason why. "

"The side effects," Eliza said, holding up her collapsed taiaha. The collected British soldiers started back as the metal baton passed through

Talwar, leaving a strange trail in its wake. Talwar's face twitched, but he appeared in no more than slight discomfort. "A bit nasty, don't you think?"

"Dear God," whispered Wellington. He dared to touch what he believed was a solid body, but Talwar was composed of nothing more than a dense mist. He held his hand in front of him, running his thumb back and forth along the inside of his fingers.

"What is it, Wellington?" she asked. "Something on your skin?"

"No, they are tingling." He waved his hand back and forth. The sensation crawling against his skin was not painful. It was unsettling. "It's not stopping."

"It will in a few moments. I think your fingers have been ionized," Vania said as she lowered her head closer to the ground. "What does this to a man?"

"An overabundance of æthergate travel," Wellington began, mirroring Vania, who was looking at Talwar at a low angle. Indeed, she was right. Talwar's outline appeared solid from above, but at this lower angle he appeared to shimmer. The edge of his robes, even his face, danced and undulated before him. "This is why the Ministry uses æthergates only in the direst of situations. Prolonged exposure to its radiation makes one's existence…unstable."

"That's why he looks so terrified," Eliza said, looking up at O'Neil. "He is caught—now how did Axelrod explain it to me—between two points of reality. He can see past, present, and future, passing in flashes, but in our time, Talwar is caught at the moment his body hit the ground."

Vania looked back and forth to each of them. "I thought the Ministry had locked down æthergate technology."

"We had. Initially." Wellington looked over to Eliza. "Weren't you on that mission when the Ministry tangled with the House of Usher?"

"No, but Harry was. He told me about it," Eliza said. "The Ministry had secured the Atlantean generators…"

"Atlantean?" O'Neil asked, as if he thought he'd misheard. "As in Atlantis?"

"Now you understand, Lieutenant, why we are not called The Ministry of Everyday Occurrences," Eliza quipped. "The House managed to steal the original parchments. There was one problem, though—Poseidon's Key. The Atlantean Rosetta Stone. They didn't have it. We did."

Wellington looked to Vania. "This didn't leave Usher so easily discouraged in cracking the mystery of æthergates."

"London, 1871?" Eliza asked.

"Splendid," he said with a smile. "Case Number 18710520UKMG. Mercury's Gate. The scientist's name was Sir Carroll Ludovic, and he had somehow managed to unlock the basics of æthergate travel. The problem with Mercury's Gate compared to the true Atlantean æthergates, according to our experts at R&D, was the radiation output and its effect on the structural integrity of organic matter. Sir Carroll's design was less than efficient."

Vania look at where the gate had been. "So, what we saw...?"

"A very respectable facsimile," Wellington said, returning to his feet, "but not the genuine article."

Eliza pressed the switch extending her taiaha, and placed the weapon inside Talwar again. This time, his body trembled, looking as if he were being poked or prodded with something which, in a manner of speaking, was true. "And this is what happens when that radiation is not managed properly." Her thumb hovered over the blue button in the weapon. "I'm sorry," she whispered to him.

Sparks dimly illuminated the inside of Talwar, his mouth suddenly locking in a silent scream. His eyes saw Wellington for just an instant, and then he disappeared in a wild flash of blue light.

"That was what we saw in their retreat," Vania said.

Wellington looked back to the barracks. "Where's Southerby? We need to talk to him straight away. With Featherstone so closely connected with Jekyll and this Ghost Rebellion as you call..."

His voice trailed off as O'Neil cast his eyes over to his regiment, all of which, one by one, removed their helmets and caps. Many cast down their eyes, and Wellington let out a sigh as he realised.

"Soditall," Eliza whispered.

"Determined as he was," O'Neil said sombrely, "Southerby chose to face the danger just as his soldiers would. He refused to surrender the fort to this lot. To the last."

"Very noble, save for one thing," Wellington said, "his intent. If he had lived to claim the day, he would have been hailed as a hero of the empire. With his death, he now gives Parliament the justification to bring all of its military might to bear on India." He looked around him, noting the tired soldiers carrying wounded mates to what he assumed was an emergency infirmary. "Remember Southerby and Fort St Paul. Quite the rallying cry, don't you think?"

"Either way," Vania said, "Southerby gets his wish: the subjugation of India."

"Dear Lord," O'Neil said, staring at the devastation. "I never considered that."

Wellington turned to the young officer, addressing him just as he had once done to soldiers during his days in Africa. "Lieutenant, considering the circumstances, the Ministry is assuming command of this fort."

The young man blinked. "Agent Books?"

"He is well within protocols, Lieutenant," Vania said, taking a spot at his back. "The Ministry has jurisdiction over all unusual occurrences like this. It's in the name, and even if Lockhart fights it, the Queen will remind him personally if need be."

"Do you have a photographer of any kind on the base?" Wellington asked.

O'Neil cleared his throat, and then stood a little straighter. "Yes, Mr Books."

"I want your men to check any and all of the enemy dead here, solid or otherwise, and I want them photographed."

"Yes, Agent Books," O'Neil said, giving him a salute before ordering his men to pass along his words through the ranks.

"Sorry, darling," Wellington said, giving Eliza a weak smile. "I should have let you take command as you are the senior agent."

"Old habits." Eliza patted him on his shoulder before turning to Vania. "Inauthentic æthergate technology, a man presumed dead taking up arms against the empire, and all the elements in play to throw India into chaos. What do you think, Agent Pujari?"

"Usher," she replied.

"We're going to need to see those photographs as soon as they are ready. Alert Director Smith, and send word to the home office. Inform them of the situation."

"Yes, ma'am," Vania said before heading back to the barracks.

"Well then," Wellington began, "the House of Usher is apparently supplying rebels with inferior, supernatural technology, India is on the brink of war with Mother England, all while a madman possessing the ability to turn ordinary people into ten feet monsters is on the loose."

Eliza bobbed her head, her lips bent in a smirk. "Just another day at the Ministry."

"Shall I go put the kettle on?"

"Please."

CHAPTER SIX

✦⇒◉⇐✦

Wherein Our Colonial Pepperpot and Our Dashing Archivist Face a Decision

"So now we find ourselves in command of a military base," Eliza said, behind Southerby's grand desk. "That's certainly a turn up for the books."

She turned and grinned at Wellington, hoping her attempt at levity struck home somewhere, but instead she found he was not looking at her at all. Rather he was staring out the bullet-riddled window as a small group of soldiers carried Southerby to the infirmary. Not that he was able to be helped at this stage. It was the only place to put him. Her partner had a look on his face of such pensiveness that she just knew he was imagining the worst case for this scenario to play out.

"Wellington?" she pressed, until he jerked around and stared at her.

"What...oh, I am sorry Eliza, or should I say, Commander Braun?"

The sentiment made Eliza take stock of this grand office, seeming more appropriate for an Adventurer's Club than a high-ranking outpost of Her Majesty's military. Lieutenant General Southerby may have considered himself "one of the boys," but with the stuffed lion and tiger at opposite ends of the office, the banners of past battles, and the lovely paintings all flanking the larger-than-life sized portrait of himself, Southerby made it clear: Whomever occupied this office occupied a place of power. Eliza had never been one for pomp and ceremony, but she did not necessarily feel out of place. With the general's office showing signs of the firefight, some of that pomp was dampened.

Still, the idea that as ranking field agent Eliza was now in control of Fort St Paul was ludicrous. Luckily, the solution was at hand. Lieutenant General Southerby had the best of everything installed at his base, and that included an æthermessage system, which she and Vania had made use of in summoning Director Smith.

Lieutenant O'Neil stood at the door, waiting at attention. Having an attractive man at her beck and call was something of a fantasy for Eliza, but O'Neil was so *serious*. He was making her nervous.

"O'Neil, could you please form a detail that will meet Director Smith of the Ministry? I want to make sure once he arrives, he is escorted promptly to my office." She leaned on the desk, feigning the authority she hardly felt comfortable in wielding.

"Certainly, Agent Braun." O'Neil spun on his heel and left her and Wellington alone.

Eliza would have never thought she would feel such relief at a handsome officer leaving her sight. Once he was gone, she let out a sigh and sagged into the chair still warm from the Indian afternoon.

"Starting to feel the weight of leadership across your shoulders?" Wellington perched himself on the edge of the desk. "Would you like me to rub them for you, darling?"

She wasn't positive if he was joking or not, so she tapped him on the knee. "Watch your step, Books, or I will have you thrown into the brig."

He shook his head. "The brig is for the Navy. In the Army, we call it the stockade."

"You're not helping." She rubbed at the bridge of her nose, attempting to push back a headache she could feel lurking in her skull. "I should just leave. Let O'Neil handle this."

"Tosh, you wouldn't be able to leave the fort, not with it in this state," Wellington said. "You're handling this fine, and you must until Maulik arrives. It's difficult being responsible for all these souls, believe me I know."

She sat up suddenly. "Where did Vania go?"

The two of them looked around, but the young agent was nowhere in sight.

"She was right behind us," Eliza whispered, running over to the window. If another Pujari sister died she would never forgive herself. Ihita's death was not on her watch, but Eliza carried it with her. She loved Ihita. She was a dear friend. Perhaps, if she had still been active in the field, she could have done something.

Outside, the chaos was subsiding. Injured soldiers had been cleared into the infirmary, while the dead had been piled to one side. Small fires, whether caused by the Enforcer's destruction or by the rebel attack, had been put out. When the wind blew aside the smoke, Eliza was relieved to see Vania standing with her back to them, scribbling notes. The soldiers flowed around her, but she remained where she was, head buried in her work. Ihita had been like that; committed to the detriment of everything else about. Eliza smiled at the memory of many lunches shared at her friend's desk, with Ihita sticking food in one corner of her mouth while still scribbling with her pencil at some report or other. She had possessed a mighty tolerance for paperwork, one that Eliza had never understood.

Clearing her throat, she jerked her head in the direction of the young agent. "She's out there taking notes of some kind."

Lieutenant O'Neil appeared at the door. He was holding a tape from an æthermessenger. "Ma'am, Director Smith," he announced before turning on his heel and stepping out.

Maulik wheeled into the office and took in the surroundings for a moment, slowly turning his chair in place. "I would never picture you in a posh office such as this, Eliza, but with the bullet holes this new position actually suits you."

That headache she felt creeping up on her was returning once more.

"You are here to relieve me, yes, Maulik?" she asked.

"Of course, of course," he said, waving his hand. "I'm just genuinely impressed in how you have managed to stumble upon an ongoing case while pursing a completely unrelated one. Well done."

"And I thought I had managed to cock things up here."

"By stopping this latest incursion from these elusive rebels? My dear Eliza, the fact you and Wellington were able to positively identify the æthergate—or should I say Mercury's Gate?—has provided quite the breakthrough."

"That was Sir Carroll's name for it, but if it walks like a duck and quacks like a duck," Wellington said, shrugging. "I was going to suggest making the best of our time, and show you the site of the æthergate's appearance while Eliza remains in command."

"Then I'll stay here," she said, taking the lieutenant general's seat once more. "I will do what I've done best so far as base commander and keep the chair warm." She added a broad wink. "After all, how much of a mess can one little woman make?"

Maulik tilted his head, and then looked over to Wellington. "You know, Wellington, I understand this base has an Enforcer. Quite the technological marvel."

"*Had* an Enforcer," Wellington said gently, glancing at Eliza. She managed to look not the least contrite.

"Oh yes, yes, yes," and Maulik laced his fingers together across his stomach, and looked at her. "Had."

Eliza motioned with her head to a paperweight sitting at the edge of the desk. "I can reach that, you know?"

"You said you had something to show me, Books?" Maulik asked, already backing away and turning to the door.

"Right this way, Director," Wellington said, leading the way out.

Eliza was finally alone. With Maulik and Wellington exchanging notes with Vania, Lieutenant O'Neil preoccupied with restoring operations, and the soldiers of St Paul busy licking their wounds, this was her first opportunity to enjoy a moment's peace. She would need it in order to have a clear head and search this office properly.

Leaping to her feet, Eliza stepped back to get a better look at the great desk. Six drawers, two on the left, locked, and four on the right. Across the centre section was a smaller drawer, locked. While the base could brag of having the latest in technological marvels, Southerby's office was nothing of the sort. For one thing, Southerby didn't enjoy the assistance of an analytical machine, an æthermessenger terminal, or any kind of scientific innovation. *So,* Eliza thought with a sigh, *this is going to be the old-fashioned way. That suits me just fine.*

Rolling up her sleeves to the elbow, she pulled open the first of the four drawers. This drawer, as was the one underneath it, was full of supplies you would expect: paper, stamps, envelopes, and odds and ends that told her nothing. The third drawer revealed a list of numbers, each soldier being cross-referenced rather than listed immediately. A key for the filing cabinets to her left. She let out a soft groan. Typical of the army to make things complicated.

Eliza sat back and, on hearing O'Neil bark out orders, stared at the window. Fort St Paul would have to adjust their way of thinking after today. Soldiers, generally speaking, concentrated on the here and now: who was in front of them, how much their ration of beer was, and what their next mission would entail. Often times Eliza knew she completely forgot to take into account how some of the things the Ministry dealt with on a regular basis would appear to those unaccustomed to the unexplained. She had spent so much of her life dealing with secret societies, mad scientists and unnatural beings, they had become normal to her. What Fort St Paul had seen here today would change all that, and some of them simply wouldn't be able to cope.

Perhaps they would rather wash it away with their regulation India Pale Ale, which sailed in on continuous shipments. Maybe after long enough they would be able to tell themselves they hadn't seen it at all. Everyone had their own ways of dealing with the strange, the unusual, and the bizarre.

"Right then," Eliza muttered to herself, her eyes narrowing on the centre desk drawer. "Back to business."

She did not pack her lock picking set on account of she needed to be able to move. This meant carrying only the essentials: her pistols and her taiaha. So, without the precision tools, this would mean using whatever she could find. Her eyes immediately fell on a rather lovely letter opener. From its make, quite sturdy. Then there was the paperweight she had used to threaten Wellington and Maulik—an impressive statue of what looked like Southerby, the general and his horse mounted against a wide base.

With tip of the letter opener nestled into the keyhole, Eliza lifted the paperweight up over her head and swung. The statue base slammed hard into the opener. Eliza hefted the paperweight upwards and struck the opener again. The third strike gave items on the desk a good shudder. That should have been enough.

Eliza gave the opener a hard twist, but on the second wrench, the lock disengaged. With a grin, she opened the drawer and found amidst additional writing utensils and supplies needed for one's office a folder. She placed it on the desk and flipped it open.

Those in charge of Fort St Paul had bragged of their connection with Lord Featherstone, but from the looks of these documents, it was hardly an idle boast. India had been the recipient of incredible creations of war. Along with the schematics for The Enforcer, an experimental sniper rifle that shot explosive shells, and uniforms that doubled as body armour, Eliza found in this dossier plenty of inventions waiting on approval from Parliament. Turning another page, the designs for the Gatling Garrison appeared, dated two months before the events of the Diamond Jubilee. Eliza's *déjà vu* was not unfounded.

The next schematics were of weapons that she had seen both advancing from the Thames and attacking from the air. Perhaps in six months or so, the Indian sky would be dotted with Mechamen Mark IIIs while the titanic Mark IIs lumbered along Bombay's perimeter.

"Oh, tisk, tisk, *tisk*, Doctor Jekyll," Eliza said. "You really are quite the cad."

Then she thought about Wellington's prediction. *Remember Southerby and Fort St Paul.* Parliament and the Crown would rally the spirit of the people, and in a matter of weeks…

The loud bang of a door slamming caused Eliza to start. The voices of Wellington, Maulik, and Vania were now discernible in the corridor outside the office, but Eliza could hear a fourth pair of boots with them. That must have been O'Neil.

"As Agent Books remarked earlier, this variation of æthergate these separatists are using is very unstable," Vania said, her words echoing slightly. "The ionization of the air, similar to what you felt when you touched Talwar, is still prevalent."

"Now with my own limited understanding of this device…" Maulik began.

"There you go again, being modest, Director Smith," chided Wellington. "You were on the mission that secured Atlantis."

"That will do, Books."

Eliza smiled at that retort. Maulik really did not care for his new role, but it did suit him.

"But if my own memory still serves," Maulik said, "while we might not be able to see it, the fabric of reality does take quite a bludgeoning. One wrong step outside and we could accidentally slip through an ætheric fracture, step into another dimension."

"I believe that is the great mystery at hand," Vania said as they entered the office. "We have no idea what fallout these imitation æthergates may have on the environment."

"Usher may be able to build these portals, but without Poseidon's Key they cannot translate accurately the computations for targeting, power flow regulation, or even the best current for that matter."

"They were working with Edison when we tangled with them in the Americas," Eliza offered. "I'll wager they are using direct current."

Maulik wagged a finger at her. "Books is rubbing off on you."

"On all sorts of places," she said, waggling her eyebrows a fraction. Waiting for Wellington's blush to flare, she switched her attention to the stern O'Neil standing by the door. "Lieutenant O'Neil?"

"Yes, ma'am," he replied sharply, loud enough to echo in the outside corridor.

"Oh for heaven's sake, man, at ease, relax, or just…" and she fluttered her hand around him, adding, "…stop making me so bloody nervous. I liked you better when I wasn't the ranking officer here."

O'Neil cleared his throat and removed his helmet. "Sorry, Agent Braun."

"*Much* better. Now, a few questions—The Enforcer. A lovely machine, to be sure, but I did overhear Southerby mention that outside of yourself, none of the other men here could operate it?"

"That's true. The controls were rather...difficult...to manage."

"But you did?"

O'Neil smiled. "Like you said, it's a bit like operating a tractor. Many of the officers in the ranks come from privileged homes. You and I, if I may be so bold to presume..."

"You may," Eliza said with a nod.

"We come from more humble backgrounds."

"And I noticed a few experimentals in your gun rack. Did I see a modified Crackshot?"

"Oh yes, the Wilkinson-Webley Model X. Higher velocity shells with an advanced targeting system."

Wellington leaned forward. "Advanced how?"

"Southerby told us the shells worked on a biochemical targeting formula. Provided you could obtain a blood sample from the intended target, the bullets would be able to single them out from a crowd."

Wellington and Eliza shared a glance before she asked, "And did it work?"

The question took O'Neil by surprise. "I...I'm sorry, Miss Braun?"

"Did the Model X operate as promised?"

O'Neil shifted from one foot to another, his eyes cast down to the floor for a moment. "We had a few challenges with it, as well."

"What Featherstone supplied you with was nothing like you had ever seen before, was it?"

"Indeed, Miss Braun."

Eliza turned to Wellington, Vania, and Maulik, holding up the folder of schematics. "Featherstone was offering these weapons as the latest from the Empire; but compromised by Jekyll as we knew him to be, Fort St Paul served as his personal proving ground."

Maulik leaned forward in his chair. "Neither Parliament nor the War Department would ever allow untested weapons into the field, let alone protect India."

"Not all the experimentals were so unpredictable," O'Neil protested.

Eliza pointed to the soldier with the folder. "Let me guess—the Gatling Garrison?" O'Neil's brow furrowed, but he nodded nonetheless. "That design had already been thoroughly tested, in preparation for the Diamond Jubilee."

"The Grey Ghosts?" Wellington asked.

"Yes," Eliza said, handing Wellington the schematics, "and from the looks of what Featherstone was supplying the military, Jekyll had been running this little side venture for quite some time."

"Mechamen designs?" Wellington brought the file closer to his face. "Featherstone had passed these on to Southerby before the Jubilee. Jekyll was playing both sides?"

"As if he didn't trust the stability of the Maestro." Eliza then turned back to O'Neil. "When did you say Featherstone proposed æthergate technology to you all?"

"Four months ago. I remember Southerby was quite excited over it, but as I said before, Featherstone pulled the project a month later. Southerby was furious."

"And this Ghost Rebellion you mentioned to us—when did they first start to appear?"

O'Neil shrugged. "I would say two months ago."

Vania gasped, catching everyone's attention. "Jekyll's found a new proving ground."

Wellington gently tapped Eliza's shoulder. "We should look at that personal diary of Featherstone's again. If this hunch of yours is correct, Featherstone was coming to India to aid Jekyll and this Ghost Rebellion."

"Give us the room," Maulik said, his mechanised voice sounding even and still as a lake in the early morning.

O'Neil and Vania both stepped out without question. The lieutenant closed the doors behind him as Maulik wheeled himself over to the corner of the office that had been reserved for more casual talks. There was a fine, dark wood cigar box and a crystal decanter on a small, round table here. The intimate setting was flanked by three high back, plush chairs.

"Would you mind?" Maulik asked, waving his hand at one of the chairs.

Wellington moved one aside as the Director rolled into its vacancy. Eliza took one of the remaining seats and waited for Wellington to join her.

"That was impressive," Eliza said to Maulik. "For someone hesitant in undertaking a leadership role, you know when to make your standing clear."

"I never said I was hesitant, my dear Eliza," Maulik replied. "I may not like being in charge, but I have never been hesitant. At least, until now." He patted his right hand with his left, and gave a slight nod before looking back up at the two of them. "I know that currently, you both are on the hunt for Jekyll, and I know better than anyone the high priority the Ministry places on his capture. That being said, I need your help."

"Help?" Wellington said. "Are you asking us to abandon the chase for Jekyll and assist you in dealing with this Ghost Rebellion?"

"Maulik," Eliza said, leaning in closer, "it is obvious there is some sort of connection here…"

"Yes, we had suspected that our Royal Engineer, under the influence of Doctor Jekyll, is supplying experimental technology into the hands of rebels. Rebels that, according to O'Neil, were reported to be killed in action. Now currently, your manhunt and my peculiar occurrence are intertwined. My concern is what happens when they are not.

"Since the Jubilee, the Ministry has been working to get back on their feet. Even with these many months, while I am comfortable in my position, my staff are still inexperienced. I need agents with undeniable talent. I need agents with honed instincts. I need agents with a certain *je ne se quoi*. I need—"

"What you really need are agents who can tell their arse from their elbow," Eliza blurted out.

Wellington moaned something along the lines of *"With all the grace and eloquence of a ballerina…"* while Maulik chuckled.

"You know what I need, Eliza. Can I count on the both of you?"

Eliza locked her gaze with Wellington's. They both wanted Jekyll. As Maulik said, Jekyll was a top priority—however Featherstone and Jekyll together had placed India in a delicate position. The Ghost Rebellion, whomever they were, and the death of Southerby could bring down upon the country and its people the wrath of the British Empire.

Wellington took Eliza's hand, squeezed it tightly, and then looked to Maulik. "What can we do?"

"Excellent," Maulik said, reaching into his coat pocket. "A bit of a relief as it will be easier to keep an eye on you."

Eliza inclined her head to one side. "Come again?"

Maulik unfurled the paper he had just drawn from his pocket. "Received this æthermissive from headquarters. One of our operatives, Agent Case, reported seeing the two of you in Bruges. Two days ago." He looked up. "I just need to confirm—you're not in Belgium presently, are you?"

✦═◉═✦

Wherein the Doctor Pays a House Call

" We have assembled and wait upon you."

Nahush Kari's eyes flicked open. The separatist movement he had started—born of frustration and rage—had seen a light of hope in the most unexpected of benefactors. Now, after their failed attack against the invaders, he was trapped, betrayed, and humiliated.

A trickle of sweat ran down his face, and it was not the heat in the close quarters of the building that caused it. Wiping it off with the back of his hand, he took a deep breath and pulled himself up to his feet. They were all seated in the top floor of a two-storey building, deep in Bombay, but they might as well have been in a British prison. He joined his fellow freedom fighters and saw more than disappointment in their slumped postures. He saw the edges of despair. Balaji who was the oldest among them had, as a younger man, fought in the rebellion of '58. Yet now he sat, hands over his eyes, bent and silent. He was broken.

A gentle breeze blew through the small windows and offered relief from the heat. He had not come this far to fail.

The series of houses they occupied in the Shor Bazaar were all interconnected by underground tunnels, and kept under careful watch. This was their haven, their protected place. Even with those British that dared to venture into the market for something exotic to take home, this market remained India. That, and hiding right under their noses was not only amusing, it just made sense. Let the English roam the Western Ghats, getting wet and bitten by insects. They would not find them in the mountains. They would never think to look so close.

Their location within Bombay was much better for their vaunted æthergate technology to work—and it had done so magnificently, for their recruitment needs and the raids that followed. *Without question,* Nahush Kari thought as he looked at those in his ranks, *the æthergate had been a success.* They not only increased their numbers, but he had recruited the finest soldiers. Freedom fighters like Phani Talwar. He knew, and his men knew, they finally possessed an advantage over the English.

Then came the disaster at Fort St Paul.

Not one of the assembled leaders of the rebellion could meet his eyes. They remained silent as the chatter of the bazaar flittered in from outside their windows.

At the edge of the assembled was Makeala, the sole woman, and one of the movement's greatest supporters. Her dark eyes met his in an unflinching, penetrating gaze. She showed none of the fear and anger in the others, remaining the calm centre of the group. She was neither disappointed nor in despair. She was angry.

Oddly, Nahush found her anger a small relief.

His officers had been wary of Featherstone's generous offer. The British engineer had found Nahush in the monsoon season and offered them schematics of a device that seemed to be the answer to their problems. The Imperial army was a beast with many tentacles, and though the separatists could strike at the limbs, they could never get close enough to attack the head. Featherstone's device had offered the chance to strike them in the eye, a definite step forward in Nahush's plan for India.

Nahush had shaken the white man's hand. Nahush had been the first through the æthergate. Nahush believed, as everyone before him had believed, that Featherstone had been their unexpected salvation. Now looking at the others seated around him, he could sense that they were remembering that too, rolling it over in their minds. Soon enough one of them would speak the words.

"The æthergate has failed us, brothers and sisters." He kept his voice strong, trying to remind them he was still their leader. Nahush held the eyes of his council, trying to make them see he would not turn away from the responsibility. Honesty, he knew to be an unshakeable foundation to build upon.

"We were prepared," Makeala said softly. Nahush was eternally grateful this cursed science had not touched her. Her dark eyes gleamed with pride. "The gate worked perfectly in the beginning. We only had the plans, but you made it work."

"Your pact with that English bastard has damned us all," Shardool said, breaking the silence of the other men. His friend of many decades stood, openly challenging Nahush with fire blazing in his eyes. "We came here to fight and die by your side if necessary, but instead you condemned us all."

"Shardool," Nahush began, "we were all led to believe in the æthergate. It cost us good men."

"There is nothing for our mothers to even burn and cast into the Ganges!"

"We all feel the loss. I will not presume to know the feeling of watching your brother disappear at the portal as he did."

"He was alive," his friend continued, thrusting his finger towards Nahush, "and this science you trusted, you made us believe in, killed him."

Makeala rose to her feet, her sari slipping from her sleek, dark hair while she folded her hands in front of her. "We have struck fear into the hearts of the occupiers," she countered. "They have seen what we are willing to sacrifice to rid our Mother India of them, and they too are still licking their wounds."

Some of the men frowned at this woman raising her voice in such a manner, but many of the younger ones in the room stared at Makeala entranced.

"Sacrifice for a result is one thing," Nahush said, gesturing as kindly as he could for Makeala to sit. She gave him a glare but did so, folding her sari around her and not meeting the gaze of any of the men. "My cousin is wrong, I fear. We did not destroy the fort as we intended, and we lost far too many of Mother India's sons today."

"But the English lost their leader," she stated.

The room fell silent as they considered her words. This band of passionate Indians under his rule needed to strike at a target that would cripple the British. Nahush recognised their hunger all too well. Under the Imperial yoke, the resources of their home continued to be syphoned off to the self-professed Empress of India. They possessed more wealth than the other territories of the Empire, and yet Indians were denied even the right to vote on those that ruled them. Their culture was decried as savage at every turn, their children taught European ways. The Empire had promised much and delivered very little. He needed to keep this resentment stoked as the raging fire he knew it to be.

Perhaps on this raid, they had reached for too much.

"Yes, we did take a life. An important one. An influential one." Nahush looked to each of them, finding a source of pride from what their raid had accomplished. "If we still believe the æthergate as a blessing, then yes, I would rejoice. However, I fear we killed one cobra only to have awakened the nest."

Before he could continue, a commotion suddenly erupted below them. The walls of their building echoed with shouts. They leapt to their feet, drawing various edged weapons. Even his old friend Shardool held a modified Bulldog at the ready. A few muffled yelps followed by sharp rings of metal against metal, the sickening sound of ripping viscera, and then...

Scuff. Scuff. Scuff. Someone was coming up the stairs...

"Do not fire that weapon," Nahush whispered tersely. His friend's gaze was wild, but he held a finger to him. "If you do, you will reveal our secret with an impulse, and everything ends today."

The footsteps seemed to take their time in reaching them. With his gaze locked on the doorway, Nahush expected to see a troop of British soldiers charge into the room to kill them all. How the British could infiltrate this deep into the bazaar without some warning was a mystery.

So when a tall, broad shouldered man appeared on that spot instead, Nahush was stunned for a moment. The three clicks and a compressor priming took his gaze back to Shardool. He held up his hand, warning his friend once more what was at stake. When Shardool returned the hammer back to a safe position, Nahush looked back to the newcomer.

Something was not right with this Englishman standing in the threshold. As Nahush observed him, he appeared to shrink somehow. His massive shoulders, impossible on a living man, adjusted down to diminutive proportions. He was white, not burnt by the sun or even tanned, but pale. It was as if he had not seen sun in months. Nahush could see the veins running under his skin and the blood throbbing noticeably. Such a sight would have meant he should have been breathing hard, exerting himself in some fashion. Instead, he appeared calm and collected. He wore a well cut, if slightly rumpled, beige linen suit, which now looked far too large for him.

Their gazes locked, and a shudder of horror ran through Nahush.

Once, as a young boy, he had stumbled across a tiger eating from a carcass. The predator had looked at him with these same eyes. Empty, black and pitiless. Suddenly in that moment Nahush realised how little he mattered in the greater scheme of things.

That tiger had at least been beautiful. This man was anything but. For an instant he reconsidered calling for gunfire.

Finally, Nahush asked, his own English sounding strange in this room, "How did you get in here?"

"Well, your building has this amazing innovation called 'the front door' and I am an advocate for innovation, so I used that," he said, his voice changing with each word, going from feral to civilised along the way. "I suppose you are wondering about your men. I wish I could say I left them unharmed, but...well, that would be a lie."

In the corner of his eye, Nahush saw Shardool lift the gun once more. Before anyone could move or speak, the man had crossed the room and gripped his friend's arm in a strange lock unlike any martial art Nahush was familiar with. The gun dropped out of Shardool's hand, and his friend was tossed into the far wall as if he weighed nothing.

The stranger took a breath, and the veins Nahush saw were darker. He now filled his suit properly, but then he began to shrink again. His smile was a nasty baring of teeth that made Nahush think of white, bleached bones in the desert. The newcomer's eyes raked over the gathering of leaders, seemingly weighing and measuring each of them. His eyes flickered over Makeala the longest, but he said nothing as he turned back to Nahush. What kind of demon was this man?

"I'm terribly sorry, I didn't introduce myself." The man gave a little bow. "Doctor Henry Jekyll, at your service."

Nahush had received the best education an Indian boy could expect—a British one. This strange doctor had the kind of polished accent only gained in Oxford or Cambridge. It grated on Nahush's nerves, since he had long come to associate it with oppression and intolerance. He had received many beatings as an Indian in the private schools of England. The sting of blows on his back had been accompanied by taunts with this very accent. When he spent his time studying in Oxford, there had been less beatings, but just as many cruel words flung his way. Nahush's father had thought he was doing right by his son, but most of what he had learned in Britain was hatred.

"And from that look in your eye, I can see you have deduced I am English." The doctor took off his flat cap, and held his arms outward in a shrug. "Then again I would have thought my skin colour or fashion choices would have been your first clue."

One nod and Jekyll would be made quick work of, but how did he find them? "Featherstone," Nahush guessed. "You are an associate of his."

Jekyll's eyes lit up with delight, but the levity did nothing to put Nahush at ease. "Yes, Hieronymus told me all about you, Nahush Kari. So good to finally meet the man behind the movement."

Now Makeala stepped forward, her own blade raising upward, but Nahush slipped ahead of her, shaking his head slightly. Pushing back his instinct to give the order to kill this man, Nahush faced him. "You are taking quite a risk coming here."

"Really?" Jekyll let out an exasperated sigh. "Just as you did with that rather ugly scene at Fort St Paul?"

Whatever fear inhibited him vanished in that moment. Nahush drew his own knife and was on him, blade to his throat before anyone could move. "I am sick of white men offering solutions and then letting us do the dying. From what I was told, we were nothing but test subjects for your science experiments."

Jekyll glanced down at the edge of the knife, but his breathing remained even. Nahush might as well have been holding a spoon to his flesh. "I assume you have questions about your æthergate. I have answers for you."

Nahush trembled in that moment, wondering if it would be wiser to slit the doctor's throat, or if that would result in something even more horrific happening. He didn't like being this close to the man. Where Jekyll's skin was in contact with his, Nahush could feel it puckering, quivering with strange spasms. He stepped back, glanced over to his soldiers, all of them waiting for a word, a command.

"If your answers do not satisfy me," Nahush warned, "you will disappear from this mortal plane. Completely."

"It may surprise you how resilient I am, but certainly, yes, have your way with me,"—his eyes shot to Nahush with the kind of chill calm reminiscent of that tiger's gaze—"*after* you listen to what I have to say."

"I will give you five minutes."

"Five minutes? Quite a bit can happen in five minutes. First, a goodwill gesture." He reached into his pocket and pulled out a small, brown bottle. He rattled its contents and then tossed it to Makeala. "That's for your man against the wall, for any aches he may encounter. Now, to business..." He adjusted his cravat before taking a more central point of the room. "Featherstone was a patient of mine. I had a bit of influence over him, and when I heard that he was pawning off shoddy æthergate technology to you, I made it my priority to find you and apologise on his behalf. Reckless behaviour that I cannot abide by."

"Featherstone knew this science was dangerous?" Jagish asked from Nahush's left. The faint creak of leather meant Jagish's grip must have been quite firm around his kukri.

"Yes, I am sad to say," Jekyll said. "He spun a yarn, if I am to understand correctly, about the occupation of India being too costly and therefore he wanted to help you in this quaint rebellion of yours." He nodded. "Yes, total poppycock. At great risk to my own life, I regret to inform you that you lot were test subjects in Featherstone's grand experiment."

Jagish and Omar took a step towards him, but Nahush held them back with a look. "And I am to believe you because...?"

"If you check with your spies in Bombay, particularly the contact that introduced you to Featherstone, you'll find I'm a wanted man, and rather a nasty piece of work—at least according to the British. Two peas in a pod, we are." Jekyll strolled over to the writing desk in the far corner and slid out its chair for himself. He casually glanced at the collection of books and nodded in appreciation. "Oh yes, we do share a few things in common."

"We are nothing alike," Nahush seethed.

"We both want something, something each other has." Jekyll took a seat and then checked his pocket watch. "Please, another five minutes?"

Makeala touched Nahush on the shoulder, and whispered into his ear, "The enemy of our enemy could be useful."

Nahush cast a glance over his leaders, and then took the seat across from Jekyll while they sat once more on the floor. However, this time with their weapons across their respective laps.

"The æthergates are based on rather flimsy trials from an incident involving the Ministry of Peculiar Occurrences," Jekyll stated, producing from the inside pocket of his coat a small notebook, a larger, folded parchment seeming to serve as its bookmark. "Featherstone believed he could control the side effects, but needed test subjects. Initially, it was to be the men of St Paul's, but on discovering one of your spies, he took it upon himself to kill two birds with a rather ambitious stone."

Nahush frowned and only just restrained the urge to poke the man in the shoulder. "What exactly do you know?"

"Tell me, Mr Kari," Jekyll began, considering him in a way that made him feel exactly like a piece of meat, "how many missions have you conducted using the gates?"

"Four," he replied. "Recruitment operations."

Jekyll pulled out a pair of spectacles from his jacket pocket, put them on, opened the book at the point where the parchment marked, and examined Nahush even more closely. "And I take it you did not accompany your brave soldiers on their daring raids?"

"Are you implying Nahush is a coward?" Omar asked.

"On the contrary," Jekyll said, "it is foolhardy for great leaders to charge into battle, lest they fall themselves. Who then will lead in their stead? Southerby learned that, didn't he?" His eyes narrowed on Omar, and Nahush watched his captain grow ashen as Jekyll gave the man his undivided attention. "You strike me as a man of action. How many times have you stepped through the æthergate?"

Omar swallowed. "Six."

The doctor didn't even blink. His eyes grew dark and dangerous behind his glasses, and a strange blue tint radiated over his face, yet his voice was still calm. "When was the last time you ate?"

Omar hesitated. "I...I can't..."

"Before St Paul, there was the attack on the Bangalore Club, if memory serves?"

"That was three weeks ago."

"And that was the last time you enjoyed a meal of any description. Probably the last time you felt thirsty as well." Jekyll glanced at the open journal in his hand and nodded. "Repeated æthergate travel—at least the experimental version that Featherstone offered you—comes with quite a number of side-effects, which are unfortunately striking your soldiers. Your body is—now, how did Featherstone describe it to me—confused as to exactly where it is. A very simplified description, I'm sure, but prolonged exposure to its radiation will continue to tear apart your physical presence between two locations until..." and he spread his hands open, wiggling his fingers as he whispered, "poof."

Makeala had taken a place at her cousin's shoulder. He had not even noticed her standing up. "Can you stop it?"

"Oh, that is easy enough," Jekyll said, "Stop using the æthergate. Eventually, the body heals itself, provided the side effects are caught in time."

"But we must strike now." Shardool groaned, having found his voice again as he took a seat with the others. "The army at Bombay will only strengthen if we give them time. All that we have done will be lost if we don't press on."

"You have no reason to trust me, Mr Kari, and every reason to slit my throat." Jekyll closed the small notebook, and folded his hands on top of his notes. "I will provide you a safer alternative to the æthergates, which will still allow you to transport your men to where they need to be, and I will not ask for compensation until you are certain of the technology's worth."

If Nahush were a Christian he might have thought he was faced with the devil, but there was the Nāga from his own pantheon that Jekyll resembled. The trickster. The Persecutor of All. The King Cobra of great prowess and strength, living only to devour others. Yet, Nahush was not religious in that way. Science, even for its recent failings, had taken them further than they'd ever gone before.

"Keep talking," he said, his hand nevertheless drifting to the hilt of his knife.

"This other technology, I can attest, comes from modern sciences well within our own understanding, its advancements allowing you limitless possibilities. Believe me, I want this device to work for you. If your movement succeeds, I will in turn."

Nahush leaned in close to the doctor, though every one of his senses told him not to. "How?"

"Your stand against the Empire will not only draw the attention of the crown, but more importantly the attention of the Ministry. That means I can move about with a bit more freedom. Scrutiny is not something I work well under."

"Your act of goodwill does not come without a cost?"

"Certainly not," he chuckled, slipping the parchment out from his notebook and offering it to Nahush.

His eyes glanced over the paper, and then again just to be certain. "This is what you want in exchange for your services?"

"Do we have an agreement?"

Nahush could feel the rest of his seconds staring at him, and he knew what his captains and lieutenants were thinking. Trusting another white man so soon after being duped by the previous one was insane.

However, what other options did they have?

In the manner of the British, Nahush held out his hand. "Produce results, doctor. We must strike soon, and harder than before. If the British are seeking retribution…"

"*Carpe diem,* Mr Kari." The corners of Jekyll's eyes crinkled. His smile was kindly. Nahush did not trust it. "Tonight, I shall return with a few tools of this trade. I am sure we can salvage some parts from Featherstone's æthergate to use in our new endeavour. We'll have you bringing the dickens to the army before the week is out. You have my word."

As Nahush rose to his feet, shaking hands with their new collaborator, he caught Makeala's sharp gaze. She looked as stern as ever, but he could detect her concerns. They were the same as his, he was sure, but for now there was at least a glimmer of hope that their mission could be salvaged. It would have to be enough for now.

❖⟹ ⟸❖

Wherein Our Dashing Archivist
Rallies What's Left of the Troops

The modest stack of case files landed against the desktop with a dull thump. Wellington tried to clear his head, tried to get out of his mind's eye the sight he had just left. When he first undertook his duties as the Ministry's Chief Archivist, Wellington had to set right the Archives in London. That had taken him a year. Once things were in order, he intended to travel to the larger field offices and restructure their own archival storages, starting with India. It had been a four-month undertaking; but when he was done with them, the Indian Archives rivalled London in their efficiency and expediency.

Now, thanks to the Department of Imperial Inconveniences and the reconstruction of the Ministry, his work had been reduced to a diorama of the Sacking of Rome.

There was a strange, surreal quiet of the office, broken by just a murmur from the street outside, the rhythmic tick of contraptions at the far end of the room, and the snicker of the clerk on his typewriter. The odd cacophony he found rather pleasant after the excitement at Fort St Paul and the initial investigation that followed. He rapped a knuckle against the stack of files he managed to salvage from the Archives. Anything he could find on æthergate activity could be useful.

Wellington caught himself glancing at the clock again. He was trying very hard not to wonder when Eliza would return, nor preoccupy himself in wondering what she and Vania were discussing. Wellington understood the guilt Eliza carried with Ihita Pujari, but he could not fathom *why* she blamed herself. He knew her guilt after his own time in the battlefield. Sending young men to their demise all too soon had driven him away from life in the military. Eliza's guilt, however, was unfounded. It was not as if Ihita had been following her orders. She had been a victim of the Culpepper sisters and their fanatical desire to stop the Suffragette movement. Perhaps Eliza's guilt came from the fact she was alive and Ihita was not. Far be it from him to deny her a chance at, perhaps, finding a sense of redemption with Vania.

With Fort St Paul secured under nominal Ministry control, they had returned to the office in order to access the Archives as well as search Featherstone's secret apartment. If he needed quiet, the office appeared to be the best place in India. Nearly all of the agents had accompanied Director Smith to continue investigation into the separatists' attack, anything to stave off retribution from England. Spreading the dossiers across the desk, Wellington organised the various incidents chronologically, except for this one. Case #18840716INLD.

Now, he thought to himself, *provided I can work uninterrupted...*

"Agent Books!" a voice, accompanied by a rattle of running footsteps, called from the stairwell.

Wellington groaned softly. *Sometimes, I wonder if I am not trapped in some sort of penny dreadful.*

The agent appeared at the top of the stairs, her eyes wide, back straight. She looked very young, and perhaps a tad over excited. She brushed her dark hair out of her eyes and looked like she might actually give a salute. "Agent Books, sir," she said, her voice somewhat strained. "I just picked up a surge in the ElectriFlux. A huge one."

"Excellent." They stared at each other for a moment. Apparently, this news was quite the sensation. It was just lost on Wellington, sadly. "And you are?"

She blinked, suddenly understanding Wellington's confusion. "Oh, yes, my apologies, sir. Agent Strickland. Sierra Strickland. R&D."

"Progress," he said with a nod. "So, I know who you are. That leaves the ElectriFlux."

"Yes, this reading. It is massive. Unlike anything I have ever seen."

"Excellent."

Again, they stared at each other in silence.

"Oh, yes, the ElectriFlux. Of course, you wouldn't know," she said, chuckling nervously. "Case #18710520UKMG. Sir Carroll Ludovic and Mercury's Gate. He was using super-charged ion particles for his faux æthergates, the same sort of ion activity found in thunderstorms. We adjusted the ElectriFlux to pick up similar ion emissions found within æthergates."

"Very clever, but with such an adjustment how are you certain this isn't some false positive? You could be picking up a distant thunderstorm."

"Best you come and have a look, Agent Books," she said, motioning for him to follow.

Wellington kept pace with Agent Strickland as she thundered back down the staircase. She led him to a room with a thick iron door, similar to one R&D used beneath Miggins Antiquities to contain explosions and any out-of-control creations. Branch offices did not have the resources to run large-scale experimentation as they used to at Miggins. Obviously, the Indian office stood as an exception.

Agent Strickland guided him over to the desk at the rear of the laboratory where a large battery of test equipment was spread out before them. The array was a combination of Tesla coils, a Righi electrostatic machine, several small boilers all providing power, and several heavy cables that snaked up the corner of the laboratory and disappeared, presumably outside. Wellington's gaze landed on a central gauge and immediately saw that the gauge's needle was jammed into the red—threatening, in fact, to break.

"The adjustment for detection of these imitation æthergates was rather simple: incorporate into the array a standard-issue æthermetre."

Wellington shook his head. Agent Strickland seemed cut from the same cloth as Axelrod and Blackwell. "Æthermetres are used to monitor sending and receiving of æthermail and for detecting harmful radiation emitted from newly-acquired artefacts. How can you modify it for this sort of precise detection?"

"Calibration, Agent Books. By using it in conjunction with the ElectriFlux, we can pick up *specific* ionic activity."

Letting a ragged breath escape from between his teeth, Wellington adjusted his glasses and bent over the ElectriFlux array. Three control boxes wired together were offering a set of numbers—map coordinates—in each of their displays. The minutes were fluctuating slightly, but appeared to be remaining in the same longitude and latitude.

Agent Strickland whirled him around to an unfurled map of India. "We can't seem to get a lock on to exact coordinates, but as you can see in the triangulation and taking into account of the variance, we're predicting the singularity should happen…" She pointed to the map, her eyes triumphant as she looked at Wellington. "Here!"

He looked at the map and tilted his head to one side. "The Taj Mahal? That's eight hundred miles from here. How are you picking up activity that far away?"

She looked at him, looked down at the map, then back up to him, a bit flustered. "Sorry. Got carried away there." She carefully placed her finger on the map and looked up to Wellington. "Here!"

Wellington adjusted his spectacles and looked at where she pointed. "The docks."

"The docks."

Regardless of however mad this Ministry scientist was, it was abundantly clear: something was unfolding, yet again, with the Ghost Rebellion.

And Eliza was not here to lead the charge.

Wellington straightened up and adjusted his cravat. "Then let us not dally. We must rally the troops."

Strickland suddenly went ashen. Was she in need of smelling salts? "What troops?"

"Certainly the director did not abscond with the entirety of the Indian Branch to Fort St Paul?"

"Well actually…" She really *was* in need of smelling salts.

"Right then, Agent Strickland, who is left in the office apart from you and me? Any active field agents by chance?"

Strickland straightened, a thin bead of sweat breaking out on her forehead. "Agent Donald Thorp, but he is…" and her thought trailed off with her words.

"What?" Wellington implored. "Sniper class? Hand-to-hand combatant? Bartitsu Master?"

"Clerical." She bit her bottom lip. "And I'm R&D."

"But you have field training, correct? *Basic* field training?" Wellington could hear a regimental tone creeping into his voice, but for the situation unfolding that was hardly a bad thing.

The agent's skin was nearly ghost white by now, but then came the set of her jaw as she gave a quick nod. "Yes, sir, as it is required."

"Send a quick æthermessage to Director Smith. Be brief, but let him know of our situation."

"And then?"

"And then we will—as the Americans would say—*saddle up.*"

Wellington was sure Eliza, had she been in the room, would have made much of his ridiculous use of the term, but it gave the ginger to Strickland. He gestured back to the ElectriFlux. "Do you have a way to make this portable?"

"Perhaps," she replied.

"You have ten minutes. You're a clever sort, I'm sure you will come upon a solution," Wellington said, hoping his words sounded convincing. He was digging deep for optimism. "I'll inform Agent Thorp of our situation. Meet us by the lift."

Leaving her to take care of the ElectriFlux, Wellington shot up into the stairwell to return to the office. Earlier, this reed-thin man, the burnt-red neck of a new-comer to India, had been typing away, chuckling happily to himself. He was now huddled over his paper-work, one hand leaning against his ear.

Wellington cleared his throat.

He cleared it again.

Then with a sigh rapped Agent Thorp on the shoulder.

The man leapt and nearly fell off his chair. It was at that moment Wellington discovered that the other man had an audio speaker nestled in the palm of his hand. The Ministry had been working on new methods of covert surveillance, but India, once again, appeared a little more advanced. Peering over Thorp's shoulder, Wellington could see he had been transcribing something.

"Yes, sir," Thorp said, rising so quickly to his feet that he might have been a jack-in-the-box. "How can I help? Does something need to be filed? Sorted?"

"We have an anomaly in the city, and with all other staff currently engaged at Fort St Paul, it is up to us to investi—"

"Fan—bloody—TASTIC!" Thorp chuckled gleefully as he threw a switch from underneath his desk. His desktop split in two, scattering papers and pencils everywhere, which seemed to matter very little to him at present.

Wellington looked down to where the desktop had once been and he nearly toppled over.

A pair of Webley-Maxim Mark IIs.

Three Rickies.

Five Firestorms.

Two Mule's Kicks.

Across the bottom of the weapons compartment, a Lee-Metford-Tesla. Mark V.

"I was told you were clerical," Wellington managed.

Agent Thorp was strapping on a belt and immediately holstered a pair of Mavericks. He then released the rifle from its mount, pulled it in close to him, and smiled. "Not today."

Thorp reached for a Mule's Kick. "You…can leave that behind," Wellington said.

"But it's standard issue, sir," he protested.

"It still needs field testing. Particularly in lessening recoil."

Strickland, struggling under the weight of four boxes of different lengths and sizes, appeared in the stairwell. "I'm going to have to assemble the ElectriFlux whist on the way, I'm afraid."

"This," Wellington began, motioning to all the boxes, "is portable?"

"Portable, by the broadest definition," Agent Strickland said. The main box of this "portable" array was about five feet long, looked rather heavy, and had a long, thick cable running out of one end. It was not exactly the most inconspicuous of devices, but that was nothing compared with the antenna, also about five feet long and comprised of long pieces of intersecting metal. It looked rather as if a metallic tree had gone quite mad.

"Right then!" came Thorp's voice from behind him. Wellington turned to look at the clerical agent who was stuffing Firestarters in his coat pockets. He then threw the Mark V over his shoulder and snapped to Wellington a quick, polished salute.

This is not going to be easy, Wellington realised, grabbing the last Ricky and stuffing it in his coat pocket. "I suppose we can hail a carriage of some fashion."

"No need for a rickshaw, sir," Strickland said. "There is a horseless carriage downstairs we can use." She shifted the boxes in her arms and huffed. "A good thing, too, as we won't have to trawl the streets of Bombay with these things."

The quaint, old-fashioned name did not give Wellington much hope of high technology, but it was better than the alternative. Walking the streets of the city with a disassembled ElectriFlux would probably get them killed within one block of the office. The parts alone would fetch a few pennies, to be certain. "Very well then," he said, taking a few of the smaller boxes from their precarious balance in Agent Strickland's arms. "Let's see what we have."

They crossed to Director Maulik's private lift and rode it back down to the main street level. At least, that was where Wellington believed them to be headed. Thorp flipped two switches attached to the Chadburn, and an alarm buzzed for a few seconds. Their lift reached Ground Floor, and then continued descending. A dimly lit corridor slipped into view, and on reaching this subterranean floor the lift came to a stop. The grate doors collapsed away to reveal a massive garage space illuminated by electrical lights set in the opposing walls. It could easily have housed half a dozen motor cars, or two larger trucks if required. Instead of larger transports or a collection of smaller motorcars, however, this garage housed at this present moment one very odd looking "horseless carriage," which, by design, was an insult to carriages and horses everywhere. Wellington felt now a real pang for the *Ares*, as he struggled to conclude if it was a small bus, motorcar, tractor, or some unholy conjoining of all three, covered in what looked like metallic warts all over its posterior. If there were any plans for them to arrive inconspicuously, this gigantic, combustion-powered beetle ruined that possibility.

"Isn't she beautiful?" Strickland said, still fighting to keep the ElectriFlux box off the ground. "Designed to cover all terrains, armoured for combat, and enough weapons to take on a small army."

"Rest assured, Agent Books, the *Bug* could give those House of Usher blokes quite a go," Thorp said, the tone of admiration evident in his voice.

"The bug?" Wellington asked.

"The *Bombay Bug*. That's what we christened her. Director Smith usually takes her out at night for a shakedown, but never on official business for Her Majesty."

"I call the back seat," Strickland shouted, making Wellington start. "I'll need room to set up the ElectriFlux."

"I'll stoke the boilers," Thorp said, giddy as a bride on her nuptial day.

The *Bombay Bug* measured about double the size of the *Ares*. It had treads running down its latter-half, and as the back was mercifully covered, Strickland could rebuild the ElectriFlux in privacy. The closer Wellington drew to it, though, he could see grooves across its bumpy dome. Perhaps there was a way from the driver's seat to retract it, much like a beetle's shell parts to allow for flight. If they were in fact running into another clash with the Ghost Rebellion, the *Bombay Bug* might be useful in providing some cover.

Wellington passed the boxes in his arms to Strickland and then climbed up into the driving seat, wincing as he plopped into it. The interior was bare, shafts and levers exposed, very little padding on the iron seat. Once Wellington had levered the door shut—which closed with a *thunk* that could be either regarded as very comforting, or very frightening—the driver and passenger side formed a fully surrounded shell, the only opening being in front of Wellington where a windshield would be. His own *Ares* was a luxury vehicle compared to this. Mounted just above his head was a wide mirror that allowed Wellington the ability to see Agent Strickland in the back seat, diligently reconstructing the ElectriFlux.

Gauges jumped to life. The *Bug* shuddered and rumbled. Thorp then slid up to the passenger side and gave Wellington a nod as his own door slammed shut.

Modern conveniences such as a steering wheel were apparently considered extravagant, as the *Bug* had only installed a more primitive tiller system similar to the rare motor cars he learned to operate in the military. The sequences and rhythms he knew were locked away inside him. He pushed a lever to his right and…

"Well," Thorp said, checking his collection of weapons, "are we underway or waiting for the occurrence to come to us?"

He looked over to Strickland, inspecting a component from her ElectriFlux as if she had never seen it before. *If I were Axelrod or Blackwell working on this monster, where would I put the accelerator?* Wellington looked to his left and found a crank wheel. He began turning it towards him, and after a few revolutions something growled underneath them. The *Bug* lurched then, slowly lumbering forward. Thrusting aside ideas of examining the workings under the bonnet, he set himself the task of getting to the docks at all speed, recalling how motor cars operated in Africa but thinking about how eccentric clankertons designed their contraptions. Getting out of the underground garage proved more than a little challenging, but Wellington managed it with no small amount of frustrated facial expressions that he was glad his fellow agents could not see from where they were sitting.

The *Bug* made small chugging and *clitter-clack-clickity-clack* noises all around him. In his peripheral, plenty of interesting things underfoot were happening. His curiosity was begging for him to switch his concentration from the busy Indian street to the engineering feat before him. *No time to look now*, he reminded himself again. And again.

Heads turned. Rickshaws, carriages, and the odd motorcar swerved to avoid them. While there was rarely a time in the streets of Bombay that did not see a crowd or crush of people, it would take a great deal for said crowd or crush to stop and gawk. Which was exactly what they were doing right now.

"Right or left?" Wellington asked over his shoulder.

Strickland swung the antenna up and outward. "Go right, and I'll see if we can triangulate a more precise point-of-origin from there."

Whatever was coming, it was taking a good amount of power to create it. This imitation æthergate would have to be massive. Would it be as equally deadly in its side effects?

"You want a bearing south," she said, readjusting knobs and flipping switches that earned her a spark or two from the connections, "but this reading is bloody insane."

Now trundling on a southerly direction, the *Bug* was moving at a nice clip. However, it was impossible to enjoy the ride as Wellington struggled against its hair-trigger responses. The transport's multi-directional capacity by design took all of his wits to keep the metal monster in check.

"Turn right-turn right-TURN RIGHT!" Strickland shouted as she swung the antenna back and forth, threatening to bean Wellington with it. "HERE!"

Wellington gave a high-pitched yelp as a group of schoolgirls wrapped in fuchsia saris and a lean, English schoolmarm suddenly appeared in front of them, making a mad dash to cross the street. The Bug jostled and pitched as it crashed through the corner of a building before returning to the open street.

"Told you to turn right," Strickland said.

"Do we have an exact point for the event horizon?" Wellington asked, glancing back at her.

"Definitely the army base at the port. Has to be. The port narrows down to almost nothing down there."

The words "army base" hit Wellington like a brick to the stomach, and he hoped that Maulik had received their message. If this was the Ghost Rebellion and support did not come in time, Wellington feared it might be a blood bath. A very quick and costly blood bath.

As he piloted the *Bug* around the main railway station and pointed its blunt, rounded nose towards the sea, the ElectriFlux actually let out a squawk that made Wellington start in his uncomfortable seat.

"Sorry, sir!" Agent Strickland leaned into the cabin and practically yelled in Wellington's ear. "Didn't know the damn thing did that!"

"Why did it do that?" he asked.

"All readings are peaking. We're here."

"I would dare say so," he replied, his hands shoving the *Bug's* levers into their original positions.

They came to a halt before a fine four-storey building made of beige and cream stone. The words "Army & Navy" emblazoned on the outside silently begged to make this fine piece of architecture a target. To their right was a general store, while to the left was a modest travel plaza. Two airships were floating over the harbour, but luckily none were tethered to the ground. A cargo ship was secured by the dock. No movement visible either on or off the vessel.

That could change, however, at any moment.

Wellington scrambled out of the pilot's seat, drawing the Maverick, which, depending on the size of the portal, would have been as effective as a butter knife at the siege of Harfleur. He heard the slam of another iron hatch and Thorp joined him, gripping tight the Mark V. Around them, soldiers—the ones not staring at them or their strange, armoured transport—were going about their day. Some going into the store, some chatting outside, others unloading a lorry parked just in front of the *Bug*. In short, where the Army & Navy building stood, was a hub for the military to distribute vital supplies, and where officers could buy the luxuries denied to enlisted men. Presently it was not the scene of an attack.

That did not mean it wasn't a target.

A groan came from the rear of the *Bug*, and Agent Strickland emerged with the central gauge of the ElectriFlux mounted on a small club. Extending from all points of the gauge and its housing were antennae of all makes and configurations.

"This is the place, no question," Strickland said under her breath as she joined them. "The accuracy of the device is only a hundred feet or so. We'll have to rely on our eyes."

Agent Thorp slipped the rifle over his shoulder and drew his Rickies, totally oblivious to the scattering of soldiers that noticed his weapons. "Let them come. We'll show 'em what-for."

"Very noble, Agent Thorp, but somewhat foolhardy," chided Wellington. "We—as in the three of us—may have to hope we can keep this attack at bay until reinforcements arrive. This will mean either incredible fortune upon us, or a very quick defencive stance before being overrun."

"According to the ElectriFlux," Strickland whispered, scowling as she studied the gauge, "we should be seeing something by now."

Wellington looked around the courtyard. It was just another afternoon under a blazing sun. "You are certain it was to be the docks?"

"Positive. Unless..."

Oh, how he hated it when clankertons used that word. "Unless?"

True to the form of a complete quack, Strickland was shaking her head whispering things like *"No-no-no-no"* and *"This cannot be correct,"* which did little to reassure Wellington things were going in their favour.

"Agent Strickland?" he asked, his polite veneer slipping like sand through the neck of an hourglass.

"My knowledge of æthergates is limited, so I could only go by estimation and hypothesis." She swallowed. "I may have been wrong."

Now Thorp turned around to stare at the engineer. "You may have been wrong about the æthergate appearing?"

"No," she insisted, "the event is happening, and it is happening here." Strickland now looked around, her eyes darting about as if she were a cornered animal. "I was referencing #18710520UKMG for the ElectriFlux design when I'm thinking, according to these readings, I should have referenced #18960128UKEA for better accuracy."

Case #18960128UKEA? Was she serious? "That would mean the separatists have..." and then Wellington took a step backward, the sudden chill he felt inside his veins now suddenly tickling his skin, "...an electroporter."

Wellington almost failed to get the words out as his mouth began to water, and a scent of copper filled the air around them.

CHAPTER EIGHT

⊹⋯⊙ ⊙⋯⊹

In Which Agents of the Ministry Make Some Discoveries

"I thought there would be a teashop at least," Eliza said, as they stood under the awning along with at least ten other people in the middle of the Chor Bazaar. The flow of Hindi around her was beautiful but disconcerting. Eliza had never been stationed in India, so she never learned the language. However, this was Vania's country, and the New Zealander was comfortable enough letting her lead the way.

Hindi flowed from her lips as she turned to Eliza with a smile. "Believe me, this will be even better."

An Indian man was standing before a six-foot-tall copper pot which whistled cheerily while liquid burbled and gurgled through it. Eliza could see a bright flame flickering within the pot's inner workings. Nothing like a teapot, sugar tongs, or a milk jug were in sight, but the aroma coming from the tall pot was very enticing. She detected the odour of ginger, cinnamon, and a host of many other spices she could not identify. As she leaned forward to get a whiff, the pot began to sing. When she jerked back, the crowd around her let out a chorus of laughter, Vania among them. The way she laughed, throwing back her head, was quite different to her sister's. Ihita had been afraid to show much emotion, at least at work. *Was this,* Eliza wondered, *what my friend had been like in her own country?* Masking a twitch of pain, she turned to listen to the song, a high pitched, reedy sound that belted out a jolly rhythm. The men huddled in the stall clapped their hands in time with the music, and Eliza suddenly felt an urge to dance.

"What is this?" Eliza asked Vania.

Vania gestured to the pot. "The pot plays like a *pungi*—you might have heard a snake charmer playing the instrument. This *chai wallah* is my favourite in all of Bombay because of this creation, and he made it all with items salvaged from the streets." She grinned at the man standing proud next to his pot. "I am always telling Maulik we need Harsha in R&D."

"No, Miss Pujari," Harsha waved his hand, smiling. "I cannot leave the chai."

Eliza's eyebrow shot up at Vania's casual use of the director's name. It seemed once out of the office she unwound a fraction.

Her companion sighed heavily and theatrically. "Well then, if I cannot lure you away, perhaps you would be getting my friend and me a cutting chai each."

Friend. Eliza swallowed hard on that word.

It was like magic how quick the chai wallah moved. Snatching up two clay cups, he poured a full, steaming, frothy mixture into one, right to the brim. Then he slowed down, closed his eyes for just an instant, and tipped a tiny amount onto the edge of the flickering flame.

"An offering to Agni, Lord of fire," Vania whispered to Eliza. "Now watch."

Harsha spun around, the full cup in one hand, the empty in the other. Raising the full one above his head, he poured it into the empty one, which he held on a straight arm down by his knees. The cups were small, the height great, and yet Eliza watched amazed as he hit the bottom-most cup without spilling a drop. He repeated this trick twice more, and managed to split the full cup evenly between the two.

Eliza knew her face was ridiculously surprised and took the good-natured laughs around her as Vania paid the chai wallah and guided her out.

Then she sipped the chai itself, and suddenly the performance was the *second* most impressive thing of the morning. The drink was warm, sweet, milky, and spiced in a way she had never had tea before.

"Wonderful," she said finally taking her lips from the clay cup. "My assignments in India never allowed me to take in little pleasures like this. Tea perfected by science."

Vania laughed. "Now Eliza, don't forget Harsha in the mix. It is a fine line between science and art, but art requires the human touch."

"Your sister would have said the same thing." Eliza had no idea why she brought up Ihita, but the words burst from somewhere.

Vania nodded, though her hand tightened on the cup. She did not reply.

All the grace of a wild bull in a china shop, Eliza thought, sipping her chai while she took in the street around her.

The buildings of the Chor Bazaar were not unfamiliar; she would have seen their like in London or any other English town. They were brick and two levels, though some of the embellishments were of more exotic shapes, but that was where the similarities ended. Sounds and smells of all kinds permeated the air. Some stalls offered music and songs of joy, while another stall would make her mouth water at the promise of succulent meats. Merchants, clankertons, and artisans were crowded on both sides of the streets, many of them working diligently on their wares while others employed criers that invited tourists and passers-by to come and watch the makers hard at work. Other booths relied on bright hanging awnings displaying crafts of all measure, from cloth to mechanical, to beckon customers. Eliza did not know where to focus. Red rugs, tables full of jars of spices, baskets of metal parts—it looked like everything was available in this bazaar.

The women passed an automaton shop, the scent of oil and grease tickling her nose, where at least a dozen metallic heads turned to follow their progress. Some of them had legs or wheels, but the others looked to be under some kind of rebuilding process. One called out to the two of them in a series of beeps and boops.

"Did that automaton *recognise* us as possible customers?" Eliza asked.

"It is a possibility," Vania replied. "Our engineers, especially our street scientists, are quite talented, but like Harsha, they want to make India a better place. They will never leave home."

Vania then fell silent. Even with the cacophony of the bazaar, her silence Eliza found deafening. She had to break it.

"Ihita had a good life in London," she blurted out. "She was admired and appreciated by everyone who worked with her in the Ministry. I just thought you might want to know."

Vania nodded and drained the last of her chai. "She wrote to me about her adventures there, and she did seem...content..."

They walked a little further, stepping out of the way of a couple of laughing boys riding bicycles down the middle of the street. Eliza would rather have faced a dozen House of Usher agents than have this conversation.

If she was lucky, maybe some would turn up.

Staring down into her now empty cup, Vania finally spoke. "She is the reason I joined the Ministry, I admit."

"Hardly a surprise." Eliza daringly pressed her hand on the top of Vania's. "You want to feel close to her, hold onto the bits of her that remain."

The younger woman smiled, and for a moment Eliza was back on the embankment in London, sitting by the Thames, sharing sandwiches with her friend.

Eliza sniffled, fanned herself with one hand, and gestured with her own teacup to the houses on either side of them. "This really doesn't seem to be a place Lord Featherstone would fit in. He was very fond of the better things in life."

"You'd be surprised how many rich Bombay folk have a little *pied-à-terre* in the town that no one knows about." Vania nodded in the direction of pale-skinned shoppers milling about the marketplace. "And as you can see, there are still some English about."

It was true, though they were in one of the less salubrious parts of the city, there were still tourists around them. The desire to find something cheap and exotic was obviously quite the lure. *Not so different from London,* Eliza supposed. Plenty of men went down to the fleshpots of the East End for the same reason. Perhaps this didn't look exactly like London, but people were people the world over.

Featherstone, however was a mystery, right up until the moment he was swallowed by the paddles of the steamer.

The women finished their chai, and it was Vania that smashed the pottery cup by simply throwing it to one side of the road. With an arched eyebrow, Eliza followed suit.

"You learn quickly," Vania said, smiling brightly.

"I try. And that," Eliza said, pointing to the remains of her cup, "was delicious. I could certainly get used to that flavour."

"India has many wonderful things about it. We're not all curries and cotton you know."

"I am beginning to learn."

"This way then," Vania said, glancing up a slightly smaller side street. It looked to be less clogged with stalls, though still part of the bazaar.

A young Indian man with a twitching automaton in one hand approached them, holding it aloft to demonstrate something about its workings. Vania spoke to him in quick Hindi, waving her hands, and dismissing him as best she could. However, just as you would find in London, street vendors were persistent. The peddler followed them for a few minutes, shouting something at them. It was impossible for Eliza to tell if he was simply trying to make a sale or if he was throwing insults at them. Vania looked unfazed by the whole scene, and guided Eliza up the narrow passage at a faster pace.

"Nearly there," she said.

Eliza was trying to keep her wits about her in this darker corner of India, but she found herself distracted by Vania. She sensed the other woman teetered on the verge of asking her something. Her fellow agent kept biting her lip and shooting sidelong glances her way.

"Right then, that's it," Eliza huffed, spinning Vania round to face her. "What?"

"If we are to continue this investigation, we have to trust each other." She watched Vania's skin pale slightly. "Out with it."

"Are you and Agent Books involved?" Vania asked in a rush.

It was not at all what Eliza had been expecting, and she stopped for a moment in the shade of a building and stared at her companion. "I… well…so, Wellington Books…"

Vania was blushing now. "Forgive me, it was just something Ihita mentioned in her letters…"

"Wait, *Ihita* was curious about me and Wellington? But we had not even kissed then."

"She noticed something in you whenever you mentioned his name. Ihita said it was always a very sweet smile."

"Welly gave me trouble when we first met."

"Perhaps, but Ihita saw something else."

Shaking her head, Eliza muttered to herself, "Was I already taken with him by then?"

"Then there are the rumours going around the office…"

"I beg your pardon?" she whispered tersely.

Vania held up her hands in surrender. "From all I have heard of Wellington Books, he is a brilliant man. His skills in deception, however, are amateur at best." Her hands dropped and she released a long, slow shrug. "When he looks at you, he gets this rather cute…lost puppy dog look."

That people were talking about her in India was a surprise, but she supposed it had to get out eventually. "Yes, yes, we are. It has its complications," she admitted.

"I do not mean to make things awkward, but particularly at Fort St Paul it was rather endearing how he fretted over you."

Eliza sighed. "Oh my precious, young lady, he wants to be my valiant protector. My white knight…"

"Your mother hen?"

They held a gaze in silence before bursting into laughter. "He does mean well, but Wellington sometimes forgets I can take care of myself. I have done so for years."

"But now it is you *and* Wellington. This is new. To both of you."

Eliza nodded. Vania shared that perception Ihita once possessed. "Yes. Yes, it is, but make no mistake—Wellington and I know our duty."

"Ah, yes, duty." Vania sighed. "We're all about duty at the Ministry."

"And gossip, apparently."

"I suppose we all have our vices. Director Smith is allowed his own."

"Maulik started this?" Eliza groaned in frustration. "I should have known. That man…he's worse than a fishwife."

Vania shot her a sideways smile, but refrained from making comment on her superior. Instead she gestured towards a house painted a bright green.

"This is it, I believe," Vania said.

All the houses here were three storeys high, side-by-side with no room between them, and slightly sagging against each other. It was the perfect location for someone of high standing wanting to remain anonymous. Eliza turned to Vania and caught her smiling again, but this time out of pure pride. Despite the fact that she was the senior agent, they had been only able to find this place thanks to Vania's help.

However, it was important the senior agent lay some ground rules. "No heroics. If we find anyone upstairs, you get out of the way. The person we are tracking is no one to be trifled with."

Vania straightened. "I have been through training. My combat skills are certainly up to date."

Now Eliza was reminded of Ihita's stubbornness. Vania's sister had a highly honed skill for avoiding arguments and still doing exactly what she wanted. Now Eliza wondered if that was a family trait.

Pressing her lips together, she glared at Vania. "Presently, I am the senior agent in the field, so remember the rules of the Ministry." Vania didn't reply. Eliza wasn't foolish enough to take her silence as compliance. "Are we clear?"

Vania's nod was barely perceptible.

Eliza's gaze wandered up the side of the building. No visible surfaces to scale should they come back that night. It would have to be a front entrance.

Turning to Vania, she began to lay out a plan. "If we run into anyone up there who knows Featherstone, you are the scorned young woman and I am your guardian recently arrived from York come to help you get a ring on your finger from him."

Vania adjusted her jacket. "I can manage that."

"Then rub your eyes a bit. Redness and near tears are what we need."

Vania was quick to comply, scrubbing furiously at her face until she did indeed look on the verge of crying.

"Now look distraught," Eliza instructed.

She could have been on the stage the way her expression melted into despair so quickly.

"You missed your calling," Eliza muttered as they entered the building.

Almost immediately a little round woman came racing out, yelling at them in Hindi. It didn't matter where you were in the world, a landlady was always angry.

Not missing her cue, Vania burst out into hysterical sobs, stammering in Hindi what Eliza could only assume was their hastily-formulated legend. She waved her hands in the air and then threw her arms around Eliza.

"Give..." she whispered, sobbed into Eliza's shoulder for a moment, and then continued, "...money..."

Eliza gently rubbed Vania's back, shushed her, and offered the old woman a few coins. It seemed to do the trick, and the landlady—who offered in Hindi what Eliza guessed by the abrupt hand gestures was advice on what to do to Featherstone—handed over the key. It was a delightful change not having to kick in a door or pick a lock.

The building was broken up into small apartments, and despite its appearance outside, it looked to be mostly families living here. A little girl was in the corridor with her brother as they ascended the stairs. Eliza smiled at her, and the girl gave a little wave as they went past, though her brother was tugging on her arm. With almost a visceral pang, the agent remembered her brother, Gerry, doing the very same thing when they were small. It had been a bother to have her siblings trailing after her, but Gerry in particular had always wanted to do what she was doing. The boy's innocent gesture distracted her with wonderings of what was happening back home.

Even now, from the shores of India, New Zealand still tugged on her heart.

"Eliza?" And just like that, she was back in the apartments outside of the Chor Bazaar. Vania's brow knotted slightly. "Are you alright?"

"Yes," she said, nodding. Eliza could feel a tightness in her throat. "Dandy, thank you."

They reached the second floor and walked along the landing to apartment 1F. This was according to Featherstone's notes where he would meet with Jekyll. Perhaps a perfect hiding spot from the curious eyes of the privileged either living in or visiting India. Scanning the door, Eliza could tell it had not been forced in any way. She motioned for the key while silently pulling out one of her pounamu pistols from under her jacket. Vania unholstered a standard Ministry issue Remington-Elliott as Eliza eased the key into the door. She had turned it only halfway before she paused.

"What?" Vania mouthed.

"Not. Locked." Eliza replied in a similar fashion.

Based on how well he had hidden his personal journals in his suite on the *African Sunset*, Featherstone had hardly given the impression of a man who was lax on security. Eliza raised one finger to her lips, and jerked her head towards the door. Vania's eyes locked with hers, and with a nod, Eliza eased the door open and slipped inside.

It was immediately apparent that Featherstone's apartment was much bigger than it had a right to be. Three of the walls were hung with beautiful silks, and fine Indian paintings. The fourth wall was quite different; it was lined with so many weapons even Eliza stood impressed. One glance told her that Featherstone was quite an aficionado. He had gathered a variety of Indian weapons, swords, sticks, even bows and arrows. If he were not a collector, Eliza would have easily believed Featherstone to be constantly expecting unpleasant company.

Vania brought her fist up and Eliza froze. Somewhere deeper in the apartment, unpleasant or otherwise, company was present.

Eliza identified the sound straightaway—she had heard it often enough in her time in the Archives. Papers were being shuffled, and after a moment, Eliza heard the sound of drawers being opened.

Turning to Vania, she gave her a stern look and held a hand up to her. *Stay here*, she was communicating, though it was impossible to say if her companion got it. Partnered with Wellington she had grown accustomed to making her intentions clear. *Abundantly* clear, as a matter of fact. Making the doorway in wide, soft strides, she glanced back and was relieved to find Vania right where she had left her: standing in the middle of the receiving room. Her Remington-Elliott remained primed but held down. Her stance was solid. A gleam of fortitude in her eye. Vania appeared true to form for a Ministry agent. *Ihita would have approved,* she thought.

Another rustling of paper brought Eliza's attention back to the adjoining room. With her pounamu pistol held up and outward, she continued across the parlour. She slipped her head around the threshold and, in the study, she saw no one. She could see into a washroom, the epitome of luxury with a beautiful bath in it, but no one was there either. Ahead lay the bedroom with the door open, and she could see an intruder concentrating on his task, his back turned towards the hallway. So not a professional, then.

Eliza slipped into the room, her pistol aimed on the man yanking open shelves in Featherstone's bedside table. A stack of papers was strewn across the bed. At the centre of the bed sat a portable æthermessenger. Its keys, vacuum chambers, microboilers, and visible mechanics were polished to a fine gleam. Featherstone really did have access to all the best toys. No wonder the army found him so useful.

Eliza cleared her throat, and the man spun about. He was a young man, Indian, somewhat burly, and rather surprised by her appearance.

"I am sure," she began, now hoping he understood English, "you have a very good reason for rifling through Lord Featherstone's bedroom. Don't you?"

They stared at each other for a moment, and then he suddenly dropped to his knees, his wails easily filling the room. Perhaps the entire suite.

With her pistol still trained on him, Eliza tried to keep control of a situation she knew was escalating. "What—what are you—oh for goodness' sake, stop that!"

"Please, *oh please, kind lady,* do not hurt me!" he wailed. His English was hardly fluent, but it was enough. "I have a sick mother to feed! I have been forced—*forced*—to break laws of our queen!" He held his hands over his eyes, and rocked back and forth. "I hear Lord Featherstone is dead... so I come looking for things to sell."

Quite a performance, Eliza thought. *Brilliant writing, inspired direction.* Her eyes narrowed on what he was wearing. *Pity his costumer was not up to snuff.*

"Poor man," she said, her pistol still held steady on him. "That must have weighed heavily on you when trying to take Fort St Paul." His expression switched from tormented to stunned. "Markings of the Mughal Empire, yes?"

It was only an instant, but in that instant the intruder transformed from reluctant thief to trained warrior looking for an opportunity. His grin suggested he might have found one, even kneeling on the ground.

He screwed his eyes shut and flicked his hand against the wooden floor. Eliza managed to catch a glimpse of a ring before the flash of light filled her eyes. She stumbled back a step, and then something struck her. Eliza's head rung as she toppled over, the back of her skull striking the wooden planks in the floor. His arms were around her waist, and he was leveraging all his weight into her, effectively pinning her to the ground. Though stunned, Eliza allowed her training, her reflexes, and more importantly her time growing up the middle girl between two brothers, to take over. Her fist connected with something. She hit it again, and again.

"Ow!" she heard him say. "Ow! *Ow!* You're...punching me...in the *ear!*"

As he ground his hips into her own, Eliza swung again. Harder. No, punching him in the ear would not end this fight as a solid hit to his lip or, better yet, his nose. What she did know was this would give him a hell of a headache. Rattling his own skull like this also confirmed that he had not received any of the good doctor's serum.

However, he wasn't letting go, and he kept pressing his body into hers. *You. Rotten. Flapdoodle.*

Her left hand wrapped around his head and yanked. The side of his face pressed into her chest. Looking down, her vision was still lost in a grey-white haze but she could just make out an exposed face.

"You wanted this!" And Eliza punched him in the nose. "You could have just talked to me!" Another punch. Not until she knew for certain. "But *you—wanted—this!*"

On the third punch, just over his screams, Eliza heard—and felt—the nose give way.

Bringing her knee up, she connected with his stomach. Between the assault on his ear and his nose, he finally released her. Eliza pushed him off, and continued to blink her eyes madly hoping to get her sight back while scrambling about for her dropped pistol. The weapon appeared out of the fog in her eyes, but before she could grasp it, he lunged at her again, this time locking her arms against her side and picking her up. Together, they landed hard against the floor of the study.

He turned her over and leaned close into her. Eliza thrust her forehead up and cracked him on the nose with a solid Glasgow Kiss. If his nose was not broken before, it was now. Between rapping her own head against the floor and that Kiss, the world teetered around her. She could hear the intruder let out a muffled howl of rage. His hands were probably clamped around his nose and mouth, and if he wanted to breathe, he would have to...

Crunch.

His scream was delicious.

When Eliza's vision cleared, she saw Vania bearing down on the insurgent. She heard Hindi shouted between them, and they collided into one another. The Remington-Elliot clattered to the far end of the room. Eliza staggered to her feet, sure she was about to see a fellow agent slaughtered before her eyes. He had Vania up against the wall, hands locked around her throat, but he did not keep her there for long. Vania cocked back her arm as much as she could and punched the rebel in the throat. As he stumbled back, she collapsed to the floor.

Eliza drew her second pistol and fired. He jerked back when the bullet hit his shoulder. He looked as if he was to fall right there, but instead he sprinted for the foyer. Eliza took a second shot, but this time the bullet struck only the wooden arch.

"Dammit," she swore. Pushing her hair out of her eyes, Eliza turned back to Vania. "You alright there, Pujari?"

Vania let out a little growl of her own. "I was going to ask you the same, Braun."

There was a slight ringing in her ears. Hopefully, she was just rattled and not suffering a concussion. "I really could use a drink."

"What do you think he wanted?"

"He was making some work for himself," Eliza said, pointing back to the bedroom. "Papers all over the bed, and this."

"A portable æthermessenger?" Vania reached for one of the documents on the bed. "Doesn't look like anything we don't know already. These look like notes from Mercury's Gate."

"I think finding anything here is wishful thinking, but that?" she said, motioning to the communication device. "A little treasure trove, this is. Pristine condition. Looks like Featherstone took right good care of it."

"How does this help us?"

"Æthermessengers are equipped with an internal log that can be accessed. Portable ones, the memory bricks are smaller."

Vania inclined her head. "You know how to operate one of these things? These contraptions are quite complicated."

"I am in love with a clankerton. You tend to pick up a few new skills in such a relationship. All we need are his most recent messages. Say the past month or so."

"You think he was using this to talk to Jekyll?"

"Only one way to find out."

Turning the æthermessenger to face her, Eliza went to power up the device when a rattling boom echoed through the skies of Bombay.

"Eliza?" Vania asked.

"Wasn't me." She went to the window and studied the plume of smoke reaching up to the sky. "Knowing my 'things that go boom,' that explosion did not have the concussive strength of ordinance the Ministry uses." Eliza walked to the far side of the bed and found her other pounamu pistol. Holstering it, she made for the door.

"But wait, aren't we heading back to headquarters?"

"You're going back to headquarters with that," she said, pointing to the æthermessenger. "R&D should be able to access the memory. Might be able to find out what was being shared between Featherstone and Jekyll."

Vania called from behind her. "Wait, where are *you* going?"

"Oh my dear Vania, in your time with the Ministry, you should know this is what we do. When others run away from the explosions, we run toward them!"

✦═◉═✦

In Which an Archivist-Turned-Agent
Loses Himself in a Fit of Passion

Wellington, Strickland, and Thorp were thrown backwards as the spitting, snarling sphere of blue-white electricity punctuated the space in front of the Army & Navy building, releasing rebels around the plaza in wave upon wave. Wellington sat upright to see soldiers of the Ghost Rebellion drop to the ground and roll back up on their feet. Unlike an æthergate, the electroporter deposited its contents in a singular wild burst of light, energy, and power, and in a flash, insurgents filled the courtyard before them.

Two soldiers directly across from the *Bombay Bug* were first to fall. Trained, perhaps experienced soldiers, ill-prepared to face an army appearing out of thin air. This was one of many reasons Director Sound had chosen to keep æthergate technology under lock and key in the London Archives. Such an advantage could be exploited for far more nefarious purposes. That, however, was not Wellington's primary concern. Only a handful of people knew about Atlantean technology, but the amount of people who knew about electroporters? An even smaller lot. Far smaller.

And the Ghost Rebellion had in their possession an electroporter.

The Army & Navy building itself suddenly shook with a concussive explosion from the inside. The central command burst from the back sending dust and debris high into the sky. Some of the separatists must have appeared directly inside the building itself. A show of remarkable accuracy that Wellington had never seen before.

"Bloody hell," Thorp yelled before shouldering the Mark V. "Right then, let's fight a little fire with fire." He threw another switch near the rifle's trigger, and a small kickstand extended from the middle of the barrel. Thorp propped the rifle's end on the edge of the *Bug's* front-left wheel and took aim across the causeway. "If you don't have a pair of sunspecs," Thorp said as he slipped on his own, "you might want to close your eyes."

Wellington heard the whine of the Lee-Metford-Tesla's generators, and screwed his eyes shut just before hearing the muffled thud of what he knew to be a concentrated plasma blast. He opened his eyes just in time to see the blast impact with the separatists, sending bodies flying in every direction. This explosion was only a pause for the Ghost Rebellion though, and they began their assault anew, peppering the area with rifle and handgun fire. As bullets zipped through the air, Wellington yanked Strickland behind the *Bug*, screaming for Thorp to take cover just before a Gatling opened up on them. They heard a swarm of bullets angrily ping off their motorcar's bonnet. Suddenly, Wellington wished they had more than a set of pistols and a single modified rifle to call on.

"Don't suppose the *Bug* possesses armaments of any kind?" he asked Strickland, who was looking rather pale.

A shake of the head was all Wellington got in return.

He dared a look around the corner of their vehicle, and that was when he saw Thorp sprawled across the ground, his white linen suit stained with a sheen of beige dust and five bullet holes running up his torso. Wellington took stock of where they were pinned down. Across from them, a group of British soldiers by the storehouse's door had taken cover near a stack of crates. Behind them, there was a small detail locking down the aeroport. He could not hear the airships any longer on account of the gunfire, but he could see they were gaining altitude. Separatists were still mowing down anyone still standing in the plaza. He caught sight of what could have been the remains of a squad taking shelter in a simple hardware store. Those men would not last long, so Wellington knew that he had to move.

"Thorp is dead," he told Strickland. She looked wildly about, but did not look like she would panic. "We need to help those lads across the way. Stay here," he said, handing her the Ricky he had pocketed. "Eight shots. High velocity. Make them count."

Strickland nodded quickly. Wellington recognised the sweat across her brow and neck as not coming from the heat. He gave her a reassuring nod, then crouched low and belly-crawled over to Agent Thorp's body. He was not familiar with the Mark V upgrades, but at first glance he could deduce enough to access the basic workings. The kickstand was new, and within seconds of stabilising the rifle, he loved the subtle addition. His first shot took down the separatist leading a small group towards their position. They immediately scattered, but not before Wellington felled another in their number. He then flipped up a new feature of the Mark V—a telescopic sight. Earlier models offered such an accessory as optional, but this had to be one of the upgrades. He had just slipped the bolt back into a firing position when he caught sight of a head peering from around a corner. For his pains, Wellington sent the man a bullet.

Through the scope, Wellington could see intermittent flashes coming from the windows of the Army & Navy building. Perhaps the lads still inside were putting up a fight. *Well done,* he thought.

When he pulled away his attention from the scope, he saw the separatist walking down the middle of the causeway. Even from this distance, Wellington could see in the man's eyes nothing but malicious intent of the darkest kind. The lines in his face appeared as carvings across dark wood, and watching him approach, he felt himself grow colder. Over this man's shoulder was a large backpack, connected to a series of tubes and valves that would have looked more at home in a laboratory than a battlefield. Wellington would have assumed it was one of those Havelock battle suits but instead of a Gatling, this separatist wielded a hose in his hands.

And he was alone. None of his compatriots were in sight.

Wellington returned to the Mark V's scope, and in the magnified view he watched the separatist turn a valve from where he held the hose. Bright blue flame poured out of the spout, covering the ground six feet in front of him. Wellington half-expected the man to be incinerated as he disappeared behind this wall of fire. However, when the flames dissipated, there he stood. The hardware storefront wherein the British soldiers had taken shelter was now engulfed. With a weapon of this kind, their protection had become a death-trap-in-the-making.

Wellington flipped the charging button on the transformer, and went to line up the fire-slinging madman in his crosshairs. He was about to fire when more insurgents ran past the flamethrower, using the chaos as their cover.

With heavy smoke casting shadows and obscuring possible sightlines, Wellington tugged free from Agent Thorp his belt. Once the belt was secured about his own waist, he then fished out of the dead man's pockets several Firestorms.

"Strickland!" he called as he threw the Mark V across his back. "Get back into the *Bug* and wait for me in the cockpit."

She peered around the corner. "Are you sure?"

"No, not really," Wellington said, scampering over to her, "but I'm having a thought."

He followed the engineer into the safety of the armoured vehicle. Setting the Mark V aside, Wellington settled into the uncomfortable driver's seat. "Prime the boilers, if you please."

"Yessir," Agent Strickland said as she began opening valves and flipping switches on the passenger's side. "Shouldn't be long."

"We will drive the *Bug* closer to the hardware store and rescue those held up in there. With their help, we should be able to hold position until reinforcements arrive."

"What weapons have we on hand?"

"Three Rickies, plus whatever is left in the rifle." Wellington reached under the dashboard and released the brake. "Get—"

A rush of air followed by the sound of something cutting through flesh knocked Wellington out of his seat. He looked up to Agent Strickland, and instinctively grabbed the Mark V as he slid against the floor, out of the cockpit. Had there been a windshield, there would have been a chance it would have deflected such a high velocity bullet. Instead, with the open viewport, Wellington had practically handed the insurgents a target. The back of Strickland's head spilt blood, along with small bits of bone and brain matter, down the passenger seat. This gore shattered something inside Wellington.

I failed her, he thought while shimmying to the back of the *Bug.* He reached overhead, undid the latch, and was dumped unceremoniously out into the world, the escape appearing from the outside as a short, squat, metal-monster shitting a Ministry agent against the dusty Indian plaza. *I failed them both,* he thought as he braced himself against the *Bug's* treads.

He pulled the Lee-Metford-Tesla into his chest, his eyes shut tight as he worked the bolt action. *They are dead because of me.* His thumb pressed the transformer as Gatling guns opened up on his position. *They were counting on me, and I failed them.*

A voice from the past called to him. *Go on, my son. Make me proud.*

His eyes flicked open. Wellington got to his feet, though it felt as if someone else was controlling him. He knew he was moving into the open. Was someone calling out to him to take cover? What a ridiculous notion. Based on the exit wound in Strickland's skull, he knew exactly where the sniper had taken position. The scope came in line with his eye. The man's headwrap was just visible on the other side of his own rifle, but Wellington had been a few heartbeats faster. He saw the offending sniper's head snap back before he lowered the rifle.

Immediate threat eliminated. Now to begin work on the entrenched separatists. A small team off to his left, taking position behind crates newly unloaded from the moored cargo ship. Another to his right had taken position in front of a small café, tables now overturned and serving as makeshift shields. Perhaps this had been a squad, separated into two teams in order to form a modest gauntlet.

That's it, boy, his father said, his voice strangely strong and confident. Not the voice he remembered on their last meeting. *Show these ungrateful bastards the might of the Empire they defy.*

Wellington spun up the generator on the Mark V, but slipped the rifle over his shoulder before drawing the Rickies. The calls of the separatists he recognised as the local dialect, but he did not know the particulars. His time in war made interpreting the foreign tongue's intent crystal clear to him. He pulled the trigger of the left Ricky three times, then held up the right pistol and pulled that trigger four times. Before he could confirm kills, Wellington slipped to his right behind a pair of outdoor display stands. He heard the tearing and splintering of wood from a spray of bullets. If not careful, he would find himself pinned in this position, his cover eventually deteriorating under the assault of gunfire. There came another volley, this time from the separatists entrenched closest to him. Then the gunfire ceased. They were either reloading or waiting for him to take a shot.

Wellington holstered a Ricky, and produced a single Firestorm. The canister was barely larger than his hand, and on shaking the weapon vigorously, he could feel its contents coalescing together, giving the grenade a bit of weight. He knew what it would do on impact, but he was preferring a more dramatic punishment for these insurgents.

Wellington tossed the grenade high into the air at the separatists keeping hold in front of the café. Had Wellington allowed the grenade to continue, it would have sailed far beyond the intended target. That, however, had been the intention. They would be able to tell the Firestorm would not land anywhere near them. They would enjoy a sense of confidence. They would let their guard down.

And even if their guard had remained up, they would not have any defence against Wellington's offensive.

He took aim and fired the Ricky, effectively and efficiently causing the Firestorm to explode above the separatists. The gelatinous compound mimicked a summer's downpour, only carrying an intense, hungry fire that devoured the men caught underneath it. Screams were filling the air, and one man broke free of the cover to run into the plaza.

Let him burn, boy, his father said, quite pleased with Wellington's improvisation.

Now emerging from cover, Wellington shook a fresh Firestorm, primed it, and then hurtled it towards the rebels peering from the other side of crates stacked dockside. This time, the Firestorm shattered on hitting the ground. Flame swept from the point of impact, the fire straining to keep up with the viscous substance spilling across the docks. The fire would keep them back, giving him enough time and opportunity to throw one more Firestorm. He could feel the liquid switch from one end of the canister to the other, was aware of a shift in the bomb's weight, and watched it take flight. One managed to get free of the grenade, but his escape ended abruptly on account of Wellington's aim and the Ricky's high-calibre shell.

From somewhere far off came distant *pop-pop-pop's*, but they were not firing at him. That gunfire must be coming from the Army & Navy building. Could the tide be turning in their favour?

The sounds of celebration suddenly tickled his ears. Gunfire was still coming from within the headquarters, but the plaza and dock has been defended. That was why the men were jubilant.

They are celebrating? The outrage in his father's voice Wellington knew far too intimately. *What do they think this is? Some sort of Sunday outing with tennis and croquet? They have forgotten their service, their promise to the Empire.*

Wellington felt himself toss the Ricky aside and slip the Mark V into his grasp. The generator indicated green. Ready to fire. *If it were not for their callous, careless attitude, those agents would still be alive.*

The rifle hummed gently in his tight grip.

Discipline them, my son. Remind them of their responsibilities, and the consequences of failure.

Wherein a Simple Mission
Becomes Terribly Complicated

"Right then, a factory full of Houseboys and the three of us planning to infiltrate," Bruce said as he laid alongside Ryfka and Brandon across the snow. It was still deeply dark, but the Starlight goggles were evening things out. "Can't see how this little operation could end poorly."

Ryfka rapped his shoulder. Her signing was a bit harder to make out, even with help from the Starlights, but Bruce managed. *I have watched this factory for three weeks now. This particular entry point is the most vulnerable.*

When they had left Old Blighty, Bruce and Brandon had prepared for a simple infiltration job. They were also packing light, only the barest of essentials for a quick getaway. Now, following a long night of animated conversations with Ryfka punctuated by the slumber-fuelled interjections of Grand-uncle Leib, they were planning a reconnaissance mission on an Usher outpost. No intelligence or logistics for support. No reinforcements for backup. Simply what they had in the field. Bruce had been able to enjoy the brashness of the plan, but now on the factory's perimeter, the chances of success on any of their objectives looked terribly thin. Whatever original intentions he and Brandon had in making this heist a simple, by-the-numbers grab-and-go were completely secondary. This was Ryfka's mission now.

Remember, Bruce signed to Ryfka, *you cover us. This may be your operation, but Brandon and I have done this sort of thing before. Besides, if* things went pear-shaped, it would be nice to have someone covering their sprint across open snow.

Ryfka's eyes on account of the Starlights were hidden from view, but from how slow and deliberate her reply was, the Russian could not have been happy with him at present. *Understood, Agent Campbell. Consider yourself covered. Just remember, I have been working undercover inside. Follow the map I gave Brandon, and we all get what we want.*

I know, Bruce said, trying not to get curt with their only ally here. *We get the Firebird feather while you get hard evidence for this raid you want. We're all square.*

Ryfka nodded. *Don't cock it up.*

Somehow, in sign language, the slight came across twice as insulting.

Returning his attention to the valley below them, Bruce turned the Starlight's magnification to maximum as he examined the low-lying, grey box that was the munitions factory. Ryfka had drawn a pretty good diagram of the outpost, and it looked just as charming as she had described it. For a factory that specialised in bullets, bombs, and other gadgets that went boom, it seemed rather large. On account of its size, this factory made no effort to blend into the wilds of Russia. In fact, it appeared extravagant, as if it wanted to be noticed. Bruce would never admit to it, but that unsettled him.

Usher had been quiet for many years, "quiet" a relative term at best. Bruce and Brandon had tangled with them early in their partnership across America and Canada. Usher was definitely an obsession with the Fat Man, even though their recent ventures were more characteristic of predators preoccupied in building private empires than watching the world burn. Bruce preferred them the latter as opposed to the former. Perhaps that was why the Ministry was so caught off-guard when Books was pinched. They had grown comfortable in Usher's "shadow government" schemes, and had not seen that coming. Who knew that plonker was such a high-value target?

Then he felt his throat tighten. Who knew that plonker would wind up saving his skin in Edinburgh four months ago?

Now, looking at these Houseboys patrolling the perimeter in lock-step as a well-oiled, fine-tuned machination told Bruce they were returning to that Golden Age of Chaos. Someone had given this old raven a kick up the ass.

Bruce went to give Ryfka the signal to move into position, but her pleasing figure was no longer there.

"Where did she go?" he asked.

"She slipped away just after you and she said whatever you two said to one another. The only reason I know this is I happened to be looking in your direction. Silent as the grave, she is."

Bruce swept his Starlights around the surrounding ridge. Nothing. There was no movement whatsoever. Not even a clump of snow tumbling down the hillside. Wherever she had slipped off to, she was invisible. The snow, the darkness, the wilderness of Russia accepted Ryfka into her embrace and now they were one.

Bloody terrifying—but then he had always preferred bloody terrifying women.

"Ready, mate?" Bruce asked, adjusting the hood of his snowsuit.

With a nod, Brandon flipped his weather-white hood over his head and belly-crawled out of their cover, leading the way down toward their objective. Here out of sight of the factory there was nothing but layers of snow. Bruce and Brandon slinked silently from the top of the ridge, but remaining undetected meant an achingly slow progress down their slope. They had not made it a quarter of the way before Bruce noticed the cold beginning to creep through his clothes.

Brandon was just in front of him, so Bruce was able to see his left hand slip against ice instead of the snow needed to make modest traction. Bruce's right hand shot forward like a bullwhip, his fingers clamping around Brandon's ankle. His other hand drove deep and hard into the snowdrift. They slid a few inches, and Bruce felt a lump in his throat as he watched chunks of ice and powder tumble down the hill.

Then Bruce heard a hard *pop*, followed by a sharp, almost deafening crack. A fairly heavy branch, its reach wide and many-fingered, landed just behind them and started to roll down the hillside. Bruce let go of Brandon, and began to follow the branch. He kept rolling, even as he felt the branches brushing and clawing at his suit. Then when the branches stopped, he stopped as well. Easily done as the slope underneath him had evened out. Bruce peeked out from his hood. Brandon was also hidden under the multitude of branches and a slight dusting of snow. The guards by the factory, barely visible against the surrounding snowdrifts, stood there for a moment. One of them shook his head, and with a hard rap to his mate's shoulder, they turned back towards their post at the factory.

While their backs were to them, Bruce and Brandon slipped closer in behind the fallen branch. At the break point, he could see in his Starlights the shards of wood, some of it still fresh with life, and the bullet that had weakened its hold on the tree. Ryfka really was quite a cracking shot.

"You alright?" Brandon whispered.

"Might be a bit bruised up," he replied. "None the worse for wear."

"Five minutes, then we move."

Five minutes of remaining still. It was nothing new to Bruce, but that time in enemy territory, well within range of a firearm, might as well have been five hours.

Assured that the guards were out of earshot and the stillness had returned, Bruce and Brandon crawled free of their branch cover and huddled behind a modest rise in the snow. Brandon then slipped out a Remington-Elliot, checked its processors, and passed it on to Bruce. "So, running or crawling?" he asked, producing from the haversack what looked like a shotgun case of some description.

"Considering the snow?" Bruce eyeballed it. There were still plenty of hours of darkness left to them. "Crawl."

"Very well, then," he replied, unzipping the case and producing the weapon inside.

A weapon that made Bruce's jaw drop.

It looked as large as a shotgun, four barrels arranged in a diamond pattern; but the length of the weapon resembled a pistol in some respects. A hand cannon, hastily modified in the field. There looked to be a pump-action loading mechanism to it, but there also appeared to be a variety of piping and values welded into where the chambers met. Across the top barrels was a tight coil of copper that ended just shy of a pair of metal rods that came close to touching one another.

"What in the bloody hell is that monster?" Bruce asked.

Brandon hefted the weapon and smiled at it as if it were a new lover. "This, my friend, is the Nagant-Benardos M1899 Hand Cannon. Eight shells. Combination cartridge and pump action loader with an optional carbon-cannon. The finest in Russian engineering."

"And Ryfka's lettin' you have a go with it?"

"Apparently." Brandon pulled the weapon a hint closer to him. "She trusts me with it."

"Just handle that new friend of yours with care. It looks as if it packs a punch." Bruce took in a deep breath, checked his Remington-Elliot one last time, then grinned. "Let's pay these Houseboys a call, eh?"

It had been a long time since Bruce had been down on his elbows and knees—at least in the field, on assignment. As it was under Cassandra's leadership, Bruce recalled his soldiering days, not that he had enjoyed those very much either. To add to the misery, his soldiering days were under the Australian sun, a brutal ball of heat that he truly did not appreciate until crawling the first few yards forward in the Russian snow. A good fire, nice stout, and a steak—that's what waited for him on his return to Old Blighty. Pausing, Bruce took a quick peek. Snow began to fall around them, an unexpected helping hand in concealing their crossing to the stronghold.

A sudden grunt from his partner brought his progress to a halt. Through the thin veil of snowfall, Brandon's eyes motioned towards the fortress and then he blinked intentionally three times. Bruce returned his gaze forward and noted a third guard emerging from the factory. That was going to make this simple infiltration a bit more complicated.

Before he could move another inch, a vehicle rumbled somewhere in the shadows. Had to be a truck or perhaps a large transport of some kind. The House could hardly call in an airship with such dense forestation around here. Once the three guards turned in the direction of the sound, Bruce gave a quick jerk of his neck to Brandon, and they increased the pace of their crawl.

Just ten feet away from the door, they could hear some Houseboys discussing their day.

"...and then I took off my boot, and damned if there was a hole in my sock." The voice was a deep bass, but the accent was not Russian. Bruce could detect a definite East London edge to it, which was strange; mostly the House Directors were very territorial.

"I thought you told her to darn it?" The second voice sounded *American* of all things.

"But I hate socks after they've been mended. Bloody things are always in need of attention, you know? Needin' all stitched up and such."

"Well, it's that frontier spirit like in Colorado, isn't it? You got to make do."

Like most jobs, being a part of the House had to be ninety-nine percent boredom.

"Oye, Ivan—"

"Iliad," the third man spoke. He was Russian, but the accent could not hide the man's annoyance. "I told you. My name—Iliad."

"Yeah, all right, Iliad," the Bloke began, walking up to the Russian. This blighter really did have some balls as that Russian towered over him. "Go on and drive that contraption of yours back to the hangar. Think its test in the cold is a success, seein' as its startin' up there now, eh?"

"*Khorsho,*" he replied flatly. "I will accompany Bear back to Cave."

"*Khorsho,*" he mimicked back, "you do tha'."

With the Russian lumbering away toward whatever was idling in the distance, Bruce felt that unwelcome tension ebb away. The odds for their polite infiltration were looking a lot better.

"You don't particularly care for our Russian brother, do you?" the American blurted out, causing Bruce to jump slightly.

The Bloke went to answer, but paused as he stared in Bruce's direction. "Don't care for grease bears, is all."

"Now hold on there," the American said, raising his hands slightly, "what's with the slurs?"

"Just don't trust 'em, is all," he replied, his eyes still on where Bruce remained hidden.

"I'm sure he feels the same way about you lagerheads."

He rounded on the American, slamming him back against the factory wall. "You watch it, mate!"

"Easy there, my friend. We're all one big happy Usher family now. Ragnarök, after all, depends on that, yes?"

Bruce looked over to Brandon, jerked his head towards the Houseboys, and together they leapt up from the snow. The Bloke probably got a glance at the Thunder from Down Under just before it connected with his chin. Bruce could feel some give so he was pretty sure some teeth had been knocked out. His counter-punch sent the Bloke back, his head rapping hard enough against the factory to knock him out. The poor sod wouldn't get cold as the American flopped across him moments later.

"You all right there, mate?" Bruce asked Brandon, who was shaking his hand, flexing his fingers as he did so. "That Yank built a bit more solid than you thought?"

"My speciality is knives, blades, anything with an edge. My fisticuffs needs work."

Slapping his partner on the shoulder, Bruce chuckled. "When we get back to Whiterock, I'll give you a few pointers for toughening up those meathooks." He grabbed the cuff of the American and lifted him up as if he were a weighted duffel bag. "Now, how about this lock?"

Brandon rubbed his hands together and knelt by the door. Bruce reached down for the Bloke then paused. It was quiet again. He dared to step out into the small service road. No longer could he hear the gurgling of a massive engine. Iliad and the "Bear" were now in the safety of the "Cave," wherever or whatever that was.

Two quick whistles from the factory returned his attention back to his partner, now inside. Bruce lifted the Bloke up by the collar and dragged both unconscious guards across the threshold. The Bloke was a little heavier. Maybe the American was right about this one and his love for lager. "Got a place for these?"

"We just might."

"Good," he said, passing a limp body to Brandon. "Make sure there's room for two."

Brandon cleaned out a coat closet, probably needed as watch shifts would come in from the outside or head out into the winter. He stuffed the now gagged, blindfolded, and bound American into it. "And we have enough room for his fellow."

"Good. Help me secure him." Binding the ankles and wrists, Bruce and Brandon gently folded the Bloke's legs and pressed him against the Yank. Even with hanging the coats back up, the wardrobe still managed to close. "What do you think?"

Brandon gave a slight exhale and then looked at him. "About?"

"How long, you think?" he asked, motioning to the wardrobe.

"Well, I don't know. I—look, this is more your expertise, mate."

"It's not like you've never punched a bloke, come on," insisted Bruce. "How hard did you hit him?"

Brandon's head bobbled between Bruce and the coat closet. "Forty minutes?" He then nodded. "Yes, without a doubt, forty minutes."

"Then let's make this snappy," Bruce said, drawing his pistol.

After shedding their own coats, Bruce and Brandon continued into the factory, a *thunk-thunk-thunk* of machinery heard just over the drone of what Bruce could assume was a forge of some sort. Whatever they were making here, the end results must have been impressive.

Brandon stopped suddenly checking the door in front of them. "This should be it, according to Ryfka."

"How's the security?" he asked, motioning to the door.

The Remington-Elliott felt heavier in Bruce's grasp as Brandon's jaw twitched. The doorknob was plain, and there appeared to be no keyhole in sight. The Canadian took hold of the knob, sucked in a deep breath, and turned it.

The door creaked open. No alarms sounded.

"Surprisingly light," Brandon said.

Swinging the door wider, the dimly-lit room was hardly anything to make one stop and gawk. "So if these Firebird feathers are all powerful," Bruce began, closing the door behind them, "then how come there isn't a detail on them?" He holstered his pistol. "And she sure does have a lot of access to this place. Why didn't she go on and gather evidence on her own?"

"Oh come off it, Bruce, you know what it is like to work undercover. She probably was denied access elsewhere. Considering her condition, she probably did not want to take unnecessary risks in being somewhere she wasn't supposed to be."

"Mate, her 'condition' is not as debilitating as you're insinuating. Body odour, pressure against floorboards, I guarantee ya' she can take care of herself."

"There is still a risk," Brandon continued. Bruce really wished he would stop. "She would look conspicuous being somewhere without proper authorisation."

She was deaf, not helpless. "Are you sure you're reading that map right, Brandon?" he snapped.

The dim room suddenly became awash with gold light. Bruce turned to find Brandon's face illuminated by a deep amber glow emitting from an open box in front of him. "Oh, I'm quite certain."

Bruce came around to the crate Brandon was opening. It was the length of a peacock feather; however, it would never be mistaken as being from such a common bird. Peering down at it, Bruce was almost hypnotised by the gleaming gold that shimmered across its surface. The feather looked fragile. One wrong look and it would crack under the strain. Bruce could see, though, their treasure was pressing against the case's glass top in such a way that it was secure. He took a measure of the case's depth. There was more than one of these feathers here.

"All right, then," Bruce said, lowering the lid and returning the two of them to the near-darkness of the room, "we have what we came for. We'll grab a couple of rifles from the ready room, spin a yarn to Ryfka that this is what's coming off the assembly line here, then get the hell out of this winter wasteland."

"I do not particularly care for fibbing to Ryfka."

"We're not fibbing. We're liberating the Houseboys of a few weapons, presenting them as evidence of dastardly going's-on here, and sure as Aunt Fanny's your Uncle Bob, she'll get that raid. See? All good."

"Then you carry out the feathers while I provide cover." Brandon removed the M1899 from his back holder. "It would be a shame to not take advantage of the local culture."

"Fair enough," Bruce said, throwing the feather crate across his back. "Let's get a move on, shall we?"

They slipped back out into the hallway, the factory's heart continuing to chug and churn. He checked his Mapping & Webb. It was 3 o'clock in the morning, and yet it sounded like operations were running full blast. Brandon silently led the way back to where they had left their slumbering guards. Bruce set the box down in order to slip his coat back on, but he only made it as far as one sleeve before he stopped and looked back to the innards of the factory.

What were these weaselling bastards up to?

"Bruce?" he heard his partner whisper evenly. "You need to put your other arm into the sleeve, pick up the feathers, and within two days we will be toasting to our suc—"

"You said forty minutes, right?" Bruce asked, checking his wristwatch again.

"Bruce..."

"We still got twenty for sure," he said, looking for a place within their small ready room. There were other boxes about, similar to theirs; but they couldn't afford to have some Houseboy go on and open up their prize thinking it was a crate for rifles or sidearms. He glanced into the wardrobe. The Bloke and the Yank were still unconscious. There were the extra coats and what looked like artillery belts hanging from pegs, concealing them from view.

And there was a small shelf just above the coats. Vacant, and out of average sight lines.

"Bruce, have you taken a good look at where we are?"

"That's what been buggin' me, mate," Bruce said, pushing their objective as far back as the closet allowed. "You don't think it's just a little odd that these Houseboys are sittin' on something like these Firebird feathers, and they give 'em the same security you would find at a beach house in Noosa?"

"Where?"

"Think about it—why Ryfka thought we were really here, the lax security, that bloke Iliad taking the 'Bear' back to the 'Cave' and *what the hell are they making in here at 3 in the morning?*"

Brandon raised a finger at Bruce, his lips pursing tight before his shoulders fell and he checked his own wristwatch. "We make this *quick.*"

The two agents shared a nod before sprinting back into the factory, this time heading towards the *thunk-thunk-thunk* and low rumble. The sounds of whatever the House of Usher was producing eventually grew to a point where the agents resorted to hand signals. Bruce touched a heavy door in front of them and immediately drew it back. Bloody thing was hot. *Through here,* he said to Brandon silently. *Eyes sharp.*

Brandon nodded, hefting the M1899 higher.

Bruce slipped his hand into the cuff of his coat, pulled open the door, and Brandon led the way. The two of them had not felt themselves ascend or descend, but they were on a gangplank that was passing by a massive steel oven, the heat so intense that the world around them rippled slightly. Bruce and Brandon pushed ahead through the fierce temperatures, the oppressive warmth lifting further down the gangplank.

Their crossing abruptly stopped on seeing the open cavern below. Through a large mouth at the opposite end of the factory lumbered what appeared to be something like a giant bear, forged from black steel. The tank's four legs were a series of three spheres, all connecting to a larger, central orb. Mounted on top of that were a pair of large-bore Maxim machine guns, while at the most forward point was a half-hemisphere from where a variety of rifle barrels and small cannons extended.

"So I guess this is the Cave?" Brandon shouted into Bruce's ear.

The loudspeaker overhead blared out some Russian. The Bear that had just come in from the outside now trudged its way to an open slot nested between other tanks all forged in the same style. Bruce counted at least ten of these monsters. More than enough to claim a city. Hold it, if necessary.

Bruce gestured back towards the oven, and took the lead. They had seen more than enough.

Once clear of the heat, and further away from the sounds of the factory, Bruce turned to face Brandon. "This was what Ryfka was expecting us to take care of. We need to get this intel back to the Ministry."

Brandon nodded, then brought the M1899 up. Bruce hit the deck.

He heard something crackle above his head, then there was a burst of light. He rolled over to his back and drew his own Remington-Elliott. He fired and felled a guard while Brandon took down the other with a shot from the hand cannon's top barrel.

Klaxons were now blaring all around them.

"Time to move," Bruce said, pulling himself up on his feet.

"I like this cannon," Brandon said in a conversational tone.

"Faired up nicely against those two guards."

"Three."

Bruce stopped. "Three?"

Brandon flared up the arc welder at the tip of the M1899. "Three."

He would have to hear about what happened to the mystery guard later. Bruce and Brandon were forced to sprint back to their entry point. Hopefully, on account of the late hour, the guards would be light. So far they had only faced...

Turning the corner, five guards were bearing down on them.

Bruce pulled out the second Remington-Elliott and slid feet first, opening fire as he did. Two more guards dropped, immediately followed by two more as Brandon fired off several shells. The last guard drew aim on Brandon, but not before Bruce delivered a single shot to his forehead.

"Right then, Bruce," Brandon said, "let's hope we're beyond the worst of it."

"I'm feeling pretty optimistic, mate."

They stepped through the door to the ready room, right into the sight lines of a dozen Houseboys. Bruce counted five on each side of them with the Bloke and the Yank dead centre.

Bugger.

"Guess my punch was closer to thirty minutes," Brandon admitted with a shrug.

CHAPTER TEN

⊶▸═◉═◄⊶

In Which Old Acquaintances Are Reunited

Eliza did run towards the explosion. Trousers made that so much easier, though the heat did not. Ahead the grey cloud of smoke and debris drew her on, rising above the buildings down by the waterfront, and wafting the faint scent of gunpowder in her direction. Eliza might not have Vania's understanding of the city, but she did know from their earlier arrival that the port was in that direction.

The retort of gunfire was now almost constant. As she slowed down her approach, she could identify heavy weapons, as well as handguns—that, combined with the explosion, warned of bad things ahead. As she got closer and the press of fleeing people going in the opposite direction thinned out, she drew one of her pistols and held it low and ready. Then, approaching the corner at a wide angle, she gave herself enough room to see around it, while not risking a bullet to the face. Then came an explosion she recognised as a Firestorm grenade. Another. And a third.

Then the gunfire became intermittent, sounding as if it came from inside a larger building. Leaning around to assess the situation, gun held in front of her, Eliza canted to one side, her eyes darting from one direction to another. The plaza just outside the Army & Navy building had been hit hard. There were several small fires, some of these flames were blue-green in colour.

She quickly ducked back. All those additional windows in the Army & Navy building, plus the roof, offered excellent perches for snipers. It occurred to her how ironic it was now, that she had been that sniper at the Diamond Jubilee.

Between where she stood and the remains of the fight, there were several automobiles parked: a lorry, a small open topped motor car, and a strange looking, almost military vehicle that she couldn't identify. However, that one provided the best chance of cover since it looked to have at least some partial armour.

Decision made, she sprinted from around the corner. As she approached the strange, transport from the rear she noticed a form crumpled by the driver's door. It wasn't a separatist, but neither was it military. Blood had saturated the ground under him, indicating he'd been shot were he fell. A final stand. Crouching down, Eliza touched his throat, searching for a pulse. Nothing. Bending lower, she recognised him immediately as a Ministry agent from the Indian office. What was his name again? Thorp. That's it. Don Thorp. He'd been doing paperwork when she'd last seen him. Had he seen the explosion and attempted to take on the Ghost Rebellion all on his own?

The wind shifted, carrying clouds of smoke out to sea. Eliza heard retorts of gunfire once more, then relative silence. Over the sound of the waves striking the pier and the groans of the wounded, she heard a noise that would have been more appropriate in a jungle or perhaps a zoo. It was a snarl conjured from somewhere primitive and primeval.

Easing herself around the vehicle, on the opposite side to the firefight, Eliza angled herself out wide enough to assess the situation, but not get shot herself.

Immediately she saw that there was a good reason for the silence, though it took her a moment to properly identify it. Even after comprehending what she saw, a part of her still refused to accept it. A man stood in the centre of the causeway, surrounded by downed combatants from both English and rebels. Some had been shot, others burned, and some twisted and broken as if they had been rag dolls thrown aside during a wild tantrum. Weapons of all makes and models remained scattered about. An English soldier charged for the man, his rifle with fixed bayonet extended before him, but the man's left hand swept back with incredible speed and swiftness while the right clasped around the young man's neck. The rifle clattered to the ground as he was lifted into the air.

That was when Eliza saw the profile of the mysterious man standing within the carnage.

"Wellington!" she screamed.

As Eliza stood there, pistol up and ready, her mind desperately scrambling to grasp what must have happened here, Wellington tossed the man—the *English* soldier—aside as if he weighed nothing. He slammed into a small stack of crates, and from the force of his landing and the way his body bent, his back was surely broken. From the angle of his head, his neck as well. She almost shot her lover then, but it was his eyes that stopped her cold. She'd seen passion and hunger in his expression before, in intimate moments. In the field, particularly during the Diamond Jubilee, she had seen compassion and concentration. Here, surrounded by the injured and dead, the eyes of Wellington Thornhill Books had nothing in them. No remorse. No regret. His eyes were dead, like the frozen gaze of a child's doll. He made no differentiation between friend and foe. Her love was a stranger—a terrifying vessel of death.

The moment they held between each other was abruptly fractured when he took a step towards her, and she fell back one. His smile held no mirth, but when Eliza backed away from him on his next step the smile on his face widened. There was no one between him and her, and nothing could stop him.

"Wellington," she called, despite the fact that she brought up the pistol, "calm down. All our enemies are undone, so let us go, have a spot of tea, and talk about this whole thing."

He continued to walk towards her, the gunfire from inside the Army & Navy building dying down to nothing. Now, only the hiss of the flames was audible.

"It is over, Wellington," she said, pulling back the hammer. "Stop."

Her eyes roamed over his body as she contemplated where exactly she could shoot Wellington without killing him. Had he worn his bullet-proof corset this morning? In this moment she couldn't quite recall. If she was sure then she would have planted one right in his chest. It would hurt, it would knock him down, but it wouldn't kill him.

Perhaps a bullet in the shoulder? Placed properly, if she was careful, it would not be near any major artery; and it should stop him. If the wound did not heal properly, which was always a chance, it could alter his own gunmanship. Was that worth the risk?

Maybe in the meat of his legs, maybe in his thigh. She liked his thigh, though. He did have lovely legs. And same with the shoulder wound—if the leg did not heal properly, he would be reliant on a cane, or worse.

In a moment there would be no time for contemplation, he would be on her.

The leg then, yes, oh God the leg. Please forgive me, Wellington. I love you, darling. She had to hold the gun still. *I love you, and I have never even told you.*

Her finger wrapped around the trigger when Wellington suddenly lurched backward, his hand snapping up to his neck.

But I didn't pull the trigger, she thought hurriedly. Or had she pulled the trigger on instinct and killed the man she loved?

Wellington managed one more step before crumpling face down on the ground.

"You hesitated, *signorina*," spoke a voice from behind her. Eliza would have never expected to hear this accent in India. "Deciding where to shoot him, yes?"

Eliza turned to face Sophia del Morte, her arms held up in surrender. In one of her raised hands, hanging off her index finger, was a pistol. Not the sort of weapon she would attribute to the assassin. Her fashion choice of a deep crimson jacket with matching Turkish trousers and a trilby topping the outfit was hardly appropriate for one on the run from both the Ministry and the House of Usher. Yet that was hardly surprising.

Eliza brought her own gun back up and pointed it at the centre of the assassin's forehead. One bullet and she would be done, but in that same moment she realised Sophia had been standing behind her for some time. The assassin had her, and did not take the shot. Her eyes jumped to the small pistol in Sophia's hand. It was the kind of weapon the Ministry issued to agents when targets needed to be taken alive.

"Some of Jekyll's experiments would suffer moments of passion, much like your lover here just experienced. I mastered dart guns quite quickly," Sophia said, tipping her hat a fraction. They stood there, looking at each other in silence, the Italian's smile melted away. "You can say 'thank you' at any time,"

Eliza's throat tightened. She still held Sophia at gunpoint. "What difference would that have made to you?" she managed to growl, snatching the tranquiliser gun from her hand.

Sophia made a *tsking* noise. "Quite a great deal actually. You and Mr Books are my only friends in the whole world...well, at least, the only people I can trust not to sell me out to the House."

"Are you sure about that?" Eliza wanted to do two things at once: shoot Sophia, and check if Wellington was alright, but she found herself unable to do either.

"May I please lower my hands?" Sophia asked with a twist of her lips and a shrug.

Eliza eased the hammer back to a safe position, and gave her a sharp nod.

"I cannot blame you for hesitating," Sophia said. "Shooting someone you care for is far too cold and detached. That is why I prefer the more personal approach when doing such things: poisons, blades, sharp spoons. These are the kills that are more intimate."

Dammit, Sophia always looks so smug.

"Please don't make me change my mind about shooting you." Eliza strode over to the slumbering Wellington, but then placed a hand square on Sophia's chest, stopping her in her tracks. "What are you doing here in India?"

"Looking for you."

Despite the situation, Sophia suddenly had Eliza's undivided attention. "Come again?"

"Shall we tend to your lover first," Sophia offered, motioning to the unconscious Wellington at their feet. "At your Ministry headquarters I will tell you more about my…delicate matter."

"Take his feet then," she grumbled.

A sudden flash of light erupted from the inside the Army & Navy building. Eliza and Sophia, both suspending Wellington between them, turned to see the strange light flicker and then wink out completely from the end of the plaza. They could now hear screams of confusion joining the calls for medics.

"What just happened?" Eliza asked.

Surprisingly, it was Sophia who answered her without hesitation. "It appears Doctor Jekyll has been quite busy providing your angry Indian friends here with an electroporter."

If there was any word capable of striking fear into the heart of Eliza D Braun it was the horror of the electroporter. What it had done to the Chandi sisters at the end was not something she would ever forget.

Yet looking at the destruction around them, she knew there was no time to dwell on that right now. Reinforcements would be here soon. Medical teams. Military units. Local law enforcement. All of them demanding answers. She had to get Wellington out.

"Over there," she said, gesturing with her head to the armoured vehicle.

"Can you drive that?" Sophia asked.

"We will find out, won't we?"

They carried Wellington to the odd tank and opened the passenger door. Both women jumped slightly as another agent toppled out of it. Eliza prayed Wellington was not responsible for that death. Or for the death of Thorp.

They slid Wellington into the back across the metallic bench, pushing aside the odd scientific instruments jumbled together back there. They then loaded the other Ministry agents into the cabin, placing the corpses across the floorboard underneath Wellington. This macabre clean-up made Eliza slightly ill. She had dealt with dead bodies before, but this felt deceptive and improper somehow. She knew why; Eliza, with Sophia's help, was attempting to remove their presence from this incident. She hoped Wellington left no survivors to tell tales, and that made her feel worse.

Sophia cast a wary look at the gore staining the passenger seat, but took it nonetheless. "This is new for you, isn't it?"

She looked over the collection of gearshifts and gauges. The boilers, according to the readouts, were still stoked. Wellington or Thorp had never powered down this monster at any point. They could go whenever they were ready.

"I've covered my tracks before. I've killed before. But not like this." She pulled down a series of gearshifts. The engine rumbled to life.

The tank lurched backwards. Hardly what she intended, but it was fortuitous when their transport reversed out of the plaza as locals ran past them. Eliza manage to spin the transport around to face up a street she vaguely recognized. In the distance, one building rose over the low skyline of the city. Home. They rumbled off towards the office, sharing no more words, leaving behind quite a mess for the Army, Navy, and the Ministry to clean up.

CHAPTER ELEVEN

⋅→══◯ ◯══←⋅

In Which Ghosts Take Form
and a Poltergeist is Discovered

The buzzing in his ears was the first thing Wellington became aware of, that and the sensation of drowning in a sea of light. Its radiance filled him, and it was delicious at first. Better to be carried away by this primitive tide than face a world of pain, but then as he let himself float on it for a time, he began to recall the others he'd left behind. A pair of blue eyes, which challenged and loved him. Those were the things worth fighting for, and this ocean of emptiness suddenly felt less than welcoming.

The drone changed pitch and became intermittent. There was a rhythm. Words. This sound was now becoming discernable. Distant, like an echo, but he could hear someone talking. It was a woman, and she was concerned…

"No, it is not as simple as that, sir." That was the voice he dreamt of. From a land found at the edge of the Empire. It was voice of the woman with those challenging, loving blue eyes. "He was not in his right mind…"

He almost didn't hear the respondent. Male, but there was something odd about his voice. "Agent Braun, are we in danger?"

"Stuff it, Maulik, this is Wellington we are talking about!"

"I know…"

Wellington struggled to reach this other world, swimming now instead of floating, climbing back to himself and her. The light was growing fainter. *Keep talking. I am almost there…*

He woke up spluttering and thrashing in light, but not sunlight. This was man-made. He could see windows across from him, the world outside black as pitch. It was night. Eliza was leaning over him, her hair rumpled, her linen suit stained with soot, but it didn't matter. He'd made it back. Just next to her, similarly dishevelled, was Vania Pujari.

Then Wellington's muscles stiffened, and his head throbbed with the most painful of migraines. He managed a moan which, he was most grateful, did not lead to retching. However, a good vomit might have made him feel better.

"Dear Lord," Wellington finally uttered, "what happened to me?"

"A question for the ages, Agent Books," came a mechanical voice.

Wellington looked around and realised he had been laid out across a boardroom table. He was in Maulik's office, so it was hardly a surprise to see the director himself wheel into view. The woman to one side of him, however...

"You," he gasped, sitting up and feeling about for a weapon of some kind.

Sophia del Morte, assassin and woman responsible for so much death and destruction, merely smiled. "A pleasure to see you again, as well."

"Calm down, Welly," Eliza said, taking hold of his hands. "She's the one that saved you...well, at least saved me from having to shoot you."

"What?" Wellington looked between the two women as if they had both run mad. "You were going to shoot me?"

"He doesn't remember." Sophia tilted his head and examined Wellington in a clinical fashion, most unexpected from a killer of her calibre. She then looked down at Maulik. "Sometimes that happens. It might be a blessing..."

A chill of fear ran over Wellington as he looked around the office. There were four agents, both English and Indian, present along with Lieutenant O'Neil. All of them, save for Eliza and Sophia, were watching him intently. "What—" he cleared his throat, "—what did I do?"

"That is what we are all trying to find out," O'Neil said.

Was the clasp to his gun holster undone?

Eliza let out a long sigh. The fact that she had her back turned to the assassin was some kind of strange occurrence in itself. "What is the last thing you remember?"

"An electroporter!" Wellington blurted out. "Eliza, Maulik, the Ghost Rebellion have an electroporter!"

"Easy there, Books," the director replied, slowly easing his wheelchair back. "We need to keep our wits about us."

Wellington went to continue but then noticed Maulik was only one retreating. The other Ministry agents stood stock still. That was when he noticed they all held either Remington-Elliots or Bulldogs. Drawn. And primed.

"Wellington, darling, we know about the electroporter," Eliza said, her tone an attempt to soothe him. It was not working. "What happened after that?"

"I recall the separatists, the Ghost Rebellion if you will, opening fire. I remember Agent Thorp doing the same. We were pinned down—Thorp, myself, and Agent Strickland. Thorp didn't make it. Strickland and I were going to drive the Bug into the fray, try and reach a small squad pinned down by the rebels." He paused as Eliza turned away to glare at O'Neil. The officer did not seem impressed in the slightest. "Then Strickland was shot, and then..." Wellington's face contorted. His mind plummeted into an abyss. "Nothing."

Eliza's expression went from caring to cold and hard, as if he had done something wrong. "You did it again, Welly. You tapped into your particular skills again, but this time you lost control of it."

"I lost...control?" He was hoping against hope this was some kind of test.

"You started attacking anyone near you," O'Neil barked at him, causing him to nearly leap up from the table. "You took out the rebels, and then you opened fire on your own."

"That will do, Lieutenant," warned Maulik.

The officer's Bulldog slipped out of his holster with a whisper of leather, still echoing in Wellington's ears as O'Neil pulled back the hammer. "Some of those men were friends of mine."

Eliza's pistols were out just as the Ministry agents turned their weapons on O'Neil. "Holster that sidearm, mate."

Vania remained with Wellington, her own Remington-Elliot drawn and ready with two compressors showing green.

"That will do, *everyone!*" Maulik snapped. He rolled his chair between Wellington and O'Neil. "Today's events were a tragedy, to be sure, but Wellington's condition not withstanding, we are all seeking justice for both this and Fort St Paul, now then..." He motioned to his Ministry agents, and their pistols lowered. "You too, Eliza."

"He goes first."

"Stand down, Agent Braun," Maulik ordered gently. At least, it sounded gentle, but his intent was crystal clear.

Eliza's pistol lowered with evident reluctance.

"Do not make this any worse for yourself," Maulik said to O'Neil.

"On myself?" he asked, tightening the grip on his pistol.

"You see, while we have been holding this standoff of Military versus Ministry, the formidable Miss del Morte has slipped right next to you. If you so much as flinch, I believe she will cut you with the blade she now holds."

"You will be dead before you hit the floor," she warned in her usual charming manner.

Once O'Neil's pistol retuned to his holster, Maulik let out a long breath. "So, Books, been keeping secrets, have you?"

"It's complicated. Usually, I can keep these talents under control." Wellington looked over to Eliza. "All it takes is a focal point."

"Not today, love," Eliza said, taking his hand and squeezing it. "You even turned on me."

Sophia slipped her knife back into her sleeve as she spoke. "I had to use a knock-out dart I keep in my gauntlet."

That was a bit shocking. "A *knock-out* dart? From you?" Wellington asked.

"When I need to move incognito, I must leave fewer corpses in my wake."

"Speaking of which," Maulik said, turning his chair to face the Italian assassin, "Miss del Morte, to what do we owe the pleasure?"

"If I may?" she asked, motioning to the satchel hanging across her hip.

"You're amongst...well..." Maulik looked at Wellington and Eliza, then at his own agents, and continued with "...professional acquaintances."

From the satchel came eight dossiers, all of them Wellington recognised as being from Usher on account of the raven seal seared into the leather. He slipped one of the folders out of the pile, and inspected its contents. Eliza did the same, a frown forming on her face.

"Elizabeth Case," Wellington read aloud from another dossier. "Did we tangle with an Usher agent named Beth Case?"

"The name sounds familiar," Eliza said, tapping her fingers on the folder.

"That's because," Sophia said, offering Maulik a small box, the last item in the satchel from the looks of it, "she was close to you. A colleague."

Maulik opened the box and pulled out the familiar wallet bearing the crest of the Ministry of Peculiar Occurrences.

"She was a double agent?" Vania whispered as if the mere idea of such a thing had never crossed her mind.

"And apparently, this black widow for Usher was using Bruges as her web," Sophia stated.

"Hold on," Maulik began, looking through the Ministry identification. "London Office received an æthermessage from her, stating that she had rendezvoused with Wellington and Eliza in Bruges. We immediately sent back in code that it had to be some elaborate operation to compromise her position."

"Ah, you mean," and Sophia pulled from her pocket a small piece of paper which she unfurled and read. "Have a care, cousin. We last heard Wellington and Eliza were enjoying their stay at Uncle Allan's. A safe guess things at the Hume estate are booming."

Eliza shrugged. "Fantastic code, that is. Even I don't know what it means."

"Allan Hume. One of the founders of the Indian National Congress," Wellington said. "First meeting, 1855 in Bombay."

"Now you know how I found you," Sophia said, handing the message to Maulik.

"Lovely," Maulik said. "As if this Ghost Rebellion was not enough to worry about, now we have to be on alert for double agents."

Wellington pulled himself off the long table and, with Eliza offering support, he approached O'Neil. "You have no reason to trust me, but I implore you, sir. This Ghost Rebellion of yours now has access to an electroporter. It has its own limitations like an æthergate, but not the same risks. The only people who know about electroporters are myself, Miss Braun here, and those directly involved with them."

O'Neil's eyes narrowed. "When we met, you all were investigating Featherstone. He never mentioned to us anything called by that name."

"But Featherstone was answering to Jekyll," Wellington said, pointing to a chair at the head of the grand table. Eliza helped him over to it, and he found the seat indeed as comfortable as it looked. "There has to be a connection between Featherstone, Jekyll, the æthergate, and the electroporter." He looked up at the officer. "It may seem difficult to grasp, but I am a victim in this as well. Please, help us with this investigation."

Not a word was spoken for a few moments.

"If you even show a hint of turning on us," O'Neil said, "I will end you with a bullet."

"Charming notion to carry into the fray," Wellington said with a tilt of his head, "which brings to light a more pressing matter. We have managed to contain the incident at Fort St Paul. Yet now we have an attack on the headquarters of the British military in the heart of Bombay?"

"Yes," Maulik sighed, shaking his head. "It will be all the talk in the streets and across the headlines. Parliament and the House of Lords, and possibly the British people, will demand blood for blood."

"So much for borrowed time," Eliza said, standing at Wellington's side, her eyes never leaving O'Neil. "What do we know about this Ghost Rebellion?"

Maulik nodded to his own agents, and a pair of them went to the director's desk. That was when Wellington noticed the modest collection of case files. Vania also picked up a stack of dossiers, the one atop her pile he immediately recognised as what he was about to open before being interrupted by Agent Strickland.

Case #18840716INLD, the Lilac of Durga. This was when and where Director-then-Agent Maulik Smith had confronted Dr Henry Jekyll for the first time.

"I suppose great minds really do think alike," Maulik said as he brought himself to the table. "While you were sound asleep, we were pulling any and all cases that could bring this Ghost Rebellion to light."

Wellington looked over to O'Neil. "You said the Ghost Rebellion got its moniker from your men claiming the fighters were 'ghosts' refusing to rest until India is free."

The lieutenant glowered at Wellington before finally relenting, joining the Ministry agents at the long table. "Yes, and we all saw Phani Talwar. I put a bullet in him six months ago. The body was never recovered. Missing, presumed dead."

"Here are cases of missing rebels over the past few months," Maulik said, patting the dossiers gently. "All these men were active in the rebellion against Her Majesty, and then they started disappearing, one by one. Either in situations such as Talwar's, or just up and vanished. One disappearance, quite frankly, has kept my knickers in a twist ever since it happened."

Vania pulled the file just underneath Maulik's old case and opened it. "Wellington, Eliza, meet Nahush Kari, known separatist. Fought for the Fire of Shiva."

"I've heard of that lot," Eliza said. "The Fire of Shiva are radical, even by the standards of F.I. and Mohini's Wish."

"He was the first to disappear. Seven months ago and I've been investigating it all this time. Considering how active he was, it made no sense."

Wellington's throat tightened on looking at the photograph. "I saw him. Today."

"You saw Nahush Kari at the attack on the Army & Navy Building?" Vania asked.

"I am certain of it. He was armed with a rather nasty piece of hardware that threw fire wherever he pleased."

"It is a blessing that you're here at all," Maulik stated. "Kari is known for being thorough at whatever he does." The director glanced across at O'Neil. "While he was at large, he took responsibility for several bombings. The last one particularly terrible. The Bangalore Club."

"He bombed a gentlemen's club? A civilian target?" asked Wellington.

"Enough explosives to raze it to the ground," Maulik replied, "and he was hardly concerned with whatever retribution would fall upon his people or himself. Quite the showman, until seven months ago when he vanished."

Eliza let out a long breath that sounded like she had been holding it for a while. "So what brings this separatist to the attention of the Ministry of Peculiar Occurrences?"

Vania dug deeper into Kari's file. "We were investigating another rebel disappearance last month—three insurgent lieutenants went unaccounted for after a standoff with Free India. This photo was taken at the scene." She placed a photograph of a warehouse ablaze, on-lookers crowded to one side of an empty street. She handed Eliza a magnifying glass. "Lower left, in the foreground."

Eliza pressed closer into Wellington as they both looked at the image, the glass in her hand bringing out a detail easily missed by an untrained eye. "Well now," she cooed, "hello again, Mr Kari."

"I can see several points that match, but probability and certainty are not one and the same," Wellington noted.

"How good is your probability, you think?" asked Maulik.

He looked up from the photo to the dark lenses of the director's mask. "I'm thinking my assessment won't change your mind."

"It's not just the face. Relative height to the others in the street. A blemish on the hand that just matches the pattern of a tattoo others in his order took when pledging themselves to the cause." Maulik tapped gently on the photo. "And the man you saw today?"

Wellington studied the magnified image. Even blurry, the man's eyes were unmistakable. "The resemblance is uncanny."

"To go underground for this long, not so much as a manifesto or even a whisper in the streets that he was planning something bolder than the Bangalore Club, and then out for a stroll on the streets of Bombay?"

"No," Eliza began. "Vania, after Kari, exactly when did people start disappearing?"

"About five months ago, give or take a few weeks."

Eliza then asked O'Neil, "And when did you men claim to see these ghosts?"

"Maybe two, three months ago," he replied.

She looked up to Wellington, and he knew Eliza's thoughts before she shared them with everyone. "Kari wasn't there by chance. He was supervising an operation. An extraction."

Wellington nodded, then turned to O'Neil. "Featherstone must have opened a secret dialogue with Kari months ago, offered him æthergate technology. And why not? Perhaps if the odd experimental fails on you, it can be dismissed as the risks of modifying firearms. An æthergate? I would wager Featherstone wanted to avoid attention if something like that failed."

"But now the Ghost Rebellion has an electroporter. An entirely different matter. Featherstone wouldn't know about them. Jekyll would." Eliza's look was fixed and hard. The electroporter was still a sore subject with her. Placing her hands on her hips, she glanced at Wellington. "But why would Jekyll give the Ghost Rebellion an electroporter? The Seven discovered that was how he got around London with minimal detection. What does he gain from surrendering that sort of technology?"

"Jekyll is not an advocate for independence in India," Sophia stated, making Wellington start slightly. She really could be silent as the grave. "He is more of an opportunist."

Wellington's eyes fell on Case #18840716INLD. He took it up and quickly glanced at the preliminary notes. "Maulik, when you tangled with Jekyll, it was at the Water Palace, correct?"

"Jal Mahal, yes. He was after the Lilac of Durga, a rare flower found only there. We were not certain as to why he was so desperate for that particular flora, but after witnessing first hand the science he was dabbling in, he must need it for his rather potent cocktails."

Closing the file and sliding it next to the one on Kari, Wellington locked his gaze with Eliza's. "Safe passage. Instead of risking life and limb getting to the Water Palace, he had offered the Ghost Rebellion an advantage against the English, an advantage that does not pose the same dangers as æthergate travel. In exchange, Kari gets him safely to the Water Palace."

"So Featherstone intends to test æthergates on Indian rebels, Jekyll gets wind of it, and then manipulates all parties to grant him safe passage back to Jal Mahal," Maulik concluded. "If the good doctor were not such a monster, I would applaud him for his ingenuity."

"Sir," Vania spoke up, "perhaps we should send a detail to Jal Mahal. A team of three should suffice, not to mention they will travel most quickly.

They can scout the palace, or at the very least offer reconnaissance in case the Ghost Rebellion is already there."

"I concur. You up for the assignment, Pujari?"

The young agent's back straightened, and a glimmer of pride flickered across her features. "I am, sir."

"Excellent. Take Agents Rivers and Sethi with you." Maulik slipped out a pocket watch and checked the time. "Might be able to catch the last flight out of the aeroport, provided normal operations have resumed after today's dust-up."

"Sir," the three agents replied in unison before leaving.

"So, this is what it has all led to?" Maulik said, glancing over the case files strewn across the table.

"As you said," Sophia began, "quite the manipulator. It is his way."

"And what is your way?" O'Neil asked.

The assassin gave the dashing officer a sidelong look, her smile surprisingly warm. "I'm sure you would enjoy finding out."

"You really can't turn it off, can you?" Eliza said with a dark look as she casually thumbed through the case file of Nahush Kari.

"After hiding in Bruges for so long, it feels good to be out in the open," Sophia said, making no attempt whatsoever to mask her delight.

"Yes, about your sudden return to polite society," Maulik began, "might I ask what your next move is Miss del Morte? It is asylum you are seeking, yes?"

"I am."

A bark of laughter made everyone turn to look at Eliza, her eyes still in the dossier. "If we grant her as much, then yes, I think we should all…" Her words trailed off as she pulled out a single photograph. "Where's the æthermessenger we brought in from Featherstone's?"

"I believe it was taken straight to R&D," Maulik replied.

Eliza clutched the photo close to her as she sprinted for the stairs. Wellington pushed through his own weariness and tried to catch up with her. He was dimly aware of Sophia easily keeping pace with him. She might feign confidence, but obviously she didn't want to be in a room with Maulik.

However, right at this moment, Eliza was his main concern. Over the thunder of footsteps, he could just hear his partner whispering *"No, no, no, no…"* which did not instil confidence.

The lone technician in R&D looked up from her clipboard, and Wellington could see the young Indian woman's eyes were puffy and red. This must have been incredibly difficult to return to her office and find her associate had been killed-in-action, something unexpected for this division of the Ministry.

"You were brought an æthermessenger," Eliza barked out. "Where is it?"

The girl closed her eyes and took in a deep breath. Eliza's hands clenched at her side, a sure sign she was hanging onto her anger by the barest thread. Finally, the poor technician managed, "Yes, Agent Braun. We found your æthermessenger, but we could not salvage the internal memory as per requested."

"Why not?"

"The memory had suffered some internal damage."

"Where is it?"

The technician motioned to the opposite side of the room. Wellington, with Sophia trailing in his shadow, followed Eliza to the device which looked new at a glance, its metal fixtures catching the dim glow of the workshop. It wasn't until Eliza turned it around that he saw the deep scratches and slight bending of metal along the back.

"Vania tampered with it," Eliza spat.

"What?" Wellington asked. "How are you so certain of that?"

"We found this at Featherstone's, and it was pristine. Not a scratch or blemish on it. She must have pried one of these back panels loose to access its internal mechanics."

"Wait—Vania has a working proficiency with æthermessengers? The temporary memory block is hardly common knowledge."

"It is if I tell her," Eliza seethed.

"So you have *another* spy in your midst?" Sophia let out a little giggle. "The Ministry is always trying to be so clever, but it can never seem to keep those pesky double agents out."

"Are you sure you want to take that tone with me, at present?" Eliza warned.

"Ladies." Wellington shot a glance at Eliza. They stared at each other for a long moment before they both looked away. "Eliza, to sabotage an æthermessenger, you would have to know what systems to damage."

"Look around us, Wellington. There are Tesla Coils, magnetic devices, and right behind you a carbon arc welder. It wouldn't take much skill or effort make a dog's breakfast of the internals."

He looked over Eliza and Sophia at the clankerton now engrossed in her clipboard. His voice was but a whisper when he asked, "And how do you know the damage didn't happen here? In R&D?"

Eliza held up the photo she had pulled from Kari's file. "This gentleman I met earlier today at Featherstone's. According to Kari's file, this chap is one of his lieutenants. He went missing at the same time as Kari. Vania had a bit of an argy–bargy with him while I was down, as well as a quick, little chat in Hindi. Something she knows I don't. Coincidence, mate? *Yeah-nah.*"

"Then as we are agreed," Sophia said, the tense moment shattered as her voice was at full volume, "perhaps we can set about following this little double agent of yours. I am sure she has gone somewhere interesting where you don't want her to go, and it seems you are rather short staffed. She's already got a few minutes' head start on us."

"We don't need to worry about losing her," Wellington said, holding up his hand and wiggling his Ministry ring. "She's in the company of two other agents presently. They should be wearing these, but we don't have much time."

"Where is my valise?" Sophia asked. "I had it sent here."

Eliza shook her head quickly. "I beg your pardon?"

"If we are to find this double agent of yours in the streets of Bombay, then we should wear the proper fashions." Sophia took off her hat and let her silky, dark locks fall behind her. "I have just the thing for this very moment."

◆⫷◉⫸◆

In which the Mistress of Death Comes to the Ministry's Rescue. Again.

Sophia was not going to lie—it was a joy to be back in her own skin, doing what she loved, even if presently she was not working for a bounty of any sort. She absently wondered why she felt this sudden need to help the Ministry. She did not care about earning their trust, after all they still owed her for her help in London.

As she strolled through the streets, dressed this time in a proper Englishwomen's attire of a long, pale green dress, perky little feathered hat, and long cloak to protect her from the dust of the street, she smiled. It was about control. Something about setting on this girl's trail reminded her of how much control she had when going undercover. This magnanimous gesture to the Ministry, this olive branch in exchange for their help, was part of her own reclaiming of that.

"Remember," that woman's voiced cracked in her earpiece, "you are not to engage."

Hearing Eliza D Braun bark orders in her ear, though, also served as a reminder. It was a long and arduous journey ahead to regain that control. She would have to tread very carefully.

Reaching up into her cowl, she tapped the small cup fitted around her left ear. "I have not forgotten. Now, if you wish me to remain in concealment, do be silent."

"Just know we are watching," the agent warned.

The ETS, a quaint device that was standard for the Ministry, has easily narrowed in on Pujari working her way through the dark streets of Bombay. On the small compass face that rendered a map of the city street, the tiny light representing the double agent continued on, assumingly in the company of her own fellows. Sophia would never admit this particular device from the Ministry impressed her. Secure frequencies, efficient yet compact and elegant in design, and effective in tracking agents either in trouble or, in the case of Miss Pujari, going rogue. The ETS came in quite handy…

Provided the ring bearer remained unaware of it, she thought, noticing that Pujari had stopped in a side alleyway. Sophia had to double her pace.

She had managed two street blocks before the narrow shape of Agent Vania Pujari emerged from an alleyway only a hundred feet in front of her. Sophia ducked into an alley of her own, slipping from her belt a small mirror that she used to seemingly check the condition of her make-up. Pujari's reflection glanced up and down the busy street before adopting a quick stride through the crowd. If Sophia was any judge of people, the Indian agent looked perturbed, pushing between people rather than going around. She was not completely trained then, because the first rule of any covert activities was not to make waves. Hide in the shadows, disturb no one, and certainly don't cause the population around you to yell at you. Sophia winced as Pujari forged on through a group of three men. They waved and screamed some rather rude words after her.

Closing the compact, Sophia set on the woman's heels. She was a shark following calmly behind a flapping, wounded seal. The young agent's absence of finesse made her easy to follow, giving Sophia plenty of time to contemplate her situation. She glanced at the ETS tracker in her hand. The light which had represented Pujari remained still in the alleyway from where she had emerged.

With her quarry still in eyesight, Sophia dared to tap her earpiece. "Follow Pujari's tracker. I am afraid there you will find a pair of dead agents. Continuing my pursuit."

Once again, Wellington and his tedious New Zealand lover were beholden to her with this surveillance of their little double agent. The female was most certainly not going to like it—but that made this gesture all the sweeter. As always, her timing was impeccable. A del Morte trait.

Up ahead was Victoria Terminus. It had still been under construction when she'd been here before, but even then she'd been able to tell it would be one of those grand, very English constructions; all spires and archways. The golden stone at least gave it some true Indian charm, and there were hints of the sub-continent in the domes at least. Sophia sighed a little as she continued towards it. If only the Italians had conquered India instead of the staid English, then at least they would have had some truly stylish architecture. However, Italy had been too busy sorting out its own problems while Britannia swallowed up all the treasures.

Sophia followed the agent up the steps of the railway station, and into the terminus itself. It was like most ports of entry and departure around the world: thrumming with activity. Clusters of men and woman ebbed and flowed in the main foyer, staring up occasionally at the clatter of departure and arrival signs hanging from the ceiling. As it was in Bombay, the Victoria Terminus remained a hub of humanity even after the sun set. With night now upon India, there was still so much left to be done, destinations to undertake, and homes to return to.

Within this throng, she worried for a moment that she had lost Pujari; but after a heartbeat, she spotted the agent over by the ticket counter. She was standing on the tips of her toes and scanning the crowd too.

Not exactly covert, Sophia thought to herself. *But then again, most of the Ministry is busy right now, I suppose.*

Picking up a newspaper from a little lad by the doorway, Sophia took a seat, and began her observation over the top of its carefully angled pages.

Vania Pujari looked worried, there were no two ways about that. This was not a planned rendezvous, but more one thrust upon her. The Ministry were, on a whole, frightfully clever; their ability to tie Featherstone, Jekyll, and this Ghost Rebellion together in this grand scheme was a testament to how smart those in their ranks were, in particular Agents Books and Braun. Vania had just discovered first hand how formidable Wellington and his woman were. It must have been quite a shock. Sophia watched as the agent took in one final look around the terminus before walking towards a small tea shop to her right.

The little café was a slice of London here in India, offering ridiculous white linens and delicate looking porcelain cups. What marred this illusion were its patrons. They were of different colours, different nations. A part of the same Empire? *Hardly,* Sophia noted from the disparaging glances from the tourists. New arrivals, their skin not touched yet by the Indian sun, perhaps ready to embark on an adventure, provided that adventure held little to no interactions with the uneducated natives.

Sophia tipped her head down slightly. "Still watching me?"

"Victoria Terminus sounds busy tonight," Braun replied.

"Never sleeps apparently."

"Is Vania leaving Bombay?"

"I don't believe so. At least, not yet."

Keeping her line of sight on her prey, Sophia folded up her paper and approached the café while Vania's back was turned. Once her mark was shown to a table, Sophia waited a few beats before approaching the maître d'.

"Something near the back," she said, her voice dropping into an accent similar to Braun's. She didn't want to be too close to the skittish agent. All she needed was to be able to see her.

"If that was your attempt at my accent," Braun's voice crackled in her ear, "you need to work on it."

Settling into a comfortable chair near the potted plants and the window, Sophia glanced out of the corner of her eye towards Vania. She had taken a spot further away, near the rumble of the crowd, probably to avoid being overheard. They were not the only ones seated alone, but the agent was not drinking. Another mistake. When her rather dashing waiter approached, his suit as immaculate white as the tablecloth, Sophia ordered Darjeeling and some cucumber sandwiches.

"You hate tea," Braun quipped.

How did she know that? "Just becoming part of the scenery. I take it the signal is coming in clear."

If she had been her own self she would have flirted with the waiter. He had the gleam in his eye she always liked—always wanted to find out what it was backed up with. Instead, Sophia took her tea and the dismal sandwiches when he brought them.

Vania did finally order something. Still, she was sitting on the edge of the chair, looking like a schoolgirl waiting on her first caller. *The Ministry had been gutted by the Department of Imperial Inconveniences,* Sophia supposed. *Perhaps the rush of raw recruits had overwhelmed them.* It would also explain their vulnerability. In light of Agent Case and Pujari, how many other double agents were hidden in their ranks?

The man that approached Vania and took a seat opposite her was nothing like the photograph she had seen back at the Ministry Office. He was tall, handsome, and impeccably dressed in a sleek ensemble from Saville Row. His skin was flawless, his beard groomed in a most proper fashion, no signs of warfare, intrigue, or espionage about him. Propping up a glossy walking cane and a modest suitcase by their table, he took off his top hat and smiled, something Sophia would have never expected from Nahush Kari. He was paler than he appeared in his photographs, and his lighter skin coupled with his fine fashion allowed him to pass as a tanned Englishman, or perhaps a Greek.

Sophia smiled, but covered it up with one gloved hand. That movement smoothly changed to adjusting the cloak's collar, a modification of the listening device she had used in San Francisco. She had spent plenty of time in Bruges improving and adapting her travelling kit. There had been little else to do outside of gossiping and weaving, so improving her surveillance systems provided a delightful break from the monotony of Belgium.

"Target has made contact with Kari," Sophia muttered.

"*Nahush* is there?" came Wellington's voice this time.

"Listen for yourself."

Now, with the modified earpiece she wore, both she and the Ministry were able to hear what was about to pass between Vania and Nahush.

His voice, when it crackled in her ear, was smooth, deliciously deep, and marked with the polished accent of one well-educated. "Why so surprised, Vania? Were you expecting the brave freedom fighter with sword in hand?"

Vania almost glanced over her shoulder, but caught herself. She gave a little shrug. "I guess...perhaps."

Both of them broke off when a waiter approached with tea, and two teacups.

Nahush ordered cucumber and cream cheese sandwiches as the waiter poured. When they were alone again, he reached across and boldly took Vania's hand. "It wouldn't hurt if we appeared like a courting couple."

Sophia pressed her lips together, lest a chuckle escape her. Considering how handsome he looked at present, playing such a part opposite Nahush would not be difficult.

Vania did not snatch her hand away, but merely nodded. They waited until the waiter returned with the tea setting.

"Most English food is appalling," he commented before taking a bite of a sandwich, "but I fell in love with these while at Oxford. The ones here? Unparalleled."

"Are we going to sit here talking nonsense?" Vania's back was so straight it looked close to snapping. "When were you going to tell me of your collaboration with Jekyll?"

He did not reply. Sophia flexed her wrist, arming her cog-gauntlet. The woman was sitting across from the most wanted man in India, and after today all of the British Empire; she questioned him as if he were a lowly recruit. "I was unaware you had been promoted to the ranks of my inner-circle," he returned.

Vania leaned forward. "That was not an æthergate today...that was the thing that," in profile Sophia could observe the twist in the woman's face, "killed my sister."

"The electroporter didn't kill your sister," Nahush said calmly. "Hanging from under a London bridge did that. Her involvements with the English did that. The electroporter is merely a tool that we need." Vania went to speak, but Nahush held up a hand. "We made a deal with Jekyll, and so far we have the results we desire."

"Jekyll is using you—using us—to get to Jal Mahal. We have been part of a grand confidence scheme of this doctor's making."

"If you think I am bringing this Englishman close to my breast as a brother, I am not. I am, however, a man of my word."

For a moment it looked as though Vania might stand and leave. She jerked her chin up and tensed, but his hand caught the crook of her arm. If they were not careful they would start causing a scene.

Sophia drained her teacup just in case she had to make a dash for it.

"Don't trust him," Vania said, her voice low and pained. "Don't trust any of them."

"I never do." Sophia saw Nahush's hand tighten on her arm, then he slowly released her. "Now, please, before you attract attention to us…"

Vania eased back into her chair, relaxed, adopting the semblance of a woman forgiving her lover. "I can no longer stall the investigation. The Ministry has connected Featherstone and the æthergates, Jekyll to the electroporter, and the Ghost Rebellion to it all."

Nahush gave her a nod and then took a sip of tea. "Then our hand is forced, and I need your assistance. I cannot trust anyone else with it."

Those were the words that would melt any woman's resistance; Sophia knew that from some harsh experiences of late. Vania shifted in her chair, but stayed put. "What is it?"

Nahush pulled from his lapel pocket an envelope. He slid it across the table's surface while placing the suitcase by her chair. "I need you to travel to Jal Mahal and prepare it for our arrival. You leave tonight." He glanced at a clock in the centre of the Terminus. "In fact you have twenty minutes to catch your train."

Sophia fought an urge to shake her head. She was used to being asked to do the dirty work of men, but she was curious to see how that would sit with this fledging agent.

Vania stared at the small bag as if it were a snake. "You're actually answering to Jekyll?" she asked softly.

"We had an arrangement, and while I do not trust him, I do trust his technology. Especially, as on this voyage, he is accompanying us."

"I cannot believe you are actually granting him anything."

Sophia observed Nahush's eyebrows draw together. "You are a foot soldier in our struggle, Vania, so I don't owe you any explanation of my plans."

"I have read the Ministry reports on Jekyll. He is a monster."

"Then perhaps you should return to the Ministry, seeing as they are better judges of character than I am. After all, they opened their hearts to you, didn't they?" Nahush took up his cane and hat. "I wouldn't worry about their resourcefulness in deducing where your loyalties lie. And if they do, you are more than capable of protecting yourself."

Vania toyed with her teacup for a moment, and Sophia could read, even at this distance, the distrust on her face.

Nahush's gaze slid around the tearoom, and the assassin made herself busy with the newspaper. When he found his voice again, it was so soft that even her device had a hard time catching it. "You now have *fifteen* minutes to catch that train, Vania."

Neither of her two targets moved, frozen in a tableau that could go either way.

When the woman opposite him didn't move, Nahush leaned forward. "This is a war. We have all been called upon to do distasteful things, my dear. Tell me you are up to the task."

He drank the last of his tea while Vania contemplated her answer. Her reply finally came in the form of a curt nod.

"Well then," Nahush said, getting up from his seat and executing a small bow. "Your train leaves shortly. I suggest you hurry."

Her little gasp of outrage at this abrupt remark was lost on Nahush as he had already strode away back into the crowd. Sophia recognized it for a trick; something to hurry the young agent along. He didn't want to give her time to think, only to do. Vania paid her bill and hurried out shortly after.

The assassin folded her newspaper, dropped some coins on the table for the handsome waiter, and followed at a discreet distance. Out among the crowd her surveillance cloak was a little harder to manage. It worked best when stationary, as well as with less people milling about and breaking clear sightlines. She watched as Vania presented her ticket to a porter, was directed as to which platform was hers, and then made a mad dash for the train and her latest mission for the Ghost Rebellion.

For Vania, it had been easy. No remorse, no regrets. She walked away from the Ministry.

"Target on the move." Sophia looked up at the split-flap display chattering overhead. "She is boarding the last train to Jaipur, and she is carrying the electroporter's targeting device."

"We know," came Braun's voice. From behind her.

Sophia whirled about and fired the cog from her gauntlet, but the razor-edged disc merely sailed up into the rafters of the Terminus. She was also stunned, if not impressed, to find her arm held down by her side by Eliza Braun.

"Jumpy, are we?" Braun asked.

"You were here all along?"

"We both were," Wellington said, standing back up to his full height. He straightened his bowler as he added, "A good thing all three of us have fast reflexes."

Braun cast him a sideways glance. "You didn't hit the floor too hard, did you, Welly?"

"I might be a bit tender in the morning."

Sophia looked from Braun to Wellington, and then back to Braun. "When did you get here?"

"We managed to get here in time to see you leave the café," Braun said, releasing Sophia. "No sign of Nahush, sadly."

"You would have missed him easily." The Ministry agents looked as if they were insulted. Sophia groaned softly, and said, "He knows how to blend into his surroundings, is what I meant."

Wellington looked over her shoulder in the direction of the platform. "You didn't pursue Vania?"

She glared at him. "My instructions were to observe only. Besides, we know where she is going."

"And the doctor will be there." Braun's jaw twitched, and Sophia wondered if she were thinking of the child lost to Jekyll's terrible experiments. The assassin recognised vengeance.

"So we follow her to this Water Palace, and wait for him to show his face." Sophia smiled at them. "What an adventure for the three of us."

"*Three of us?*" Wellington exclaimed. Braun rapped him hard in the arm, and he then became aware of where they were. Glancing around he cleared his throat and asked in a tone more *pianissimo* than *fortissimo*, "This is our mission. Why on earth would we take you with us?"

"What, you think I work for free?" she said with a little laugh, stripping off her gloves. "My presence is the cost of my services."

"A heavy cost, indeed," Braun muttered under her breath.

"I could be much more useful to you, especially if things go wrong. Besides, I know Jekyll, and I know his weaknesses."

"You could tell us now," Braun suggested, "or I could make you tell us."

"Oh *preziosa bambina*, what would be the fun in that?" Her stiff smile melted away as she glared at Braun. As much as she could see the woman's desire to punch her, Sophia knew she wouldn't. Despite Braun's devil-make-care reputation, she was not one to destroy an opportunity for revenge on account of their irreconcilable differences.

"Are we going then?" Sophia said, keeping her tone light and conversational, even though she knew her fate hinged on this moment.

Wellington and Braun shared a look, and this look embodied their outrage, apprehension, distrust and disgust. It was apparent the two of them were, at that point of their affair, where they could hold entire discussions without a single word spoken.

"I'll grab us a table then while we wait for Director Smith," Wellington finally spoke. "However, it goes without saying, any wrong move on your part and I will not stand in Eliza's way."

Sophia gave him an exaggerated pout of her lip. "Not even to play the gallant and rescue me from the clutches of…"

"If the words 'ugly, evil dragon from the mountains' leave your lips," Braun stated, "you will lose a tooth or two."

Sophia gritted her teeth, and managed a smile, hoping it looked sincere. She then gestured to her fine outfit. "Best then I stop. Getting blood out of this would be such a bother."

Eliza's brows lifted. She well understood the implication.

Sophia del Morte was entirely unsure how a knife fight between her and Eliza D Braun would go; their one time at the opera had been a bit of a draw.

Still, if she was helpful, polite even, perhaps it wouldn't come to that.

Perhaps.

※=◎ ◎=※

Wherein the Ministry's Finest Experience a Taste of the Local Culture

Bruce looked over to Brandon. He was adopting the "Find a fixed point and make that your world" discipline, which he'd adopted from time to time when captured. There were several strategies when facing interrogation. Brandon's fixed point was one. Another was the "West End Method," where you act like you're in a panic, ready to talk, and you string along your interrogators while working them for information and casing the cell for any possible vulnerabilities. What Bruce was employing, however, was a method reserved for a select few: The Achilles Method. He would look around their cell, maybe make eye contact with the on-looking Houseboy, which could risk further interaction between one's face and a hostile's rifle butt. His expression needed to remain constant. No fear. Total defiance in light of what appeared to be a hopeless situation.

While appearing insolent, Bruce took full note of where they were being held. Any little detail could help. A set of wide windows. Tempered glass covering most of the window while the top third appeared to be simple panes. Hinges by the smooth panes insinuated that those could be opened, maybe to vent out any access heat. Granted, in this winter those windows probably stayed shut. Aside from the two chairs where he and Brandon were secured, there was one other chair in the far corner of the cell, two modest electric lights on either side of the door.

One door. One way in, one way out.

The Houseboy watching them wore black, no surprises there. The weapon of choice looked like an 1891 Mosin-Nagants, using interchangeable bolt heads like the Lee–Enfields. No visible modifications for these M1891s, so the House was keeping it simple. Made sense after seeing those monster-tanks lumbering into their respective maintenance bays. They were focused on committing resources into building those Bears. A very practical, very reasonable strategy from the House of Usher.

That Bruce found utterly terrifying.

His concerns scattered as locks began disengaging at the door. It was time to meet those in charge or, at the very least, a liaison to the big boss.

He cast another glance at Brandon. Fixed point. Completely in a different world than from where they were, at present. Guess he would be doing the talking.

The door swung open, revealing a Houseboy that was familiar to Bruce. Could this be Iliad? He was flanked by another guard and a tiny, rotund woman, her head protected by a kerchief that was as traditional as her fashion. Among the giants dressed head to toe in black, she was a strange contrast of bright colours. In fact, she looked like the cliché of a typical Russian grandmother. She was pushing a properly set tea trolley with a gleaming copper samovar in the centre with a teapot sitting proudly on the top. The tall container was making bubbling noises, indicating the water was very hot; and the tray on which it sat had several small glasses, and a bottle of what could have been water, wine, or some other libation.

Bruce didn't fool himself. He was in the Russian Empire. He knew *exactly* what was in that bottle.

Iliad towered over them all. Even if Bruce were not secured to a chair, Iliad would have at least five inches on him. The man was a walking testament to his country—massive, rugged, and harsh. Bruce knew from a few tangles in Norway and Finland that these blokes were never to be underestimated. Certainly, it was better to be either behind the Russian throwing the punch, or nowhere in the same country if a Russian punch was coming at you.

"All right then, Iliad, right?" The mountain of a man blinked, surprised to be addressed by his name, or maybe it was the fact that it was the captured, not the captors, that were starting off the interrogation. "Been wondering just how long it was gonna take before I got to sit down with those in charge and have a heart-to-heart. So, how about we formerly introduce ourselves?"

"Da," the old woman said as she straightened the trolley, and poured two small tumblers with a few shots of vodka for each. "We should get to know one another, understand each other's minds. I think that would be good start."

Bruce looked up at Iliad, whose gaze immediately hopped from the crone up to a point on the far wall. The other guards, like Iliad, were all now stock still and at attention.

"*You're* the one in charge of this operation?" Bruce asked, turning back to the old woman.

"You seem surprised," she said, as she poured some of the teapot's contents into a cup. "Little old Russian lady not what you think leadership material?"

Bruce guffawed and eased back into his chair as much as his restraints allowed. "You strike me more as better off in a kitchen somewhere, baking gingerbread cookies and knitting scarves. You know, all Hans Christen Andersen and the like."

He snickered, but his laugh faded on hearing one of the Houseboys groaning softly. He cast a glance at the other one, just behind Iliad. The guard looked at Bruce and ever so slightly shook his head.

The woman's face wasn't "aged" so much as "chiselled," no doubt by many harsh winters. Her eyes, dark as they were, sent a slight tingle of fear through Bruce when they met. She was sizing him up within seconds, and every flight instinct in him was screaming to run fast, run hard. A tiny voice in his head also chided him for not employing Brandon's approach to this interrogation.

She glanced at Brandon, his own stare still fixed forward, and shook her head. "Arrogance. Caustic manners. You must be part of British Empire." Her eyes narrowed. "New Zealand?"

"Australia," Bruce said, feeling his hackles rise a bit.

"You are long way from Great Barrier Reef." The old hag was certainly not what she seemed. She turned the spigot on the samovar and poured hot water into the teacup. "What brings you to my beloved Russia, Australian?"

"Well, it's bleedin' hot this time of year in the Land of Plenty. I was lookin' for cooler climates. That's how I came across your lovely corner of the world here."

"Really?" The old babushka motioned to Iliad who moved the remaining chair in the cell to a spot before them. Taking up the cup of tea, she hopped up into the chair, her feet dangling above the floor as if she were a small child. "And you come in to see what we make in factory out of curiosity? We have saying in Russia. I will translate: The more you know, the closer you are to death."

It was a shame; Bruce could have done with a cuppa right at this moment.

"Seeing what the different corners of the world have to offer has always been a fascination to me," Bruce said, working up his courage with each thought. "In India, you got all them fine silks. In America you got manufacturing of all kinds. I tell you, the things I have seen in Detroit? Amazing. And now, with all the sciences Old Blighty has brought to the world, it looks like you all here in Poland are embracing it."

"We in *Russia* are believed to be, how you say, behind times? As you see, we are stepping into brave new world now." She took a long sip of her tea and smiled. "So, Mister World Traveller, what should I call you?"

"Acquaintances call me Mister Campbell. Seeing as we are getting to know one another, why don't you call me Bruce?" Bruce gave the old woman his best smile. "And what should I call you, beautiful?"

"I am not permitted to give real name," she said, her words sounding a little sad that she could not afford the same intimacy. "You call me Mama Bear."

"Mama Bear?" Bruce repeated, nodding. "Well, all right then, Mama Bear, how are we going to handle this rather sticky wicket we find each other in?"

"We?" She motioned for Iliad and murmured something. Her Russian was soft but clear in its intent. With a quick nod from Iliad, the soldier disappeared. "I do not think you understand problem, Bruce."

"Aww, now come on, Mama B, I understand the problem all too well. You all are up to no good out here in the woods. My mate here and I are having a butcher's on behalf of curious parties." He gave a shrug of his own massive shoulders. "And something tells me if we were to not let our superiors know of our well-being, your little operation here will warrant a lot of attention."

"I see," she said, with an incline of her head. "Perhaps I should let you know a bit more of our operation then?"

Bruce allowed his smile to brighten a bit. Didn't matter the age, he could always charm the ladies.

His attention jumped from Mama Bear to the door as both the Bloke and the Yank, immediately followed by Iliad, all entered the cell. The two guards' faces darkened on seeing the stoic Brandon and him sitting there, but their simmering anger lasted for only a moment as they suddenly noticed the old woman sitting in front of them.

"Gentlemen," she said, putting her teacup back on the trolley "you recognise our guests here, yes?"

"Tha' I do, Mama Bear," the Bloke growled. "Got scores to settle with the both of 'em."

"Indeed, you do, but first—" and she motioned to the tea and vodka by her side, "—what would you prefer?"

"I'm not one for tea, Mama Bear," the Yank said, "so I will gladly partake of the vodka."

"The same," said the Bloke.

She turned to the tray and took up the glasses, passing one to each of them.

"Ta, mum."

"Da, nyet," the old lady said, chuckling. She motioned for the two of them to come closer. "I give you drink—good Russian vodka—and you say 'Ta,' when you should say *'Nosdrovia'* which is Russian 'Cheers' when drink offered. Come, come," and she waved her hand, beckoning them even closer.

The two men lowered themselves to one knee in order to accommodate Mama Bear. She took up the bottle and toasted to the two men, and much to Bruce's surprise, tipped the bottle back and enjoyed a good-sized gulp of the spirit.

The Bloke forced a smile and repeated, "Nosdrovia."

The American followed suit. "Nosdrovia."

They were in mid-drink when the old woman switched her grip on the bottle's neck and shattered it against the leg of the seat she occupied. The jagged edge of the vodka bottle sank into the Bloke's neck, but it was the twist Mama Bear gave the glass that proved fatal. Blood was now gushing into the bottle fragment, pouring out of the still-intact glass neck. Bruce then watched Mama Bear, calm as you please, reach into a compartment of the tea trolley and produce Bruce's own Remington-Elliott.

The Yank stumbled back to find himself trapped in the corner of the cell. "Mama Bear, please—" was all he was able to say before she fired off a single shot, decorating the dark corner with a think texture of skull and brains.

"Perhaps House of Usher could equip us with such fine sidearms, da?" she asked no one in particular as she studied the light pistol in her hands. "You say you understand problem when there really is no problem." She hopped back into her seat and looked at Bruce. He could see it in her gaze—she was talking to a dead man. "You see what you should not see. You die. Secret kept."

Bruce looked back over to Brandon. Nothing. Still staring forward. He was really taking this method to heart.

"Now just a moment, Mama B," Bruce said, trying to keep calm. "My silent partner and I are just curious travellers, that's all. Those who employ us—"

"—will know to stay clear of Usher business," she said as she raised the pistol.

"You really are thick," a voice from behind Bruce stated.

Bruce was on the verge of soiling his trousers, and Brandon just throws the gauntlet down like that? *He's finally cracked,* Bruce thought as he looked back to his partner.

Brandon's expression was as menacing as Mama Bear's. He remained fixed on the babushka, his smile confident, his outward demeanour that of one completely and utterly in command of what was a completely-out-of-control scenario.

"Fine," Mama Bear conceded. "I shoot you first."

"Kill us," Brandon said, "and you commit your operation here to a full-scale assault from our replacements."

The Remington-Elliott lowered slightly. "And why would your replacements mount full assault? They know nothing."

"They know about Ragnarök," he insisted.

"Goddammit, Brandon, " Bruce blurted out, "now they know why we are really here! If you had just given me a few more minutes—"

"Bruce, I know you wanted to handle this without heavy loss of life, but we've got no choice in the matter. We've tried solving it your way. Now we let Her Majesty's military handle it."

Mama Bear tossed the pistol to Iliad and then slipped out of her chair to stand between the two men. "So you are British military, after all."

"In a manner of speaking," Brandon stated. "We're independent contractors from the Department of Imperial Inconveniences. Some of my connections in the higher ranks got wind of Ragnarök and sent us in for confirmation. We have, depending on the last time I consulted a timepiece, twelve hours before we are counted as overdue. Once that happens, you call down the might of the Imperial Army on this location."

"You have seen what we are doing here, yes?"

"And you know full well what our military is capable of when properly motivated."

Bruce nodded. "Rest assured, Mama B, if the military is willing to send in blokes like us, the reputation of the Department as it is, Her Majesty is properly motivated."

She looked at the two of them for a moment, and then barked something in Russian. Iliad and one of their cell guards grabbed the corpses and dragged them out into the corridor as Mama Bear dealt orders to the remaining man. Once the guard snapped her a salute, she turned to face them again.

"Then I have twelve hours to decide what to do with you," she said evenly. "My initial option perhaps brings on more problems. We shall see, yes?"

She spared one final look to each of them, and then turned to follow the other two guards. Bruce shot Brandon a hot, angry look, but then loosed a wink. They had just bought themselves time.

With a deep breath, Bruce resumed his own casing of the room. Not much different from before, except now for the presence of a tea trolley. He craned his neck to look at the window behind them. No snowfall. It looked as if the sky cleared up as there was moonlight coming in and falling on Brandon's hands.

He looked back towards the window again. Clear night. Moonlight.

From the talk with Mama Bear, the Houseboy's primary language was Russian. Maybe he knew enough English, though, to make the next part of his plan work.

"You know French, German, and even Spanish," Bruce chuckled, "and you're still wanting more?"

Brandon blinked. "Come again?"

"You're wanting to learn sign language. You deserve a hand. I mean, that's good of you, mate. "

"Be quiet," their guard barked.

Bruce looked over to Brandon. "Got to hand it to ya." Brandon's brow furrowed. "Knowing sign language? It's going to come in quite handy."

"QUIET," the guard snapped.

Bruce kept his gaze with Brandon. Then he watched his partner's brow relax and his eyes go to Bruce's bound hands.

One. Guard.

On the second time signing this, Brandon mimicked the gestures with his own bound hands.

Watch. Door.

"What if I don't want to be quiet?" Bruce asked.

The guard stomped in front of Bruce. "Mama Bear want you alive. Mama Bear do not care if you are injured."

"Really?" Bruce barked out a laugh. "Brave man, talkin' to a guy all tied up."

"You forget," he said, lifting up his M1891, "I also have gun. Does not make me brave." The guard then swung the rifle butt around, clocking Bruce in the temple. "Does make me in charge."

Bruce blinked, trying to ignore the stars merrily dancing in front of him. "Good on you, mate."

The guard snorted, then took a few steps towards Brandon. "You have anything to say?"

Glass shattered, and the guard's head snapped back. A single bullet to the brow, and she had even compensated for trajectory through tempered glass.

Brandon, after a moment, said, "I do. Cracking shot, Ryfka is."

Bruce twisted in his chair, turning his own binds towards Brandon. "Right then, work on these knots for me, would ya?" He heard the grinding of metal against concrete, and then felt fingers start to work against the knots out of his reach. "Since we have a moment, what the hell were you all on about?"

"What? Ragnarök, you mean?"

"Yeah."

"Not a bloody clue. It was something that Yank said just before we jumped him and his mate. *'We're all one big happy Usher family now. Ragnarök, after all, depends on that, yes?'* I'm thinking this is what Usher is up to here."

"That explains why there was little to no security on them Firebird feathers. Not sure if them feathers are part of the plan." Bruce felt his rope slacken, and then he was free. "It's all about those tanks."

"I'm still trying to understand what it was we saw. Tanks are unstoppable, after all, so why reinvent the wheel?"

"Tanks are unstoppable monsters on the battlefield," Bruce began, freeing his ankles, "but what about the terrain around here? Those treads and all that metal they're carrying wouldn't fare so well."

"Build something that can climb, that can manage steep vertical inclines."

"Those Bears would do quite well for themselves in cold, mountainous regions." Once free, Bruce kicked aside his chair and started on Brandon's bonds. "Russia. Germany. Parts of Spain."

"Blimey," Brandon whispered. "They could revolutionise war with technology like that."

"But what was it you said—one big happy Usher family now? Something tells me these Bears are only part of this Ragnarök."

Once Brandon's wrists were freed, Bruce stepped into the moonlight. *Amazing shot, Ryfka,* he signed. *We're making our way back to the east entry point. Meet us there. Urgent.*

With Brandon back on his feet, Bruce motioned to the dead guard. "What do you think?"

"Come on, look at those shoulders," Brandon said.

"Right then," he grumbled, taking his own coat off, "since I can't do any sort of Russian accent to save our lives, and yeah, I mean that literally, I think you should be responsible for any sort of cover story, if we get stopped."

"How's this for a cover story? I lead with a punch and you shoot anyone else who happens to be there?"

Bruce slipped into the Houseboy's long black coat, and hefted the M1891. He took the offered munitions belt from Brandon, and passed the rife to him. "I like the sound of that cover story."

"The coat should suffice," Brandon said. He returned the rifle, along with a wide, black scarf. "Try to conceal that ridiculous jawline of yours."

"I'll have you know," Bruce began, tightening his fist around the thick scarf, "that this is a good, solid Australian profile I have. It's a trademark of the country."

"Unfortunate we're in Russia at the moment then," his partner quipped. He pushed back the folds of Bruce's coat, and found in one of his belt's pouches a series of long, thin instruments probably used in maintenance for the rifle's scope. "Now give me a few minutes with this lock, and then we're getting out of here."

"East entry point. Ryfka's meeting us there."

"What?" Brandon asked, nearly dropping his makeshift picks. "Are you mad? We need to find the closest exit."

"Nah, mate, we meet Ryfka at the east entrance." Bruce tightened the grip on the M1891. "Mission parameters have changed."

CHAPTER TWELVE

In Which Our Intrepid Agents
Enjoy a Most Extraordinary Train

S tanding on the private platform, wreathed in steam on this warm evening, Eliza counted the number of carriages, while Wellington disappeared to examine the working end of things. This was her second stroll along the impressive locomotive belonging to the Indian Office of the Ministry. It was not a hypersteam, but she somehow felt there was an incredible power in this train. Something not only about the engine but the cars had a unique design to them. In particular, the car directly behind the coal car. That particular segment was twice the length of a normal car, and it seemed—somehow—to be *floating*.

"My, my, so many handsome men—and in uniform too," Sophia said, her tone resembling a hungry purr.

Eliza tried not to think of the assassin standing behind her; that would only make her back itch. In normal circumstances, she would keep Sophia well within eyesight. So far, this operation had been nothing but odd and unpredictable, even for the Ministry. They originally came to India on the hunt for Henry Jekyll. An æthergate, an electroporter, and a double agent later, she was about to bring to justice a group of rebels comprised of those listed as missing or dead, who might or might not be completely in this world. She had seen a grand number of fantastic things in her time with the Ministry, but this case felt like a perfect storm of insanity.

Out of the corner of her eye she observed Sophia move to stand next to her, looking over the impressive locomotive from end to end. Eliza cast her gaze downward to the two suitcases flanking the assassin. "For someone on the run, you're hardly travelling light."

"India provided me an opportunity to replenish my wardrobe," Sophia returned. "And resupply myself with a few necessary sundries."

Eliza nodded. "Excellent. Then as you have been on the run, carrying your own luggage won't seem out of the ordinary." Sophia's expression hardened and that was a reward in itself. "Best get yourself settled then."

Her companion did not reply. Straight away. A devilish gleam accompanied her smile. "It is London all over again, isn't it?"

"Could be."

Sophia took stock of her suitcases, then said, "On this mission, I will tend to my own fashion. I prefer not to have my movements monitored once we part company. A valiant attempt though, Miss Braun."

So that's how the Ministry lost Sophia's signal in Cologne, she thought. Granted, with the Diamond Jubilee and the Maestro's mayhem unfolding around them, planting that particular tracker had not been her best work.

It was then Eliza realized she was clenching her jaw, a sure sign that things might go badly this time out. She felt skittish, off somehow. Like she didn't know which way to jump, and it wasn't just the presence of the Italian assassin.

She watched O'Neil and his men at the "floating" car loading weapons and supplies. Maulik, on joining them at the Victoria Terminus, had informed them this was not to be solely a Ministry mission. Alongside twenty of their agents, a full platoon under O'Neil's command would be joining them. By their set expressions they were men after vengeance.

Wellington returned, shaking his head. "I admire Maulik's transport here, but a private train seems very…impractical. The length of the engine is absurdly long. Longer than a hypersteam. Utterly ridiculous."

"Oh, Wellington," she heard Maulik say, "you cut me to the quick."

Emerging from the clouds of vapour, Maulik joined the two of them, and that was when they noted his chair seemed larger than the one he had been using since their arrival. Then Eliza could see housed in the chair's arms a set of Gatlings. Everyone appeared armed, armoured, and hungry for battle.

"Trains are the very best way to keep a low profile in this country. Airships, while faster, attract far too much attention," he pointed out.

"And Gatling guns in the armrests?" Eliza asked. "That also the best way to keep a low profile and not attract attention to yourself?"

"Oh no, this is my personal statement to the opposition. So, with a double agent already en route, two days to reach our location, and picking up a few more agents along the way, we should get moving."

"Has the Ministry enabled sufficient delays so that we might catch up with Vania?" Wellington asked.

"Yes, we considered that, but there's a problem. Vania is well versed in our procedures. She would notice any kind of manipulation like that," Maulik nodded, but then he added cheerily, "so we will rely on the next best thing."

Sophia crooked an eyebrow. "Which is?"

"The efficiency of the Great Southern India Railway Company, which is slowly transitioning to the control of the Indian government."

"Ah," Wellington said, nodding. "Say no more."

Eliza patted his hand, and led the way onto the train. She did not even look at Sophia. "Come along then."

"Yes," Maulik said, rolling on to a platform. "Meet me in the Strategy Room." The platform slowly lifted the director up towards the car as Wellington and Eliza ascended its steps. Sophia was a few feet behind them, struggling with her luggage, much to Eliza's amusement. "That's the one to my left," he added.

This carriage was all set up for business—that much was immediately apparent—as there were few seats set in the walls. Oddly, these seats came equipped with harnesses. Perhaps, as this was a train designed for operations, they expected rough travels. That must have been why this car only had four windows. Seeing the size of them, they were less for enjoying the view and more for allowing limited light into the car. Most of the wall space was covered in maps of India and images of the Ghost Rebellion ringleaders. The centre of the carriage was dominated by a large brass periscope.

Naturally, Wellington gravitated to it.

Eliza turned to Maulik. "So, this is the Strategy Room. What is the larger car forward of us?"

"The Training Carriage," the director said, his pride quite evident. "A real accomplishment on the part of R&D. It is our mobile training facility. It can be converted from a modest shooting range to an obstacle course to an open sparring centre."

Sophia dropped her cases. "On a moving train?"

"That's the ingenious part. The car is actually kept steady on its truss through high-powered magnets. The field actually dampens the inertia transferred to the car, stabilising it as if it is standing still."

"But wouldn't the magnetic field throw bullet trajectory?"

"An excellent observation, Miss del Morte. R&D lined the bottom of the car with a compound that deflects the magnetic field. The power is concentrated on keeping the car steady, which is what we need, after all.

I'm hoping to see if our Ministry agents will take on Kalaripayattu on this mission. This particular style is from the Northern region, and it would be wonderful, Wellington, if you could join us. The evasions and jumps have an elegance about them—"

"No, thank you, sir," Wellington replied quickly. Eliza glanced over her shoulder. He was busy moving dials, and peering through the periscope. A good gadget, that was all it really took to pique his interest, or at least that was what he was trying to convey. "That will not be necessary."

"Oh…what a shame," Maulik rolled forward towards the opposite door. "Then let me show you all to your berths."

The director led the way down the train. They still haven't started moving yet, but through the soles of her feet Eliza could feel the engine start to chug faster. It wouldn't be long now.

"Here you are, Miss del Morte," Maulik said, stopping at one cabin. A tight fit, even for one. "I hope you find it to your liking."

Sophia slid into the cabin and looked about. "Hardly the Ritz…but I'll manage."

"Excellent," he said, watching her move around her luggage in the tight space. "And now to you two. I hope you don't mind sharing with Wellington, Eliza. Quarters are tight after all, what with the military joining us."

"Sir," Wellington said, "what of our things? We did not have time—"

"Oh, not to worry, I called for your things and had them brought to your cabin." The huff took Maulik's attention from them to Sophia. "A benefit in serving the Ministry, my dear."

They continued deeper into the passenger car, stopping at a cabin door identical to Sophia's. Maulik slid open the door revealing a cabin twice the size of the assassin's. It was still a tight fit but it was hardly the cramped berth Sophia was settling into with her suitcases.

"We had this room designated for visiting dignitaries, so I thought it would be appropriate for you two." He gave a gentle tap to Eliza's forearm. "Get some rest. Breakfast will be served at eight, two cars up. Follow your nose."

Casting a quick glance at them both, Maulik continued deeper into the train. On account of his mask and the artificial reproduction of his voice, Eliza could not tell how the director felt about this mission. Returning to her own comparison of this visit to India as a perfect storm of calamity, Maulik had to be at his wit's end. There was Vania. There was the Ghost Rebellion. And there was Jekyll. He had seen Jekyll for the monster he truly was. He had faced him once at the Water Palace, and then faced his creation inside St Paul's Cathedral in London. The first encounter had left an impression on him while the other sentenced him to a wheelchair. Whatever was running through the director's mind remained a secret, but it couldn't be pleasant.

"We should manage here quite well," Wellington said, snapping her out of her trance.

"Better than being in a room within reach of that woman," Eliza said with a growl.

"I understand Sophia del Morte is not the most trustworthy or virtuous person," he began, slipping out of his coat, "but she has come to our aid before."

"Let's not forget she killed Harry," she seethed.

"Let's not forget she helped us prepare for the Diamond Jubilee."

She stopped, let out a sigh, and stared at Wellington. "I'm sorry. I don't mean to talk about Sophia all the time, but I swear she is like a splinter under my nail. I just…"

The train lurched forward suddenly, sending Eliza into Wellington, and both of them into a small couch. For a moment she was still, stiff as a board in his arms, and then after a moment something miraculous happened; she relaxed. He didn't say anything, simply held her, swaying a little bit, and stroking her back as the train began to pick up speed.

"Featherstone, Jekyll, æthergates, Sophia, electroporters, and then Vania," he said finally, tossing his bowler across the cabin. "Even for us, it's been a difficult few weeks."

He was right. All these old issues that she thought she'd put to rest were now coming back, and she never really addressed that. Eliza slipped one leg across Wellington's lap, straddling him, and ran her fingers through his hair. She inhaled his scent, feeling some level of calm return. Looking into his eyes, she examined his dear face.

"I know I didn't say so at the time," she muttered. "Ihita…it was… well it was difficult for me."

"You didn't need to say it. I knew."

It suddenly came to her how much she enjoyed this moment of privacy, a moment of intimacy. "You're good for me, Wellington Thornhill Books. I don't know if I have told you that, but you are."

He brushed a strand of hair off her face. "We're both rather good for each other I think."

She was damned if she knew what waited for them in this mission ahead, but she did know one thing. "I need you too, Wellington," she said, and pulled his lips to hers.

The kiss was fierce and hungry, even as the train lurched suddenly. Eliza's teeth rapped hard against Wellington's, but the tiny jolt of pain was insignificant compared against her desire for this man. Wellington managed to reach out with his foot and slide the bolt lock in place. His resourcefulness was another reason she loved him.

Eliza reluctantly pulled free of his lips, but she needed to see his eyes, those beautiful hazel eyes of his. Usually, they were her focus, a haven for her. Just as he knew her mind all too often, she always knew his when she took a moment to look into his gaze. Right then, what she saw was honest desire, but also something more. She didn't want to be the one to say it first, but she didn't want to be the one that let a moment pass.

That had been the lesson of Paris. Never again.

"I do love you, Wellington," she said, running her fingers along his cheek.

He stared at her for a moment, his hand tightening on her waist as the train reached a smoother rhythm. "I have always loved you, Eliza. Right from when you came down into the Archives."

"Even when I broke that blasted vase revealing the location of El Dorado?"

He kissed her soundly, taking his time, before pulling back to assert, "Yes."

"And when I overloaded your analytical engine with commands, even after you had warned me?"

He pulled her closer to lick and nibble her neck, sending tingles down her spine. "Even then, too."

"What about when I misfiled all those cases from 1867?"

Leaning back, he examined her as if she were a strange creature he had just discovered, before clasping her against him, and kissing her again. This time his hands roamed over her body, trying to find closures he could loosen. "That was quite trying, I must admit, *but I still loved you,*" Wellington insisted. "Besides, I knew it was only because you did not want to be there."

Eliza tugged at his ascot, and grinned slyly down at him. "Well, I learned to love the Archives almost as much as you. My only regret is not taking advantage of the privacy and enjoying amorous fantasies down there with you." She leaned forward. "Alone, in the shelves, the smell of old books all about us..."

Wellington let out a low groan. "Eliza, darling, you don't need to further inflame the situation. It is quite warm enough in this little room as it is." He cast his eyes up to the berth suspended above their heads. "Shall we take the director's advice and get some rest?"

Eliza gave a little pout. "We'll never make it."

"Whatever do you me—"

She tightened her legs against Wellington's hips, pulled him close with one hand while he grabbed the edge of the berth with the other. Eliza yanked, using Wellington as his own counterweight to pull him down to the floor.

"I think you will find," she said, gripping his shirt and tearing it open, "that we are still young and spry enough to take advantage of this floor."

How long had it been since she had touched Wellington's skin? She ran her fingertips across his smooth, muscular torso. Her feather touch eventually became firmer, her palm pressing into his flesh. Yes, fieldwork most definitely suited him.

"You didn't wear your bullet-proof corset," she said, bending down to place a soft kiss against his chest. Her tongue flicked his nipple, earning a little jolt from him.

Wellington pushed her up and frantically pulled at her blouse.

His smile melted away. "I see you wore yours."

She motioned to the line of hooks running down the front of her reinforced undergarment. "It's standard procedure—but you will notice, this shouldn't be such a chore to get me out of."

Wellington flipped the top hook of her corset with a single finger, revealing the inner curves of Eliza's breasts. She let out a little gasp as he undid the second and third hooks.

"Yes," Wellington said, releasing the final hook, "hardly a bother at all."

Feeling his fingers on her skin brought a delightful rush to Eliza. She tipped her head back and leaned into his warm, delicate touch. There was always a struggle with how she enjoyed her Wellington. Did she want him to ravish her, leap upon him herself, or enjoy each other slowly, savouring one another like a fine wine or cognac?

Always a dilemma.

She bent down to kiss him again, a wildfire rippling through her flesh as her naked breasts touched Wellington's chest. His hands pushed away the creation of fabric, leather, and steel from her, and their kissing grew hungrier on feeling their bodies press harder into each other. He descended lower along her torso, taking her breast into his mouth and teasing her nipple with his tongue. Eliza was always pleasantly surprised at how knowledgeable he was at certain pleasure points. He was a learned man, a graduate from university, and by profession an archivist. He utilised all that knowledge on how the body worked to figure how she would react to certain stimuli.

He continued to move his tongue uninhibited, tasting all of her, savouring what her body yielded to him. Her cries. His fingertips digging deep into her skin. The delicious tremble they shared against each other. She craved his touch, and drew a sweet satisfaction from feeding his pleasure.

"Do have a care, Eliza," he gasped suddenly. They were sitting up, facing one another, and Eliza had no recollection how they got to this position, not that she minded. "We might disturb the other berths in this car, and the cars connected to us, and possibly trains passing by."

She could feel his hands on the backs of her thighs. Both of them were still wearing trousers. They had to remedy this. Quickly.

"Actually, Wellington," Eliza whispered, as she reached between them and started to unbuckle his trousers, "I wish to be so improper and inappropriate that we risk exile from the Empire."

He wiggled his eyebrows. "Tallyho, then."

Her mouth was on his again, her tongue probing and desperate. That was exactly how she liked it.

INTERLUDE

In Which the Thunder from Down Under
Rages against the Russian Storm

Ryfka's eyes went to each of them. She was a reflection of Brandon, who was also looking between her and him. Once again, Bruce found himself on the unpopular end of an argument.

"Are you mad?" Brandon asked.

Are you mad? Ryfka signed quickly, her face completely flabbergasted.

"Look, I didn't say this was going to be an easy operation. Worst case, the extraction team gets you out of Łódź," Bruce said, sliding the body of the perimeter guard to a far corner of the foyer. They were probably both expecting to make a hasty retreat after Ryfka's latest kill, but now he had to convince both new-ally sniper and long-time partner that he was not tempting fate. "We need to get the Firebird feathers back to the Fat Man. That's our priority." After throwing a tarp over the poor bastard, Bruce turned to the wardrobe where he had left the Firebird feathers hidden. As he had hoped, they were still there. Sliding them free, Bruce passed the crate to Brandon. "Once we send the signal, we have forty-eight hours to get to the extraction, right? Ryfka and I are gonna take part of that forty-eight hours to make things difficult for Mama Bear."

Ryfka rapped Bruce hard against his arm. *We do not have the resources to take down this factory,* she signed.

I know that, Ryfka, he replied. *That's not what we should do. We're going to slow things down here.*

"Ryfka was expecting a demolition squad," Brandon said. "You're wanting to accomplish the same thing with the two of you?"

"What I'm saying is if we can slow down operations here, we have time to debrief the Ministry."

"But then Mama Bear will just pack up and move once we get a proper operation together."

"That's a possibility," he admitted, "but regardless of how this plays out, you've seen the operation here."

For the first time since their rendezvous with Ryfka, Brandon smiled. "It's a stalemate for Usher. Stay here, take the chance of a strike team. Or attempt to move all operations elsewhere which, judging by what's here, would take months. That's bloody brilliant." He fixed his gaze with Bruce and the smile disappeared. "Still bonkers, but brilliant."

Ryfka stomped her foot. *Exactly how are you planning to cripple operations?*

Bruce shrugged. *Making this up as I go,* he signed in reply.

"You're not making this up as you go, are you?" Brandon asked.

"Nah, mate," Bruce said with a snort, "why would you think that?" Brandon went to reply, but Bruce pushed him towards the door. "You just focus on getting those feathers to the extraction point. We will cover your exit and you send the signal first chance you get. Right, then?"

Brandon threw the box of Firebird feathers over his shoulder and shook his head. "Doesn't seem like you are giving me much of a choice."

"I'm not, mate. I'm trying to have my cake and eat it, too." Bruce clapped his partner's shoulder. "I'll see you in Łódź."

"I'm going to hold you to that." Brandon opened the door, revealing the dull glow of fresh snow against pitch darkness. The star-filled sky just visible through the forest canopy revealed a virtual road map for his partner. He knew Brandon's tracking skills were top notch, even on days when a thunderstorm raged. A night like this more than guaranteed Brandon a clear direction. "Two days."

"First pint is on me."

With a quick nod to Ryfka, Brandon glanced outside, then slipped into the dark, appearing only for a brief moment under the illumination of a perimeter light before disappearing completely.

Ryfka tapped Bruce on the shoulder. *What about any additional guards? Won't Mama Bear be on high alert?*

Bruce shook his head. *They're focusing on making tanks. Additional guards are only going to draw attention to this facility.* He motioned to the dead Houseboy, then continued to sign. *This kill, though, I'm worried it's going to make things difficult. There's going to be a check-in soon. We've got to move quick.*

Signalling her to follow, Bruce re-treaded his steps back to the centre of the factory. They came to stop at the door where he and Brandon discovered the Cave.

Now what?

Push the oven to critical?

Grab a tank and take out a few of the other units?

Or, if he could find the munitions...

The tapping on his shoulder made him jump a bit. Ryfka was looking at him somewhat incredulously. *So, this was about as far as your plan reached?*

A muscle in Bruce's jaw twitched. Reluctantly, he signed in reply, *Noticed that, did you?*

We have plenty of options.

He stared at the door. *Going this way doesn't feel quite right. It would simply put us on a perch in plain sight. What do you think? Something subtle,* he signed with a slight grin, *or something a bit more direct?*

It was the first time he had seen the sniper smile, and it suited her quite nicely. *You seem to be a more direct gentleman. I can take a spot above you, provide cover.* She gently patted on her sniper rifle.

On the other side of this door is a gangplank. If my distraction is enough, you should be out of sight. I will rendezvous with you at the east entry point.

We will have to make this fast, she returned.

Agreed. He glanced at his watch. *Ten minutes, then move into place.*

Bruce slipped past Ryfka and found a stairwell leading down to the lower levels of the factory. He cracked the door open and saw only a few Houseboys milling about. The majority of crew for this overnight shift apparently were focusing attention on the forge and construction of two more Bears. Flipping up the coat's collar and tucking his chin close to his chest, Bruce made his way deeper into the Cave. Up close, Usher's monstrous tanks were even more imposing.

Then he heard her just up ahead. Mama Bear. She was speaking in Russian, but he recognized the cold efficiency in her voice. She would spot him in a moment.

Bruce ducked into one of the bays, countering the sound of her voice by moving along the tank's length. He was on the back end of the Bear when he suddenly heard the babushka switch to English as the small party stopped by his hiding place.

"Exactly what does your Mr Fox want of me?" the old woman asked.

Bruce ducked behind the back leg of the Bear, but leaned around its spherical form to see if he could catch a glimpse of who Mama Bear was talking to.

"We want results." The bloke was an Englishman. Had to be a Houseboy high in the ranks. Bruce was guessing this tosser went with a bald look to appear more intimidating. It wasn't working with Mama Bear, from the sounds of things. "We've reviewed your preliminary findings and everything looks promising, save for the omission of Element X. We're not pleased with that whatsoever."

"When you say Element X you mean Firebird feathers, yes?"

"Legend tells of the Firebird feathers granting strength to those who possess it. The idea that we could break down the feathers and smelt them into the same metal armour for the Bears—"

"Do you hear yourself, Brother Streeper?" the old woman scoffed. "You speak of legend. We work in science. Da, Firebird feathers are a marvel. Apart from glowing they have no place in Bear. We must make sure Bear works better than prototype. After Bear succeeds, then we try magic feathers."

"The House of Usher respects the supernatural. If these models pass the next trials, I strongly suggest your next phase includes the Firebird enhancement. We need to know if we can make these creations of yours indestructible."

"We only have five feathers to work with," she stated.

"Five?" This Houseboy Streeper now looked annoyed. "I will need to see them. Based on their quality, we may want to consider other ways of employing them into Ragnarök."

"If Mr Fox wants Firebird feathers so badly," she said, "Mama Bear will give them to you as gift."

"I think he would consider that quite the peace offering."

"Let me take you to them then." The party resumed their walk.

Bruce had hoped for thirty minutes. He would be most fortunate now if he had fifteen.

"Time to make an interruption," he muttered to himself as he climbed up the tank's back leg.

The "body" of the Bear was not so much a sphere as it was shaped like a giant black egg. The "head" was nothing more than another sphere cut in half. Obviously, that would be where he would need to end up. Directly underneath him was a hatch, a handgrip just above it that probably unlocked it. Bruce gave the grip a twist, and the hatch split in two. He jumped into the beast, and found a corresponding hand-lock inside which shut the hatch with a soft hiss.

Lights flickered to life inside the Bear. Easily this machine needed to be manned by a crew of four. An engineer to check boilers, make sure systems were running properly. Two gunners, for obvious reasons. And finally, a pilot. Bruce hunched lower as he walked towards the cockpit, which was hardly what he expected. Whomever piloted this behemoth had to lie flat on their stomach. While the larger cannons were the responsibility of the gunners, the pilot operated the front-mounted Maxims. That would help in their escape, but as far as inflicting damage on the factory, he would have to be nimble in such tight quarters.

Bruce wiggled into the pilot's space and opened up valves overhead. Gauges jumped from red to green and in his body he could feel a rumble. The Bear was waking up.

His hands gripped the control sticks, each of them capped at their ends by a button. Instincts assured him that if there were buttons within reach of his thumb, then they had to be firing mechanisms of some fashion for the machine guns mounted on either side of him. His feet, snug in what felt remarkably like horse's stirrups, must have a say in the legs and how they operate.

"All right then," he whispered to himself. "Probably like driving a lorry. How hard can it be?"

Bruce flexed his right foot forward, and the Bear lurched backward, slamming into the bay's retaining wall. The impact rattled his teeth, and caught the attention of the Cave's personnel.

"So, not quite a lorry then," he said, pointing his right foot downward. The Bear heaved again, this time forward. He repeated the gesture, this time on the left, and the left side of the tank also moved forward. To make this thing move, he would have to mimic a belly crawl.

The shouts at his Bear sounded soft, muffled; but from the looks of the ground crew, mallets and spanners held over their heads as if they were pitchforks and torches, Bruce was not making any friends.

Fine. That made pushing forward without caution just that much easier.

His Bear lumbered free of its bay and, with a twist of the bars and leaning left, turned a corner that brought the forge into view.

Something landed on top of his Bear. Whatever it was, it was well over ten stone. A heartbeat later, whatever had landed on the tank collapsed and then slid free. Through his viewport, Bruce saw the workers running in a wild panic. Another thump came from the outside, followed close by the sound of a body falling against the Bear.

"Thank you, Ryfka," he muttered. "Now we just back up a bit here," and the Bear stepped back slightly. Bruce could imagine this thing leaning back on its haunches much like a real bear. "Let's complicate things."

Both Maxim guns underneath his cockpit roared to life, their muzzle flashes sparking just at the bottom of his peripheral. Against the forge, he could see sparks dancing about its many pitted surfaces. He was not expecting to pierce any part of this furnace, as it was designed sturdy enough to contain melted iron ore. That didn't mean he couldn't slow down the manufacturing process.

The spray of bullets was now catching what appeared to be walkways, exhaust pipes, and a pair of control centres on either side of the forge. He could see some workers making a run for it. Again came the thumping against the Bear of one or two brave souls attempting to gain access, only to have a bullet end their impromptu assault. A light flashed yellow in front of him. If he knew Russian, he might know what the light was signalling, but he was going to guess "Low Ammunition" for the Maxims. Thick steam began seeping out of several pipes of the forge. He could also see one of the control stations appeared shattered and ruined. It was a start…

Then the guns stopped.

He pressed the triggers again. Nothing.

His eyes jumped to the control panel. The yellow light had now switched to red.

"Lovely. Now what?"

He then looked around himself. He was in a bloody tank.

Bruce opened the throttle up and the Bear broke into a sprint—or at least, a sprint for a tank—forward. He watched the distance to the forge disappear, and then felt every inch of him jostle on impact. He could hear metal grind and groan as the Bear tried to continue on, but the forge would not relent. Good.

Ignoring the muffled calls for help and thumping from outside, Bruce shimmied out of the pilot's seat and crawled to the back of his tank, his eyes frantically searching for anything he could use out in the Cave. His eyes went over the gunner's chair and there he found a small case of grenades. He freed two from their casings, and then he turned around to the engineer's station. This, due to his lack of knowledge on the Russian language, was the tricky bit of his improvisation.

"You sit here, you're the engineer," he said to himself. "Now if I wanted access to a button, but only if things were a complete cock-up, I would make it look like…"

The red button was one of the larger buttons on the control panel. It was framed by yellow and black stripes, and housed under a small glass cover. The Cyrillic label underneath it was printed in large, red characters.

"Yeah, exactly like that," he said, ripping off its cover and pushing it.

The Bear's interior lights switched to a deep red. Next to the engineer's panel, the clock's hands reset to midnight. The hour hand suddenly locked itself at the three o'clock position while the minute hand started ticking backwards.

Bruce scrambled for the main hatch, opened it to the outside world, and then hurled out a grenade. The club-shape object sailed up into the Cave and disappeared from view. The explosion that soon followed offered him a moment to hoist himself up through the exit. He slid down the back-end, and on reaching terra firma, lobbed the second grenade. Once he heard it detonate, Bruce sprinted. He could try for another Bear, but that would have been pressing his luck. He needed a transport, preferably one faster than these monsters.

Run, he told himself. *Just run.*

The gunfire was coming now, too much for him to try and discern which one belonged to Ryfka and which were trying to pick him off. It all came down to this hare-brained scheme of his, and how much distance he could put between himself and his tank.

He found the bay where his Bear had come from and dove inside it. He felt the explosion through the ground. Parts of his tank flew in every direction, a good amount of this shrapnel tearing into the forge. Now cracked, it released super-heated iron ore that poured across the Bear's burning husk, consuming it greedily as if attempting to reclaim it from whence it had come.

Damage done, he thought. *Time to pick up Ryfka.*

The Cave was Bedlam, and he was no longer a priority to the Houseboys. The damaged forge was now putting out even more heat, and the other Bears in their maintenance bays were potential hazards with the ordinance on board. There was also the forge itself, and the dangers it posed to crew and completed tanks. Bruce kept running towards the mouth of the Cave, the air tasting less and less harsh the closer he drew. His run stopped at the *chug-chug-chug* of a lorry attempting to start. It was a truck the likes of which Bruce had never seen before. He had seen vehicles with canopies covering the beds, certainly, but never with broad, wide wheels in the front and a series of smaller wheels in the back, all of which turned a wide, sturdy tread. This odd transport was just pulling away when Bruce grabbed hold of the bed's tailgate and hauled himself up.

He had only just laid back against the truck's bed when someone pulled him up to his feet.

The Houseboy was about Bruce's size. So were the other four blokes sitting closer towards the cab.

"You alright there, mate?" he asked. The thick accent jolted Bruce harder than a kick to the bollocks. He had better opinions of his kinsmen.

"Yeah," Bruce said, nodding quickly. "Things going tit's up out there, eh?"

The Houseboy blinked. "Crikey, another Australian? Here?"

"Got another surprise for ya, mate," Bruce said before planting a solid right against the man's jaw.

The Houseboy toppled back into the other four, giving Bruce a chance to throw the bloke closest to him through the bed's canopy and out into the dark. He didn't see who it was or where it came from, but someone managed to plant a good hit to the kidney. It winded Bruce, but he pushed forward from the legs, shouldering his opponent out of the way and ploughing into the remaining three Usher sods. Suddenly he was being picked up, and Bruce grabbed for any kind of purchase. He latched onto a heavy wool coat, similar to his borrowed one, and he dug his fingers deep into it as he was pushed out of the canopy's hole. They both were suspended outside in the cold morning, but Bruce's other hand caught the truck bed's frame. Tightening his grip on the man's coat, Bruce heaved, and pulled himself back into the truck.

A fist came out of the shadows, but Bruce ducked, hearing the attack sail overhead. He pushed and a Houseboy slapped into the other side of the canvas, which ripped away and sent him sprawling into the snow.

Arms grabbed him from behind and held him fast. Bruce couldn't see this bloke, but he could see his countryman returning to his feet, wiping away the blood from the corner of his mouth.

"Nice punch there, mate. What—Sydney? Melbourne?"

"Brisbane, ya wanker," Bruce barked. "You Townsville?"

He nodded. "What gave it away?"

Bruce spat on the man's foot. "Any pisspot throwing his hat in with Usher can't be all that smart. So, Townsville."

He drove a fist into Bruce's gut. Bruce doubled-over, and the man holding him struggled to keep his footing.

"Well, Brisbane," Townsville said to Bruce, leaning close to his ear, "you're not long for this world."

Bruce jerked his head up, clocking Townsville while also knocking the bloke holding on to him back a few steps. They both hit the cab hard, causing Houseboy to lose his grip. Bruce's elbow connected with the Usher agent's temple, stunning him enough for Bruce to toss him out into the dark.

And then there was one.

"That's the problem with Townsville," Bruce scoffed. "You lot never know when to shut it."

Bruce drove his fist down onto his fellow Australian, but he only heard the sound of his fist slapping into an open palm. Townsville grunted as he pushed Bruce backward, and then charged at him. Both men fell to the bed as their lorry rumbled around a corner.

One hit to the kidney. Another hit to the kidney.

Yeah, this bloke was definitely from Townsville.

"Breaks my heart," Townsville said as he shoved Bruce back into the cab, pinning him against it by his throat, "to do this to you, mate."

Bruce worked against the man's wrist but then braced his hands against Townsville's elbow and heaved. Under his grip, Bruce felt a joint pop, and Townsville's hold was no more.

"Breaks my heart, meetin' you here," Bruce wheezed before grabbing Townsville by the collar and pulling him in for a right nose-ender. Under Bruce's forehead, something snapped.

It had been a long time since he had used the Thunder from Down Under on a fellow Australian. For this plonker, it felt amazing.

Once Townsville slipped free of the truck bed, Bruce grabbed hold of the frame that defiantly attempted to keep what was left of the canvas. It was plenty sturdy, so swinging into the driver's seat shouldn't be a problem. Bruce took a deep breath and sent himself around, his grip switching from the frame to the driver's door handle.

The gun discharged over his head, but the shift downward opened the door, sending him swinging out and into the hood. A thick plume of smoke rose from underneath the truck, and the vehicle accelerated. Bruce swung back towards the cab, but not for long as something—a safe and sure assumption it was a foot—kicked the door away, slamming him into the hood again.

This Houseboy had a bit of smarts about him as the lorry surged forward, uphill.

Bruce was swinging back, faster this time, but just before another kick sent him out once more, he reached around the door and grabbed the driver's leg.

"Gotcha!" Bruce said.

Then he caught a glimpse of the gun. The one that he had seen earlier.

Bruce kicked off the side of the cab, and the Houseboy slipped off his seat. From the look of this sod's landing, his neck had broken for sure. The door swung back and Bruce hopped up into the cab. He opened up the boilers and the truck continued forward, unfaltering against the snow. Something about those treads must have been helping them along.

The hill he was climbing levelled out, and the East Entrance appeared in front of him. Bruce maneuvered the truck closer to the access door just as it flew open. Ryfka stepped into view and pointed her rifle at the cab.

Bruce slammed on the brakes and raised his hands into the air. "It's me!"

Ryfka lowered her weapon and let out a long breath, mist lingering around her as she did so.

Bruce beckoned her into the cab. She had not even settled into her seat before he brought the boilers up to maximum and launched them forward.

Glancing above his head, Bruce found a small light, probably used to check maps in darkness. These Russians were crafty buggers. He leaned into the light, making sure she could see his lips. "Bloody good shooting, Ryfka."

He glanced over to her. *Any pistols on you?*

Bruce dug into his pants pocket and fished out his Remington-Elliott. Leaning back into the light, hard to do while driving, he said, "All I got, love."

He caught sight of the chambers before handing it to her. Only two bullets.

She rapped him on the shoulder. *How fast can this...thing...go?*

His eyes looked at the variety of gauges. Ryfka slapped him on the shoulder again and pointed to a round window with a single needle that was hovering around the number twenty.

"The velocimeter claims she can get up to thirty. Let's find out."

A roar thundered behind him, and a red-orange glow briefly lit the snowy road stretching before them. Glancing in the mirror suspended between them, Bruce could make out the factory receding in the distance, the wing where he knew the Cave was located appeared shrouded in flame.

Bruce then leaned forward in his seat. The perimeter gate was up ahead, but there was someone standing in the middle of the bloody road.

"Oh, you have got to be joking," he swore.

The short, squat shape was unmistakable. Mama Bear stepped into the light, cradling in her hands a union of a small Maxim, a Mosin-Nagant, and from the looks of the odd cage-funnel underneath, a Tesla attachment. Her hand pulled back the pump action underneath it, and lights of all kinds flared to life.

Bruce tightened his grip on the steering wheel.

The bolt from the Tesla attachment struck the hood, cradling the front of their truck in a web of electricity that danced back and forth. Inside the cab, gauges bounced back and forth, and the light above Bruce blinked before everything went dark.

Mama Bear pushed the pump action forward and levelled the rifle. Bullets ripped through the windshield and hood.

A door opened, and Bruce saw Ryfka lean out and fire the Remington-Elliot twice. He sat up straight just in time to see the perimeter gates snap open on their impact. There was no way to tell how fast they were going, but everything felt steady. They now had to get to the extraction point. In roughly thirty-six hours. Provided nothing went...

The Maxim snarled angrily behind them, and Ryfka let out a scream. She was slipping out of the cab, but he managed to catch her by the wrist and haul her back in. A pair of bullets had torn through her right shoulder. While there were exit wounds, the amount of blood coming out of her was a bit alarming.

"Ah, dammit," Bruce cursed as he wriggled out of his coat. He balled it up and pressed it as best as he could against Ryfka's wounds. "Help me out here, love. Push against that."

Ryfka's hand joined Bruce's. He quickly slipped his hand free and pressed hard against hers, earning a small yelp.

"As soon as I know we're clear," Bruce said, knowing Ryfka couldn't see his lips, "I'll patch you up. Just stay with me." She couldn't hear him. This was more for himself. He knew that. "Just stay with me."

He looked in the rear view mirror. The glow of the factory was growing dimmer by the second, but he couldn't stop. Not now. They had to get to the extraction point.

"Just stay with me, Ryfka."

⊷══◉══⊷

In Which the Ministry of Peculiar Occurrences Makes a Grand Entrance

After two nights on the floor with Eliza, Wellington could feel a muscle in his back twitching. Still as he looked across the Strategy Room to where she was studying the map of India, he could only smile as his eyes followed the curve of her backsides in the trousers she wore. *So improper and inappropriate that we would be exiled from the Empire,* she had asked of him.

What he was presently thinking was *highly* inappropriate, and he did not mind in the least. It was so satisfying to tell her the truth of how he felt, and just as good to seal their sharing the way they had. It had been very much worth it.

Wellington took a turn at the periscope to get his mind off of his lover and back on the mission at hand. Sweeping the landscape revealed green hills slipping by and open skies overhead. No peril on the horizon. He flicked the scope's arms and sent it back into place in the ceiling. The train was an impressive feat of technology, ingenuity, necessity, and luxury...but it still bothered him: Why wasn't it a hypersteam?

Sophia del Morte appeared in the entrance, rather incongruously pushing a tea trolley. At his raised eyebrow, she said, "Just making myself useful, and besides, the coffee was atrocious."

Wellington observed the narrow form of a coffeepot right next to the one for tea.

"Which would you like?" Sophia's grin suggested both might be scandalous.

Wellington could feel Eliza's gaze fixed on him, and for a moment he was torn.

"You should have the coffee," Sophia said, inhaling the scent. "Wonderful, a roast so dark"—she glanced up and shot the two of them a wicked look—"Like my soul."

Eliza gave a little hiss of annoyance, but Wellington was relieved to see she didn't reach for one of her pistols. That was an improvement, certainly.

"I think I will have tea," Wellington said, taking hold of the pot himself. "More my speed."

Sophia gave a little shrug and poured herself a coffee. "I sincerely hope your director is right about this leisurely pace." She took a sip. "Jekyll has given these insurgents an incredible power."

"Indeed they have, Signorina," Wellington agreed, "which can sometimes give men—and yes, women—a false sense of confidence. From what we heard, Nahush's confidence in electroporters must be what allows him to entrust his Ghost Rebellion to Jekyll."

"Perhaps after facing you at the Army & Navy Building, he is willing to work with Jekyll as the electroporter offers them an advantage."

"Tosh, my condition does not play in this whatsoever."

"Your *condition?*" Her left eyebrow raised. "Is that what you call it?"

Wellington felt himself clench.

"Fan-bloody-tastic, Sophia," seethed his partner. "You might want to consider helping him."

"I am," Sophia replied tersely. "Instead of treating what happened as an affliction, Wellington should embrace it. What he can do is nothing less than astounding, and it will serve us well in the battle ahead."

"Not if I can't control it," Wellington stated.

"But you can," Eliza said, placing her hand on his arm.

He looked at her. So beautiful. So trusting. "How can you be so certain, Eliza?"

"Listen to yourself right now, Welly. There is a control there." She touched his cheek. "Jekyll does not have a hold on you. Neither does your father. You cut those ties many years ago."

He placed his hand over hers. "And you said I was the one good to you. You are rather special to me, as well."

"Shall I leave you two alone?" Sophia asked with a tilt of her head.

Eliza kept her gaze with his. "Think of all the times I've gotten the better of that disciplined exterior of yours."

He blushed. "Well, yes, you have me there."

"I know how strong you are, even if you do not."

"I believe," Sophia groaned, "I am going to be ill."

The two women stared at each other, but so far no one was throwing knives. *Maybe*, Wellington thought, *they were starting to actually like each other.*

Maulik, flanked by Lieutenant O'Neil, rolled into the Strategy Room, thankfully breaking the tension. "Good morning, all. Rested and ready for an exciting day, I hope?"

"So, what is the plan, Director?" Eliza asked, turning her back on Sophia. "Are we planning to stop somewhere in Jaipur City, or are we coming at the Water Palace from a different angle?"

"You didn't read the case file provided in your cabin?" Maulik asked.

"I…" Eliza gently bit her bottom lip. "I lost track of time, what with all the excitement in leaving Bombay."

"Two days and two nights," Sophia stated with a sly grin, "on a train, and you didn't find a moment?"

"She does have a point," Wellington agreed…

…and immediately regretted it. Eliza shot him a look that could have been classed as a lethal weapon.

"I didn't see you reminding me about any case file last night when we were naked and wrapped in one another's loving embrace," she snapped at him.

"Eliza…" Wellington whispered through clenched teeth.

"Oh Wellington, please, don't act so shocked. Eliza Braun and I are powerful women and we have voracious appetites in all things." She went to take a sip of her coffee, and paused. "I know of at least three of your Ministry agents, director, who are more than relaxed and ready for this mission."

"Yes, well, that is far more than I need to know about what is happening on my train," Maulik said, clearing his throat. "Anyone else have anything to share?" He looked over his shoulder. "O'Neil?"

"I'm trying to stay focused on the mission," he replied. O'Neil's grip tightened on his pith helmet. "I'm wondering if I'm going about this the right way."

"Eliza," Maulik began, "to answer your question—our plan for today faces it first challenge in Jal Mahal's location. There is a reason it is called the Water Palace."

"It is completely surrounded by Man Sagar Lake," Wellington said, "so, Director, how are we going to get to the Water Palace undetected if the Ghost Rebellion may be there already?"

"The solution is all about you," Maulik said, motioning around him.

"This train? We are going to catch the Ghost Rebellion off-guard with a train?"

"That we are, my friend." He wheeled to one side to face O'Neil. "Make yourselves ready." The lieutenant placed his helmet back on his head and exited in the direction of the passenger cars. Moments later, O'Neil reappeared, followed by Ministry agents and British infantry. They filed through the Strategy Room, and proceeded towards the engine.

Once the last man disappeared, Maulik went to the map of India. He flipped a few switches, making the map's tiles spin and flip, the image of India shimmering out of focus. The rotating tiles now slid up and out of view, replaced by other tiles forming a new map of the city of Jaipur, Man Sagar Lake, and Jal Mahal. Outside the city, a series of lines connected and branched off to points beyond the map.

"We are here," Maulik began, placing a small two-part woodcut of their train onto one of the railroad lines heading to Jaipur. A few moments later, it began inching closer to the city. "As you said, Wellington, avoiding detection is the trick."

"This train," Sophia said, looking around her as if studying the Strategy Car's integrity. "Does it have æthergate abilities?"

Maulik let out a sharp laugh. "I would never endanger my agents with any of the adverse effects of æthergate travel. I have something better in mind." He pointed to a small junction the train magnet was approaching, then pressed two red buttons in his chair's armrests. "I recommend you secure that tea trolley and hold on to something. We're about to detach."

Sophia pushed the trolley out of the carriage and returned quickly, an excited grin on her lips. Wellington had just fixed his grip onto the periscope's housing when the train lurched. The magnet depicting their train split, the engine proceeding around the city perimeter while the second half—the passenger cars—continued to Jaipur.

"The passenger cars will be picked up by Ministry operatives," Maulik assured them. "Right now, our team await deployment in the next car up."

"Deployment?" Sophia asked, and even she looked impressed.

"Since we are now considerably lighter, we should be in position in roughly half an hour." He motioned to the seats fastened against the wall. "More than enough time for you lot to secure yourselves."

As the three of them slipped into these chairs and accompanying harnesses, Maulik retracted the metal blinds covering the windows. Sunlight suddenly filled their car, blinding them for a moment. On the map, their train continued at a quick pace around the city.

"Wellington, do you feel that?" Eliza said. "We're on an incline."

He nodded, though he didn't have any time to reply, for moments later a low droning sound reached his ears, and the pitch grew the higher they continued upward. Maulik threw a switch on his armrest, and the door leading to the engine hissed shut. The whine was not as piercing anymore, but still present.

They were also slowing down.

Maulik looked over to the map as he locked his chair in a small nook next to theirs. "Right then, any moment now..."

The incline levelled out and then turned quickly into a decline. With that change came a sudden increase in their speed. A hard, sharp eruption roared from the engine, shoving them forward. The train shook and shuddered madly all around them, as if it would tear itself apart, but they were still continuing downward, although the present momentum felt different than before.

Then the sunlight disappeared.

Sand, soil, mud, and crushed rock smeared along the window. The odd pen or ashtray that thudded against the carpet now trembled its way across the room seemingly of its own accord as they rumbled their way downward into India.

"You mentioned back in Bombay about the engine length being absurdly long. Longer than a hypersteam, but no, this train is no hypersteam," Maulik said. "If it were, we would not have room for the drill bit."

"We are *drilling* our way to the Water Palace?" Sophia asked over the rumble of their excavation.

"Thrilling, isn't it?" Maulik let out a delighted laugh, but it stopped abruptly. "Granted we have never attempted a dig quite this far..."

Eliza glanced over at Wellington, and he patted her hand. Though she really didn't look worried.

"Hold on," Wellington said. "A drill bit certainly isn't enough to keep us moving forward."

"Always the tinker, eh, Books?" Maulik motioned to the front of the train. "The drill bit applies the principles of a hypersteam engine. We capture, recycle, and condense steam from the engine, and send it through the drill bit. The soil is softened, the bit catches, and we achieve forward momentum. To add to that, our wheels are now at a ninety-degree angle and assist in digging. When I commissioned this train, I had high hopes." Maulik sounded pleased as punch. "R&D actually surpassed them!"

He'd become quite different in India, Wellington observed. *Or perhaps he's always been like this?*

"I would advise you all to stay secured," he warned. "As we are dealing with geology, Mother Earth can sometimes throw rather nasty surprises when subterranean."

On the map, their train approached the banks of the Man Sagar Lake. Wellington gripped the armrests, and now it was Eliza who reached over and brushed the side of his face.

"No need to fret, Wellington. The lake is man-made, not terribly deep—only fifteen feet at the most. We have dug three times that depth. That should prevent cave-ins." Maulik shrugged. "According to the math."

Wellington swallowed and hoped the director's math had been sound before leaving Bombay.

The train slowly progressed under Man Sagar Lake, until a yellow light set in the side of the map suddenly flared to life. "That's the engine." Maulik gripped the arms of his chair. "We're about to slip underneath the foundation. Hold on to something."

Wellington watched loose items dance over the floor again toward the far side of their car. They were definitely ascending, the angle growing steeper with their increasing speed.

"We're ready to breach," Maulik called over the growing rumble around them. "The booster rocket should engage any moment now."

The yellow light in the map switched to red, and they all lurched as a deafening roar came from the rear of their car. Wellington feared the Strategy Room would be torn apart, but the thrust lasted only a matter of seconds. A dull explosion ran through the whole structure before the carriage righted itself and became level with a sharp thud.

"Well, that was exhilarating, wasn't it?" Maulik said, releasing himself from the nook. "Shall we go?"

Wellington unbuckled himself from the seat and offered Eliza a hand. Once she came to her feet, he did the same for Sophia.

"Always the gentleman," Sophia purred as she stepped closer to him.

Eliza glared at the assassin.

"Ladies, please," Wellington said, before violence broke out. He then looked up in the direction of where the troops had gone. "No gunfire. A good sign, yes?"

"Could be the calm before the storm," Eliza replied, drawing her pounamu pistols.

"Or merely a tempest in a teacup," Sophia said.

Maulik waved a finger at the ladies, and surprisingly they subsided before punches were thrown.

Relieved, Wellington led the way into the empty training carriage. It had its walls down on the ground, acting as ramps that bridged the damaged landscape underneath. He proceeded down the platform, out of the car, and into the courtyard of Jal Mahal palace. They had missed the centre by a few hundred feet, emerging from one of the four grassy quadrants that surrounded a central octagon. Each corner of the Water Palace was decorated with domed pavilions, *chhatri* in Indian architecture.

"Charming spot, Jal Mahal," Maulik said, trundling up alongside Wellington, "for gatherings or ambushes."

"No one here, Agent Books," came O'Neil, appearing from behind one of the Palace's stone pillars. "Nothing out of the ordinary. I'll have my men take position."

"Something's not right," Wellington muttered.

Eliza looked up to him. "What are you seeing that I am not, love?"

"Nothing, and that is what scares me." He looked around the entirety of the Water Palace. "Vania had a good four-hour head start. Even with delays from the Railway Company, I am sceptical."

"You don't believe that maybe we've just hit on a stroke of good luck?" Eliza asked. "We actually beat Vania here…"

Wellington gave her a crooked smile. "Darling, if you really believed in good luck, you would have holstered your sidearms by now."

Eliza looked down at her weapons, then to Wellington. "I do hate it when you're right."

"We have the ElectriFlux that Agent Strickland designed," Maulik said, approaching from across the courtyard. "If the Ghost Rebellion appears, it should give us a few moment's notice."

"Director!" a voice called from behind them in the courtyard.

"Yes, Agent Gadhavi," Maulik said, "what have you got for me?"

"We just connected the leads to Strickland's device," the young man said, "when everything in its display lit up."

"Have you had time to calibrate it?"

"Sir, I would not know where to begin calibrating this thing. I just wanted to get it to work."

"No, this is all too easy," Wellington said. "Sophia, what were Nahush's orders to Vania?"

"She was sent ahead to place the targeting system for the electroporter."

He shook his head. "What were his exact words?"

She furrowed her brow, and twisted her mouth. "He needed her to travel to Jal Mahal and prepare it for their arrival."

Wellington looked around again, the growing dread in him now turning into a full-fledged panic. "Damn."

"What is it, Books?" Maulik asked.

"Vania didn't come to the Water Palace to set a targeting device," he said, catching the faint scent of copper in the air. "She came here to make the Water Place itself a targeting device."

Eliza saw what he was getting at immediately. "Call back your men!"

Maulik pressed a yellow button in the left arm of his chair, and a high-pitched whistle sounded twice. From surrounding alcoves came the scuffing of boots against stone.

"Director," Gadhavi began, "what about you?"

"Do not leave his side," Wellington insisted.

No sooner were the words out of his mouth than a crackle of white energy joined the corner pavilions and the main chhatri, creating an arc of light that circled the perimeter. The bolt of electricity froze there for several seconds before a sudden breeze swept through the courtyard. The branches of energy and light began to multiply, creating a blinding chain around the battlements of the Water Palace. Faster and faster the tendrils wound around them until light swept through the corridors encircling the courtyard. With a deafening thunderclap, the glare exploded, tossing the handful of men and women sprinting into the courtyard forward. They were the Ministry agents and cavalry that had heard the Director's call.

Wellington could see O'Neil helping those around him up to their feet. "Make for the train!" he cried out.

When the blast finally dissipated, he quickly took stock of their numbers. Combined, they now only numbered twenty-six. The electroporter was a two-way device, and the rebels had used that to their advantage, ripping away over half of their enemies in one strike.

In fleeting moments, Wellington saw they had gone from possessing the upper-hand in numbers, munitions, and tactical advantage, to taking a final stand in the centre of a killing box.

CHAPTER FOURTEEN

Wherein an Audience Is Held

Around them echoed the footsteps of what they knew to be the Ghost Rebellion. Wellington could not be certain if this was Nahush's phantom army in their entirety, but it was a good number of fighters, to be sure. With their limited ranks now huddled by the mole train, it would not be a final stand so much as a massacre. Their massacre.

They were well within sights of rifles. They had to be. So far, no one was daring to shoot.

"We can try to get back inside the train," Eliza offered up, her eyes tight on him. "Hold out from there."

"To what end? Provided we can get inside before being picked off like targets in a shooting gallery, any stand we make is our last."

"What about following the tunnel we made to get here?" Sophia asked, her grip tightening on her own pistol.

"Yes, a clever thought," Maulik said, "but there is the matter of that forty to fifty feet of distance between us and where the tunnel levels out."

Ranks of soldiers lined up, three deep and ten in length, at the far end of the courtyard. Moments later, Nahush Kari emerged from the perimeter. His tall, broad figure was hard to miss, but from where Wellington remained sheltered, the rebel's expression was impossible to read. Even harder to read was Vania Pujari, accompanying her true commander as they walked along the ranks.

It shouldn't have been a shock, but for a moment Wellington could have sworn it was Ihita. He could only imagine what Eliza might be thinking.

Sophia's eyes narrowed on the open corridors immediately across from their train. "We could make for that junction. It's close and there are not as many soldiers."

"No need to flank us" Eliza added. "They have at least four guns to our one."

"More importantly," Wellington said, "why haven't they opened fire, be done with us?"

"Wellington Thornhill Books," Nahush called out, his voice echoing across the courtyard. "I seek an audience."

All eyes slowly turned to Wellington.

He patted his left breast pocket. Excellent, he still had a few announcement cards there.

"Pull your men back from here," Wellington began, "and I will gla—"

A gunshot thundered in the courtyard, and a soldier next to O'Neil crumpled.

Maulik quickly hissed, "Do not return fire! Hold, everyone! Hold!"

"Mister Books," Nahush stated, "you are in no position to dictate terms, and I do not like to be kept waiting."

Wellington nodded to Eliza. She pointed her own pistol to the corridor across from them, and fired. A rebel slumped over the low stone wall.

"And you, sir, have chosen the oddest time and place to demand a social call," Wellington said. "I suggest you indulge me."

Eliza pulled back the hammer of her pistols during the silence. As much as Wellington loved chess, he did so hate stalemates.

Nahush finally spoke up, and Wellington took in a breath. "*Quid pro quo* it is then."

"Pull your people out of this junction, and I will gladly hold an audience with you."

Time crawled by. Nahush Kari was the kind of gentleman, apparently, who did not believe in giving any quarter to an opponent. "Come along," Wellington whispered, "how badly do you want this audience?"

The revolutionaries holding the junction across from them pulled back their weapons, and disappeared from view.

"Ready when you are, Mister Books," Nahush called.

"When you find a moment to get to that junction, Director," Wellington said, "do not hesitate."

"Are you seriously going off to entertain this known anarchist?" Maulik asked.

"I am a gentleman. I keep my word."

"You are gallant to the point of stupidity, Welly, do you know that?" Eliza snapped, locking her hand on his wrist. "I'm coming with you."

"Really?" he asked. "You think you are just going to saunter along with me, up to the leader of the Ghost Rebellion?"

"Actually," Sophia said, "Eliza will be to your right. I will be to your left."

"Now just a moment—" Wellington protested.

"Books," Maulik interrupted, "Kari is waiting."

His eyes jumped between Eliza and Sophia. For two women who loathed one another, they really were two peas in a pod. Quite insufferable.

With a final glance over his suit, just to make sure he was presentable, Wellington looked over their small number, tipped his bowler to them, and then started across the courtyard.

"What's your plan, Welly?" Eliza said, holstering her pistols.

"Working on one," he replied.

"Quite quickly, I hope," Sophia muttered.

The three of them remained quiet as they closed their distance with Nahush and his army. Wellington reached into his coat pocket and produced one of his announcement cards. Holding it between two fingers, he presented it to one of the most wanted men in the Empire.

"How civilised," Nahush said, holding up Wellington's card.

"Nahush Kari," Wellington said, clearing his throat and elevating his chin slightly, "I suppose there is no way I, as an appointed agent of Her Majesty the Queen of England and Empress of India, could convince you to surrender peacefully?"

"Let me see now," he said, tapping the announcement card in his open palm. "On account of the electroporter I have the English outnumbered four to one..."

"Well done, that."

"Thank you. I was rather proud of that tactic myself." When Nahush smiled, Wellington thought it suited him. "So, considering the circumstances, I think not."

"Right then." He glanced to either side of him, both ladies looking at him in anticipation. "So much for Plan A."

"*That*," Sophia whispered, "was your plan?"

"Keeping it simple," he replied. "Sometimes, simplicity is the best plan."

"I am siding emphatically with the Italian on this one," Eliza said with an angry shake of her head.

"Please," Nahush implored softly, "stop."

"I am hoping you and I can reach a peaceful resolution to this. We are, after all, part of the Empire," Wellington insisted.

Nahush's eyebrows rose. "You truly believe that? Even when you see how we are segregated in our own country, exploited for our resources, and repeatedly denied our own culture and prosperity, you still believe we are all part of some glorious utopia?" He closed in on Wellington, staring deep into his eyes.

Wellington found it difficult to hold the soldier's gaze. He believed in the idea. The reality was very different.

"So I thought," Nahush said.

"Is that why you betrayed the Ministry then?" Eliza, her voice carrying an edge as sharp as one of Sophia's blades, asked Vania. "Your friends, your colleagues, did you think of their families when you planned on killing them?"

"No more than the Ministry thought of mine," she replied, her voice low but angry.

"Hard to know what Ihita would say, considering—"

"She wanted what I want—a free India."

Wellington was trying desperately to keep his attention on Nahush and Vania, but something beyond the obvious was very wrong. The Ghost Rebellion, as Nahush had successfully done, held a clear advantage.

"So what exactly are you waiting for?" Sophia blurted out. The tirade between Eliza and Vania stopped abruptly. Nahush kept his own gaze fixed on Wellington as she continued. "You're here. We're here. Can we just move things along?"

"You could have gunned us down without a fuss after you arrived," Wellington stated, "but instead you call for an audience?"

Eliza looked to Vania, then to Nahush. "And we've been posturing like peacocks. Why?"

Movement from behind the ranks stole Wellington's gaze from Nahush. Four soldiers, armed only with large jugs, appeared from the open corridors of the Water Palace. He could see inside the containers gallons upon gallons of water sloshing back and forth.

Then came the slight man in their wake, dressed in a fashion proper for India. Linen suit. Pith helmet. High boots. Tinted spectacles that stood out in stark contrast against his own pale skin. In each of his hands he carried two sturdy cases. Wellington recognised them at a glance from his time collecting insects. They were designed for delicate work in collecting specimens, be those specimens fauna or floral.

"Oh, look at you," Dr Henry Jekyll gasped. "Even with our little dust-ups these recent years, we have been ships in the night. I never expected to see you again."

Wellington had only seen the good doctor from a distance—through the lenses of binoculars. Now, this close, a memory rushed towards him. He was just a boy, but he didn't like Uncle Henry. He especially did not like Uncle Henry when he smiled. His father always told him that this man would be his best friend. Yet every time Jekyll came to visit, he would place a tight grip on Wellington's shoulder. So tight, it scared him; but *she* was always there to intervene.

His mother's eyes would always follow Uncle Henry.

"Little Wellington," Jekyll said gleefully, "all grown up." Perhaps what stunned Wellington more than the vivid recollections of his childhood was how Doctor Henry Jekyll looked presently. It was as if his memory had come to life. Somehow Jekyll had avoided the touch of age. "It has been some time, hasn't it?"

"I—" Wellington cleared his throat, hoping that would make his words sound less faltering. "I would not forget you no matter how many years have passed, Doctor."

"Doctor? Not Uncle Henry?"

Every instinct inside Wellington was now begging for him to run. A bullet in the back was preferable to talking with this monster.

"Perhaps we should start with formalities and work our way back to familiarities," Wellington said, even as Eliza draw a little closer to his side.

"Very well," Jekyll said with a shrug. "We will not be taking up too much of the Queen's valuable time. Speaking of which, how is my royal patient?"

"Better," Eliza said with a dark frown, "now that you are no longer tending to her."

Jekyll crooked an eyebrow as his eyes turned to her, and Wellington's hand itched for a weapon. The flight instinct was now replaced with a hard, deep-seated urge to protect.

"We have not formerly met, have we?" He looked her over, and then said, "Henry Jekyll, doctor, physician, and atypical mad scientist."

Eliza nodded. "Eliza Braun. Agent of the Ministry, proud daughter of New Zealand, and regretful I did not place that tracer bullet between your eyes."

"Oh, that was you? Excellent shooting."

"This is why no one has fired a single shot," Wellington said, turning to Nahush. "Jekyll wanted to see me?"

"Well actually," Jekyll spoke before Nahush could answer, "I wanted to extend to you an invitation to join me."

"What?" came Wellington, Nahush, and Eliza, all at once.

"Oh dear," he groaned, "so dramatic."

"This was not what we agreed to," Nahush insisted. "You wanted me to bring you here for your precious flowers and water. Bringing this Englishman back was not part of the bargain."

"Nahush, old chap," Jekyll said, "you wanted an advantage in today's fight, and I believe I delivered what you wanted with great aplomb. Consider this a tip of the hat for a job well done."

"And what makes you think I will surrender to you without a fight?" Wellington asked.

Jekyll wore that smile Wellington remembered from his childhood, from terrible dreams he was now uncertain if they were merely dreams or something far worse. "Wellington, my boy, the choice is not yours to make."

"So, even if I were to ask in exchange for me, safe passage for the ladies and those with us?"

"I would guarantee it," Jekyll said, "but Nahush would be the one with a final say in the matter."

Sophia's blade caught the light for just an instant. The blade, a gear with its cogs filed down to a fine edge, sliced cleanly into Vania's hand, embedding itself into her flesh. The distraction of her howl and her crashing into Nahush was enough room for Wellington to charge the soldier closest to him.

The distraction also gave Eliza a moment to slip up to Jekyll and bring her knee square into the good doctor's crotch.

Gunfire rippled through the air, the Imperial forces and the Ghost Rebellion exchanging volleys as Wellington fell to the ground, wrestling the rifle out of the soldier's grasp. He shoved the fine wooden butt of the rifle into the man's face then quickly rolled to one side, firing round upon round in quick succession. He wouldn't know exactly how many he would manage before someone would take him out, but he was determined to take down as many as he could.

Something thrummed in his ears and rippled across his back. The concussion wave knocked a handful of soldiers in every direction. Wellington pulled himself up to one knee and cast a quick glance back to the train. A Ministry agent, her blonde hair still tossing in the breeze and armed with what had to be a Mule's Kick, was braced against the Training Car's ramp. Bravery was never in short supply with the Ministry.

A pair of hands grabbed Wellington under the arms and hoisted him to his feet. "We move," came the command, draped in a rich Italian accent, "now!"

"Bloody brilliant, taking a shot at Vania," he gasped as he followed on Sophia's heels to the outer wall.

"I was going to kill Jekyll," she snapped, "but too many eyes were watching. That was when I realised no one was paying attention to that irritating Vania woman."

"I didn't even consider that." He then looked around them, and grabbed hold of her jacket, spinning her to face him. "Where's Eliza?"

Sophia motioned with her head in the direction from where they had come. "I never interrupt a lady when she is enjoying herself."

Wellington's eyes went wide as he saw what she meant. Eliza was demanding Jekyll's full attention, spinning on one foot, her boot connecting—rather soundly—with the mad doctor's jaw. She stopped in her assault and said something to him, but from where they had taken shelter and the surrounding gunfire he could not make out exactly what.

The rifle came up to his shoulder, but then paused as he looked at Jekyll. "Sophia, give me a pistol."

"I beg your pardon? We are in the middle of—"

His tenor, he knew, could not have been more than a whisper, but she heard every word. "Dammit, give me a sidearm."

Sophia's lips pressed together.

"Please," he said as calmly as possible.

Her eyes narrowed as she flipped open a pouch on her belt. "Can you do this, Wellington?"

"He's turning," Wellington said, looking over the contraption that Sophia offered him. "I suppose we will find out."

The odd device looked appropriate for the assassin. At a glance, the weapon appeared as a set of knuckle dusters, but on closer inspection, folded within it, was a rudimentary blade and a detachable cylinder. He extended the knuckles fully, and quickly evaluated the pistol's balance. Crude, low calibre, but it would have to do. He now had six shots along with what was left in the rifle.

"Make every one count," Sophia said as if addressing a schoolboy.

"Always," Wellington replied.

I'm coming, Eliza, he thought as he stepped out of hiding, and into the mouth of madness.

Wherein Bruce and Ryfka Make a Friend

Just stay with me, Ryfka.

It had become Bruce's mantra since abandoning the truck. He had not stopped until the sun was up and the boilers were depleted. With the dashboard completely shorted out, there was no telling how close they were to the extraction point. Łódź could be just around the corner. It could be another day's travel. It was impossible to tell, but he had hoped for the former rather than the latter. They had been on the move for well over thirty hours, as far as Bruce could estimate. In the mad escape from Mama Bear's Cave, he had forgotten to wind his wristwatch.

Ryfka had been patched up as best as Bruce could manage, using snow to clean the wound and bits of the truck's canopy to bandage it. She needed stitches. She needed a clean dressing. She needed a proper doctor. Bruce had done what he could, and in the back of his mind, he knew it wasn't enough.

What…are you…doing, Bruce? Ryfka asked, her signing an effort akin to mountain climbing.

"We are not having this conversation again," Bruce both spoke aloud as well as signed. He couldn't be certain what she was able to see through exhausted eyes. Her complexion matched that of the snow as well. He just had to get her to the extraction point. "I am seeing this mission through, and I will not take any losses. Ya follow?"

Her head lolled from one side to the next. "Stubborn," she managed in an affected speech.

Bruce hoisted her up, managing a groan out of her. "Yeah, one of my more endearing qualities."

They pushed on through the thicket of trees, fallen branches cracking and snapping underfoot. A few yards ahead, though, Bruce noticed the trees were thinning out. A field was about to open up before them. Blessing or curse, Bruce wouldn't know until they got there.

"Ryfka, we're about to lose our cover," he said, stopping just short of the forest's edge. He peered through the barren branches. "There's a farmhouse up there. They might have something for you. Shall we give it a go?"

Ryfka looked up at him. *Your mission. Your call.*

He chuckled. "That's got to hurt, admitting that."

She furrowed her brow. *Poor choice of words.* Then she managed a wry grin, and signed, *Mate.*

Bruce nodded, and led her around the perimeter of trees to the farmhouse. With a glance to Ryfka, the two of them broke clear of the forest and hobbled over to the modest structure. The doors were secured with a lock. A lock Brandon could easily pick, but for Bruce? What he wouldn't give for a sidearm of any description.

"Wait a minute," he whispered, staring at the padlock.

The lock, the longer he looked at it, was a reminder of where he was. Welded and forged into it were buttons and gauges of all kinds. It appeared to be a pressure lock, albeit not one as sophisticated as you would find in Pommy-land but the same principle.

Bruce tapped Ryfka on her good shoulder, snapping her awake. "Do you still have the Remington-Elliot on you?" he asked her.

Ryfka motioned with her head to her pocket where Bruce fished out the pistol. Cracking the small weapon open, he pried out one of the spent shells. "This just might work."

He took the open end of the bullet casing and worked it between his teeth, folding the thin brass once then twice, making what appeared to be a less-than-precise lock pick. Ryfka watched as Bruce continued to work the metal as best as he could until finally the casing resembled nothing more than a crude nail.

That, she signed, *will never crack the lock.*

Bruce carried her to the other side of the barn and gently set her down. "Who said I was going to crack it?" he asked her, winking before heading back to the barn doors.

The sun was about to set. Extraction had to be closing in, and what he was about to attempt would either be a waste of time, or attract the attention of whomever lived here.

"Here we go," Bruce muttered as he jammed the ragged pick into the keyhole.

He waited for a few seconds, and then noticed one of its two gauges jitter. The needle was trying to accurately read pressure but couldn't quite understand if the lock was being tampered with, or if there was an actual key. For more sophisticated pressure locks, there were safeguards against what Bruce was doing. As this was a *schlockwork's* approach to security, he was banking on this sort of reaction.

He whipped back around to where Ryfka was trying to breathe through her pain. Seconds later, a loud crack like that of a bullwhip's strike echoed into the oncoming dusk. Bruce peeked around the barn to see a small mist of smoke around the padlock, now hanging useless on the chain.

"I'll have to pass this story on to Brandon," he said to himself, lifting Ryfka back to her feet.

His gaze went from left to right. Someone would be coming, for certain. Even in the case of one as homemade as this, a pressure lock would not be used to keep simple farm equipment in check. This bloke had something in there he wanted to keep under heavy guard. The door rumbled off to one side, and in the dim light coming into the barn, Bruce could make out a workbench and several mechanical creations of various sizes and shapes. These technological curiosities had been all cobbled together from appliances, tools, and devices never meant for cobbling together. Bruce could see clearly an automaton wheat thrasher. The scythe was expertly welded into a chassis that connected to a small steam engine. From the looks of the various axels and cogs, the scythe would make easy work of several acres. The engine also appeared to be connected to treads similar to their truck's, and behind all of this was a place for a driver.

"That's bloody clever," Bruce muttered as he dragged Ryfka to the workbench.

She winced on removing her coat. The shreds of canopy covering the wound were now saturated with blood, and that was not good. Russia's harsh winter had helped a bit in keeping the wound under control, but it would not heal her. He had to close that wound. Fast. He would have been concerned about his odds in helping Ryfka had it not been for the various tools and machinations in sight. All these little metallic beasties sported expert welding techniques.

His gaze fell on a bottle that was set apart from the wrenches, pliers, and spare parts. He removed the cork and took a whiff. The aqua vitae of Russia.

Bruce stepped in front of Ryfka and handed her the bottle. "Here," he said, stopping her hands as she was attempting to remove her blood-stained shirt. "Pull a few from this."

Ryfka let out a breath, her whole body trembling as she did, and then took a swig from the bottle. Her face twisted in disgust.

"It's vodka," he said, slowly lifting the shirt free of her body. "Thought you all loved that stuff." Ryfka shook her head. "You're joking, right?" She took another drink from the bottle and groaned after finishing the gulp. "This place just doesn't quit with the surprises."

He gently guided her arm free of the wide shirtsleeve. Normally, he would never be so gentle with undressing a lady, but considering the circumstances—and the fact she was a crack shot—he did his best not to glance at Ryfka's more intimate attributes.

"Well," he said, taking a closer look at the wound, "good news, the bullet's gone clean through, but you're still bleeding out." Bruce took the bottle from Ryfka, then he looked over to the worktable. He found a small belt the length of his forearm and offered it to her. "I need to perform some field medicine," he said, shaking the bottle lightly in his hand.

Ryfka nodded and folded the belt once before placing it in her mouth.

He poured the libation over the exit wound, and heard the belt she was biting into strain under her teeth. For her part, the sniper merely exhaled. The rush of pain was figuratively slapping sense back into Ryfka as she looked quite alert suddenly.

After a few deep breaths, she gave another nod and Bruce repeated the pouring, this time on the entry wound. After a few seconds, he traded the belt for the bottle.

Right then, that was the easy part.

"Ryfka, I have to cauterize the wound," he said to her, signing alongside his words. "There's an arc welder over here. Once I stop the bleeding, I hope to patch you up properly. Then we need to get going. Extraction is coming up quickly."

She nodded, even as she sagged backwards; exhaustion couldn't be far off for her. Time was running out.

Bruce flipped switches along the rusted, metallic box, his lips whispering a prayer that he was not simply firing up what could potentially be a small bomb capable of taking them out with the barn. The goggles left on top of the power supply clicked and clacked in his hands as he slipped them around his head. *Just stay with me, Ryfka,* he thought to himself as he waited for the welder to give him some indication it was ready. Lights were now changing from green to yellow, then red, the Russian script under them not his concern. He just wanted the bloody thing to work.

As it was with the experimental Brandon had employed in the factory, Bruce eased the ends of the welder itself together until they flared brightly. He looked along the worktable and found a slim strip of metal, which should do for the cauterizing. Bruce passed the end of it along the flame, watching carefully through his goggles to make certain he did not melt anything. Once the glow was consistent, he parted the rod tips and brought the goggles up to rest on his forehead. The small strip, even held out at arm's length, was putting out a lot of heat.

"This is going to hurt," he began, ignoring the pounding in his chest. "A lot."

Ryfka took a swig of the strangely dark vodka, then returned the folded belt back into her mouth.

"All right, here we—"

"*STOP!*" came a voice from behind him.

The command nearly sent Bruce toppling into Ryfka. He spun around to stand at his full height, the red-hot strip of metal held over his head as if it were a club. Albeit, a very small, very hot club.

If Bruce had sneezed, he believed it would have knocked the frail man to the ground. He was shorter than Ryfka, his skinny frame barely filling the grey overalls of what Bruce assumed would belong to a factory worker. The stranger peered at them through spectacles that not only covered the entirety of his eye sockets but magnified his eyes, making them appear bloated and freakish. He looked to be in his forties, and he also looked tired. All these things—his fatigue, frame, poor eyesight, and height—would have made this bloke an easy target for Bruce...

...except for the rifle-like weapon he held them under. The same kind of creation he saw Mama Bear use on them in their escape. That could not be a coincidence.

"What—" he began, his fingers splaying slowly around the rifle, "—do you think you're doing?"

He must have overheard him speaking English. Lovely. "I need to cauterize this wound, or she's gonna die."

The weapon powered down and was then leant up against the inside of the barn door in one swift act as the man shook his head madly from side-to-side. "No-no-no-no-no, are you mad?" he asked, his accent rolling and flowing even through the broken English. "You will only infect wound and make things worse for poor girl."

Bruce lowered the strip of heated metal. "Well then..." He pulled the goggles off his head, watching the Russian scamper throughout the workshop. Wasn't he about to gun them both down? "What do we need to do?"

"First," he said, "we must cauterize wound."

He held up the metal in his grasp, its red glow dimming but still putting out a good amount of heat. "Isn't that what I was doing here, mate?"

"Da, but you cauterize wound as *kak karova ha l'udi*," he said, snatching the strip from Bruce's gasp. Little bugger was quick.

"What the hell does that mean, mate?"

"Like cow...on ice."

The man tapped on Ryfka's good shoulder, making her start slightly. "I will cauterize wound. This will hurt." He then beckoned Bruce over to them. "You will want to hold her steady."

Bruce's brow furrowed as the man poured onto a small cloth a white, powdery substance. He shared a look with Bruce who put his arms around Ryfka to brace her.

There was no hiss of heat against skin. There was no smell of burnt flesh. The Russian merely applied the kerchief of white powder against Ryfka's exit wound. With the belt trapped between her teeth, Ryfka let out a muffled scream, and jerked madly.

"Hold her!" the man insisted, keeping the kerchief on her. "Must keep it on wound for few seconds."

Good to his word, the man removed the cloth from Ryfka, and Bruce stared at the blackened, soot-like appearance where the kerchief had been. The exit wound was now closed.

"What is that stuff, mate?"

"Silver nitrate," he replied, pouring a fresh new helping of it on to the kerchief. "You cleanse wound with vodka, *da?*"

"How did you know?"

"I only have two drinks from that bottle," he said, motioning to the bottle in Ryfka's firm grip. "Bottle nearly finished. Lady still sitting upright, meaning she does not drink much."

"Good eyes, mate," Bruce said.

"One more time," he said to her, just before applying the powder to the back of her shoulder.

Again, Ryfka bucked and growled, but eased into Bruce's hold once the man removed the kerchief from her. He tossed it aside and then reached for what looked like a replacement shirt. "This for you, once I bandage you." She looked up at him, confused. "Your friend, here. Must be hard of hearing."

"Who the bloody hell are you, mate?" Bruce finally asked.

"Dmitri Vladimirovich Yurganakov," he said as he started winding fresh, proper bandages around her shoulder. "I work at factory you nearly destroy."

"Hold on," Bruce said, glancing at the rifle-creation by the door. Might as well had been in London. "You work with the House of Usher?"

Dmitri looked at Bruce with his magnified eyes, then spat on the ground. "I say I work at factory. Not the same."

"So what do you do at the factory?" Bruce asked.

"I design weapons for Bears. As you can see, I like to tinker." he said, motioning around him. "When you tinker, accidents happen. So I know what to do." Dmitri tightened a strip of gauze in place before tucking it into one of its folds. Once the bandage was secured with tape, he motioned to the shirt in Ryfka's lap, then turned to join Bruce. "Give lady privacy while we talk."

Bruce nodded to her, and then turned to peer down at Dmitri. "Should I ask why you are helping us, mate?"

"What these Usher people do, is not good." Dmitri glanced out of the half-open door. "What you do to Usher, I like. Instead of many Bears, Usher now have four."

"Four?"

"And all are looking for you. Following east as you leave through East Perimeter. You are now south. This buys you time."

"Not a lot," Bruce said. "They'll probably look at closest towns, villages, and the like. And we are running out of time. Our extraction won't wait for us."

"Girl must rest."

"That's not going to happen," he returned. "I've got to get her out of here."

A hard knocking came from the worktable behind them. Ryfka was now in the new shirt, presumably Dmitri's although she filled it far more impressively, Bruce believed, than Dmitri would.

"You need to travel quickly?" he asked Bruce.

"Yeah, we do, mate."

The small man nodded, then walked past the two of them. He grabbed the corner of a tarp and pulled, sending dust and hay in all directions. For a moment, Bruce couldn't see their unexpected saviour. Then, the dust settled and he could see Dmitri gently stroking the handlebars of an impressive motor-bicycle. The design was a bit reminiscent of the Excelsior & Eureka's latest model he'd seen toodling around the countryside, but with a few modifications. This motor-bicycle was broader, both in the frame and in the engine. The other difference was, evidently, Dmitri's touch with a sidecar welded to the right of it. It was a thing of beauty, it was. Just a sight for...

"Mate?" Bruce called out to Dmitri. "You all right there?"

"Da." Dmitri had removed his glasses and was now staring at the motorcycle, his gaze not one of pride but of loss. "This—" He cleared his throat, and then went silent. Bruce was suddenly afraid to move. "This was something I made with my wife. Kristina loved rides across countryside."

Bruce had seen that look before. In Brandon's face. "That's why you're helping us."

"Usher did not appreciate Kristina's engineering talent. They had her working on Bear prototype. Hull design inferior. She say so. As design belong to Mama Bear, she insist Kristina pilot prototype. First test run, Bear collapse on itself. Mama Bear send wreckage to forge for repurposing."

"She didn't bother to get Kristina out of the wreckage, did she?"

Dmitri took a deep breath. "Motorcycle ready to go. If Usher comes, I will stand ground."

Bruce nodded. "Thanks."

"You slow down Mama Bear," he said, walking over to the rifle. He picked it up and then looked back at the two of them. "Next time, kill her. She will not stop until mission complete."

"What mission?"

Dmitri looked across the snowy field outside the barn. The light was dying, but Bruce could see in his eyes an acceptance. There would be consequences, but Dmitri was ready.

"Ragnarök," the Russian muttered.

⤙⟾ ⟾⤚

In Which Our Plucky Pepperpot and Alluring Assassin Strike an Unlikely Accord

"This is for Callum," Eliza growled as she slammed her knee into Jekyll's crotch.

The howl he let out was satisfying, but her appetite for revenge was barely sated.

"This is for Her Majesty," she said, before leaping into the air. The leg she had bent served as an extra pivot in her hips for her trailing leg to strike out whip-like. The top of her boot connected with the underside of Jekyll's chin. His head snapped up, and he staggered back a few steps.

The sensible thing to do would have been to take cover as gunfire ricocheted around the courtyard, but this felt far too satisfying.

When Jekyll climbed upright again, Eliza spun on one foot, while the other swung up, and now it was her boot heel that connected with his face.

The bastard was still standing.

Jekyll chuckled just a little as he rubbed his jaw. "Is that for little Wellington?"

"Oh no," she said, with a wag of her finger. "Recompense for that is going to take much longer."

He didn't see the blow coming as her fist connected soundly with his hawk-like nose. Blood splattered over her knuckles, and the crack that sounded made her smile.

"Oh you're a feisty one," he gasped as he wiped his lip. "Have you taken a shine to my protégé?"

"If Wellington Books is anything to you—" And this time, without flair or fanfare, Eliza kicked him in the chest, not quite centre but where she knew it would deal the most damage. The strike knocked him back several feet. "—he is the one that got away—*far away*—from you."

"And yet—" Why was this wanker still laughing? He had a broken nose. From the sound of the rattle coming from his breathing, he had at least one broken rib, and yet he found all this funny? "—here we are. You think it merely Fate or Chance that brings us here?"

"Bad luck," she said, before running at him and firing off another kick for his ribs. "For you."

The slap of her leather boot against his hand rang clearly over the gunfire around them. She had come to a stop, nowhere close to her mark. His fingers tightened around her foot as he held her there, studying her as if she were a specimen under glass. Then his cold eyes went black. Completely black, making the orbs appear like hollow pits set in his face.

"Bad luck?" he asked her, blood spraying from between his lips. "Allow me to show you just how bad your luck is today, missy."

A shot sounded behind her, and Jekyll's body jerked back. She stumbled and hit the ground. Jekyll only sank to one knee.

Then something cracked. It sounded again, and again.

Eliza knew gunfire, but this noise was like taut rope snapping when pulled beyond its breaking point. She then realised the sounds were coming from Jekyll. His bones were cracking, his muscles stretching. He was growing before her.

Another shot rang out as Jekyll thrust out his monstrous hand. His laugh now sounded more like deep grunts as he slowly opened his undulating fist. The bullet fell from his hand and bounced against the courtyard.

"Get to cover, darling," Wellington called, working the bolt of his rifle. "I have an appointment with the good doctor here. One a long time coming."

It was Wellington coming closer to her, but she didn't recognise him. He had a dead stare in his eyes, that same one as he had at the Army & Navy Building. In his words and inflection, though, she heard him. It was her Wellington. She hoped he could keep control of whatever this doctor had created in him.

The archivist shouldered the rifle and fired again. His hand worked the bolt so quickly, it caused Eliza to blink. That was just not humanly possible. The next shot knocked Jekyll over, but he leapt upright just as quickly. It was not a mistake or her eyes playing tricks: Jekyll had doubled in size, and his smile stretched literally from one ear to the other.

The rifle was ready for another shot, but this time, only the *click* of the trigger came.

"Trust me, Eliza," Wellington said, tossing the rifle aside, while his gaze never left Jekyll. Instead he drew from his pocket an Apache revolver—God only knew where he got one of those. "I will be fine. Take cover, stop the Ghost Rebellion. This is my fight."

She had never seen that look on his face. Complete and total commitment. Far be it from her to deny him this.

"Little Wellington," roared Jekyll. "Come sit on Uncle Henry's knee?"

Eliza was transfixed. She watched as her lover held out the revolver and began shooting, quickening his pace towards Jekyll with each shot. The monstrous man swung an arm, now the size of a tree trunk, across Wellington's path. However, the archivist slipped beneath the backhand attack, tucking and rolling under the arm and firing two shots into Jekyll's chest. Perhaps it was the calibre he was using or the massive flesh Jekyll's torso was comprised of, or a combination of both, but the mad doctor only stumbled a step backward.

"Stings a bit," Jekyll growled.

Wellington slipped his fingers into the knuckle duster. Unless he could get another weapon with a bit more stopping power, it was going to be fisticuffs, which would not last long against this monster.

She couldn't stay here to watch. Bullets were eating their way closer to her. Getting to her feet, Eliza sprinted for the closest cover. Shots whizzed by as she zig-zagged across the courtyard and found a corner shielded from the Ghost Rebellion's ranks.

It was there she stumbled over Sophia del Morte. *"Vaffanculo!"*

Eliza drew her own signature pair. "Must admit—never pegged you for a pistol girl."

"I adapt to my surroundings," she stated, half-climbing over Eliza. "Now, if you will excuse me."

She popped her head out only for a moment, ducked back, raised her pistols, and on leaning out released an impressive volley from their vantage point.

When Sophia returned to their shared hiding spot, Eliza watched her for a moment as she quickly replaced spent shells with fresh ones. "You know, this is an excellent hiding spot, but I for one would rather not stay here if we don't have to."

Sophia looked up from her pistols, green eyes flashing. "Meaning?"

It was time to trust her enemy. Again. "We need to get around them, box them in."

Sophia raised an eyebrow at the notion. "Really? And for this risk, exactly what am I to gain?"

Eliza's forearm struck Sophia's chest, pushing her against the Palace's red sandstone. "Wellington needs our help as do the members of Her Majesty's infantry and the Ministry of Peculiar Occurrences. Performing a selfless, heroic act for these brave men and women could change their perception of you, wouldn't you agree?"

Eliza was able to read the flickers of emotion on the assassin's face. Rage, comprehension, and then finally, chilly acceptance. They both knew the odds.

However, when Eliza released Sophia she gave her a slight shove as a reminder of who was in charge. "Follow my lead," Eliza said.

The two women emerged from their corner, four pistols firing into the melee. Shadows were appearing from the palace's surrounding archways. The rebels were fortified, for the time being.

"Focus on visible infantry," she called out to Sophia as they continued backward.

"Contact Left," Sophia called, turning one of her pistols on a target taking aim from a pavilion.

"Go, run!" Eliza called to her, firing a final shot before sprinting the remaining feet to an open corridor of the palace.

"Eliza!" a voice called out.

From the opposite end of the hall, she could see O'Neil waving.

"Keep firing," she reminded Sophia before sprinting towards him.

He and Director Smith had taken a position in an alcove connecting two corridors. Both seemed none the worse for wear, though O'Neil kept his rifle at his shoulder.

"Now would be a good time for the appearance of your Queensbury Rules, Maulik," Eliza said, checking her own pistols.

"I dare not on account of Wellington in the fray," the director said, patting the mounted Gatling cannon in his chair.

Sophia ran up to join them, her pistols now dumping empty shells at her feet. "Eliza suggested a pincer movement," she said while reloading.

"Our intention as well," O'Neil replied with a frown, motioning to the eight others with them, "but our numbers are rather thin. We have a unit of twelve attempting to hold that junction while we work our way around to the other side of the palace."

"What about that Mule's Kick?" Eliza asked. "That could give us quite an advantage."

"Agent March!" Maulik called out.

The young agent stepped forward, her blue eyes bright and her blonde hair loose around her face. From her expression, combat such as this was something new and she was enjoying it immensely. "Yes, sir?"

"Agent Ellie March, this is Agent Braun. You two should get along swimmingly."

"Excellent shooting back there," Eliza said. Her smile faltered as she saw the young agent armed with a standard Bulldog. The odd experimental Wellington had used on the *African Sunset* was dangling from March's belt. "Why aren't you using the Mule's Kick?"

"The charge," she said, glancing down at it. "It takes a spell or three before she's ready."

"Any way you can speed up the process, perchance?"

March bit her lip, a sweet gesture in the midst of a firefight. "The clankertons did give us a basics in maintenance, but when it came to modifications, they were insistent about us not tinkering with its inner-workings."

"Well damn that," Eliza said, removing the weapon from March's belt. "At this point we need to get creative."

"O'Neil, I suggest you give Wellington cover fire," Maulik said, wheeling over to the open junction of their corridor. "I will make sure we have no unwanted callers."

"You heard Director Smith," O'Neil called out. "Find a window. Cover Books."

Eliza whacked the handle of the pistol against the floor until one of its wood panels popped off, revealing a wide array of wires, gears, and small orbs that pulsated in time with the slow, rhythmic ticking of its mechanics. Two she immediately identified as leading to power sources, based on the heat and light the orbs gave off.

"Exactly what are we looking at?" Sophia demanded, peering into the Mule Kick's inner workings.

"Safety measures, power regulators," March replied. The young girl knew her weapons. "Or more importantly things to insure you don't go 'boom' when you pull the trigger."

"These bits and bobs are reasons I am not particularly happy with experimentals in the field," Eliza said, following the wiring with her eyes. "They are supposed to make weapons like these work efficiently, but not to their potential."

"Are you tinkering with an experimental during a combat situation?" Sophia asked.

"Oh bloody brilliant, this is!" March said excitedly.

Eliza rather liked this girl.

"It's not like I've done it before," Eliza assured them as she held a pair of fingers over one of the glowing orbs. Then, on moving to the other, "All right then, this one is the temperature regulator."

Sophia fixed a hard stare on her. "You do understand these sciences, yes?"

"Hardly," she said, pinching the small orb between her fingernails until it finally popped out of its housing, "but I know enough about modifying weapons to be dangerous. It's all a matter—oh bugger all, these wires are small!" she swore.

Sophia reached up and pulled out two hairpins from her head. "I do hope you are a fan of Far Eastern cuisine."

"I am from New Zealand, so I have run missions in China, Japan, and Korea," Eliza replied, taking the two pins into her free hand and balancing them between her fingers. She tested the pinching action she could manage from them and nodded, "and I adore sushi."

The hairpins dug into the mess of wires, weaving their way through to the one Eliza needed. The red one. How she loved the colour red.

"Right then," she said, capturing it in her grasp. "Just give it a little *tug*," and sparks flew from the array. "Now I just need to find—" and her hairpins trapped a green wire and pulled it free as well. She returned the fine pins back to Sophia and then, with her fingertips, Eliza twisted the frayed ends of each wire together. "This is what we call a Christmas Surprise. The green wire is usually tied in with the firing mechanism. In a sense, what I am doing—"

"You are bypassing the temperature regulator," Agent March spoke quickly, her cheeks seeming to glow as she added, "which was slowing down the energy build process. This Christmas Surprise has now cut the charging process to half the time. It could also increase the Kick's output." Eliza and Sophia stared at the young agent for a moment. Agent March giggled. "I really do love Science."

Once the connection was secure, Eliza flipped the Mule's Kick over to look at the power gauge. It was quickly reaching a maximum charge.

Eliza called out, "O'Neil, are you ready?"

"Yes, ma'am!" he replied. He got in one more shot before calling out, "Move people. To the junction!"

The mix of Ministry and military sprinted for the junction where Maulik waited, his gloved fingers tapping nervously against the triggers of his Queensbury Rules. Ahead of them, they could hear the rebels coming. "I do believe the Ghost Rebellion are on their way."

"Agent March," Eliza said, releasing the safety on the Kick, "back to the front lines with you. Sophia, get behind me."

The assassin inclined her head. "I am using you as a shield?"

Eliza gave her a wry grin. "Not today. Just brace me. There's a reason it's called the Mule's Kick." She then called out to the troops as Sophia took position behind her. "Hold your fire on my mark!" Eliza glanced at the Mule's Kick and took in a deep breath. "Ready, Sophia?"

"Ready," she replied, her breath hot on Eliza's neck.

Eliza pulled the trigger, and waited. The seconds ticking by felt like those when facing Featherstone.

The cries of the rebels echoed around them as the first of their numbers came out of the shadows.

Then the handle began to vibrate.

"Now!" she shouted, leaning forward.

Sophia's hands pressed against Eliza's shoulders as the blast from the Mule's Kick threatened to send her back into the junction. Instead she remained upright as the energy rippled along the walls, floor, and ceiling, knocking all the rebels in every direction. They were either given a good thrashing when thrown into their comrades or a quick death when thrown into the ceiling or wall.

Military and Ministry charged into the falling dust of the experimental's attack, leaving Sophia and Eliza behind. The Mule's Kick weighed incredibly heavy in her hand, but had most assuredly proven its worth.

"Well done," Sophia said. "We are still alive. That is an accomplishment."

Eliza felt a reply on the tip of her tongue, but then her hand—or the object in her hand—began to vibrate. She looked down at the Mule's Kick. It was powering up once again.

"What is the matter?" Sophia asked.

Eliza swallowed hard. "We might have a problem."

⊷⊜◠⊷

Wherein the Ministry's Finest Make a Noble Final Stand

The Russian winter tore at Bruce's hands and cheeks. Through the riding goggles, the light snow did not seem to be falling so much as it was rushing at him. It gave him the illusion that he was moving faster than he actually was, but much to Dmitri's credit both he and Ryfka were making incredible time. The darkness and incoming weather, however, did very little to boost Bruce's confidence.

He pried his eyes away from the road to look down at the sidecar to his right. Bundled in blankets was Ryfka, and from the looks of how she was sitting, it was impossible to tell if she were conscious or even alive.

Stop thinking that way, Bruce chided himself silently. *If she were dead, she'd be flopping around like a damned fish on the pier. She's still with you. Still in the game.*

He glanced down at the compass set within the dash of the bike. They were still on course. The road Dmitri had told them to follow was just as he said—a straight path to Łódź. Just follow the road, keep an eye on the compass, and stop for nothing. So far, the plan was working. Bruce had promised his mate Brandon a pint. He was determined to make good on that promise.

A dull thud cut through the sound of wind and motorbike engine, and then a tree in front of them burst into flames, knocking branches, snow, and sheets of bark in front of him. Bruce swerved, feeling the bike threaten to spin out of control. Another thud, and then another. Patches of trees disappeared behind walls of dirt, smoke, and flame. He glanced down at Ryfka, who was straining to look behind them. She forced herself to turn an inch further and then she slumped back into the sidecar. Her hands worked free of the blankets and she signed just one word.

Bear.

Bruce had to hope they were close. If they could just get to Łódź, they could have a chance of evading Mama Bear and her Houseboys. Right now, on this road, they were a peach ripe for the picking.

The trees suddenly disappeared, and up ahead they could make out the dim lights of a city, dark rooftops with smoke slipping out from chimneys, the spire of a church reaching high into the darkness. Bruce could also see the silhouettes of factories, all of them dark. The people of Łódź were either enjoying a nightly round at their favourite pub or settling in for a good night's sleep.

What a shame. The Bears thundering behind them were not going to be so considerate of the time.

Another thud, and to their left snow, dirt, and flame exploded into every direction. The Bear's arsenal was impressive, but their targeting systems needed work. Still, their motor-bicycle was far easier to narrow on, now free of the forest cover. Bruce fixed his gaze on the outskirts of the city. He could see the details of the factories emerging from the shadows. This close to the extraction, he was not going to give Mama Bear any opportunity to steal this great escape from him.

A wall of fire rose from the road in front of him. Bruce turned the handlebars to the right, and then leaned left. The sidecar lifted up along with Ryfka shifting in her seat to provide a better balance. Bruce scrunched lower in his own seat as the fire attempted to snatch him off his bike, but it could not claim him or fail to throw his balance and concentration. The bike's two wheels continued to grip the snowy road as they maneuvered around the shell's impact. Ryfka bounced lightly in her sidecar as her wheel returned to the ground. Moments later, they were speeding down a snow-covered street surrounded on either side not by trees but by white stone buildings.

Bruce checked the compass. Once in the city, he had to reach the town centre, and from what Brandon had told him in their trip to Germany, Łódź made for an exceptional extraction point as the main street—the one he was on—eventually led to a circle in the heart of the city. That was where Brandon would be, provided they were not too late.

"Almost there," he muttered to himself as the buildings disappeared by him in a blur.

Łódź's town circle open up before him, all its surrounding structures appearing as stone giants gathered round a central point. Bruce throttled back the motorcycle, bringing their ride to a halt at an obelisk set in the centre of the courtyard.

Snow languidly fell around them. The quiet was unsettling. Bruce wriggled his fingers, a hint of warmth returning to his digits. His cheeks stung. Nothing a bit of salve and a good shot of whisky couldn't cure. He looked up at the stone pillar looming over them, his eyes stopping at the illuminated clock near its top. 9:18. Had they missed the window?

Bruce stepped out into the courtyard, casting his eyes everywhere. Nothing moved. All the windows were dark. They were alone here.

Damn.

The snow crunched underfoot as he returned to the motorcycle. He knelt by the sidecar and pushed back the covers. *How are you, Ryfka?* His fingers felt stiff, but he knew signing would bring some life back to them.

Exhausted, Ryfka signed. She looked better than she did on arriving at Dmitri's farm, but it wasn't as if she were ready for a night of dance, drink, and song. *You did it.*

Bruce bit his bottom lip. *In a manner of speaking, yeah.*

Ryfka stared at him for a moment, then reached out and touched his cheek. He suddenly became aware of how long it had been since he shaved.

"I'm sorry, Ryfka," he admitted, not bothering to sign. She would know what she said.

The woman smiled, and shook her head. The smile faded as she looked over his shoulder.

They are coming.

Bruce tilted his head to one side, but a tightness welled in his throat as he heard a rhythmic *thump-thump-thump* coming from all sides. The first Bear appeared in the street just ahead of him. There were two others, one pounding up on the left with another coming in from the right. Perhaps the fourth one was outside of city limits, just in case Bruce pulled a magic trick out of his hat.

Oh yeah, that's right. He wasn't wearing a hat.

The Bears all hissed to a halt. Their Maxims were not trained on them, however. They just sat there. It was not as if they had cut off all exits, but Bruce would not have been able to get the bike up and running again before these beasties cut him and Ryfka down. Still, they were making no movement closer. They were watching him. Perhaps, assuring themselves it was all over and done with?

The centre Bear hissed again, and emerging from it was the babushka. Mama Bear was still short, still squat, still a little old lady cut from stone harder than granite, only this time her head was covered not by a kerchief but a soft helmet, its ears flopping as she walked towards him. He would have laughed at her if he didn't know what a monster she truly was.

Bruce stood, but Ryfka gently took hold of his wrist. He looked down at her. *Stay,* she signed.

Of course, he replied.

Yeah, let that little terror come to them. Don't make this easy for her.

She came to a stop and looked him over from head to foot. "You are most impressive, Bruce," she stated.

"You too. Mate of mine told me you didn't stop until the mission was done."

She looked at their bike, and nodded. "Dmitri was quite talented."

You old bitch. "Good value, Dmitri. So was his wife."

The corner of Mama Bear's mouth twitched at that.

"Long way from home," she said, pulling out from her coat a pistol. No mods. Just a simple, six-shooter pistol. Very practical. Very Russian. "To die so far from there. Must be heart-breaking."

Oh, so she wanted to gloat a bit? "You think I'm dyin' tonight, Mama Bear?" Bruce gave a gruff laugh. "I'm not gonna give ya' that sort of satisfaction. Besides, we're not done with ya' from where I stand."

"Bears surround you from three sides. You try to run, we shoot you in leg. We drag you back to girl. I shoot girl in head, then finish you."

"That's what I want you to think," Bruce said. "This was all part of my plan. I gotcha right where I want ya."

The rocket sailed from somewhere above him and struck Mama Bear's tank. Its explosion made both of them jump along with the Bear itself. The machine then collapsed after returning to earth.

"Crikey," Bruce said. "I was bluffing."

Mama Bear turned her pistol on Bruce. However, the opportunity to end his merry chase disappeared in a flash. The darkness around them suddenly became nothing but brightness. Bruce was knocked back into the sidecar where Ryfka's arm went around him. Once the grey and black spots faded from his view, he could just make out Mama Bear on the ground. She was merely dazed, but now unarmed. Her gun sizzled against the fresh snow on the ground. The sidearm appeared to be warped in some way. It was bowing at the centre from where whatever stuck it and sent them both flying.

"Bruce!" a voice called from across the courtyard.

He made the mistake of following the voice and the second flash blinded him again. He slipped against the sidecar, fighting back those damned black and grey spots on hearing the sound of crackling electricity and generators spinning down.

Bruce's vision had only just returned for him to catch sight of a small rocket sail across the town circle and strike hard into another Bear. The remaining tank had managed to lumber backward, catching only a glancing blow from the attack.

"Bruce," Brandon said, lifting him up to his feet, "you had me worried there for a spell."

"Get Ryfka. She's coming with."

Brandon gingerly took her hand. "Poor thing's cold to the touch."

"It's Russia, mate. *Everyone's* cold." He turned to the final tank and could just make out its cannons coming to bear. "Time to run," he said, draping Ryfka's bad arm over his shoulders.

The three of them hobbled in the direction from where Brandon had appeared. Behind them, the motorcycle erupted. Bruce's footing slipped a bit when the concussion wave slapped into them, but he pushed forward, an operative waving ahead of them serving as the carrot to his horse. He didn't know if there was a medic or a full extraction team on the other side of that door, but whomever waited for him, he knew, would be of a better disposition than Mama Bear and her remaining tank.

Stepping into the dark, Ryfka was suddenly jerked from between him and Brandon, and then...

"Hello, sweetie."

A sudden desire to dash back outside and take his chances with Mama Bear nearly overwhelmed Bruce. "Beatrice?" he asked.

Still a foot taller than him. Still imposing, especially with the Lee-Metford-Tesla in her grasp. Still a befuddling—if not completely stunning—mix of lethal force and graceful beauty, Beatrice Octavia Muldoon considered him with her brilliant blue eyes. Bruce was frantically trying to recall how Beatrice and he parted after the events of the Diamond Jubilee. He remembered her standing over him as if she were a child of Ares and Aphrodite, her high cheekbones appearing even harder in the early shadows of a magic hour just after she had knocked him on his ass. The cross to his jaw had served as a harsh reminder not to make bold assumptions of the lady.

"What the bloody hell are you doing here, Bea?" Bruce finally managed.

She was about to answer, but through the floor he could feel that rhythmic *thump-thump-thump* again.

"Priorities, Bruce," she said, throwing the rifle over her shoulder. "We've got a flight to catch. Party of two."

"Three," Bruce quickly corrected her as he motioned to Ryfka under what looked like the care of the extraction team's medic. "Górski here is coming with us."

The woman's face darkened slightly before turning to the bloke checking on Ryfka. "Fischer?"

"I don't know about three," he replied. "Weight concerns."

"We'll make it work," Bruce insisted. "Let's get a move on."

Beatrice shook her head, then beckoned them to follow her. "That tank will be upon us in a few, so come on. Through the back door."

Bruce and Brandon took up Ryfka, and followed Beatrice and the one called Fischer—a sturdy gent that didn't look like he could move fast, but his pace was damn impressive—to a solitary door at the back of the building. Beatrice was frantically shooing them across the threshold as the thumping underfoot grew stronger.

"They're getting closer," Fischer said. "From the feel of the floor, five minutes, if that."

"How did you convince the extraction to stay put?" Bruce asked Brandon as they climbed into a truck cab. It was going to be a tight fit for the three of them.

"Miss Muldoon took one look at me and asked 'You're the mission?' to which I replied that I was working with you." Brandon shrugged. "Suddenly we weren't leaving until you got here."

Well, fancy that.

The building behind them exploded, a large plume of smoke and fire rising from where they had all been.

"Hang on, everyone," Beatrice called over her shoulder as their transport lumbered away into the night.

"What about your men with the rockets?" Bruce asked.

"Autolaunchers." Fischer said, opening the throttle to coax more speed. "Designed them back in my Department days. The targeting system is based on a network of magnets." He craned his neck to talk over his shoulder. His smile puffed out his already round cheeks even more. "As the surrounding buildings were mainly comprised of white stone, those tanks made for an easy lock on. You see, I had originally calibrated the autolaunchers for trucks like this one. You can see with the amount of metal that—"

"Fischer," Beatrice said, spinning up the transformers mounted in the stock, "you're doing it again."

"Sorry, Miss Muldoon."

"Just keep your eyes peeled and get us out of town."

If there was no resistance, it would be a smooth, uninterrupted drive from here to the German border. So far, from the sounds of where they left, Mama Bear was determined to raze anything to the ground between her and Bruce. For their own part, their truck was now only a block from the edge of the city. Bruce could only assume it would be a trip down this road to an awaiting airship, cross over the Germanic border, and then a lovely cruise home. Easy as pudding.

"Contact," Fischer said.

Up ahead, a line of Houseboys took a position across their path. Mama Bear was obviously leaving nothing to chance.

"How far away is our airship?" Bruce asked.

Beatrice kept her eyes fixed on the road ahead. "We're not meeting an airship."

"Come again, Bea?"

"Be a dear, Bruce, and shut it!" she snapped. "Do we have enough road?"

"With the extra passenger? I'm not certain," Fischer replied. He stroked his blonde goatee, then took hold of a red lever over his head. "We could just barrel right through them."

"No, Paul," she said as she released the safety on her rifle. "We need to clear the tree line."

"Care to let me in on this little plan of yours?" Bruce asked.

"Just hold on and pray," she replied.

Their truck was picking up speed. Bruce could see Houseboys now completely blocked the road returning them into the forest cover. It was impossible to see exactly what kind of guns they were brandishing, and that was a bit irksome.

"Give the word, Beatrice," Fischer said.

"Not yet."

They pressed on. Bruce could see Fischer's hand gripping something under the dashboard while his free hand kept the wheel steady. "Anytime, Bea."

"Pull that now," she warned, "and this will all be for naught. Hold. Steady."

Their truck continued to rumble forward. Bruce could now see the House shouldering their rifles, the lights of mini-generators flaring to life causing Bruce's throat to tighten.

"She knows what she's doing, Bruce," Brandon said. His mate leaned forward in his seat and then said to Beatrice, "You do know what you are doing?"

"Not now, Hill," Beatrice muttered as she pulled her own rifle closer, flipping a third switch in its main transformer. Bruce knew the Lee-Metford-Tesla Mark IV, thanks to Shillingworth. That feature was something new. "Bruce, love, can you reach my coat?"

"Sure thing, Bea," he said, leaning forward as best as he could to take hold of Beatrice's coat tail. He wrapped it several times around his hand and wrist. "Hope your tailor is worth their salt."

"Gieves & Hawkes," Beatrice said as she opened her door. "Paul, get ready. This is going to go quick."

As she leaned out of the cab, Bruce's grip tightened on the thick fabric of her coat. He was expecting the pop of stitches, a strain against the fabric, but Gieves & Hawkes were true masters of their office. Henry Poole and Company knew what he liked, and they could make him shine like a newly minted shilling; but maybe these blokes could give him something more appropriate for the field.

Beatrice aimed just over the Houseboys' ranks and fired. From the Tesla modification. What came from the bell-shaped cage was a blue sphere, its glow so muted that it disappeared only a few feet into its launch.

"Pull me in, Bruce." He heaved, and Beatrice slipped back into her seat. "Pull it, Fischer. Goggles down." She placed dark lenses over her eyes and turned back to the three of them. "Shield your eyes."

Bruce and Brandon pulled themselves into Ryfka as Bruce heard a series of latches unlock all around them while a loud hissing filled their cab. Even through the strain of his screwed-shut eyes, Bruce could see the glare of something bright appear. Right ahead of them.

"Just keep your eyes shut, Campbell," he heard Beatrice shout.

She knew him to a fault.

An odd lurch, and his stomach dropped a few inches to bop his bowels. Ryfka's grip tightening on him served as a strange reassurance. Throughout this fresh slice of madness, she was still with them, still alive.

Bugger it, he thought to himself as he dared to open his eyes.

The pearlescent fog in front of them was dazzling, if not slightly disorienting. There were brief flashes of red, blue, green, and violet within it, these other colours dancing through the luminescent mist as would the hobby lanterns of Ireland. The blinding light did not unsettle Bruce. The occasional bursts of colour coming from the strange cloud did not unsettle Bruce.

It was that their truck—or at least part of it—was quickly rising above this strange fireworks display. That unsettled Bruce. Quite a bit.

"Get ready to feel a little jolt!" Fischer called as he pulled hard against that red lever over his head.

Bruce, Ryfka, and Brandon were thrown back into their seat. The strange luminescent cloud slipped quickly underneath them, followed moments later by the sound of something scratching underneath their cab.

"Paul!" Beatrice snapped. "Pull up!"

"I am pulling up!" he returned. "The extra weight is not helping."

She looked at Fischer, her eyes noting that rather solid frame he himself sported.

"Not a word," Fischer warned, "about that extra helping of apple strudel I had last night." He shook his head. "Not. One. Word."

The scratching grew louder as their cab trembled, threatening to shake itself apart. Bruce pulled Ryfka even closer to him as they climbed higher into the night. Then the rapid scraping sound subsided, and their cab tipped forward ever so slightly. The pull of the seat eased up, and with the gradual release of pressure Bruce could hear a low rumble of rockets coming from either side of them.

"You call that a little jolt, mate?" Brandon barked.

"The Sunburst would stun those Usher blokes for only a spell," Fischer spoke over his shoulder. "We needed to not only get beyond the infantry but clear the grove. Our ascent was a bit dicey, but none the worse for wear. I'll let the boys at Section P know we are en route."

"Nice work, Paul," Beatrice sighed, storing her rifle in the door.

Bruce leaned forward slightly to peer out of the cab window. Far below was nothing but darkness accented by patches of snow. From the looks of how quickly these brief glimpses of white passed by, they were still moving at a fast pace. He looked up and could make out a balloon—and judging from what he could see and the lack of a curve, a massive balloon—overhead. A low drone still tickled Bruce's ears amidst the groaning and creaks of cables and struts attached to their cab.

No, not a cab. A gondola.

"You like it?" Beatrice asked. "The latest in German engineering. Section P needed a thorough field testing so I obliged."

Bruce blinked. "Field testing? You mean those blighters at Section P had no clue this bloody thing would even work?"

"Well," Fischer began, even though Beatrice's mouth was open as if she were about to answer the question, "Section P's engineers test their equipment up to, and sometimes even beyond, the point of failure. This field test was really just a chance to open this little wonder up and see what she could—"

"Fischer," warned Beatrice.

He paused in mid-thought. "I'm doing it again?"

"You're doing it again."

Fischer stroked his goatee. "Right then. I'll just pilot the dirigible, shall I?"

Beatrice nodded.

"Estimated time of arrival in Breslau, one hour. We should be switching to prop power in the next ten minutes or so."

"Good man," she said.

"Can either of you do me a favour?" Bruce asked. "Do we have any kind of light for our...gondola?"

Beatrice opened up a small compartment in front of her and produced a torch. With a twist, one end illuminated the lower corner of their gondola.

"Just focus it on my hands," he said as he maneuvered around to face Ryfka as much as he could.

Beatrice's head tipped to one side as she obliged. Bruce gently placed two fingers under Ryfka's chin, bringing her eyes to his own. He then motioned to his hands.

It's over, he signed. *We will be in Germany soon.*

Ryfka smiled, looking up at him. "Thank you," she managed, and then pulled him close to kiss his cheek.

Go on and rest, he signed.

The sniper nuzzled closer to Bruce and closed her eyes. It wouldn't take her long to get to sleep.

The light flickered off. "Still making friends wherever you go, Campbell?"

"You know me, Bea," he said. "All about improving global relations."

"One bird at a time?" she said, rolling her eyes.

"Not this one, Bea," he said. "This one saved my hide." He then settled back in the seat as much as he could. It was going to be a long hour in the air. "I guess I owe you, as well."

"Leave you to be tortured by Usher? I couldn't let that happen." In the dim light of their cabin, he could see Beatrice smile. "That's my favourite hobby."

Bruce nodded. "I know a good wine shop in Breslau."

Beatrice purred. "I do love a good Riesling."

"Then how about I make things square between us once we get back down to earth?"

"Love to."

From the other end of the gondola, Brandon groaned. "No way this could end badly."

CHAPTER SIXTEEN

⊰⇒◉⇐⊱

Wherein the Will of the Empire Is Made Known

"You're being quite terrible to your Uncle Henry, Wellington," Jekyll said, his face musculature attempting to grow larger, even though his size had doubled in the short time they were standing in front of one another. "How disappointed your father would be."

"If memory serves," Wellington said evenly, "you and my father had a bit of a falling out. I happened to be back from school for a holiday." He nodded as he circled his opponent. "I was fourteen, but I remember the huge row you two had."

"Your father was narrow-minded!" Jekyll snapped. "He refused to see beyond his commission to the House of Usher. It was all about delivering results and preserving his legacy. I wanted to evolve those we deemed fit. Don't you see, Little Wellington?" Jekyll motioned to himself and to the archivist as he said with that bizarre smile of his. "You and I? We are gods among scuttling ants."

"If that is the case," Wellington said, tightening his fist around the knuckle dusters, "then please do refer to me with something far more reverent than 'Little Wellington'."

Bringing his fist up, the punch he delivered was given a touch more pep thanks to the brass encasing his fist. Jekyll stumbled backward, tripped over his own feet, and landed soundly on his back. The impact was also enough to cause Wellington to lose his balance.

A most fortunate happenstance, as a rebel turned his pistol on him and fired. The bullet tore through his shoulder, a hot, searing shock that sent Wellington—even in his battle trance—down to one knee.

The roar he easily mistook for a lion's cry, but looking up, all he saw was Jekyll grabbing the soldier, his meaty hand wrapping completely around the Indian.

"I am having a conversation with an old family friend," he growled to the man. "Do you mind?"

Jekyll's arm cocked back and he tossed the poor sod high into the air. The soldier's arms and legs failed wildly as he tumbled before crashing through one of the Palace's pavilions.

"Now," Jekyll said, turning slowly around to face Wellington, "we were discussing the issues I had with your father."

Wellington went to get back on his feet, but then noticed two more insurgents running at Jekyll, their rifles up and ready to fire.

Jekyll's arm came around and swept across the two men, shooting them into the sandstone walls. The subtle, tan colour of the Water Palace now found itself decorated with splatters of blood.

"KARI!" Jekyll howled. *"DO NOT TEST MY PATIENCE!"*

Nahush Kari appeared on the far stairs, flanked by nearly a dozen men. Wellington could hear his army engaging the Ministry and the military across the courtyard and in the palace's corridors, but these rebels were all pointing their weapons at Jekyll. "You kill my men without provocation and expect me to be compliant?"

"They are not to harm Wellington Books here," he warned, his eyes still bulging with a wild fury. "My interest in him should be indication enough that he is a priority."

"I have brought you here and fetched what you desire, as you wished." Kari motioned to Wellington. "This Ministry agent was never mentioned."

Jekyll took in a breath before bellowing even louder, *"I'm mentioning him now!"*

A soldier fired his rifle, and the round harmlessly bounced off Jekyll's chest. Kari whirled around and shouted to his men, his hands out. Wellington could only assume he was trying to calm them.

What Nahush should have done was try and calm Jekyll, who appeared to gain another foot in height to his already massive size.

"Bloody savages," Jekyll growled. "I should have known!"

Jekyll lumbered up to Kari's men, and grabbed one of the soldiers by his legs. The monster swept this resistance fighter across the ranks, scattering insurgents as if they were pins on a bowling pitch. Bullets pelted Jekyll, but they were nothing more than bothersome gnats to this giant. The melee now descended into complete mayhem as the Ghost Rebellion did not know where to focus their attention and their firepower—the unseen Ministry-military forces, or the mutated monster within their midst.

"I know I will regret this," Wellington said as he got to his feet.

He imagined himself at that fateful rugby match hosted by Eliza's countrymen. She had watched as he surrendered to baser emotions—jealousy being at the forefront—and make a rather unsporting tackle against that rather pompous wanker, Douglas Sheppard. Wellington let this specific training of Arthur Books take hold. His muscles tensed and turn his body into an armour of flesh similar to Jekyll's, turning Wellington into that cad fulfilling the Forward position on that day.

This time, however, his intentions were completely and utterly malevolent.

Wellington led with his good shoulder, his eyes narrowing on the massive knee joint just visible through Jekyll's torn trousers. He felt flesh and muscle underneath him give way to his momentum. Something inside this tree trunk of a leg cracked sharply.

Jekyll's deafening scream drowned out the gunfire.

Rolling away from the toppling behemoth, Wellington scrambled to his feet. He truly hoped he had not made the wrong judgment call.

Now staggering, Jekyll tossed the solder still in his grasp aside and struggled to take pressure off his damaged knee. He stumbled, then collapsed, his body smashing into one of the wooden cases he had been carrying.

"Wellington," he heard a familiar voice call to him, "take cover!"

The Mule's Kick appeared in the air and remained suspended there for a moment, tumbling end over end. As it did, Wellington noticed a glow coming from it. That was to be expected, but this glow was far brighter than he had ever seen.

Then the sun caught its handle. Someone had modified it.

"Bloody hell, Eliza," Wellington swore as he ran for the nearest window and leapt through.

Sandstone walls buckled and cracked as the concussion struck them. The sound wave ripped through the windows, knocking over any insurgents entrenched there.

Wellington remained low to the ground as gunfire soon followed. Cries of "God save the Queen!" and the report of what Wellington recognised as Maulik Smith's Queensbury Rules echoed through the palace. Despite their small numbers, O'Neil and his men were making a final push.

Wellington dared to look up just as Nahush Kari emerged from the dust and smoke. He looked a bit bruised, but none the worse for wear.

With a glance over his shoulder, the rebel leader sprinted into the corridor just ahead of him.

Returning to his feet, Wellington made chase. He picked up a rifle off a dead soldier, and quickly checked its chamber. He had at least one round at the ready. This wing of the Water Palace appeared deserted, save for Nahush running ahead of him.

"Nahush Kari!" Wellington shouted as he stopped and shouldered his weapon. "Stop!"

The man continued down the hallway. Wellington gave him three steps before pulling the trigger.

Nahush's steps never faltered.

I never miss, Wellington thought quickly as he loaded what he hoped would be another round. He resumed his pursuit, playing in his mind over and over again what should have been a debilitating shot. Were the sights off on this rifle?

Nahush's hand came up, and Wellington could see a box of some description. A wireless device. A light flickered on its surface, and a rush of cool air struck Wellington in the face as an æthergate appeared at the end of the corridor. He braced the stock into his good shoulder and fired again; but his quarry merely turned to face him, Nahush halfway between the Water Palace and wherever this personal portal led. He then tossed his device into the air before proceeding through. Once the box shattered against the palace floor, the portal collapsed on itself. Nahush Kari, at an extreme risk to himself, was gone.

"Welly?" Eliza called. "Wellington Thornhill Books, if I find you dead, I will never speak to you again!"

"Sorry to disappoint," he replied, his eyes going back and forth the length of his rifle, "but I'm here, alive and well."

Eliza came around the corner, her face a twisted expression of concern until her eyes came to his own. There was elation, immediately followed by shock. Wellington felt his shoulder throb, and understood. She went to say something, but a blinding light suddenly swept through the hallway. The sudden flash was accompanied by a chilled gust of wind, and Wellington tasted copper as he heard a wild crack of electricity.

"Jekyll," they said together.

They both ran for the opening of the corridor, but on reaching the courtyard the light disappeared. Through the odd patches of grey floating before him, the palace centre was littered with insurgents. Some were bent in abnormal fashions while others were trying to summon the courage to continue. The small number of British and Ministry rushed across the courtyard, scuttling to a halt, holding the rebels at bay with their own rifles and sidearms.

Sophia emerged from the corridors alongside Maulik and O'Neil. "The doctor came prepared with a contingency, it would appear," she stated sourly.

"Well done," Maulik said, although he did not sound like a man who had just captured a movement against the crown. "A shame to lose Jekyll again. Something about this place. Jekyll's good luck charm, I suppose. And Wellington, kept your wits about you this go round?"

"I will feel a touch wittier once I see a medic," he winced, tossing his rifle aside.

Maulik motioned with his hand. "Follow me, everyone. We will patch up Books here and make him right as rain."

The three of them followed Maulik on a slow walk back to the train, while O'Neil and his men led at gunpoint the few remnants of the Ghost Rebellion to a far corner of the courtyard. They stopped on seeing Vania Pujari led to where her other compatriots were held. Sophia smiled slightly at the bloody bandage around her left hand.

Eliza's blue eyes locked with the treasonous agent's. Wellington knew that look from his partner. She was searching for some sign of regret, but he knew her search would be in vain.

"Why?" she finally asked.

"If you have to ask 'why' then you truly are ignorant. You believe we are all happy citizens, equal in every way?" Vania spat into Eliza's face. *"That* is how you see us."

Eliza took a moment. She slowly dabbed off the spittle with her sleeve. "Your sister never showed such resentment to the Empire."

Vania's eyes narrowed, "I am not her."

"No," she spoke evenly, "You most certainly are not."

A soldier nudged Vania in the back with the butt of his rifle. With a final look to Eliza, she was led to where the rebels sat, most of whom Wellington recognised from various photos and daguerreotypes. She soon joined their ranks without question or protest, her look one of hardened resolution, as it was with all of them.

"The Lieutenant has taken command of the palace, Wellington," Maulik said in a low, stiff tone. From behind them, O'Neil shouted orders to his men. On account of the echo, it was hard to hear exactly what those orders were. "As this is a military operation now, the responsibility of the Ghost Rebellion falls upon O'Neil. Now let us tend to that shoulder of yours. We would hate to have it infected, now wouldn't we?"

Wellington cast a glance at Eliza and Sophia, who had their gazes fixed on Maulik.

"This is Agent Kessler," Maulik said, motioning to a Ministry agent coming out of the train, carrying an assortment of bandages and dark bottles. In the growing shadow of the Strategy Car, there were a few agents and soldiers with bandages around eyes, heads, and one soldier who had a tourniquet around his leg. Wellington knew he would not keep that leg for much longer. By the junction where they had begun their push, four bodies lay motionless. All things being as they were, Wellington considered himself most fortunate. "He will fix you up straight away."

"Excellent," Wellington said, taking a seat on the edge of the ramp.

"This shouldn't take long at all, Agent Books," Kessler told him.

"The Ministry is done here?" Eliza asked Maulik.

"Of course. Your part in this mad caper was to find Jekyll, and you found him. Our part was to understand exactly who or what the Ghost Rebellion was, and we did just that. Peculiar occurrences resolved. Now we debrief and collect our train while the military steps in—"

"When did this become a military operation?" Wellington asked, grimacing as Kessler worked on bandaging his wound.

That was when Maulik stopped, and his chair turned to face Wellington. Had that been the wrong question to ask?

"If you must insist on knowing, Agent Books," Maulik began, his tone sounding particularly authoritative, "it was the attack on Fort St Paul and the Army & Navy Building. The moment Kari spilt the blood of Her Majesty's soldiers, it became a military matter." He steepled his fingers as he sat deeper into his wheelchair. "Any other questions you may have concerning protocol between branches of Her Majesty's government?"

Wellington swallowed. He cast a glance to Eliza, who merely shrugged. His eyes then went to Sophia. A single eyebrow angled itself sharply, and her silent reply to his look spoke volumes. "No, sir."

O'Neil's order suddenly rang out across the courtyard. _"FIRE!"_

Gunshots rippled through the air, and seconds later came a succession of clicks—bolts of rifles —and then, O'Neil's voice came again. _"FIRE!"_

From their vantage point at the train, they watched as a line of insurgents, this one with Vania Pujari at its centre, rocked back into the wall behind them, spots of crimson decorating their heads, necks, and chests. They remained standing for perhaps a second before collapsing on the corpses strewn in front of them.

"Before you say one word, Eliza," Maulik began, "do keep in mind the innocent civilians caught in the crossfire. Consider the agents cut down today, and how many were compromised in the field, on account of her actions. We have no idea the damage done from Miss Pujari's actions." He paused. "Consider your words carefully."

The response did not come from Eliza. Or Wellington. "You are no better than those you fought today."

All eyes turned to Sophia.

"Madam, you are a guest of the Ministry," Maulik stated. "That can change."

"You will hold court as did your military just now?"

"There is also the matter of both æthergate and electroporter technology," the director returned. "We could not afford to have this knowledge fall into the hands of other scientists."

"And you think for a moment, Maulik, it *justifies* what we have done?" Eliza asked. "The Empire—"

"—is whole once more," he said.

"Not this way!" Eliza insisted. "Sophia is damn well right. We are no better than the Ghost Rebellion!"

"On the contrary," O'Neil spoke, making them all turn to him, "we are far better than Kari and his lot. It was what helped win the day."

"What gives you the authority, Lieutenant, to serve as the final word?" Eliza demanded.

"My service and loyalty to the crown, Agent Braun. And my new rank as captain."

Eliza took in a breath, cast a glance to Maulik, and then stormed off, disappearing into the corridors of the Water Palace.

"She isn't taking this well," Maulik said with a sigh.

"Truth be told," Wellington said, looking between both Captain O'Neil and Director Smith, "none of us should."

In Which Predators Gather and Plan for the Future

Mr Fox took a sip of the tea at his elbow, and glanced nervously at the ceiling for the fourth time. Jaipur, for this godforsaken country, was surprisingly beautiful, full of tourists, plenty of activity, and a delightful display of culture nestled within signs of British innovation. All these things and more made Jaipur the worst place to be after the events at the Water Palace.

And of all locations to meet—a hookah café. They may as well had been wearing pith helmets and draped in the Union Flag.

"Relax, Jeremy," Holmes said, a curl of smoke rising up before his face. "That's the whole idea of places like this, you know."

Jeremy shot the Lord of the Manor—no, the *Chairman*—a glance. For an American, he enjoyed playing king just a little too much. He got them a private corner in the café, sitting on scarlet cushions, with the setting sun dappling over his feet and across the hookah's ornate water jar. The device seemed to sparkle in the dying light, attracting what he believed unwanted attention to themselves. Henry did look content, but Jeremy wasn't fooled.

"Indulge a bit in the local culture," Holmes said, offering Jeremy the pipe.

Not daring to argue with the Chairman, he took the hose, and drew from the mouthpiece. There was, oddly enough, something relaxing in hearing the water burble from within the brass bowl, and the smoke caressing his tongue was cool, sweetened with flavours of cinnamon, ginger, and cumin. He did not want to relax, especially within reach of the Chairman.

"See? Wonderful smoke, this is, and quite impressive that they have updated their hookah to these hoses. It does make it easier to share," Holmes said before finishing off his cup of tea. "And no, I would not even think of using this advancement as a garrotte. That would ruin the experience."

Jeremy exhaled, decorating the air around them with a veil of smoke. As wonderful as this indulgence was, he could not afford to relax around this man.

"Quite a display today." Holmes' eyes were slitted, like a cat at rest, but just like one he could pounce. "Arthur Books' theories of indoctrination, physical training, and Jekyll's serum creating superb fighting men does seem to have merit."

The Chairman did not make a comfortable travelling companion, but at least he had witnessed the wonders of Project Achilles. Jeremy tapped his satchel where two film reels were kept dry and cool. "And I have the evidence to show to the rest of the board."

Holmes waved his hand as he drew from the hookah. After a long exhale, he said, "This super soldier project between Arthur Books and Doctor Henry Jekyll was started by your predecessor, so you've inherited this albatross. The disappointment of Project Achilles is not yours."

"Perhaps the inbuilt loyalty to the House we desire can be pushed harder during the indoctrination phase. When we lost Wellington Books against all odds, the project was closed. The doctor slipped into anonymity, pursuing his own projects we discovered with the Diamond Jubilee."

"And now we know the younger Books had become, to an extent, what the House set out to create. Imagine if we can fetter this power, discover its secrets. Imagine a whole army of Wellington Books' fashion, obeying only the House of Usher. We would no longer have to hide in the shadows. We could build an empire to make the British one seem timid." His grin was wide and directed at no one in particular as he leaned back among the cushions. "Life is full of surprises, isn't it?"

Jeremy found, even though it was quite comfortable in the café, he was sweating. "You mean, like the presence of Sophia del Morte?"

"Well, not all surprises are welcome. This camaraderie with the Italian was not anticipated. Fascinating, if you linger on the details." Holmes glanced at his watch. "I think I shall have Mr Badger send a quick message to her."

Jeremy straightened up immediately, sending cushions tumbling. "Are you sure that is wise, concerning the events at the Draycott? We lost six Brothers that night."

"Six members of the House who severely underestimated our dear Italian asset. To reach the formidable Miss del Morte you must speak her language." He gave Jeremy a wink. "No need to worry. I'm fluent in it."

"Yes, my L—yes, Chairman."

"Now we have to set ourselves to finding and capturing Mr Wellington Thornhill Books, Esquire."

Jeremy was just about to ask how Holmes wanted to achieve that where so many had failed, when a tall form blocked the sunlight falling on them. "After what we have seen today, a rather tall order, do you not think, Chairman?"

His hand gripped the gun under his jacket, but then after a moment Jeremy was able to make out the clean-shaven features of the newcomer, his hair perfectly coiffed, the tailored black suit befitting of a proper gentleman.

"Mr Cobra," Jeremy said, sliding his hand away from the pistol.

"Nahush, at last," Holmes said, shaking the man's hand. "Wonderful to see you still in one piece."

"Just barely," Kari said, joining the two gentlemen at the hookah. "You would think with Nahush Kari trapped at the Water Palace, the military would have proven better shots." He adjusted his spectacles and chuckled. "They needed more time on the firing range."

"The æthergate we supplied you did not have any adverse effects, I hope?" Jeremy asked.

"After I noticed my own issues with Featherstone's imitation, I refrained from using it. When you have a potential candidate pinned down by gunfire or overwhelming opposition, any loyal soldier appearing from the other side of a tear in time and space will do." Kari took the offered pipe and drew, savouring the smoke's taste for a moment. "That's why you have your pawns on the chessboard. Before every good leader is quality cannon fodder."

"After all that time serving as the driving force behind Indian independence," Holmes said, "I regret seeing your plans quashed today."

"On the contrary, the Ghost Rebellion was a rousing success," Kari stated proudly. "Consider what we have left in our wake between the attacks against Fort St Paul and the Army & Navy Building. Parliament will be in an uproar, screaming for justice. They will tighten their noose around India's neck, which will hopefully birth new movements, all of them evoking the name of Nahush Kari, gone missing since the Massacre of Jal Mahal."

"I don't think you can hardly call a military skirmish a massacre," Jeremy said.

"You can if your men have no way of fighting back." Kari passed the pipe on to Jeremy and picked up the small tongs hanging against their hookah. He gingerly arranged the coals atop the head, turning them as he spoke. "I had planned for an altercation like this between us and the military. Only few of my soldiers were armed with working rifles. My dear cousin Makeala—the last survivor of the Ghost Rebellion—is now feeding the streets with stories of how we underwent a peaceful pilgrimage to Jal Mahal and were ambushed by the military."

"And Sister Raven? You will be rendezvousing with her soon?" Holmes asked.

"Pakistan, a week from today. Her sudden disappearance will carry consequences, as well."

"Excellent, Nahush."

"Tut-tut. Mr Cobra, if you please," Kari said with a slight wag of his finger. "We must keep up appearances."

"Yes, of course. I suppose this means we will see more of you at the conference table?"

"I would suspect so, Chairman."

"Very good," Holmes said, delighted. "With the Ghost Rebellion now a closed project, we can work with all in attendance, whole and complete, dedicated to one purpose."

Jeremy could see, even in the dim light of the café, a look of hope in Cobra's eyes. None of the other board members had spent much time with Holmes; they couldn't know him as Jeremy had grown to over these many weeks. They probably only thought of him as a murderer and a bit of an amateur architect. They could not truly understand his genius; he could be convivial, and charming, all the while manipulating pieces into place. Holmes did not care about the status or class of whom he manipulated. Be they rail tycoon, shopkeeper, or mill worker, people were merely means to an end. As Jeremy took another long draw of the hookah, he wondered what all the men and women lodging in Holmes' castle had thought when they finally realised how he had tricked them, their final thoughts as gas claimed them, their revelations when coming to on his examination table.

He wondered if his fellow board members would one day undergo the same revelation.

Mr Cobra, usually the subtlest of their number, looked to be swallowing the bait hungrily. "Before us, Chairman, is a very exciting time."

"That's the spirit, old chap." Holmes smiled. "Now, concerning Wellington Books, I would like to leave this café tonight with options on how to recruit him."

"Since I am still unacquainted about this Books fellow, outside of what I learned from Jekyll, why are we so interested in recruiting instead of killing this man?"

"Gentlemen, Wellington Books may be seen by some of our numbers as the product of a failed venture and a menace to our operations; but after today, you will stand in agreement when I say Books would be an excellent addition to our current endeavour."

Jeremy and Cobra looked to one another. How Jeremy had not thought that far ahead with Project Achilles failed him. A brilliant notion. Holmes was freshening their tea as both men shared a silent agreement.

"Then I propose a modest toast, gentlemen," Holmes said, raising his cup. "To Ragnarök."

CHAPTER SEVENTEEN

⊹⊷⊜⊶⊹

Wherein a Message Is Keenly Delivered

Travelling with Sophia del Morte was rather like sharing a carriage with a barrel of black powder. It was quite impossible to relax for a moment, just in case something happened to cause it to explode.

Eliza cast their companion a covert look from the other side of the swaying carriage, and when Sophia turned to lock eyes with her, she cast her gaze outside to the Italian countryside passing by quickly.

With all our accomplishments and accolades, Eliza contemplated, *I find myself asking repeatedly "If we are so bloody brilliant, how in the name of God on high do we continue to find ourselves in the field collaborating with her?"*

It wasn't like they didn't have enough to worry about, what with Dr Henry Jekyll and Nahush Kari on the loose, and her lover's personal demons coming to the fore. Now, compounding on all of this, they were charged by Director Smith to escort Sophia del Morte back into Europe, to wherever she wished. Eliza tried to hold onto her hatred for this known assassin, the woman who silenced Harry.

Harrison Thorne. Her partner when she arrived in London on permanent assignment. One of the finest figures of manhood she had ever known. Forever trapped in a prison of madness. Perhaps Sophia had done Harry a favour. He would not have wanted to live that way.

Dammit, Eliza swore. *Was she actually putting up a defence for this Italian tart?* Much as she hated to admit it, there was something compelling about Sophia. Perhaps it was the adventurer in her, living with the constant danger of getting a dagger through the eyeball.

The other precarious ingredient in the mix, the source of her own ignition perhaps, was also watching Sophia. Wellington, sitting opposite her in the carriage, did not turn away from the assassin's eye. Instead he leaned across, and offered her a cup of coffee. The trolley lady had only just been down the swaying carriage, and Wellington was as reliant on tea as any citizen of the Empire, not to mention kind enough to order from the trolley a coffee. Chivalrous to the very end. One of the many reasons she loved him so.

They were cutting through the lovely Italian countryside at the always-reliable pace only hypersteams could deliver, and she was hoping they might be able to drop off their charge in short order. Wellington had already shared his desire to get back to Whiterock, hopefully unearth some more information about Arthur Books' legacy, embodied in his only son. It was an inconvenient truth he had to deal with, and hopefully keep in control.

"Thank you," Sophia said, as Wellington handed her the drink. "I have become quite used to this little ritual." She tilted her head. "It is wonderful to have you...how do you say...*play mother*."

Wellington let out a breath, long and slow, but her lover did not rise to the bait; instead, he offered Eliza a cup of tea and a cucumber sandwich before resuming his own seat. "Well, since we have been charged with your safe arrival to wherever this final destination of yours may be, we wanted to be certain you have the best trip possible."

"We?"

"Yes," Eliza said, turning her gaze back to her. "I am leaving the personal service to Wellington. Had I been serving you coffee, I could not guarantee offering it without using said coffee as a weapon."

The assassin gave a little shrug and stared out the window. "I expected no less."

A surge of guilt rushed through her. Eliza did not want to feel any sort of admiration for this cold-blooded killer, but Sophia had come to their aid again. Yes, for self-serving needs, but she could have remained in hiding. Instead, she had applied her own unique skills in restoring the Empire.

That stuck her even harder. The Empire. After what transpired at the Water Palace, was the Empire what she believed it to be?

She went to ask Wellington his thoughts on the matter, and noticed he was not drinking his tea, merely staring into it. "That's good. Keep an eye on that tea. Can't turn your back on it, lest it goes cold on you. Ever vigilant."

"That will do, Eliza," he grumbled.

"Darling," she urged, giving him a light tap on his arm. "Would you let it go? You missed a shot. It happens to the best of us."

"I missed Kari twice. He was well within range. There was no wind to speak of. I had the shot and I missed. *Twice*."

"Considering the day, you may have been rattled." Eliza shrugged. "But it could have been worse."

Wellington's eyes widened. "Worse? How?"

"You could have been one of those poor sods snatched up by the electroporter."

He opened his mouth to properly debate her on the point, thought about it for a moment, then said, "Find myself teleported into an empty warehouse on the docks of Bombay, or face the terror from my childhood?"

Damn, he did have a point. "At least from the sound of the æthermail Maulik received, all our men and women were present and accounted for."

"Indeed. I know the feeling of an unexpected trip via the electroporter." Wellington finally took a sip of his tea. "Most unpleasant."

"Hopefully," Eliza said, turning her attention to Sophia, "it is much nicer where we are going…which is where exactly?"

"Eliza," Wellington began, "the ticket reads—"

"A destination," Sophia interrupted just before taking a long sip of her coffee. "I would no be so foolish as to trust your Ministry without question. You have a wider problem with double agents within your ranks."

"You are right about that," Eliza returned.

Her dark eyebrows raised slightly. "I never thought I would hear you speak those words to me."

"We may have harboured differences in the past, but I would never deny you the truth. Vania. The Case woman. We should have been better in our vetting process."

Wellington raised a finger. "Well, the Ministry was not the only branch of Her Majesty's government playing *Spellicans* after the Diamond Jubilee. If we did not have double agents before then, it is difficult to say how compromised we are as an organisation."

Eliza took a bite of her cucumber sandwich. It was a bit soggy for her liking. "But you are trusting us?"

"Why shouldn't I?" Sophia asked. "You have not only been loyal to me, you have risked your lives in keeping me safe. I find the notion somewhat foolish, but endearing."

"So where are we going?"

"Home," Sophia said with a wicked smile. "I am taking you home."

The gentle hills of Tuscany rolled past, an endless expanse of beautiful farmland, charming villages, wine and cheese. However, with their true destination revealed, Eliza suspected what was in store for them would be nothing as tranquil or serene. Rumours of the del Morte's home, its location, and its security, could never be confirmed by any of the Ministry or any other clandestine organisation for that matter. No one had ever seen it. Or at least lived to tell.

A part of Eliza was incredibly chuffed about this opportunity, most rare indeed, but she kept her thoughts on the matter to herself. She found herself jealous. *Incredibly* jealous. Sophia del Morte was a known assassin, her dossier documenting numerous deaths at her hands, leading to toppled monarchies and governments thrown into chaos, and yet she could go home. A family waited for her, offering safe haven in the worst of storms. Eliza silently pined for her own family, wishing she too could have a homecoming like Sophia. It certainly didn't seem fair that this assassin should earn or even deserve such a thing, but she could not.

His hand slipped over her own, and squeezed. She looked up into his hazel eyes, and felt a single tear escape her. Eliza believed herself to be travelling in a very ladylike fashion, buttoned and corseted, proper skirts made for hypersteam travel, but it was evident by Wellington's gesture that he wasn't fooled by the cool mask she presented.

"Ah, young love." Sophia's green eyes sparkled with amusement. "I do hope my presence isn't intruding."

"Not at all," Eliza replied. Then she leaned across and delivered a deep kiss to Wellington that put her mind in a whirl for a moment or two, pushing back melancholy thoughts. When she released him, he dropped back into his chair, and adjusted his cravat. Was that regret she saw flicker across Sophia's face? Eliza could not be certain as Sophia turned back to the window, watching Italy rush by in a blur.

The train pulled into Siena by midday, and thankfully by then they had managed to remain polite as they sipped tea, and simply ignored each other. Despite the warmth and comfort of their private carriage, a palpable tension lingered. At this particular station, however, Sophia rose from where she sat.

"We have arrived," she stated, grabbing the small suitcase from her overhead compartment.

Emerging onto the platform, Wellington took charge of their small amount of luggage. He disappeared for a few moments, perhaps to find any kind of transportation that did not involve a driver. No need to put anyone else at risk.

"Despite our current worries with Jekyll being at large and this Agent Case business coming to light," Director Smith had said to them in confidence before setting off, *"the del Morte clan have always been a threat. Wherever she is taking you, learn anything you can about her, and how her family operates. Anything we can glean from her might prove valuable and worth the bother."*

"You have our word, Sophia," Eliza said. "We take you home. No trackers. No report filed with the Ministry. Your secrets are safe with Wellington and myself."

Sophia looked Eliza from head to foot, then back again. "You surprise me, Braun. This seems out of character for you."

"That's a bit of a lark coming from you."

"People can change."

Did *Sophia del Morte* just say that? "Really?"

Wellington had returned with some sort of news—and not good news, from the look on his face—but was silenced before sharing it when Sophia offered them something totally unexpected. "Would you like to meet the family, and perhaps join us for dinner? No tea though, only wine." She held her hands up. "And I promise, no poisons."

"What about blades or guns?" Wellington asked.

"Mr Books, this is *my* family. Do not ask for the impossible."

Sophia's smile was beautiful, and yet also somewhat alarming. In a remote village, populated with an unholy legion of deadly women, surely they would not last long? Yet there was the offer right before them.

Eliza tilted her chin upwards. She never said no to an adventure. "Yes, let's."

"Follow me," she said.

"But that is what I came to tell you," Wellington said. "I cannot find proper transportation for us."

"No need to worry, Mr Books. *Mi familia* has standing arrangements here."

Sophia led the way to the local stables across from the train station, where she procured horses for the three of them. By the sweat on his brow, the owner seemed to recognise her straight away. He handed over mounts quickly, took the money offered, and then retreated. It was hardly a surprise the del Morte family were known in Siena.

Eliza looked at the tossing head of the stallion she had been given. As New Zealand was a country with few roads and endless countryside, equestrian skills comprised some of her earliest memories. However, with Wellington's influences, she had grown more comfortable with the steadiness of a motor car. They were, after all, predictable. Horses had minds and instincts of their own.

"Isn't there a place where we can hire a motor vehicle for the trip?" Wellington asked, looking over his shoulder as if his steed would magically change into one.

"Nonna does not care for them," Sophia replied, already gracefully arranging herself atop her bay mare. "Besides, anything motorised would be futile. No roads."

"Come on, Welly," Eliza said with a laugh, as she clicked her tongue to urge her horse forward. "Better than camels, you must admit."

Wellington appeared not to like her reminding him of that particular endeavour. Reluctantly, with reins clasped easily in one hand, he joined Eliza and Sophia on their way out of the stables.

On the open road, Sophia led them leisurely a mile or two before reaching a grass-covered goat track taking them deeper into the countryside. To say this ride was a beautiful, well-earned respite from their investigation in India would be an understatement. Somehow, it made perfect sense to Eliza that Sophia, with her singular, unique charm, came from such a place.

"Have your family been in the area long?" Wellington said. It was a delight to see him so relaxed, at peace.

"My Nonna came here when she was first married. My grandfather's people have been here since recorded history. Nonna doesn't like to talk about where she came from." Sophia shot him a wry grin. "I suggest you don't ask her."

"No questions for Nonna," he muttered to himself. "Duly noted."

"I hope you don't mind the question, but it's the elephant in the room." Eliza could see in the corner of her eye Wellington's grip tighten on his reins. "Are all your family killers?"

Sophia's smile was quite proud. "If you hadn't asked, I would have thought you far too trusting. The answer is no. Our village, Monteriggioni, is a rather peaceful place. And you are guests. You have nothing to fear."

The wistful note in her voice nearly took Eliza's breath away. There was also a hint of longing that she recognized from when she spoke of New Zealand. Again, a part of her ached.

Thank goodness Wellington was in a curious mood. "So do you have a plan for when you get there?"

Sophia shrugged. "I suppose I will take the path my Nonna did when she retired: find a husband, raise a new generation of del Mortes, and teach them how to weave and throw knives."

It was quite a picture, and Eliza could easily see it. Who the lucky, or unlucky, husband would be was another thing altogether.

Twilight was just stealing over the hills, colouring the landscape with shades of turmeric and saffron. Eliza was about to ask Sophia about the wines of her home when the assassin suddenly kicked her horse into a gallop. She caught on their guide's face a hardened expression, one Eliza had never seen during their trip from India.

Then, in the air, she could smell smoke. Not the kind reminiscent of winter bonfires. This was stronger, heavier.

Immediately Eliza was after her, with Wellington just behind. However, they didn't have to chase Sophia far as she had galloped to the top of the next hill. As both agents pulled up next to her, they saw why she had stopped.

On the opposite hill was the town they assumed to be Monteriggioni, small but with walls. The sounds of wood crackling and roof beams falling could be heard across the narrow valley. Tall flames and thick, acrid smoke reached into the indigo and violet sky above. Eliza could tell the town had been burning for some time. Nothing moved within the village walls, apart from the flames. No people were fleeing into the valley. No cries for help echoed up to them.

The firelight reflected on Sophia's face, catching the tears in her eyes. Her shock surrendered to sadness and mourning. She shook her head, her hands clenching on the reins. "Nonna warned me about Usher," she said, her voice cracking. "She warned me and I didn't listen."

Eliza dared to place her hand on Sophia's shoulder. "You don't know that it was—"

Sophia let out a howl, a primitive scream that made the horses jerk sideways in alarm. When she turned to her, Eliza saw an incredible, raw rage. "I know! I know *them!* I know they came here for me!"

She could think of nothing to say in response. It was most likely true. Considering how Sophia had cost the House of Usher in her partnership with the Maestro, it would not be unexpected for them to strike against her.

This tactic, however, was shocking. Even for Usher.

As Sophia kicked her horse forward, Eliza called out to her, "Do you want us to come with you? They could still be there."

The horse stopped, then turned around. The look on Sophia del Morte's face was one Eliza would never forget; it was naked pain, lit by fire and destruction. "*No,*" she spat. "This is my business. *La Cosa Nostra.* My family, my revenge."

Wellington trotted his horse forward. "Sophia, please, let us help you."

"Do not get in the way!" Her warning made Eliza pull back instinctively on her mount's reins. "If I need you, I will find you. Rest assured."

And with that she urged her horse into a mad gallop towards the burning Monteriggioni.

"Does she really intend to take on Usher alone?" Wellington asked.

Eliza's gaze travelled across the destruction. "She'll do whatever she has to, Welly." Reaching over she gave his hand a squeeze. "Let's go home. We have a madman of our own to catch."

CODA

In Which a Mad Doctor Sees the Light

Paris, *La Ville Lumière.* One of the touchstones for the Age of Enlightenment. Just in the distance, rising from an ocean of gas lamps, stood the pride and joy of the city and, of course, the architect Gustave Eiffel. Now ten years old, the wrought iron lattice wonder straddling Champ de Mars stood as a testament to what was possible if man were given no boundaries or inhibitions. Though it was true, while the Tower was being constructed, its creator took more than his fair amount of grief and scorn from the Paris Elite. Architect Charles Garnier and artists such as Maupassant, Massenet, and Bouguereau mounted protests against its construction, attempting to halt what they believed would be an abomination, a bastard creation of science and art, of form and expression, of design and creativity.

These prominent men had been wrong. So very, very wrong.

The Eiffel Tower, even at this distance, stood as an inspiration to Henry Jekyll. Those who had opposed Gustave Eiffel's legacy would have denied their fair city the distinction of having the tallest man-made structure in the world. The Tower was a breakthrough of art, architecture, and ingenuity, and Eiffel had proven to be right.

Just as he would be. One day.

Jekyll turned away from the inspiring view of the City of Lights and took his fresh cup of tea from the automaton. Head tilted, he examined the mechanical manservant, took his first sip, and then winced at the sharpness of the brew. Once again, it had steeped for too long. A human servant would only need one or two brewing attempts before comprehending what constituted a perfect cup of tea.

This was the automaton's fifth attempt.

"I thought we had remedied this," Jekyll muttered to himself as he limped around the metallic valet to the tea tray. He dropped in two more sugar cubes, stirred it into the leather-coloured liquid, and then took in a sip.

Absolute swill. He dropped in another two cubes.

Still terrible.

Three more. That should do the trick.

Better.

Well, perhaps one more.

The taste now replenished his soul. The perfect cup of tea. Finally.

Jekyll took another long sip of the Darjeeling and then stared into the drink. Eight cubes. Dammit. He was going to need another regimen. This would make the third on a weekly basis. The only other choice was to skip the treatment and allow himself to run loose in the streets of Paris. If that was his choice tonight, he would have to secure his dwelling and find an overnight boarding house as a beginning and ending point for his exploits; his alpha and omega for a night of unleashed debauchery. Possibly spilling blood. Whether that blood would be innocent or not, was impossible to calculate.

He set the cup and saucer on the end table, and taking up his cane, followed the servant's passage down to the kitchen. The automatons stood here like skeletal soldiers, silent and dark in the shadows. To some, it might have been unnerving, these metallic creations just standing there, waiting for a command. To Jekyll, they were merely furniture, so he continued through to the butler's quarters where the only light was present.

Outside the door this automaton was active, its gears and cogs clicking while lights flared and dimmed in their simple sequence. The automaton's eyes glowed green as its head slowly and smoothly turned to look at him. On recognizing that someone was standing in front of it, the eyes switched from green to yellow.

"Henry Jekyll," it stated.

The automaton held its stare with him as a pattern of bips and beeps softly ticked in its head. Jekyll was not familiar with Morse code or the ways of wireless communication, but its creator had told him this was the sentry's particular routine, or was it sequence? He couldn't recall the proper terminology, but it was still nothing less than ingenious how this machine communicated with its brethren on the other side of the door.

Those yellow eyes, still trained on him, switched back to green as it stepped back.

"Just incredible," he whispered, taking out the ornate key from his pocket.

Jekyll inserted the key and turned it twice to the left. Levers snapped inside the lock, then Jekyll grabbed the bow and pulled. The key's stem split, gaining another half inch of length. Now he turned it counter clockwise.

From the doorway came a sequence of low, deep strikes as the extra bolts disengaged. In his early experiments, he'd contained himself behind this door, back when he'd still fought against his breakthrough. That was before he knew the exquisite joy of being a god amongst mortals, before he knew the taste of the purely primal.

The room served him well back then as a prison for himself, and presently it fulfilled this need once again for one of the world's most ingenious and famous individuals.

The door swung open, revealing its sole human occupant, with three metallic servants watching over him. Thomas Alva Edison sat on the bed, and his scowl deepened with every step Jekyll took into the room. Had he not possessed the amazing vision and intellect of tomorrow, Jekyll would have already dispatched him simply for his petulant demeanour. His resources were, perhaps, not as vast as the Maestro's, but Edison's comforts were being seen to—at least on a basic level.

"How are we tonight, Thomas?" Jekyll asked with a cheery smile.

Edison gave a slight snort, crossed his arms, and fixed his gaze on the footboard of his bed.

"Dissatisfied, are we?" Jekyll's smile faded. "What a surprise."

The inventor merely looked up at him, one eyebrow lifting at Jekyll's sarcasm.

"I know that this work environment is hardly conducive to your personal taste, but think of it this way," he said, spreading his hands wide, "now you can truly empathise with your staff at Menlo Park."

Edison returned his eyes to the footboard. The man was highly unpleasant, which meant Jekyll rather enjoyed cracking his defences.

"Your work with the electroporter has been outstanding," Jekyll continued. "A true accomplishment, particularly in how you increased the power output and thereby increased the range. However, it must be quite humbling to know Tesla was right. Not only was he a better engineer, he was smarter as well."

"You son of a bitch," Edison growled, finally turning towards Jekyll.

His feet had not even slipped free of the bed before the automatons trained their eyes on him. The green lights that had shone were now deep red.

"These Shockers of yours," Jekyll said, chuckling as he looked one of them over, its eyes focused on Edison, "are just as amazing—however they still cannot make a proper cup of tea."

Edison's shoulders drooped. "That's why I have the pleasure of your company tonight? The tea sequence is still off?"

"Yes. I think it is a matter of steeping. The brew is just too—"

"I'll tend to it," he grumbled, waving his hand dismissively. "Tell me how long you want your damn tea to brew and I will—"

"Let. Me. Finish."

Edison's mouth closed, and on watching a pallid cover wash over the inventor, Jekyll experienced a slight rush of delight. "The brew is a bit too strong, and could be sweeter. My condition warrants a rather insatiable sweet tooth."

"Is that what you call it? Your condition?"

Jekyll was finding his flippancy a tad irksome. "I do so appreciate your eye for detail and attention. I also appreciate our gentlemen's agreement by not insulting my intelligence. I know you could quite easily take the opportunity to turn your Shockers against me."

"Believe me," Edison said with an angry twitch of his lip and slipped back onto the bed, "if I were dealing with you and only you, I would have parted company in Madrid."

The Shocker's eyes dimmed from red to yellow. Jekyll had not lied to Edison; he was impressed at the technological creativity these Shockers displayed, especially in the tiniest of details. "They are still in an alert mode."

"And they will stay that way until you leave and the cell is secure. Once their eyes return to green, I can move about without fear of a few hundred volts coursing through my body."

"Inspired," Jekyll remarked.

"Motivated, is more like it," Edison said, adjusting his somewhat dirty collar. "Your associate is most persuasive."

"Thomas," Jekyll began as he took a seat in the high backed reading chair. As he did so, he noted that the bookmark from Edison's current read had not moved from its place. Just as the night before. And the one before that. "You and I are men of science, but as you are more of a businessman than I am, you are in total denial of that darker side of your personality. You must be loved by your clientele, admired by your workers, and revered—if not reviled—by your peers and competitors. I, on the other hand, have embraced my darkness.

"True, I didn't at first. I came up with a separate, and somewhat pretentious identity. Different dwellings. Different wardrobe. And of course, the name." He laughed, recalling the utter ostentatiousness of it all. "The whole charade would have bankrupted me had Hyde not been so...uninhibited? Yes, uninhibited. He was everything I was not. Much like the dearly departed Duke of Sussex. I knew his madness all too well when I saw it."

"Knew?" Now it was Edison's turn to laugh. "You're speaking as if it were past tense."

"But it is, Thomas," Jekyll insisted. "You see, I was working so hard to keep that darkness under control that it was pushing me closer and closer to the edge. The breakthrough was when I watched myself transform back. While I had seen myself turn, I had never been fortunate to watch myself turn back." Edison's brow furrowed. Perhaps asking the inventor to understand psychology was too much. "I made the connection. Full circle. I had not purged my darker yearnings, nor had I isolated these base emotions and personified them as another being. I had mastered these suppressed wants and desires. They were still a part of me, ergo I could control them instead of burying them. Once I understood these were not two separate personalities but merely a fractured one, I could repair it."

"Repair your personality?" Edison shook his head. "You really are a lunatic."

"No, I am whole. I accepted my darkness," Jekyll said, spreading his arms out wide, "and now I am simply Jekyll. Your host," he inclined his head slightly as he rose from the chair, "and your master. Which facet of Jekyll you do business with is up to you."

Edison shifted in his bed. His eyes were now going to the Shockers, looking at them no longer as his captors, but perhaps more as if they were his protectors.

"I will send the valet down," Jekyll said before turning back to the door. "Be ready to move. We cannot afford another encounter with the Ministry."

"Are you saying—?"

"Nothing, Thomas," Jekyll replied, spinning on his heel at the doorway to face him. The inventor's flinch was most satisfying. "We may be in Paris for a few days. We may leave at first light tomorrow. Either way, you will tend to the tea algorithm and be ready to move on my word."

Edison's jaw twitched, but he replied gently, "Yes, Doctor."

"And please, do not strain your intellect," Jekyll said, pointing to the book by the reading chair. "You will not find a way out of here, even if you spend your hours looking for one. I made this room escape-proof long before you even cracked the riddle of the light bulb."

Edison could not have looked more surprised if Jekyll had hit him with the reading chair. Jekyll knew his apparent youth had caused many great minds consternation; it felt satisfying to know now Edison was among them.

With a final look at his reluctant partner-in-crime, Jekyll limped back to the parlour. There, he instructed the valet, "Go to Edison. Repair Protocol Delta."

The automaton turned and proceeded at a steady pace down the servant's passage.

Now alone, Jekyll turned back to the singular wooden case and two large jars—each of them twenty-four ounces—which contained the sacred ingredients procured from India. It was a great deal less than he had hoped for. It would make at least a year's worth of the regimen, if he could space out the doses in the right cycles. This would set him back, but perhaps when his supply began to dwindle, he could return to India and help himself. By then, the dust would have settled and the Ministry moved on.

Now his tea was cold, but the sweetness reminded him of what was in store for tonight. Pulling opened his Gladstone bag, he took out the small leather pouch holding five syringes. Yes. Medication. Meditation. And then...

Jekyll folded the pouch shut as he walked back to the view of Paris, and his heartbeat quickened. His head was swimming, so he gently placed the pouch on the small end table, next to the drained teacup. The sweet taste of the sugar still filled his mouth. However, it was another taste he now craved.

No. No regimen for tonight. La Ville Lumière called to him. Tonight, he would let random chance decide who would live, and who would die. Who would embrace his darker nature, and who would see the sun rise once more.

Tonight, he would live.

BOOKS & BRAUN WILL RETURN
IN 2017

Operation: Endgame

ONE FINAL MISSION...

photo by J.R. Blackwell

New Zealand-born fantasy writer and podcaster **Philippa (Pip) Ballantine** is the author of the *Books of the Order* series, and has appeared in collections such as *Steampunk World* and *Clockwork Fairy Tales*. She is also the co-author with her husband, **Tee Morris,** of *Social Media for Writers.* Tee co-authored *Podcasting for Dummies* and has contributed articles and stories for numerous anthologies including *Farscape Forever!, Tales of a Tesla Ranger,* and *A Cosmic Christmas 2 You.*

Together, they are the creators of the Ministry of Peculiar Occurrences. Both the series and its companion podcast, *Tales from the Archives,* have won numerous awards including the 2011 Airship Award for Best in Steampunk Literature, the 2013 Parsec Award for Best Podcast Anthology, and RT Reviewers' Choice for Best Steampunk of 2014.

The two reside in Manassas, Virginia with their daughter and a mighty clowder of cats. You can find out more about them and explore more of the Ministry at **ministryofpeculiaroccurrences.com**

Made in the USA
Middletown, DE
27 June 2016